With

CW01476789

A LIGHT IN THE DARKNESS

6,000,000 horses and mules were slaughtered in the Great War.

'It was not their war, Mrs Hooper.'

George Bowman

A LIGHT IN THE DARKNESS

John Kidd

The Book Guild Ltd
Sussex, England

First published in Great Britain in 2004 by
The Book Guild Ltd
25 High Street
Lewes, East Sussex
BN7 2LU

Typesetting in Baskerville by
Keyboard Services, Luton, Bedfordshire

Printed in Great Britain by
Antony Rowe Ltd, Chippenham, Wiltshire

A catalogue record for this book is available from
The British Library

ISBN 1 85776 842 6

For our three grandsons: Jacob John, George Christian and Thomas Rory.

To my best friend.

With grateful thanks to Pat Chaffey and Norah Lees for all their help and encouragement.

CONTENTS

1

A Sad Event

I made idle notes on my desk pad as I formulated in my mind a list of items that I would bring up at the next finance committee meeting.

As borough engineer of a small market town, I was well aware of working to a strict budget within the government's guidelines. Even so, there were certain items of a capital nature that were required, and my thoughts turned to the most cost-effective. In the present financial climate I had to consider which ones might receive capital approval, and this depended on the finance committee's members' own particular requirements. It was all a matter of juggling who would be the chancellor: certainly not me.

I glanced out of my office window, which overlooked the market place. It was a pleasant, early spring day. The overnight rain had cleared and the morning sunshine caused the stone cobbles of the market square to glisten. Bulbs could be seen pushing through the soil of the concrete containers that had been placed at intervals around the market-place, and I lapsed back into my thoughts.

I began thinking of my own garden, when there was a knock on my door, which immediately opened to reveal my secretary: a pretty redhead in her mid-twenties.

'I'm going down to the yard shortly, Jane. I'm expecting a rep from an industrial mowing machine company to turn up. When he does, send him down to me.'

'Yes, sir,' replied Jane.

'There's a report for the council on my tape, and some letters. Will you get on with them please?'

'Which shall I do first?'

'The report. The meeting's tomorrow, and I may need to alter it.'

'I'll get on with it straight away,' smiled Jane.

'Good girl,' I said, getting out of my chair.

'Make twenty-six copies. All the council will want to see it, and make their comments, no doubt.'

'Yes,' said Jane as she left my office.

Having told Graham, my assistant, where I was going, I left the building and made my way to the council's plant yard. I was checking the maintenance rosters and spares requisitions lists when the rep appeared on the scene.

Having discussed my requirements with him and arranged for quotations, I was about to return to my office when Graham came running towards me.

'Will you ring home immediately? It's important,' he said breathlessly.

'Yes, thank you, Graham,' I replied, my brow furrowed.

Since the yard's telephone had been disconnected recently as part of an economy drive, I went to the nearby crematorium and used the superintendent's telephone.

My wife, Elizabeth, answered the phone immediately.

'What is it, Liz? What's all the panic?' I asked, concern in my voice.

'It's your mother, Teddy, she collapsed in Lord Street this morning. She's had a stroke and she hasn't got long to live, so the hospital told me.'

There was a silence as her words sank in.

'Teddy, Teddy,' Elizabeth's voice rose.

'Yes, I heard, I'm on my way home,' I said quietly. 'I'll just leave some instructions for the yard foreman.'

I put down the phone and dialled the office. Having made the necessary arrangements, I drove home.

Liz was in the hall as I opened the front door.

'I'm sorry, Teddy,' she said, kissing me.

'Any further news?' I asked.

Liz shook her head. 'No. Shall I come with you? I can get Mrs Loan to come in.'

'No point, love,' I replied. 'I'll just pack an overnight bag.'

'I've already done it.' She pointed to a holdall in the hall.

'I'll just change, then I'll be off,' I said, bounding upstairs.

'I've made you some sandwiches and there's a flask of coffee.'

'Thanks, pet,' I replied.

I drove steadily up the M6, my mind on my mother and my life so far. I was forty-four years old, happily married with three children, and a job that I thoroughly enjoyed. I had been the borough engineer for the past eight years: true it was only a small market town in the heart of Cheshire, but it was a good place to live and I was happy.

I found the council most reasonable and no one interfered or tried to subvert my position. To a large extent, I was my own boss, without the usual associated financial worries. I glanced out of the window at the lush Cheshire countryside. I loved it, and made no secret of the fact. Liz would laugh at me if I eulogised about it, but I just shrugged.

'Sounds strange coming from a Londoner,' she would tease.

'Perhaps so, but I mean it,' I would reply.

My early years had been spent in south-east London, Queen's Road in Peckham, to be exact. A run-down area, as I recall, one that had seen better days.

'It was when they took the railings away in 1940 that started it,' sniffed my mother. 'It was almost posh round here when I was a girl.'

I had looked doubtfully at her but had not replied. The house and shop had belonged to my paternal grandparents. My grandfather had been killed during an air raid in 1940, and my grandmother had died soon after learning that my father (who was in the army) had been killed in action. I did not know either of them, as I was only a year old when my father was killed. From what I gathered from my mother, my grandmother had no wish to live after the death of my father. My grandfather's death had been a tremendous blow to her, as they had been very close, and the loss of my father was too much for her.

'Not that she was soft,' my mother had breathed in deeply through her teeth, making a hissing sound. 'Oh no, she was far from that, go to the end of the world for her George and Edward, I wouldn't cross her, not me, a terror when she was upset, I can tell you.'

I had gained the impression that my mother was very fond of my grandfather, but with my grandmother her situation was always uneasy; perhaps living in the same house had not helped. The property had been purchased by my grandmother, and had been a sweet and tobacco shop with a lending library, built up by my grandparents and my grandmother's youngest brother. My grandfather ran the shop, as he could do little else; he had been badly wounded in the First World War. He had lost his left eye and arm and was stone deaf, yet he could lip-read to an amazing degree.

'Got a string of medals he had, not that it did him

any good, poor old chap,' my mother had once said to me. 'Yet he was such an unassuming man, everyone liked and respected him, and your grandmother, give her her due, thought the world of him, not that it stopped her from ordering him about.

'George, do this, George, do that. Mind you, she had to lip-read – quite funny it was at times, particularly if he didn't want to do something. Afterwards, he would wink at me if her back was turned.'

My mother never talked much about my grandparents, but whenever she did I always found it interesting, as I longed to learn more about them.

My mother had never remarried, preferring, I think, the security of her army widow's pension to the doubtful security of another marriage. What's more, she made a good profit from the shop, which she ran, so we lived comparatively well.

I had worked hard at school, and with some assistance from the Army Benevolent Fund, was able to go to university and qualify in engineering.

Much to my surprise, my mother decided to move north when I obtained my present post, and in no time at all we had sold the property in Queen's Road and bought her present house in Southport. I should say that my grandmother had left the property to me, which perhaps might account in part for my mother's antipathy for her.

However, her move caused no problems, since my mother had not remarried and it seemed that my parents had spent their honeymoon in Southport, my father having been stationed not far away, and over the years my family and I had enjoyed many happy holidays there. My mother and I had little in common besides my children; it might seem strange but it was a fact. Why, I do not know. Perhaps it was my fault. Strange how one only thinks of these things at such times.

Since living in Southport, my mother had worked at a family florists. Her job was her main interest, outside the Baptist Church, and to both she gave her undivided loyalty. I was glad she had these interests, since it took some of the responsibility off my shoulders.

My visits were frequent but never, it seemed, frequent enough.

I drove straight to the hospital and was immediately taken to the intensive care unit. The doctor in charge came straight to the point. 'I'm sorry, Mr Bowman, your mother has had a massive stroke. It can only be a matter of hours, I'm afraid.'

'Thank you,' I murmured as he led me to my mother's bed.

I hardly recognised her, she looked so old and frail. There seemed to be a whole array of tubes and wires coming from her; she was getting every possible help, I told myself. The sister led me from the unit and pointed to a chair.

'You may sit there, Mr Bowman,' she said kindly. 'I'll have someone get you a cup of tea.

'Sister, will she come round?' I asked.

'It's most unlikely,' she replied.

'I've just remembered, I'll have to feed her cats. I'll go there now. Will you phone me if there is any change?'

'Certainly, that would be best, but you're welcome to stay.'

'If she wakes up, the first thing she will say is, "Have the cats been fed?"' I replied.

The sister smiled faintly. 'I understand. What's the number?'

She made a note of it and I retraced my steps to the hospital entrance, still a little dazed by events, and then drove back to my mother's house. I parked my car outside in the road as there was no garage or drive. It was a compact little semi with three bedrooms. More than big enough for her and not far from Lord Street, the main shopping centre of Southport.

Her neighbours were not in when I called to tell them of mother's condition. I let myself into her house; there was no sign of the cats, but that was typical of them anyway. It was just after three so I decided to have the coffee and sandwiches that Liz had prepared for me. It was pointless ringing her so I went into the sitting-room and lit the gas fire. I sat by the fire eating my sandwiches and drinking the coffee as I looked at the photos in the Victorian silver frames that had once belonged to my grandmother.

There was one of my father in his army uniform and one of the children with Liz and me. I felt suddenly very lonely, so I decided to ring Liz. I had no qualms about it, as I always paid my mother's phone bill, and it was only at my insistence that she had had it installed in the first place.

'What are you doing about a meal tonight?' asked Liz.

'I'll go to that fish and chip shop down the road, the one we use when we stay here,' I replied.

'Make sure that the spare bed is aired,' said Liz.

'Yes, love,' I replied. 'I'll ring again if there's any more news.'

'Yes, do. I'll be in the garden until it's dark.'

'Bye, love,' I said quietly.

'Bye, Teddy, take care,' replied Liz. I put down the phone.

I wandered into the kitchen and looked out of the window. I could not see either of my mother's cats in the garden. I wanted to use the toilet, so I went upstairs, and having done so sorted out some bedding from the airing cupboard. Having made up the bed in the spare bedroom, I went into my mother's bedroom; the cats still hadn't

7

made an appearance. I gazed about the room at the familiar furniture, which seemed to fill every square foot of floor space. In one corner was her old tin trunk, as ever covered with a faded tartan travelling rug. As a boy, I remembered that my mother told me not to look inside it, and there it was, after all these years, just the same.

Some morbid curiosity drew me to it. As I removed the tartan rug, I half expected my mother to come into the room and reprimand me. The battered tin trunk had a hasp and staple, but no lock. As I guiltily opened the lid, I heard a noise from the kitchen. I closed the lid and rushed downstairs, a cat had come through the back door cat flap.

'Oh it's you, is it?' I said, as the cat glared at me. 'I'll feed you in a minute.' I left the kitchen, went back upstairs and opened the trunk again.

It seemed something of an anticlimax as I peered inside. Apart from a cashbox that appeared to be locked, and a folder of papers, all I could see were two large cardboard boxes. I carefully lifted out the contents of the trunk, placing the cashbox and folder on my mother's bed. The cardboard boxes were collectors' pieces, as they had contained goods, the makers of which had ceased to exist sixty-odd years ago.

On one of the boxes was written in now almost illegible ink, *The Diaries of Cpl George Bowman, RAMC*. Carefully, I opened the box, unsure what to expect. Perhaps I had imagined leather-bound volumes; if so, I was to be disappointed. They were not neat diaries in the modern sense, with each page marked with a date, phase of the moon, and any important event. No, they were just stiff, covered notebooks, the sort available in any stationers. On their faded red covers were written dates and place names, and presumably, the names of his comrades.

There were bundles of letters tied with knitting wool, and a blue velvet-covered box. I opened it. Inside were a number of medals, carefully attached to the silk lining of the box.

As I had never served in the forces, at first they meant little to me. I closed the velvet-covered box and put it back in the trunk. I also replaced the cashbox and folder, closed the trunk, and covered it again with the tartan rug.

With the box containing the diaries under my arm, I went downstairs. I must admit I felt a little guilty, but I consoled myself with the fact that it was my grandfather, and I was entitled to know something about him.

The first notebook was marked *1916, The Somme.* My grandfather, I knew, was called up in 1916 when the Conscription Bill was passed. Unlike most eighteen-year-olds, he did not wish to join up, and registered as a conscientious objector. This seemed to enrage my great-grandfather, who then refused to have him in the house or, to put it more bluntly, threw him out. He went to live with his eldest sister, Amy, who had married a local Baptist minister.

It seemed his initiation into the army caused him little enough problem; but for the occasional bullying, because of his views, it all passed without incident. He then joined a Royal Army Medical Corps unit where he was given basic medical instruction and taught how to lift men with the minimum of effort and discomfort to both the patient and himself.

I turned up the gas fire and settled down in my mother's armchair. I glanced at the telephone as if expecting it to ring, but it remained silent. I suddenly remembered the cats and quickly went into the kitchen to feed them. Having done so, I returned to my chair and opened the first notebook. I turned a page; there was a brown stain on it. Was it blood or mud? It could have been either, I thought. There was an entry – 19th June 1916 – I embark for France.

2

The Somme

It was raining and the Channel crossing was miserable. We landed at Calais, and to my surprise were loaded into London buses. We were on the top, which was open, as the lower deck was reserved for some nurses who were being escorted by our officers. I thought we were going towards Ypres on the Flanders battle front, but the bus turned south and we headed in the direction of the River Somme.

I sat next to my pal, Victor Lascelles, whose father was a doctor in Wanstead. We were both eighteen and listened to the distant rumbling of guns above the whine of the bus engine with mixed feelings, and it is not surprising that we had little to say. Though I had seen wounded being brought home, I was quite unprepared for the battles that were to lie ahead.

Everyone was expecting a major battle, as there was a constant stream of vehicles of every sort going up to the front. Buses, lorries, smart staff cars and horse-drawn transport of every description clogged up the roads. Sweating teams of men and military police pushed to one side any that broke down. We at last reached the town of Doullens, where our nurses disembarked. We were told to stay on board, and the bus filled up with men returning to the front. We rejoined an even denser throng going towards the Somme. We passed villages with men in a variety of uniforms sitting at tables outside bars and cafés, drinking wine and beer. The guns seemed to be getting louder. We passed a large field hospital, but the bus did not stop. Eventually it did, but it was still about five miles to our rear positions, so we were told.

'Out you get. The joy-ride's over, 'urry up and form up,' came the loud voice of Sergeant Jobbins.

As we marched up the road towards the front, the sun came out and the guns were suddenly silent. I could hear birds singing; it became a lovely summer's day. But for the fact my boots were a poor fit and my kitbag seemed like a ton weight, I could have said I was reasonably happy. We arrived at a forward field hospital, and after a quick meal, were allocated our duties.

'You two come with me,' said a corporal to Victor Lascelles and myself.

We picked up our gear and followed him up a now muddy track.

'You two report to the Lancashire Fusiliers. A Corporal White is in charge of the RAMC unit.'

So began our initiation. Chalky White was a little, dark-haired man in his late twenties, old by our standards, so we tended to listen to him, which was just as well because he had already served a year in France and seemed a born survivor.

20th June 1916. They say you get used to the smell. I don't believe that because I never got used to the smell of the forward trenches; it would always haunt me.

That night, the fusiliers sent out a patrol. It so happened that the German Brunswick Regiment directly opposite us did exactly the same thing and the ensuing encounter set off our artillery, to which the German guns replied.

When it had all died down, Vic and I went out into

no man's land for the first time. The pitiful cries and groans in the darkness led us to the wounded and dying, and for the next three hours we did our unpleasant but necessary job. We came across German stretcher bearers; I jumped with fright when they came out of the gloom. I pointed to a dying German infantryman and they indicated one of our sergeants lying in the mud. We picked up our charges and said, 'Good-night'. It seemed so incongruous in such circumstances.

We met a number of times after that. The Germans were called Hans and Christian to which Vic remarked, 'We only need an Anderson.'

'Anderson?' I frowned.

'Yes, Hans Christian Anderson – get it?' grinned Vic.

'Yes, of course,' I replied.

About a week later, after an attack and a counter-attack, we found ourselves in no man's land again. Before we could get all our wounded back, the artillery started again.

We dived into a shell hole almost at the same time as Christian and Hans. There was a pale moon, and by its light we could see that we were all young and scared. I took out my cigarettes and offered them around. Christian could speak reasonable English.

'*Mein Gott*, this is terrible,' he muttered as a shell exploded sending a screeching hail of metal over our heads.

'Bloody awful,' I replied.

'This tobacco is good,' he smiled.

I nodded disinterestedly, gazing up at the flashes in the sky. The shelling suddenly stopped.

'Better get back,' said Vic, clambering up out of the shell hole. We followed him and picked up our stretchers, the Germans then going towards their lines.

'Good-night, Christian, Hans.'

'*Gute Nacht*,' they replied.

As we stumbled back, I almost tripped over a body. I could see a white smudge that was a face. I bent down and put a hand on it; there was some warmth there.

'Vic, Vic,' I hissed, 'one here, give me a hand.'

We picked up the man and put him on the stretcher.

'He's a mess my end,' whispered Vic.

We struggled back to our barbed wire and stumbled into the forward trench with our load.

'It's Captain Featherstone,' said a voice.

'Make way,' said another, as we moved down the trench. We left him at a forward dressing tent and then returned to our quarters, such as they were. I had a drink of tea and immediately fell asleep on my makeshift bunk.

During the following days, when I took wounded back to the field dressing stations, I observed more guns being brought up, and new regiments joined us. Mainly conscripts like myself – the regular army had by and large been wiped out by this time.

A big attack was expected. Word got about that it was to be on 1st July. I found this incredible, but as I was no military man, I made no comment. The weather was good during these last days of June, though I still wore my greatcoat at night when I went into no man's land. It appeared that the Germans also expected an attack because two days before it actually began I saw banners over the German lines saying, 'Come on, you English pigs' and 'We are waiting.'

It mystified me: did they actually know, I wondered?

Our shelling began late on 29 June. I'd never heard such a noise or indeed believed that it was possible to make such a sound. It continued all the following day and until dawn on 1st July, then it stopped. My ears were hurting with it; I put my fingers in them but it made no difference.

Then our men left the trenches; hundreds of them, then it seemed like thousands, were going over the top. The officers blew their whistles and bravely led them on.

When the German machine guns started I could tell their sound, which was different from ours. Wave after wave of our men were mown down, and still more followed to share the same fate, and then more, still more went forward. I just could not understand it. There was a never-ending flow of men. It was unbelievable. None got through the German wire; some reached it, but not many.

Later, we went out to find wounded. I could not believe my eyes.

'Oh, my God, look at them, hundreds and hundreds,' I muttered.

The scene was indescribable. I still dream about it, and it is just as awful, even after the passing of years. We had not gone thirty yards from our wire when we began our grim task. We worked until it was almost dark, and we had hardly reached the men in no man's land. I could hardly walk, my knees were shaking with fatigue. We got them back to our first trench, then infantrymen carried them to the dressing stations, leaving us the task of bringing in more casualties. It was a terrible business, and by this time I seemed to be immune to human suffering. I had seen everything that could happen to a man.

Suddenly, we heard a whistling and screeching in the air.

'Run,' shouted Vic, as he hared back to our trenches.

I followed as fast as my legs could carry me, my fatigue suddenly gone. Our guns had started again. As I fell into our forward trench, there was a crescendo of noise, and my ears began to hurt again. I staggered after Vic along trench after trench, until I found my billet and collapsed, shaking, on my bunk. The ground seemed to be moving. I pulled my greatcoat over my head as if I could drown the noise, but it made no difference.

'Oh, God, this is hell,' I gasped. The barrage continued until dawn, then it stopped. My ears hurt, but the silence was wonderful. Then I heard the shrill whistles; another attack had started. The staccato noise of the German machine guns penetrated my painful eardrums. I knew that sound.

'No, not all over again,' I groaned.

Unbelievable as it seemed, I must have dozed off. Vic shook me awake, I could hear his voice, 'Come on, George, we've got work to do.'

There was a lull. The machine guns were sated, so it seemed. Platoon after platoon lay on the soft ground. We wore white painted helmets and armbands with a red cross painted on them. We went unmolested about our grim task, almost up to the German wire. I knew they were watching us but I was too busy to be afraid. I tried to lift a sergeant off the barbed wire: the barbs held his coat. He was a heavy man. I turned him – his jaw was gone and he was dead. Almost thankfully, I pushed him back on the wire. I turned to a body that seemed to move. It was a private, scarcely eighteen, by the look of him. His left leg was shattered, and there was a pool of blood under it. Quickly I tied a tourniquet, then lifted him over my shoulder, my boots slipping on the ground.

'Put him down, George,' said Vic, carrying a stretcher.

I put the lad down on the stretcher and we carried him back to our lines, past the heaps of bodies that lay the length of our trenches, a seemingly never-ending line of death.

I just could not believe it, as the same thing happened all over again that night: the barrage then the dawn attack, with the same appalling result – hundreds more

16

killed. For a whole week this went on. How many died I just could not hazard a guess, and still more men came up from the rear, a never-ending procession to the slaughter.

'You can go to our reserve position, Bowman, and have a wash.'

It was Corporal Chalky White talking to me. I could not hear him even though the guns had stopped. He understood, so he beckoned me to follow him. I carried my bowl of water as if it were a precious possession, as indeed it was; I had not washed properly for two weeks.

I got behind the medics' tent and stripped off, screened by a stack of makeshift coffins. I washed myself down, then soaped my hair and at last washed my underwear and socks. By this time, the water was a dirty grey and had a thick scum on it. With clean underwear and socks from my kitbag, I felt a new man, and returned my bowl to Chalky White.

I was about to go back to my billet when he told me to report to the transport officer. I could not hear him but Vic grabbed my arm and we both reported to the medical transport officer. We were told to go with two lorry-loads of wounded to a rear hospital and then return. Vic, too, was partially deaf, and I assumed we were being rested until our hearing returned.

The hospital, some twenty miles from the front line, had been a nobleman's country house, not quite a château in the accepted sense but a very large mansion none the less. It was here that I first met Amelia. Amongst all the pain and suffering, I first set eyes on the love of my life.

Amelia Hooper, for that was her name, met us at the bottom of the stone steps that led up to the front entrance of the mansion.

'You go through the side door,' she said, pointing to an entrance past the steps.

17

I pointed to my ears and shook my hands. She understood and smiled. Taking me by the arm, she pointed to the entrance.

I thanked her, then joined Vic at the rear of the lorry. There was a constant stream of men and lorries coming and going. We offloaded our wounded, then reluctantly clambered aboard to return to the front. Amelia saw me. I quickly waved to her – she gave a brief response, then turned to another batch of arrivals.

It was dark when we returned to the front. There was a lull in the artillery barrage, though there was machine gun fire, or so Vic indicated to me. We got some food at a field kitchen then returned to our billets. So ended for us the first week of the battle of the Somme.

3

The Slaughter Continues

7th July 1916. I knew that my days must be numbered. I just could not expect to spend so much time in no man's land and not be shot at – it just was not logical.

That night, after collecting about thirty wounded, Vic and I met Christian and Hans, the German stretcher bearers, and together we crept into a shell hole to have a smoke. Christian spoke good English and mentioned that we were safe if their men knew that we were medics. I said, with less confidence, our men took the same view. His words, however, put an idea into my head.

Later that day there was another attack by our men – to no avail, of course, followed by a similar attack by the Germans. It was a Guards regiment that had gone over, and their CO and adjutant had not returned. I had obtained some white paint during the day and I had painted my helmet again; also my coat front. It had been my intention to paint a red cross on it but I had not been able to find any red paint, so the white paint would have to suffice.

I elbowed my way past guardsmen at the foot of the home-made ladder, pulling my stretcher as I did so.

'Let me by, will you?' I snapped.

I climbed up the home-made ladder to the parapet and pushed up my stretcher poles. Any sniper would see them first, I reasoned with hopeful optimism.

'Come on, Vic,' I shouted, clambering out.

'They'll see you all right, mate,' said a voice.

'Yer like a bloody snowman!'

'It's what I'm hoping,' I muttered anxiously. It was still daylight, but there was a slight mist. Quickly we picked up our first man – or to be frank – what was left of him, though he was still alive and I did not wish to waste our time as there were so many to bring back.

The smell was appalling, but unless there was a gas attack, we did not wear our gas masks as they were uncomfortable and breathing in them was difficult enough, without carrying a stretcher.

We worked for about three hours at a time, right up to the German wire. I knew they were watching me, but I was past being afraid. I seemed to be in a void. I found the Guards' CO right up to the German wire – poor bastard. It was incredible, but he was still alive. I could not see Vic so I put the man over my shoulders and staggered back to our trenches. When the guardsmen saw me, two clambered out and took my load.

'Thank you, laddie,' said a Guards officer from the trench.

I returned to my task in a dip in the ground. I found more men. They were dead but there was a German officer lying amongst them. I bent over him – his face was as grey as his greatcoat, yet he was still alive, though his left leg was at a strange angle.

I examined him quickly. He was still bleeding from his thigh. I tied a tourniquet with a handkerchief, then began to lift him. The man groaned as I put him over my shoulder. His helmet fell off, and I then struggled to the German trenches. I heard the man groan, '*Danke, danke,*' as I approached the German lines. Puffing and blowing, I heard voices.

'*Gut, Englander,* go that way to your left.' I did as I

20

was told and was soon between their first wires. Again I was instructed; then I reached their trenches. I lowered the man into willing hands and heard the words '*Herr Graff.*' As I turned to go, a German officer spoke to me.

'Thank you, *Englander*, you are a brave man.'

'Good night, sir,' I replied, touching my helmet.

As luck would have it, I stumbled across the Guards adjutant. I knelt by him, as the guns started.

'Oh Jesus,' I groaned as the earth shook. Dirt rained down on me as I lay face down, shaking.

How long it lasted, I don't recall. I thought I would die. Then it stopped. My hearing suddenly improved, I could hear rifle fire, and it was dusk.

The Guards adjutant groaned. I could hear the word 'Father'. I could not see Vic. I could not see anyone, just bodies all over the place. It seemed quiet. I got to my feet, then lifted the Guards officer, his uniform covered in blood. I did not know who he was, just another officer. I got him on my shoulder. The guns had stopped. It was so quiet from the German trenches. I heard a cheer and I thought they were about to attack.

'Oh God, I hope not,' I groaned, trying to quicken my pace.

I heard a German voice, '*Schnell, schnell Englander.*'

The man was heavy and I was almost on my knees when I reached our trenches again and the guardsmen grabbed at my charge. I almost fell in after him, as I was weak with fatigue. I must have been a sight, my white painted coat covered in blood.

A hand steadied me as I got down into the trench. My face was covered with mud, sweat and blood. I tried to wipe my eyes.

'Here, laddie, what's your name?' A Guards officer handed me a khaki handkerchief. I wiped my eyes and handed it back.

21

'Keep it. What's your name?' he asked.

I came to attention. 'Bowman, sir. Private George Bowman 6543788, no. 342 Field Hospital RAMC, sir.'

The Guards officer nodded. 'Thank you, Bowman. We are grateful to you.'

I nodded, unsure what to say. 'Yes, sir,' I muttered and gave a salute.

I staggered back to my billet completely exhausted. Vic was sitting on his bunk; he seemed in a daze, his eyes stared straight ahead, seeing nothing.

'Vic, Vic, Vic.' There was no response; he seemed in a state of shock. I lay back on my bunk, too tired to go and eat. There was the sound of rifle fire, then the rat-a-tat of a Vickers machine gun. Almost immediately I slept and did not awake until Chalky White shook me.

'Come on, Bowman, get cleaned up and go and eat. There will be work for you shortly over the top,' he said.

There was nothing malicious in his words, just the plain fact of the matter. I staggered towards the latrine, after which I drew my ration of water and tried to clean myself up. It was dawn and the Guards had just begun another attack. Further up the line a Scottish regiment had gone over. Both had suffered appalling casualties and I had just finished my breakfast of bread and jam and a mug of tea when Chalky White ordered Vic and me to go over the top.

By this time the attack had petered out and it was quiet. I pushed up my stretcher poles first, then held up my white helmet. I was learning caution as I was certain I had used up my nine lives. The guardsmen nodded affably as I climbed out of the trench. The Germans must have seen Vic and me as we retrieved the wounded, but nothing happened. Other stretcher parties joined us. For two hours we worked in the warm July sun. One of the guardsmen spoke to me as we carefully lowered a badly wounded man into the trench.

'Have you been near their wire yet?'

'No, not yet, haven't got that far yet,' I replied.

'Some of the lads got there,' said the guardsman.

I knew what he meant, but he had not liked to suggest I go to the enemy wire.

'I'll go and have a look,' I said, picking up my stretcher.

'Take care lad,' he replied.

The warm sun was pleasant but I sweated and the appalling smell of decomposing bodies almost made me throw up. I plodded towards the German wire. I held up my stretcher poles so that they could be seen, and hoped that they would not fire at me. I was now beyond fear. I expected to die at any time. I just prayed that it would be quick.

I found a number of guardsmen. The first I examined were dead, then I turned one over that had been lying face down. The man was alive – just his uniform was covered in blood. It was the officer who had given me the handkerchief. I looked around for Vic but I could not see him; where was he? I thought I could hear a rifle bolt being drawn back. Why was my hearing now so good, I wondered? My heart stopped.

'This is it,' I thought. Then I heard a guttural voice say, *'Nein Nein, der Englander.'* I heard no more and I put down my stretcher and started to lift the Guards officer.

The man groaned but I got him over my shoulder and staggered to my feet. I slithered and stumbled over the uneven ground of the dip in no man's land. I saw some German dead and a fair-haired lad whimpering. I staggered on to our trenches.

'It's the major,' said a voice as I eased him down into the willing hands of his comrades in the trench.

I stretched my back and turned to go as one was about to speak. 'There's another man alive out there,' I said in answer to their enquiring looks.

I plodded back into no man's land towards the group of dead Germans lying in a dip. The fair-haired German boy, who looked younger than myself, moved slightly. I bent down and touched him. He opened his eyes; they were filled with fear and pain. I touched my chest and pointed to their wire.

'I take you,' I smiled.

'*Danke*,' he murmured. I quickly got him over my shoulder – he was no weight at all. I was concerned that our men would fire at me, even though he was not wearing their conspicuous pointed helmet, he did have a grey greatcoat and they would recognise that.

Nothing happened, thank God, and I reached the German lines. Two German infantrymen clambered out of their trench.

'*Danke*,' said one.

'We take him,' said the other. I nodded.

'What is your surname?' he asked.

'Bowman. Why?' I said curiously.

'Our officers wish to know,' he replied.

'Oh!' I shrugged, looking at some of our men that were lying in front of the German wire. I saw a hand move slightly. The man was alive, but he was a huge Guards sergeant. I knew I could never carry him back on my own. I looked around and shouted for Vic. I walked back towards our lines, still shouting.

'Vic, Vic, Vic,' I bawled. I was sure I was being observed by snipers on both sides. 'Vic!' Suddenly Vic appeared out of a dip.

'Come on mate. I can't lift this one on my own,' I said.

With Vic's assistance we got the man on a stretcher

and we staggered back to our lines. When we got him into our forward trench, I remarked, 'God, he was a weight.'

'Should be,' said a voice further down the trench.

'The RSM's full of shit.' There was some laughter.

'Who said that?' demanded one of their officers.

'Was it you Skinner?'

'No, sir,' replied what sounded like the same voice.

Suddenly a shell landed close by and I almost dived into our trench and was only saved from hitting the duck boards by two guardsmen, who grabbed me.

'All right, mate?' said a voice.

'Yes, OK,' I replied, though I felt far from it.

We took the RSM to the dressing station, then went to the field kitchen. The sergeant cook looked at me and my blood-covered face and uniform. He knew where I had been without a word. He gave me a billycan of warm water to clean up and a mug of hot tea. I thanked him and picked up a thick slice of bread and returned to my bunk.

The artillery had started again. Within minutes I could hear almost nothing – it was some consolation, I suppose. Having cleaned up the best I could, I began to write in my diary. It seemed to soothe me as I wrote down what had happened. Why did I do it, I asked myself? Perhaps one day, if I survived, I would convince myself. It all seemed as if in a dream – that man could inflict such suffering on his fellow man was beyond my understanding. We had carried a never-ending flow of broken, often limbless young men, to the forward clearing station. It was just not believable, yet it was happening day after day.

Though I could hardly hear the guns, I could feel the ground move. The German artillery had obviously got our range. I lost all sense of time. Suddenly Vic appeared.

His face deathly white, he beckoned me to follow him. I put my diary away and grabbed my stretcher. A salvo of shells had hit our forward trenches. I cannot describe the carnage that met our eyes. I was now immune to any sight. Methodically we took those that had not been buried and were still alive, to the dressing station. It was dark by the time we rested. What time and what day it was, I could not say. When our reliefs arrived, I returned to my bunk and collapsed exhausted into a deep sleep.

It was 24th July when I was taken out of the line and sent back with a batch of wounded to a hospital outside Amiens. On my arrival I was given a disinfectant bath and clean underwear; then I had a haircut and was told to clean up my uniform. This proved impossible, the blood on it had gone hard. My white painted helmet and white painted coat I kept in a separate kitbag. My sergeant looked at it and nodded.

He spoke to me but I pointed to my ears and shook my hands. He understood – it was not an uncommon complaint for a stretcher bearer. I gathered he was telling me to draw a new uniform. I did not need telling twice, I can tell you.

Vic had continual shakes. He spilt his tea and had a job to feed himself. No one commented, it was to be expected. There were men far worse still in the line.

We were quickly found work to do, as a constant stream of wounded came in. Those that could be moved were sent to the railway station where they began their journey home in special trains. Beds were so desperately needed that they were not kept a moment longer than was necessary.

It was during my second week at Amiens that I was told to report to the chief medical officer. My heart sank. Was I going to be sent back to the line? The chief medical officer was a grey-haired surgeon from a London teaching hospital. He looked tired, as he was entitled to be, considering the hours he was at the operating table. I saluted as I entered his office. He nodded as he sat at his desk, then he spoke and stood up and held out his hand. I was mystified. The orderly sergeant spoke to him. The CMO nodded again then smiled and wrote on a pad, which he handed to me. It read: *Congratulations, you have won the Distinguished Conduct Medal and the Military Medal.* I touched my chest with my hand.

'Me, sir?' I think I said.

He nodded and he held out his hand again. I shook it in a numbed fashion, the sergeant also shook my hand. I could not believe it. 'Must be some mistake, sir,' I said.

The CMO smiled and shook his head. 'No mistake, son, you have deserved them. One was a recommendation from the Guards and they do not do that lightly.'

The sergeant pointed to the office door. I came to attention and I saluted. The CMO gave me a tired smile and I left his office.

Two days later as I was helping to unload an ambulance, I saw the nurse I had spoken to at the other hospital.

'Hello,' I said familiarly. 'Are you coming here?' I asked, for want of something better to say to her.

'Yes,' she replied.

She began to talk. I shrugged my shoulders and pointed to my ears, then I shook my head. She smiled, indicating she understood and pointed to a casualty on a stretcher. I bent over the man – he was dead. I closed the man's eyes and turned to her. She was biting her lower lip. I stood up and faced her.

I put my hands on her upper arms and squeezed gently and winked at her. She smiled gratefully at me and lowered her eyes. We started to unload the rest of the wounded. She then picked up her case and went into the main entrance of the hospital, now in complete control of herself. I saw her look fleetingly at me, then the doors closed and she was lost from my view.

Vic and I took the dead man to the rear of the hospital where a corporal took over and wrote down all the man's particulars.

During the next two weeks I saw Amelia quite frequently and she told me that she came from Blackheath, which was not far from me. Her family were wine merchants, so she told me, and she had three brothers, also in the Army; two were in the Flanders section of the front.

'I hope they are never brought in here,' she told me one evening. I was learning to lip-read and she helped by speaking slowly and emphasising each word to me.

'That's not very likely is it, they are much too far north,' I had replied, rather thoughtlessly.

It was now early August and though it was warm, the rain had been continuous for days. My hearing had improved, and I knew it was only a matter of time before I returned to the front line. I said as much to Amelia one evening. She tried to smile encouragingly at me as she said, 'I am sure that you will be all right, George. When do you get your medals?' It was the first time that they were mentioned; in fact I did not know that she knew about them.

'I've no idea, Amelia,' I said, dolefully.

'I must go now, George. Sister will be back soon – 'bye for now,' she said, moving past two wheelchairs.

'Bye Amelia,' I murmured.

I went back up the line during the last week in August. My hearing seemed to be restored, but I had a continuous earache. Vic had developed a nervous twitch, though his hearing, like mine, had improved.

The battle on the Somme had gone on for almost two months, and as far as I could see, nothing had been gained, but the casualties had been unbelievable, and still a continuous stream of new men were moving up to the front.

Amelia had given me her London address before I left. She did not look well. In my opinion, I think the never-ending suffering of the men preyed on her mind. Like many of the nurses, she was a wartime volunteer, not a professional nurse, and this must have made a difference.

We went back to a different section of the Somme front and this concerned me as I knew every square yard of the previous line. I had now put a large red cross on my white helmet, which gave me an illusion of security.

This time, the first regiment that we were attached to was a Highland one. Their pipers would lead them forward, usually with fatal consequences. After my first trip out into no man's land I established myself. I carried back one of their pipers, but when they saw me take a German officer back to their wire, I was taken to task about it when I returned with the next wounded Highlander.

'Yon Hun should have been left,' said one man, belligerently.

'What have ye tae say?' demanded another.

'The man was dying. He was entitled to die with his own comrades,' I said, quietly.

There was no reply for a moment, then an officer spoke.

'Quite right, son,' said the red-bearded officer. 'The man was entitled to that, and you brought back Piper Dewar from their wire; we're in your debt, laddie; we've nae right tae criticise you.'

'Thank you, sir,' I said, saluting.

The Highlanders now nodded affably as I moved past them down the trench to the forward dressing unit.

In the coming days I was to establish a rapport with these fearless men who took such heavy casualties. I seemed to bear a charmed life, as the enemy rifle fire seemed to virtually stop when Vic and I went out with our stretcher.

On one occasion, when I took a wounded German back to their wire, I heard a voice call out *'Danke, Englander Bowman.'* This surprised me but I had no time to reflect on it as I had to take one of our wounded back with me. I could not be seen not carrying anyone – that would invite a shot. Finding one was never difficult – within six paces I always found some unfortunate.

I was with the Highland Regiment for about three weeks. What was left of it was then withdrawn, and a regiment of the Rifle Brigade took over. They suffered as badly, and when they were taken out of the line, Vic and I were also sent back to the rear hospital. I was as deaf as a post, and Vic had the continual shakes. I'd almost forgotten Amelia, and to my disappointment found that she had gone on leave to Paris.

It was now the middle of September, and besides losing my hearing, I had a cough that I could not shake off. I was given a bath and deloused, issued with some new kit, and after a few days at the hospital felt almost human again. The sister, who was Amelia's superior, was a forbidding woman but since she did not fire bullets or shells, did not bother me. I asked when Amelia would be returning – she snapped an answer but I could not hear her. I pointed to my ears.

'Will you write it down, please Sister?' She seemed to soften, then she wrote on a pad: *On leave. Her brother has been killed, and her mother is very ill.*

'But I thought she was in Paris on leave, Sister.'

She wrote again: *That was Nurse Warrener.*

'Thank you, Sister,' I muttered, as I began to cough.

Then she looked at me and took hold of my arm. Before I knew it she had put two large spoonfuls of a

30

vile-tasting cough mixture down my throat. 'Ugh!' I gurgled, my face screwing up.

'Come back later,' she said, pronouncing her words so that I could understand. I nodded and thanked her.

The days passed quickly. There was much to do. The sister, whose name was Austell, and who I judged to be about forty, was a kind capable woman, under her hard exterior. Very efficient and most capable, was the general opinion of her. She was kind to me in her bluff way and in return I always lifted men or heavy objects if she attempted to do so. One day she gave me two pairs of socks. How she came by them I've no idea, but I took them gratefully.

I had not written to my parents since I had been in France. I had no time for my father, and my mother was too timid to say boo to him. I had no intention of ever going back to see them.

I had written to my sister, Amy. I said little, our letters were censored, and since I was a registered conscientious objector, I knew that everything I wrote would be carefully read.

This was the reason that I kept a diary. I had to put down my thoughts as a record of what I had seen. At times it seemed like a mad dream, but also seemed to soothe me.

Some men wrote poetry that was quite beyond me. Any creative thought for me was numbed by the noise of the guns. When I could hear, the pain in my ears at times became unbearable. The days now passed quickly. We were in the first week of October and it was getting colder. The conditions in those trenches must be becoming unbearable, I thought, as it had been raining almost continually.

I had expected to see Amelia any day now, and I looked anxiously at every new arrival, but there was no sign of her. The battle on the Somme continued. Still more men were committed to the struggle, as fresh regiments were thrown in, more casualties flowed back to us. A never-ending stream of misery, which at times became a torrent. It had to end soon, I told myself. Before long, at this rate, there would not be an eighteen-year-old left in England.

By the end of October, we had news to expect an even bigger influx of casualties, and every man that could be moved, was taken to a waiting hospital train. To our intense joy, Vic and I were given orders to go with it.

My hearing was beginning to return, and I was going home. When I told Sister Austell, she smiled for the first time at my beaming face, and said kindly: 'Enjoy yourself, George, you deserve it. Would you post some letters for me in London?'

'Yes, Sister,' I replied, eagerly.

I took the letter out of my tunic pocket, confirming my medal awards, and opened it up.

'I'll let you see it, Sister, and no one else,' I said, giving it to her. She glanced at it briefly, then folded it again.

'Very good, George, very well done,' she smiled, handing it back to me. I put it in my breast pocket and shuffled my feet.

'Now take that basket of soiled linen to the laundry, please.'

'Yes, Sister,' I replied, picking up the basket.

4

Home on Leave

3rd November 1916. We are going home at last. I still could not believe it. Last night I did not sleep at all, even though I had been on duty over sixteen hours. Yet this morning, I feel as right as ninepence and my hearing is a lot better. Yesterday, I wrote three letters for wounded men. I had a number of letters to post – the censor officer had given them all just a cursory glance, before I sealed them. I did not ask about Sister Austell's letters – they were already stamped and sealed.

'Just pop them in the first box you see in London.'

'Yes, Sister,' I had replied, putting them in my battledress breast pocket.

The railway station was packed, as trains arrived with more men for the front line. They spewed forth, a khaki stream of shouting, jostling figures. At the far platform was the hospital train, almost in a siding. It was hardly an encouraging sight for the barely-trained recruits going into action for the first time. It had four guards' vans, which were reserved for the more serious stretcher cases. Those that could move needed no encouragement to try and get aboard the train. Limbless men were carried from the platform into the carriages.

'Leave those wheelchairs here,' bawled the transport officer, a swagger cane under his arm.

'They will be provided at the other end. Now get a move on.'

The stretcher cases were put on the platform in a double line. Some ladies from the French Red Cross tried to give out drinks, but seemed overwhelmed by it all.

I bent down to one stretcher. It looked as if the man had died. I felt his pulse – there was nothing. I looked up at the transport officer standing importantly behind me.

'Well?' he demanded.

'I think he is dead, sir,' I replied.

'Put him to one side then,' he snapped. 'It will make room for another man.'

'I'd like the sister to see him first,' I said quickly.

'Sister,' I shouted above the din. 'Here, please,' I beckoned.

The sister hurried across the platform towards me.

'I think this man is dead, Sister.'

Without a word, she bent over and felt his pulse, then touched his neck and chest. Satisfied, she lifted the blanket over the man's head, then returned to the other side of the platform. Not a word had been spoken. Perhaps it was appropriate – there were no words left to say.

'Is he dead?' asked a cockney voice from the next stretcher.

'Yes,' I said shortly.

'We'll all be bloody dead by the time this train moves.'

The transport officer glared at the cockney, then strode importantly down the platform.

'Give me a lift, Vic, to shift this man,' I said, bending down to lift the dead man's stretcher.

We carried the unfortunate man to one side and put him down.

'You can't leave him there,' bawled a voice. 'He's in the road.'

'We'll put him in that room,' said Vic, pushing open what had been the ticket collector's office.

'Not in there,' roared the transport officer.

We had lowered the stretcher to the floor and left it.

'That's my office,' he shouted, striding down the platform.

Vic and I moved quickly back to our stretcher cases.

'Don't leave me, don't leave me,' cried a voice.

It came from the stretcher beside the cockney who had answered the transport officer. The cockney, I could tell, had lost his legs, while the man who had cried out appeared to be a young officer. His head was heavily bandaged, as were his eyes, and he had lost an arm. I bent down and put a hand on his shoulder.

'No one is going to be left,' I said, quietly, as the man tried to sit up.

'Look, I can walk, my stomach's all right,' he pleaded.

I gently held him down. 'Stay still, sir, I'll put you on board.'

'Look there's money in my wallet, take it and get me on board,' he said, desperately.

'I don't want your money,' I snapped, glancing at the cockney.

'I'll get you on board.' The cockney lad touched his temple with a forefinger, indicating his opinion of the young officer.

I thought he was right, and nodded my head.

Vic was now arguing with the transport officer.

'I said move it,' bawled the transport officer, as Vic came towards me.

'Come on, Vic, let's get these aboard. We'll take this man first.'

'Right-ho,' replied Vic, picking up the other end of the stretcher.

As we carried the stretcher into the first guard's van,

the transport officer strode towards us, his face red with anger.

'Stop this. I said remove that stretcher at once,' he roared.

We both ignored him and went into the guard's van. As I lowered the stretcher I said to the wounded officer: 'You are on board now, sir. We will be off soon.'

'Bless you,' he murmured, his one good arm shaking.

The transport officer awaited us out on the platform.

'Are you deliberately disobeying an order,' he snarled at me.

I touched my ears, shook my hands, and shrugged my shoulders.

'He's deaf,' snapped Vic. The transport officer turned on him.

'What's your name, rank and number?' he demanded.

'Next one, Vic,' I said, turning to the next stretcher.

'Right,' replied Vic, ignoring the transport officer.

'I said...' began the transport officer, grabbing Vic's arm and preventing him from moving. At this point one of the senior sisters joined us frowning.

'What's all this?' she demanded. 'Get these stretchers on board. The train is ready to leave.'

'Nothing is going to move until that stretcher is removed from my office,' snarled the transport officer.

'Your office?' frowned the sister.

Vic quickly explained what had happened, and it appeared that the sister sympathised with him.

'The body will be removed shortly,' she snapped, glancing at the transport officer. 'Now get a move on with these stretchers.'

'I want it removing now, Sister,' he growled.

The sister took a deep breath before she replied, sarcastically: 'Are you expecting the Brigadier for tea and cucumber sandwiches?'

The transport officer's eyes glinted. 'I said...' he began.

'If you don't stop interfering I'm going to blow your head off.'

Eyes turned in the direction of the voice. A young man lying on the second stretcher had pulled out an officer's pistol from under his blanket, and it was pointing at the transport officer.

'I mean it. If you don't buzz off I'll let you have it.'

'Aye, give 'im one mate,' said the cockney lad.

'Should be up the line, the bastard.'

The transport officer stepped back a pace, his mouth open, at the same time the sister, without any ado, stepped towards the man with the gun and took it from him.

'I'll have this, if you don't mind,' she said, severely. 'Now get these stretchers on board at once,' she snapped.

The incident over, we carried on loading while the transport officer, somewhat shaken, strode down the platform.

I thought that we would never reach London. We seemed to be hours at Calais and the crossing was rough, which did not help with badly wounded men. However, at last we did, and it was on a foggy November afternoon that we arrived at Charing Cross station. A fleet of ambulances were parked in a road adjacent, well out of public view, and the train pulled in at the furthest platform, so that the wounded could be secreted out of the station. The travelling public would be practically unaware that we had even arrived.

Such sights were unlikely to boost public morale, which was already at a very low ebb, now that the horrific casualty figures were filtering through, no matter how hard the Government tried to suppress them. Gone were the brass bands, with laughing crowds lining the streets, waving flags, waving on the boys. Now it was the far platform at Charing Cross station with a line of ambulances at the side of the station. Those travellers who stopped to stare were politely asked to move on by police constables. It was as if we were lepers or convicts going to a penal settlement.

Ladies from volunteer organisations served tea and buns. All, I could tell, were moved by the pitiful state of some of the men. One elegantly dressed young lady was about to give some tea to a badly injured stretcher case. I touched her shoulder and she stood up, a bewildered look on her pretty face.

'Don't try and wake him, Miss, he's better off asleep.'

'Er, yes of course, I was only...' she began in a Belgravia accent.

'Those lying down, leave. They'll end up choking and spilling tea everywhere, and that will upset Sister. Just give tea to those sitting up,' I smiled.

'Yes, of course,' she said, fluttering her long eyelashes. Her perfume smelt of another world and I was sorry when she moved away from me.

At last the convoy of ambulances slowly made its way to the Woolwich Barracks and hospital complex. I could see passers-by stop and stare at us, then shake their heads and carry on with their business. I began to think about my leave. Did it commence when I left Amiens, or was it to begin when I arrived in Woolwich?

The day after our arrival, Vic and I were given new uniforms, which we were told to wear for a parade at the barracks, as a General would be taking the salute on the following day. The parade duly took place, and I fell in with a company of RAMC stretcher bearers and orderlies, then a sergeant swooped on me and told me to get on the front row. I was unused to parades. There was a band, a guard of honour and a large number of new recruits. I thought I could be better occupied in the hospital with our new influx of wounded. I could see the General and his aides a short distance away, and we stood – a bored, impassive look on our faces.

A drill sergeant marched towards us, his pacing stick under his arm, then he came smartly to attention in front of us.

'Private Bowman – attention,' he shouted.

I automatically came to attention. 'Yes, Sergeant,' I replied.

'Follow me, left, right, left, right, left, right.'

I endeavoured to keep up with him until we reached the saluting base.

'Halt!' he bawled over his shoulder, almost too late, as I avoided bumping into him.

'Private Bowman – attention,' he shouted.

I came to attention in front of the saluting base, unsure just what to expect. The General came down from the saluting base, his aide-de-camp following, carrying a velvet cushion. He stood in front of me. I could smell his breath – a mixture of cigars and spirits emanated from it.

'Private Bowman, it gives me great pleasure to present you with the Distinguished Conduct Medal and the Military Medal.'

After he had pinned them on my uniform, he shook my hand.

'Well done, Bowman,' he said, giving a faint smile.

I was then marched back to the ranks and other men were decorated, after which the General made what he thought was a patriotic speech, then we were dismissed.

Back in the billet, I sat on my bed sewing on my medal ribbons.

'What does it feel like to be a hero?' sneered one man.

'I'm just glad to be alive,' I said quietly.

The man said no more, as others in the barrack room shouted at him to be quiet.

Later that day I was given a fourteen-day leave pass, and my back pay. I said goodbye to the lads and packed up my gear. Vic also had a leave pass and we parted company at the main gate.

My sister, Amy, lived in Lausanne Road, which was off Queen's Road, Peckham, and she was married to a Baptist minister. They had three children, two girls and a boy. Hector, her husband, was a very serious man, but I liked him. My father could not stand him. Perhaps it was because he did not drink or smoke, and was a parson. Three good enough reasons as far as he was concerned, but Hector was a kind man and was good to Amy.

I got off the tram at the bottom of Lausanne Road and swung my kitbag over my shoulder. It was a late, foggy afternoon and getting dark, but it was so peaceful, I just could not believe it. I walked slowly up Lausanne Road, as if savouring the quiet. My sister's house was a better type of terraced property with a bay window and porch. It also had a front garden with railings. My brother-in-law opened the front door and peered at me through his thick glasses. In the dim light, I thought he had not recognised me.

'It's me, Hector – George,' I exclaimed excitedly.

'George! George – come in dear boy, come in. Amy,' he called out. 'Amy, it's George.'

Hector shook my hand as Amy ran down their long hall, wiping her hands on her apron as she did so.

'Georgie, my love, Georgie,' she gasped, reaching up to put her arm about my neck and kissing my face.

I put my arms around her, my eyes full of tears.

'Oh, Amy, I thought I'd never see you again,' I sniffed.

Hector picked up my kitbag and closed the front door.

'Come in and get warm,' said Amy, wiping her eyes on her apron, and then taking my hand and leading me down the long hall to the kitchen parlour at the back of

40

the house. The three children were having their tea in the parlour.

'Look who's here! It's Uncle George home from France,' announced Amy, proudly.

'Hello!' I said, hesitantly.

The children left the table to greet me. The eldest, Alice, put her arms about my neck as I bent down to kiss her. She was seven, her sister, Ruth, was a year younger, and Jimmy, the youngest, had just had his fourth birthday.

They each kissed me and then returned to the table.

'Let me take your greatcoat,' said Hector.

I undid the buttons and belt and he relieved me of it.

'Thank you, Hector.'

'Sit by the fire, Georgie, I'll make our meal when the children are finished. Have some tea to be going on with.'

I sat by the kitchener drinking my tea, listening to the chatter of the children. At times I stared into the coals of the fire, then I noticed my sister and her husband exchange glances from time to time, but they did not intrude on my thoughts.

Amy then put the children to bed, and Hector went upstairs to tuck them in. He was understanding, was my brother-in-law, he knew I did not want to talk, and when he came back to the parlour, calmly read his ever-open Bible.

Amy came downstairs and, as she passed me to go into the kitchen, she bent down and kissed my cheek.

'It's good to have you home again, my dear,' she smiled.

'Thank you, Amy,' I murmured, tears in my eyes.

'We've got stewed lamb and dumplings, Georgie, all right?'

'Smashing,' I replied, my mouth watering.

'I'll just make some more dumplings for you. More tea?'

41

'Please.' I stood up and took my teacup out to the kitchen.

Amy, her sleeves rolled up, was mixing suet dumplings in her pastry bowl.

'I've put you in Jimmy's room. Your bed is still made up there. He's as pleased as punch that you are sharing with him again. You must go up to him, or he will never sleep. I'll make some more tea,' smiled Amy, glancing at my medal ribbons, though she made no comment.

'I'll go up and see Jimmy,' I smiled.

'Yes, do that, Georgie, the kettle will be boiled then.'

I went through the parlour and out into the long hall, then climbed the stairs. Jimmy was lying in bed sucking his thumb; Hector I could hear, was in the girls' room.

'Uncle George,' gurgled Jimmy, as I sat down on his bed. I noticed my old slippers under the other bed on which Hector had placed my kitbag.

'I'm going to take off my boots,' I said, untying the laces. Jimmy giggled and climbed out of bed.

'No, you stay in bed, Jimmy, it's cold.'

I put on my slippers and placed my boots under the other bed.

'Now into bed, Jimmy. Let me tuck you in. I'll be up soon, so you had better be asleep,' I said firmly.

'Kiss,' said Jimmy. I bent down and kissed his cheek. As I closed the bedroom door, the girls' bedroom door opened and Hector appeared.

'I've just said good-night to Jimmy,' I said.

'Then you had better say good-night to the girls as well,' smiled Hector. 'Glad you've taken those boots off,' he added.

'Yes,' I murmured apologetically. I went into the girls' room. Their beds were against opposite walls, much better than Amy ever had. She had shared with her two sisters, whilst I with my three brothers. I approached Alice, the eldest child. She was dark-haired like her father, while Ruth, the youngest, looked the image of Amy, with the same chestnut hair and blue eyes.

I kissed them both then followed Hector from the room.

'Off to sleep now, girls,' said Hector.

'Night night, Daddy, night night, Uncle George,' they giggled.

'God bless girls,' I replied.

Amy's stewed lamb and dumplings were marvellous. I had cleaned my plate and was chewing the bones long before Amy and Hector had finished their meal.

'There is a little more,' said Amy, looking around the table.

'I'm sure George can finish it off,' smiled Hector.

'Thank you,' I said quickly, handing Amy my plate.

They watched as I finished the remains of the stewed lamb. Hector, who wore thick glasses, peered at me from time to time. 'Is it as bad there as I've heard it is, George?' he asked.

I was chewing at a soft neck bone. I stopped and looked at him.

'Yes,' I nodded. 'If I told you what I'd seen, you would not believe me. It's just unbelievable.' I shrugged and carried on chewing at my bone.

'No,' murmured Hector, slowly shaking his head.

'Jam roly-poly and custard anyone?' smiled Amy.

'No,' I beamed, 'really?'

Amy nodded and winked at Hector. She left the table and then brought in the puddings. She gave me what must have been her portion as well, as I had a real plateful.

'I've had enough,' she said, looking at Hector, who smiled affectionately at her.

After my pudding, I felt blown out; never had I been so full.

'That was wonderful, Amy,' I said, struggling to hide a yawn.

The kitchener was making me drowsy – I was unused to such warmth. I could feel myself drifting off in the chair. I tried to stay awake, but my eyes kept closing.

'You go to bed, George, if you are tired,' said Hector.

'Yes, you do,' smiled Amy. 'I'll fill a hot-water bottle for you.'

'I will if you don't mind. I'll come down later,' I replied. I struggled to my feet and made my way out of the room.

'There's pyjamas under your pillow,' said Amy.

'Thank you,' I yawned, 'I'll go and lie down for a bit.'

When my head touched the pillow I remembered no more until I awoke at midday the following morning. In my drowsy state I did not know where I was. It was so quiet. At last I gathered my thoughts and sat up. It all came back to me. I was in Amy's house.

I looked over at Jimmy's bed but there was no sign of him and his bed was made. Amy was in the kitchen when I went downstairs. I could not hear the children. The house seemed so quiet, it seemed to pain my ears.

'Hello, Georgie,' smiled Amy. 'You slept well.'

'Yes, I did,' I yawned.

'Do you want some warm water for a wash and shave?'

'Yes please, I'll go and get my wash bag.'

I returned to the bedroom, took it out of my kitbag and picked up my wallet at the same time.

'I put some hot water in the bowl in the scullery, Georgie. I'll cook you some breakfast when I've got this pudding on,' said Amy.

I opened my wallet and took out three one pound notes and put them on the table in front of Amy.

'That's for my keep and something for you, and here's my ration card for two weeks,' I said.

Amy looked at the money.

'I don't want all this, dear,' she protested. 'Ten shillings a week is more than enough.'

'No, Amy, you take it. I had some back pay.'

'Are you sure?' Amy looked uncertain.

'Of course I am. I'll have my wash now,' I replied.

I didn't say 'shave' because I had no beard as such yet – just a few sparse fair-haired bristles. Amy made me a large breakfast of bacon and bubble and squeak – it was marvellous.

'Where are the children,' I asked.

'Hector's taken them to the park. He writes his sermon on a Saturday afternoon so I'll take them to the shops with me later.'

'I'll come with you,' I replied.

'Lovely,' smiled Amy. 'Are you going to see them at Holdens?'

Amy was referring to the firm I worked for prior to being called up. It was a jam factory. I worked in their small laboratory as an assistant. Their works was further up Lausanne Road on the other side.

I shrugged my shoulders. 'Don't think so.'

'Why ever not?' frowned Amy.

I shrugged again and slowly shook my head. Amy, hands on hips and her face set, looked at me.

'Because you registered as a conscientious objector, I suppose, and some of them laughed at you. Well they won't laugh now. Hector says that you have the Distinguished Conduct Medal and the Military Medal as well. That will make them laugh on the other side of their faces.'

Amy wiped her hands on a towel before she continued.

'I just can't wait to tell old Hopkins the manager, when I see him,' she said, satisfaction appearing on her face.

'I shouldn't get too worked up about it,' I grinned. 'I still don't want to see them.'

'What about Jeannie Uden? She asked after you when I saw her the other day. It was her eighteenth birthday last week. It was a shame, they had a telegram the previous day to say one of her brothers was killed at Ypres.'

'Which one?' I queried.

'Ernie, I think, the second eldest.'

'It was Ernie who punched me on the nose before I joined up – called me a bloody coward,' I said without feeling.

Amy flushed slightly, and looked uncomfortable.

'Georgie, you won't swear in front of Hector, will you?'

'No, of course not,' I smiled.

'Are you going to see Ma and Pa?' asked Amy, suddenly.

'No.' My reply was sharp as my face set.

Amy chewed on her lower lip, unsure what to say.

'Have you seen them lately?' I asked.

'I saw Ma outside the fishmonger's in Queen's Road the other day. Pa was looking at the fish on the slab and didn't see me. He looked a bit Brahms to me, and Ma was little better.'

'I've no wish to see them again. They threw me out, Amy, remember that. But for Hector and you I'd have nowhere to sleep.'

Amy lowered her eyes, but did not reply, her face now flushed.

'I'm going to see Mr Latimer at the polytechnic, though. I want to go back when I leave the Army.'

'That's good, Georgie. Hector says education is the road to a better life,' smiled Amy.

'I'm sure he's right,' I murmured.

Our conversation was brought to a halt by the return of Hector and the children. They ran down the hall, the sound of their boots making an echo on the linoleum-covered floor.

'Quiet. Quiet,' said Amy, putting her arms around Jimmy.

'George is coming shopping with me this afternoon, Hector,' said Amy, as she began to remove the children's overcoats.

'Is he?' smiled Hector, faintly. 'I can write my sermon then.'

'What's it about?' asked Amy, as she began to lay the table.'

'The power of prayer,' replied Hector, a little patronisingly.

'Do you pray, Georgie?' asked Amy, looking at me.

'Yes,' I said shortly.

'There you are then,' said Hector triumphantly, 'and you are home safe and well,' he beamed.

'Um,' I grunted. 'A lot of the lads prayed harder than me, Hector, and they won't be coming home.' Amy looked at me quickly and then went into the kitchen.

Hector cleared his throat, 'Er, well,' he began, 'let me take your coat, Ruth dear.'

'Yes, Daddy, Alice has lost a button off her coat – look!'

'I haven't,' retorted a red-faced Alice. 'You have.'

'Let's be a little quieter shall we?' said Hector patiently.

I sat down and read the newspaper. The news was not good. We had made little progress on the Somme. I almost smiled, I could have told them that.

All my clothes were in the cupboard in Jimmy's room. Amy had put my jacket and trousers on a hanger for me. Next to it was my old overcoat which had taken me weeks to save up for. I tried on my trousers; they would have fallen but for my braces; they seemed much too big for me now.

'Aren't you wearing your uniform, Georgie?' asked Amy, as I returned to the kitchen after our midday meal.

'No,' I replied, looking down at my trousers.

'My trousers seem too big now,' I said, looking at Amy.

'You have lost weight, hasn't he Hector?'

Hector peered at me for a moment, then nodded. 'He has indeed.'

'Put your uniform on if it fits better,' suggested Amy.

I could see Hector almost smiling, but he did not speak.

'It doesn't,' I said shortly.

Amy pursed her lips. 'All right then,' she said. 'Put your overcoat on, it's cold out, then we will get off.'

'I was thinking of getting Hector some second-hand books from that shop in Queen's Road, Amy.'

We were almost at Queen's Road. I was pushing Jimmy's pushchair and the girls held Amy's hands.

'He'll like that, Georgie,' smiled Amy.

'Walk properly, Ruth, you'll be tripping me up,' she scolded, pulling at Ruth's arm.

'Don't spend too much of your money,' she added.

While Amy did her shopping, I carried on to the second-hand bookshop in New Cross Road.

'I'll meet you outside the butcher's on my way back,' I said, hurrying away since I could spend hours browsing among books.

'All right, but don't be too long,' smiled Amy.

I bought Hector six second-hand books that I thought he would like, for one shilling and fourpence, and five for myself, which cost me a shilling. When I paid for them, the owner of the shop gave me a piece of string to tie them up in a bundle. I then returned to find Amy in the draper's shop, Jimmy was outside in his pushchair. To my surprise Jimmy was asleep, so I carefully moved past him into the shop. The draper was cutting up some net curtaining for Amy as I entered the shop.

'Hello,' I said, touching her shoulder and grinning.

Amy turned to me, looking a little embarrassed.

'You got some books then?' She looked down at the bundle.

'There you are, madam, that's one pound seven shillings and sixpence,' said the draper, folding up the curtaining and putting it in a paper bag.

'And the rings and wires?' asked Amy.

'They are in the bag, madam,' he replied.

Amy handed him two one-pound notes.

'There we are, madam. Twelve shillings and sixpence change.'

'Thank you,' smiled Amy.

'And thank you,' beamed the draper.

I picked up the large brown bag off the counter, as Amy put her purse into her shopping bag.

'I'll carry this, you've got enough to carry there.' I nodded at her shopping bags.

Outside the shop we put the books into the bag on Jimmy's pushchair and I took more of the shopping.

'I've spent some of that money you gave me on lace curtains for the front room. I've never been able to afford them on Hector's stipend, he is not paid very much in the Baptist's, you know.'

'You spend it on what you like, Amy. I understand,' I replied.

'Thank you, Georgie,' she smiled.

'I'll just call at the greengrocer's first, then we'll go home.'

The greengrocer had much of his display on the pavement and as we looked at it, came out of the shop.

'Seven pounds of potatoes, and a cabbage, please,' said Amy. The greengrocer – a man in his forties – weighed the potatoes, then put them into Amy's shopping bag. 'And one cabbage,' he said, eyeing me. 'Anything else?'

'Yes, two pounds of eating apples and two pounds of cooking,' said Amy, quickly.

The greengrocer looked at me again, then weighed the apples. When Amy had paid him, he spoke again. 'Should have thought a fine upstanding lad like you would have been in the Army,' he said sarcastically, a grin on his face. I sniffed, but did not reply.

Amy, however, turned on him angrily: 'He came home yesterday from the Somme, and he's got the DCM and Military Medal to prove it.'

The greengrocer was taken aback by this outburst. 'Sorry, mate, didn't know,' he muttered.

'I've seen older men than you out there. We need more men at the rate they are being mown down. There will be none left before long,' I said.

The man mumbled under his breath, then went back into the shop.

The fishmonger, in the adjoining shop, was listening intently as he served a customer.

'Like some fish for tea, Georgie?' asked Amy, having given the greengrocer a departing glare.

'Fine,' I replied. As Amy was buying some fish, Jimmy was pointing at a large crab in the centre of his display.

'Do you like crab, Amy?' I asked.

'Yes, but...' she paused.

'Does Hector?'

'Oh yes! But it's expensive,' she replied.

'How much is the crab?' I asked, pointing at it.

'A shilling,' replied the fishmonger.

'Tell me, son, 'ave you got the DCM and MM?'

I nodded.

'Can I see 'em?' he asked, putting his hands in the small of his back.

'I haven't got them with me,' I replied.

'I tell you wot, son. I'll let you 'ave that crab fer a

50

bob and if yer bring them 'ere fer me ter see, I'll let yer 'ave yer bob back. 'ows that?' the man smiled.

'Done,' I grinned, taking a shilling from my pocket. 'What time do you close?'

'Half six on a Saturday, son.'

'Right, it's four now by your clock, I'll be back by five-thirty, OK?'

'Good lad,' grinned the fishmonger, wrapping up the crab.

'I've dressed it fer yer,' he said, taking my shilling.

I could see Amy almost bursting with pride.

'See you later,' I said, nodding at the fishmonger who, by the look on his face, appeared doubtful.

We walked slowly up Lausanne Road. It was slightly uphill and with our load of shopping and three children, progress was slow. It was now almost dark and a fog was coming up the street; the other side of the street was almost a blur.

When we arrived home Amy was full of what happened. I gave the books to Hector and went upstairs to change.

'Cup of tea, George?' said Hector, calling up the stairs.

'I'm going back to that fishmonger first to get my shilling,' I replied, pulling on my boots.

I could hear Hector laughing in the hall. I finished putting on my uniform, then slipped my medals into my pocket. I had been given a velvet-covered box to keep them in and I could now feel the box in my overcoat pocket, as I went into the parlour where Amy and Hector were drinking their tea.

'You haven't shown them to us yet, George,' said Hector.

I took the box out of my overcoat pocket and put it on the parlour table, then opened it. They bent forward to look at them more closely. Hector turned them over

51

to see the inscription on the back of them. Having read, he put them back in the box.

'I'm very proud of you, George,' he blinked, patting my arm.

'And so am I,' echoed Amy, kissing my cheek.

I could see the tears in her eyes as she handed me the box.

'Take good care of them, Georgie,' she smiled.

The fishmonger did not recognise me for a moment, when I stood beside his stone slabs with their now diminishing variety of fish. Sprigs of parsley now occupied most of the space. Then he recognised me and came forward, smiling.

'There y'are, son,' he greeted me.

Without a word, I opened up my greatcoat and pointed to the ribbons on my tunic, then I took the box from my pocket, opened it and held it under one of the paraffin lamps that lit his marble slabs. I could see his eyes open wider as he turned over the medals.

'Private Bowman – that's me. I got them yesterday morning.'

''Strewth,' muttered the fishmonger.

'Charlie, Bill, 'ave a look at these,' he called to his mates. Both men looked at the medals, one shook his head.

'Cor, never seen 'em before,' said Charlie.

'Nor me, mate,' said the other one.

They were joined by the greengrocer, who was equally taken aback.

'Here's yer shilling, son, and another one fer a drink on me,' smiled the fishmonger.

'Thank you,' I replied, taking the florin and putting it in my pocket with my medals.

'Like kippers, son?' asked the fishmonger. I nodded. He wrapped up two pairs of kippers in newspaper and handed them to me. 'Fer yer breakfast,' he grinned.

'Thanks very much,' I replied.

The greengrocer who had been watching, beckoned to me.

'Here y'are, son, some nice pears for me special customers,' he said, winking at me.

'Thank you,' I said, taking the bag.

' 'Ow long 'ave yer got leave, son?' asked the fishmonger.

'I go back two weeks on Monday,' I replied.

' 'Ave a good time and good luck,' he smiled.

'I will, thanks,' I replied. 'Bye.'

'Cheerio, son, and good luck,' they replied.

Hector was looking at the books that I had bought him and Amy was cooking when I returned.

'More fish,' she laughed when I gave her the kippers and she opened the bag containing the pears.

'Lovely pears, too.' There was a note of satisfaction in her voice when I told her what had happened.

The girls were playing with their chalks and boards on the parlour table.

'Like a pear, girls?' I said, smiling at them.

'After their tea, Georgie,' said Amy before they could reply.

'Thank you for those books, George,' said Hector suddenly. 'Your choice was excellent – Dickens, Trollope, Hardy – could not be better,' he smiled. 'And you were given two shillings by the fishmonger, well done.'

'Plus two pairs of kippers, and a bag of pears from the greengrocer,' I grinned, happily.

'Cup of tea,' said Amy, coming into the parlour carrying a tray. 'Here we are, my pet,' she said, handing a cup and saucer to me.

'Thanks, Amy. I think I will go and get changed first, and get my boots off,' I said, getting to my feet.

'I should,' she replied, smiling at Hector.

'Have your tea first, George,' said Hector, 'or it will get cold.'

Having been to an obligatory two services at the Baptist Chapel on Sunday, I spent the rest of the day reading. During the evening I sat by the kitchener and it was so pleasant that I fell asleep in my chair. Amy woke me with a cup of cocoa, which I took to bed.

I did not sleep well that night. I dreamed I was back in France and fell out of bed with my blankets. By the dim light I got under my bed, where I slept until morning. When I awoke, Hector was in the room with a cup of tea for me. Jimmy's bed was empty and I could hear him downstairs.

'All right, old chap?' asked Hector kindly. 'A bad dream?'

I yawned and nodded, then crawled out from under the bed.

'Drink this then,' he said, offering me the cup of tea.

'Thank you, Hector.'

I sat on the edge of the bed with the blankets around my shoulders, drinking my tea.

'No need to get up yet, you know,' said Hector. 'It's not a nice day, raining hard.'

'I'll get dressed shortly,' I replied.

Hector left the room, and I sat thinking of Amelia Hooper. I had her address in my wallet and I could not make up my mind if I should go and see her. I could smell bacon cooking, so I put on my army trousers and vest and went downstairs for a wash. Amy greeted me.

'Hello, Georgie, are you all right?' she asked, kindly.

I kissed her cheek. 'Yes, fine. I'll have a wash and shave now.'

'I've put some hot water in the bowl in the scullery. Your breakfast will be ready in a minute,' said Amy. 'You come out of the way, Jimmy.'

'He's all right, Amy,' I smiled.

'Shoo him out if he gets in your way,' she replied.

Amy, I think, was surprised to see me in my uniform as I sat down to breakfast, though she made no comment. It was Monday and washday. Besides being a wet day, the fire under the copper in the scullery was taking a time to get going, and the water in the copper was still stone cold.

'I lit the fire under that copper an hour ago,' she complained, 'and the water is still cold. It's not drawing.'

I looked out into the scullery as I ate my breakfast.

'Did you clean it out well?' I asked.

'I think so, there was some ash at the back though,' she conceded.

'That's probably the trouble. Where's Hector? Are the girls at school today?'

'Yes,' replied Amy. 'He took them, then he was going to the church. He's got a visiting this afternoon. What are you doing?'

'I think I'll go to Blackheath,' I replied.

'Blackheath?' frowned Amy. 'In the rain?'

'I'm going to see someone,' I said quietly.

'Are you? Who do you know in Blackheath?' asked Amy curiously.

'A nurse I met. She gave me her address.'

'Did she?' smiled Amy. 'Well I never, surely she will not be there now.'

'She is. She went home on compassionate grounds. She was a VAD.'

'A volunteer nurse, you mean. I see,' nodded Amy, her eyes twinkling. 'So that's why you are wearing your uniform. When you go for the tram, will you call at the photographers in Queen's Road and get your picture taken for me. I'll pay for it.'

'No need,' I replied, 'I'll call in for you.'

I left Amy still struggling with the fire underneath the copper, put on my overcoat and hat, then left the house. It was a miserable wet morning, but I did not notice it.

55

I felt good as I walked briskly down Lausanne Road, my studded boots rattling on the pavement.

The lady at the photographers knew exactly what I wanted as soon as I entered the shop.

'You would like your picture taken before you go back, young man?' she said sadly.

'Yes please, it's for my sister,' I replied.

'I think Mr Stebbings is free now, he usually is on a Monday morning. I'll just go and ask him.'

She pulled aside a green velvet curtain and went into the back of the shop. Moments later she reappeared. 'Mr Stebbings can fit you in now. Step this way, please.' She held aside the velvet curtain to allow me to pass into what was a studio.

Mr Stebbings, a tired look on his lined face, looked at me over his glasses, then spoke with almost an effort.

'Do you want it wearing your overcoat and cap, or without them?' he asked.

'Without, I think,' I replied, taking off my cap and unbuttoning my greatcoat. 'How much will it be?'

'Postcard size, sixpence, eightpence with a mount, minimum three off.'

'Oh!' I murmured, taking off my greatcoat.

As the photographer adjusted his camera, which was on a tripod, he noticed my medal ribbons.

'Sit down on the chair, son.' He pointed to a high-backed dining chair with a leather seat.

I sat down on the chair and he stepped towards me still looking at the medal ribbons.

'What medals are they, son?' he asked, peering at the ribbons.

'Distinguished Conduct Medal and Military Medal. I got them on Friday,' I replied.

'Where were you, son?' he said, in almost a whisper.

'On the Somme. I came home on Thursday with a hospital train.'

'Ruby, Ruby,' he called out. The green velvet curtain was pulled aside.

'What is it?' asked the woman.

'Have a look at the boy's medal ribbons.'

The lady, who I had spoken to earlier, came towards me and peered at my chest.

'The DCM and the MM, would you believe,' said the man, proudly.

'Do you live around here?' asked the lady.

'In Lausanne Road,' I replied.

'He was on the Somme,' said Mr Stebbings, quietly.

The woman's eyes filled with tears. 'Our youngest son was killed there three months ago' she murmured.

'I'm sorry,' I said, averting my eyes.

The lady, without a word, produced a comb from her coat pocket and then straightened my hair.

'There, that's better,' she said, returning the comb to her pocket.

Mr Stebbings quickly took the photographs.

'Be ready tomorrow afternoon,' he smiled.

'Thank you,' I said, putting on my greatcoat and picking up my cap, then pulling aside the velvet curtain.

'Good luck, son,' said the photographer.

The lady wrote out a receipt and I took some money from my pocket.

'When do you go back, dear?' she asked, sadly.

'In fourteen days' time. Three with a mount, please,' I said, handing her a florin.

'It's half price to you, dear,' she said, handing me two sixpences.

'Thank you very much,' I replied. 'Goodbye and thank you,' I said, leaving the shop.

'Goodbye dear, and God bless, lad,' she said.

I boarded the tram at New Cross and as it clattered its way through Deptford and Lewisham, I studied for the hundredth time the piece of paper on which Amelia had written her address. By the time we reached Blackheath, the drizzle had increased somewhat, and having asked my way from a shop assistant, I walked quickly towards the Heath.

5

Cedar Lodge

Amelia's home was as I expected, a large detached residence in its own grounds. It had a low wall around it and green, painted, wrought-iron railings that were head high. Inside the wall were rhododendron bushes, which gave a considerable privacy and no doubt a fine display in summer time.

I pushed open the heavy wrought-iron gate, which creaked on its dry hinges, and having closed it again, I approached the front door, my army boots crunching on the gravel path. I rang the bell, then removed my cap and tried to shake the water from it. I stood in the porch and waited. At last an elderly maid opened the door. She peered at me.

'Good morning,' I said politely. 'I wonder if I could see Miss Amelia Hooper?'

'Who are you?' she asked abruptly. The maid looked me up and down and did not seem too impressed.

'I am Private George Bowman. I met Miss Hooper in France.'

'Wait here, please,' she said, closing the door in my face.

I was gazing at the shrubs in the borders when the maid came to the door again. It was opened less than two feet.

'Miss Amelia has been ill, and Mr and Mrs Hooper say she cannot see anyone, good-day to you,' she said quickly. Before I could say anything, the door was closed again. I walked dejectedly down the gravel path and pulled on my wet cap. Having closed the gate, as per the instructions on a neat metal tag that was attached to it, I walked back to the tram stop.

'Never mind, Georgie,' said Amy sympathetically, as I sat in front of the kitchener trying to dry my trousers. 'Perhaps it's all for the best. I've hung up your greatcoat in the scullery. It should soon get dry there, my copper fire is still burning.'

'Um,' I mumbled, looking into the fire.

'You had your picture taken them?' asked Amy.

'I had to have three done, but they are only charging me half price,' I replied.

'That's good, isn't it? I'll give one to Ma and you will want one, won't you,' smiled Amy.

'I wonder what was the matter with Amelia,' I mumbled.

'Perhaps you should call again and take her some flowers,' suggested Amy, as she took a hot iron off the kitchener.

'That's a good idea,' I said, brightening, 'I'll do that.'

'Are you meeting the girls, Georgie? It will help me if you do, I've a pile of ironing to do and I'm all behind through that wretched copper this morning.'

'I had promised the girls anyway, "in your uniform too", so Alice informed me, "and mummy will remind you", she said to me.'

'Mummy is reminding you now, Uncle George, it's nearly three o'clock,' laughed Amy.

'Your greatcoat's almost dry,' called out Amy from the scullery.

'Yes, all right, Amy, I'll get off in a minute. It won't take me long to walk to Waller Road.'

'I'll start the tea as soon as I have finished this ironing. Hector doesn't like me doing it in the evening,' said Amy, taking something out of Jimmy's hand. 'Jimmy mustn't touch, naughty boy.'

I put on my greatcoat and left the house. It was still raining, so I pulled up the collar. The children were coming out of the primary school just as I arrived, and the girls, who quickly spotted me, ran towards me.

'Hello, Uncle George,' they chorused. I kissed them both, then each holding my hands, we walked home. We passed a paper shop that sold toys and sweets. Alice pulled me towards the window. Ruth did the same thing and pointed to something in the window. 'Look, Uncle George.' They both pointed to a cut-out circus outfit that was in the window. 'Look, Uncle George, it's a circus with a tent and all the animals and their cages, you cut them out and stick them,' explained Alice, her face flushed with excitement.

'Do you like them, Ruthy?' I smiled.

'Yes, there are clowns, too,' she said, nodding her head vigorously and pointing at the box.

'Let's go and look at it then,' I said, pushing open the door and ringing the bell that was attached to the top of it.

The shop seemed filled with light after the drab twilight of a damp, foggy, late afternoon in November.

'How much is the cut-out circus that you have in the window?' I asked the man behind the counter.

He scratched at the back of his neck before replying, 'Er, one-and-six I think, including glue. I'll just check.' He walked around the shop and looked into the window. 'Yes, that's it, one-and-sixpence – the old price. They've gone up; still what hasn't with this war,' he sniffed.

'I'll have it then,' I said, looking down at the girls' smiling faces.

'Oh goody,' Alice clapped her hands.

The man took the box out of the window, then wrapped it up in a piece of brown paper.

'Anything else, son?' he asked.

'Yes, I'll have three sherbert dabs and some aniseed balls, a quarter please.'

'Right, son.' The man weighed out the aniseed balls and put them in a bag with the sherbert dabs.

'That's one-and-ninepence please.'

I handed the man two shillings and he gave me threepence change.

'On leave, son?' he asked kindly.

'Yes, that's right,' I replied.

'Are you going to carry the box, Alice?'

'Ooh, yes,' gasped Alice, putting out her hands.

'Sherbert dabs, Uncle George?' said Ruth looking up at me.

'After tea, Ruthy, you can have them then,' I replied, opening the door of the shop.

'Bye,' I said over my shoulder.

'Cheerio son and good luck,' replied the shopkeeper.

'What have you got there?' asked Amy looking at the parcel that Alice had in her arms.

Amy had met us at the front door and the girls could not wait to show the cut-out circus to her.

'Uncle George bought it for us, it's a circus,' said Alice.

'Georgie, you shouldn't have,' said Amy as she closed the door.

I took off my cap and greatcoat and hung it on one of the hooks in the hall, then bent down to unfasten Ruth's coat.

'Let me help you with your coat, Ruthy,' I said, unfastening the top button.

'Uncle George bought us some sherbert dabs for after tea,' said Ruth, her face beaming.

'Did he? You are lucky girls. Let's wash your hands, then you can have your tea,' said Amy.

While the children had their tea, I read the paper. It was *The Times*, as Hector purchased it. The front page had its usual list of casualties. It made depressing reading and the nonsense about successes would have been a laugh, if one did not know of the human sacrifice being paid.

'Cup of tea, dear?' said Amy, smiling.

'Thank you.' I put down the paper.

'Hector will not be back until six, he has got a funeral at Nunhead cemetery at four today.'

'Anyone we know?' I asked.

'Shouldn't think so,' said Amy. 'If they don't go into the Golden Lion or The Anchor, our family won't know them.'

I started to laugh – Amy still had her sense of humour.

With the girls and Jimmy clutching their sherbert dabs, we at last opened the box on the parlour table. Amy watched as she sorted out her half-dry washing. The scullery had lines of it hanging up.

'Do the animals first, Uncle George,' said Alice.

'No, do this,' chimed Ruth, holding up a piece of the circus tent.

'All right, all right, we'll do a bit at a time,' I said, my ears beginning to ache.

'Don't touch that, Jimmy.' I winced a little as I spoke. Amy seemed to understand as she looked sympathetically at me. Jimmy had grabbed the scissors and a clown almost lost his head, before I retrieved the situation.

'Leave everything alone,' said Amy severely, 'or you will go straight to bed, Jimmy.'

'Send him now mummy, he's a nuisance,' said Alice, sticking her tongue out at her young brother.

'Any of that, miss, and you will go as well,' snapped Amy.

'Put that tube of glue down, Ruthy, there's a good girl,' I said, patiently, though it was wearing a little thin by this time.

Amy was now smiling as I tried to control the work that was taking place on the parlour table.

'Now leave that, Alice, don't touch that please, Jimmy.' Amy watched for a moment, then went into the kitchen still smiling. I began to cut out the animals, watched attentively by the children. At five-thirty Jimmy was put tearfully to bed.

'Look, Jimmy, when the first animal is stuck, I'll bring it upstairs for you to see,' I said, kissing him good-night.

'Promise?' he said, his tearful blue eyes wide open.

'Yes, promise,' I smiled, touching his nose playfully.

'Nighty-night,' he called out as, in Amy's arms, he went out into the hall to begin the climb upstairs to bed.

'God bless,' I replied.

'Can I cut one out, Uncle George?' asked Alice.

'Yes, all right, if you are careful, but just along the dotted line.' Thus we continued until the girls went to bed.

After our evening meal, I stuck more of the circus together, while Amy sat darning and Hector read the evening paper. I sat, elbows on the table, my hands over my ears. I could feel a pain in them again. Amy spoke, a look of concern on her face. She touched my arm. 'Are you all right, Georgie?'

'Yes,' I murmured, 'it's inside my ears – they hurt from time to time.'

'Have you seen an Army doctor?'

I nodded. 'Yes, he said it was the guns and that it would wear off.'

'Do you want anything?' asked Hector.

'No thanks, Hector, it will go.'

We lapsed into silence, though I was aware of Amy constantly looking at me.

'It says in the evening paper that our offensive on the Somme has now ended,' said Hector.

'Probably run out of men,' I muttered.

Hector looked curiously at me, as I cut out a sea lion. 'Either that, or the hospitals are full up,' I added morosely.

'Is it that bad, George?' asked Hector quietly.

'You would not believe it, Hector, if I told you of the amount of casualties. I found it unbelievable,' I murmured. 'And it was there it...' I did not finish. 'Our officer said we were not to tell anyone, and Vic, my pal, said nobody would believe us anyway, if we did tell them.'

'What did the officer say?' asked Hector.

'He did not reply. I think I will go to bed,' I said, getting out of my chair.

'Yes, you go, Georgie. I'll bring you up a cup of cocoa,' smiled Amy, sympathetically.

'Good-night, Hector.'

'Good-night, and God bless, George,' said Hector kindly. 'Hope you feel better in the morning.'

That night I slept well and I did feel better. Amy brought me up a cup of tea and I stayed in bed until nine o'clock. As I came downstairs, I could see Amy in the front room. I put my head round the door.

'Hello,' I grinned.

Amy turned. 'Ah! You're up,' she said, cheerfully. 'I'm just measuring the windows before I cut up my curtain material,' she said, looking out of the window.

'What are you looking at?' I asked, following her gaze. 'The telegraph boy?'

Amy nodded and lowered her eyes. Until she informed me I could not understand her sudden embarrassment – what had it to do with the telegraph boy?

'Why?' I frowned.

'Everyone looks out for the telegraph these days,

Georgie. No one wants him knocking at your door,' she said in a husky voice. 'It's only bad news, and everyone has got someone in the army.' There were tears in her eyes and I moved towards her and enfolded her in my arms, dear Amy.

'You must not worry – I'll be all right,' I smiled as I released her.

'I pray for that,' she murmured.

'He went up the road though, to the top end of Lausanne, or even one of the other roads off it,' I said, peering out of the window.

'I'll get you some breakfast in a minute,' said Amy, using her tape to measure the bay window.

Amy had cooked me a plate of bubble and squeak. She knew I liked it, though Hector did not. I could tell by his face, as he looked at it.

'I'm helping Hector move some furniture for the afternoon prayer meeting this morning, Amy, then I'm getting my photos this afternoon. I'll take Jimmy if you like and collect the girls from school at the same time.'

'Will you, Georgie, you don't mind?'

'No, of course not,' I replied.

'Bless you, dear, it will help me, I can get my curtains started this morning and then I serve teas this afternoon with the other ladies.'

'I could take Jimmy up to the church with me this morning, if it helps,' I suggested.

'It would, but don't let him run about in church; Hector wouldn't like that,' said Amy.

I smiled, but made no comment, to Amy's relief, I think!

'Yes, I'll see he stays in his chair. Anyway, I'll not be long there, then we'll go to the park.'

'Park, park, Unca Georgie,' began Jimmy.

'If you're good,' said Amy, wagging a finger at him.

'He will be, mind you one of the circus lions has lost his head,' I grinned.

'Oh no ... the girls will be upset,' frowned Amy.

'I'm not saying it's Jimmy,' I smiled. 'I have tried to stick it with a piece of paper. Let's hope that they do not see it.'

'Some chance, with those two,' smiled Amy.

Hector's church was in Gautry Road, less than five minutes away, and I found him in the little vestry, sorting out some papers.

'Hello, Hector. Ready to move this furniture? I said I would take Jimmy to the park.'

'Yes, of course, my boy, just give me a moment. I've mislaid something for my sermon.'

'I'll wait outside with Jimmy,' I said, backing out of the room.

'Is Jimmy with you?' Hector put down the bunch of papers.

'Yes,' I replied.

'I'll come straight away,' he said, following me out of the vestry and into the main hall.

In a few minutes the work – if you could call it that – was done, which to me was nothing, but to Hector was hard work. I left him wiping his face with a handkerchief in quite a lather.

'Put your coat on, Hector, or you will catch a cold or worse,' I said, as I left him.

'Thank you, George. See you later,' he replied.

I pushed Jimmy up Gellatly Road, then down Drakefield Road to the park. He thought it was great fun. We sat on a park bench looking at the ducks on the pond. Two old men came and sat next to me, the war was their topic of conversation, then one turned to me.

'We're showing them on the Somme, aren't we?' I did not speak. 'That right, son?' said the other, looking at me.

'Are we?' I replied tiredly.

'Aye, says so in the paper.'

'Does it?' I remarked.

I got up and began to move Jimmy's pushchair. I did not speak.

'Probably hasn't been up to the front yet, Albert,' remarked the first old man.

'No,' agreed his companion.

I did not even bother to indicate that I had heard them. It would have been a waste of time anyway. I pushed Jimmy to the other side of the park and found an empty seat. We did not stay long, as it was cold, and I made my way down to Queen's Road to collect my photographs. They were better than I expected and Amy was pleased with them.

'They are very good, Georgie, you do look handsome,' she smiled.

I did not say anything as I sat finishing off the cut-out circus, my face flushed, and watched by an attentive Jimmy.

Later I took Jimmy to meet the girls from school, while Amy was at the Baptist Church serving teas with the other ladies. Outside the school, and about to return, Ruth looked up coyly at me and said in a quiet voice, 'Can we have a sherbert dab, Uncle Georgie?'

'Mummy said we were not to ask Uncle Georgie,' said Alice, severely.

'Sherbert dab,' yelled Jimmy, shaking his pushchair and going red in the face. I knew I was beaten. 'All right, but behave,' I said, quickly. 'It's starting to rain. Hold my hand, Ruthy, let's get a move on.'

That evening I read an article from the front telling of the mud and the appalling conditions.

'Is it that bad, George?' asked Hector. He had already read the article. I put the paper down.

'It's worse, Hector. I've seen men drown in the mud and you could do nothing to help them. I'm surprised this was printed.'

'Are we winning, do you think?' Hector looked at me.

I shrugged my shoulders before I replied. 'I honestly don't know, Hector. We attack, lose hundreds of men, perhaps win a trench, then they attack, lose hundreds of men and take it back again. Then we attack and the process starts all over again. I suppose the winner will be the one in the end who has any men left. It's been going on for months.'

'That's a terrible prospect. On that basis I cannot see any end to the war,' said Hector as he removed his glasses and carefully wiped the lenses with a clean handkerchief.

'Neither can I,' I said, miserably.

'I liked your photograph,' said Amy, in an effort to change the subject.

'Did you?' I said, patiently.

'Yes, it was very good, wasn't it Hector?'

'Excellent,' he agreed, as he picked up the newspaper again.

'They charged me half price for them,' I said, a proud note in my voice.

Hector and I relapsed into our reading, for as much as I loved my sister, I had to admit that Amy had no conversation.

The following morning I again went to Blackheath. At Amy's suggestion, I bought a bunch of flowers and I hoped to be able to give them to Amelia. It was raining, and I wore my uniform and greatcoat, which kept me dry. My boots were highly polished, and as I walked through the puddles on the pavement, I thought of my unfortunate comrades on the Somme.

'Is it still raining there?' I asked myself. It just did not bear thinking about.

When I glanced out of the window of the tramcar at the falling rain, I thought how lucky I was to be out of it. As I alighted from the tramcar the rain came down even heavier, and by the time I reached Amelia's house there was a continual drip of rain falling from the peak of my cap. I pushed open the heavy iron gate and marched steadfastly up the gravel drive; my flowers by this time were beginning to look a little bedraggled to say the least. I pulled at the bell-handle, and the same maid answered the door, looking down her nose as I said: 'I've brought some flowers for Miss Amelia.' She took the flowers and the sodden piece of paper that was wrapped around them almost with disdain, and without a word she closed the front door. I was left standing in the porch wondering if I should leave. At last, I decided to do so and I was halfway to the gate when the front door opened, and a voice hailed me.

'I say...' It was an educated accent and I turned to see who had spoken. It was a young man in an army officer's uniform.

'Come back, old chap.' The greeting was friendly.

I hurried towards him. 'Sir!' my hand went instinctively to my cap.

'Come on in,' he smiled.

I clattered up the three front steps to the front door. The young officer held out his hand.

'I'm Edwin Hooper, Amelia's brother.' He grasped my wet hand.

'I'm George Bowman, sir.'

'Come on in out of the rain, you look soaked.' His friendly manner did much to dispel the poor opinion I had formed so far of the Hooper family. However, I have since learnt that one should never judge people by the manners of their servants, who are invariably worse snobs than their employers.

The hobnails of my boots screeched as I moved on the black and white tiled floor of the hall.

'Take your coat off, George,' said Edwin Hooper.

I struggled out of my greatcoat and handed it with my cap to the maid, who took it with ill-disguised distaste. At that moment we were joined by Amelia and an older lady who was introduced as her mother. Mrs Hooper was dressed in black and she was holding a handkerchief in her left hand. She did not look well.

'It's nice to see you, George,' smiled Amelia. 'The flowers are lovely.' She held out her hand, which I enfolded in my own.

'This is my mother, George.'

'How do you do, ma'am.'

'I'm pleased to make your acquaintance, Mr Bowman,' she said in an almost toneless voice.

'You must tell me all your news, George,' said Amelia, as she took her mother by the arm and led us into the drawing-room.

'Would you like some coffee, George?' said Amelia, when we were all seated.

'We have recently had some refreshments, but you are most welcome.' I could see that Amelia looked far from well. She was pale and her face was drawn.

'No, that's all right thank you,' I said in a confused fashion.

'You will stay for luncheon then?' smiled Amelia.

'I ... er...' I began.

'Of course he will – I insist, George,' grinned Edwin. 'You can then tell me all about it.'

I exchanged a glance with Amelia, who lowered her eyes almost in embarrassment.

'Yes, you must stay, Mr Bowman,' said Mrs Hooper, who gave me a weak smile.

'Yes, thank you, ma'am, if it's no trouble,' I replied.

71

'You are very welcome, George,' said Amelia, who immediately summoned the maid.

'Yes, Miss Amelia?'

'Alice, tell cook we have a guest for luncheon.'

'Yes, miss.' The maid stared blankly at me, then left the room.

'Would you like a whisky, George?' asked Edwin.

'I ... er...' again I was unsure what to say.

'I'm having one,' said Edwin, going to a carved oak cabinet. 'Warm you up, George,' said Edwin as he poured some whisky into two cut-glass tumblers. 'I'll put a spot of water in for you.'

Before I could reply, the door opened and a grey-haired middle-aged man entered the room.

'Ah! Hello father,' said Edwin cheerfully.

'Edwin,' said his father quietly as he approached Mrs Hooper, bent down and kissed her cheek.

'My dear,' he murmured. Mrs Hooper acknowledged him by a faint nod of the head.

'James,' she said at last, 'this is Mr George Bowman, a friend of Amelia's.'

I flushed slightly at her words and rose to my feet.

'Sir,' I muttered.

Mr Hooper held out his hand and smiled, somewhat tiredly.

'How nice to meet you young man,' he said, kindly.

My hand must have felt cold to Mr Hooper, as he said to Edwin, 'Give the lad a whisky, it will warm him up.'

'Just doing so father. Will you have one? The ladies are having sherry.'

'Just a small one, Edwin my dear,' said Mrs Hooper.

'Sit down, lad. George wasn't it?' said Mr Hooper.

'Yes thank you, sir,' I murmured, glancing at Amelia, who gave me an encouraging smile.

'Here we are, George,' said Edwin breezily, as he handed me a tumbler of whisky.

'Thank you,' I said, gripping the cut-glass tumbler for fear of dropping it.

Mr Hooper sat down in a high-backed leather armchair and proceeded to fill his pipe from an ornate tobacco jar. I carefully sipped my whisky, not that I liked the flavour, but it did warm me up.

'Do you smoke, George?' asked Mr Hooper, holding out the jar.

'No thank you, sir,' I replied. 'I got a niff of gas recently and smoking now makes me cough and it hurts my chest.'

'Best not to then,' said Mr Hooper, kindly.

'Was it their gas, George?' asked Edwin.

'No – ours,' I said quickly.

'Are you the young man who is a conscientious objector, yet has won all those medals?' asked Mr Hooper.

I glanced at Amelia, who flashed me a smile as she said, 'Yes he is, father. He is a stretcher bearer in the Royal Army Medical Corps.'

Mr Hooper nodded as he lit his pipe.

'I see,' he said, looking at me curiously.

'How much leave have you got, George?' asked Amelia.

'I go back next Monday week, I replied.

'Are your ears better now?' she asked.

'A bit. They've not bled lately, but I get rotten earache from time to time, and I go quite deaf.'

Mrs Hooper looked at me sympathetically, then she asked, 'Can you not take anything for it?'

The doctor gave me some tablets, ma'am,' I replied. 'They help a bit, I think.'

'How did you hurt your ears, Mr Bowman?' enquired Mrs Hooper.

'I was...' I began, as a tap sounded on the door and the maid entered and announced:

'Luncheon is served, madam.'

The Hoopers' dining-room was the grandest room in which I had ever eaten. The walls were half-oak panelled, and there were oil paintings on the wall above the panelling, country scenes and seascapes, mainly. I tried to tread as lightly as I could on the parquet flooring, but I felt that I was walking on ice.

'Mr Bowman can sit...' began Mrs Hooper.

'Call him George, mother,' said Amelia, quickly.

'George, then, can sit next to you, Amelia.' Mrs Hooper smiled faintly at me as she spoke, and indicated the high-backed dining chairs on the far side of the table. I looked down at the array of cutlery on the table, as the maid placed a plate of soup in front of me.

'Thank you,' I murmured, still looking at the cutlery.

Amelia must have read my thoughts, as she leaned towards me and smiled. 'Have you got a soup spoon, George?'

'Ah, yes you have,' she said, picking it out from among the cutlery in front of me and placing it in my hand. Her action was not unnoticed by her father, who smiled faintly in some sort of approval.

'You were telling us, George, how you hurt your ears?' said Mrs Hooper, looking at me.

I put down my soup spoon before I replied. 'I was caught in a barrage in no man's land.' I gripped my soup spoon again, aware that everyone was looking at me as I continued. 'There had been an attack and some of our men were lying wounded on the German wire. I had picked up a wounded German officer and was carrying him across no man's land when the barrage started. I was blown off my feet and lay in the mud until it lifted, then I carried on with the German to their wire and lowered him into their trench and then brought back one of our men.'

'You took a Hun back?' frowned Edwin Hooper.

'Yes,' I replied, 'that's why the German snipers let me take our own wounded back. I've taken a number of German wounded back.'

'That's a bit irregular, surely, George,' smiled Edwin Hooper.

I shrugged. 'Perhaps it is, but I've not found a better way of getting to the German wire unharmed and getting our wounded back. If I didn't do it, they would die.'

There was an embarrassed silence. No one was eating.

'Well, I think it is very commendable of you, George, dear, very,' said Mrs Hooper, wiping her eyes. 'Please excuse me,' she sniffed, then blew her nose.

Amelia stretched out a hand and touched her mother's forearm. 'Mother, dear,' she said softly.

'I'm all right now, Amelia,' said Mrs Hooper in a firm voice. 'We've just been informed, George, that our second son, Edgar, has been posted missing.'

'I'm very sorry, Mrs Hooper,' I replied.

'We heard two days ago,' said Amelia. 'I've told mother that he must be a prisoner.' Amelia flashed me a sidelong glance.

'Do you think so, George?' asked Mrs Hooper, an almost pathetic look on her face.

'Oh yes, Mrs Hooper, a lot of men are taken prisoner, and it could be months before you hear anything,' I added.

'Is that so?' she said, her voice brightening.

'Oh yes,' I said in what was, I hoped, a convincing voice.

My mind was full of images of piles of dead, unrecognisable and unknown men of both sides who would go to their graves, marked only by a plain cross, with the words: *KNOWN ONLY UNTO GOD. REST IN PEACE.*

We finished our now cold soup in silence, and Edwin had now become subdued. The main course was a leg of lamb, and Mr Hooper went to the sideboard to carve it.

'Do you like roast lamb, George?' he asked.

'Yes thank you, sir,' I replied, my mouth watering.

'Edwin, go down to the cellar and bring up that bottle of claret that I had put to one side. I was not aware that we were having a guest for luncheon.'

'Father,' replied Edwin, getting to his feet.

'What do your parents think now that you have won medals, George?' asked Mr Hooper.

'I don't know, sir, I haven't seen them. I stay with my married sister since they threw me out.'

'I see,' murmured Mr Hooper who avoided looking at Edwin, as he moved around the dining-table with a broad grin on his face.

'George's father asked him to leave,' said Amelia, quickly, 'when he registered as a conscientious objector,' she explained.

Edwin left the room, having given Amelia a broad wink that caused Amelia's cheeks to colour. I noticed, but did not comprehend the reason.

'What does your father do, George?' asked Mrs Hooper, kindly.

'He's a carter, Mrs Hooper. He has three horses, my sister says.'

'Got one, father,' said Edwin coming back into the room holding up a dusty bottle.

'Yes, all right,' said his father.

'You were saying, George?' said Amelia, quietly.

'My sister Amy says he is offering my Bessie to the army. She's old – she couldn't pull a gun, she would drown in the mud.'

'But the army needs horses, George,' said Edwin, pompously.

'They don't want Bessie. I saw our cavalry charge in September, it was awful.'

'Why?' demanded Edwin, his voice rising.

'They charged into the German machine guns, it was terrible – those poor horses, it's not their war you know.' When I thought of it, as I often did, I was close to tears. I brushed my eyes with my left hand, unaware that Amelia had put her hand on mine.

'You are quite right, George, it is not their war; poor animals to suffer so,' said Amelia, squeezing my hand.

'Quite right, my boy, quite right,' said Mr Hooper, placing a dinner plate with a large portion of lamb on it in front of me. I could see that the Hoopers were a little affected by my words, and Amelia busied herself piling vegetables on my plate. Edwin poured the wine, and when he had sat down, raised his glass, looking around the table.

'To our guest, Amelia's friend, George.' They all raised their glasses: 'George, George, George.'

I was both surprised and overcome at their words.

'Thank you,' I managed to croak.

'Where do you report to, George?' asked Edwin.

'Woolwich,' I replied.

'Did you go to Buckingham Palace to receive your medals, George,' asked Mr Hooper.

'No, sir. On the parade ground at Woolwich,' I replied.

'Who presented them to you, George?' asked Amelia.

'Some General. I did not get his name, he smelt of cigars and whisky, then he gave a speech that was a load of old rabbit!'

'It did not inspire you, George?' said Mr Hooper, endeavouring not to laugh.

'No, sir. It was a lot of cobblers,' I replied.

Amelia and Edwin were now both laughing, but not so Mrs Hooper, who frowned as she said to Amelia in an enquiring tone, 'What is old rabbit and cobblers, dear?'

'It's cockney slang, mother,' said Amelia, looking at me.

I took the hint. It was the drink that I had been given that had loosened my tongue.

'I'm off to Aldershot next Tuesday – you never know, we might run into each other,' smiled Edwin.

'I hope for your sake we do not,' I said briefly.

'I take your point,' he replied, his smile somewhat forced.

'You are staying with your married sister, George?' queried Mrs Hooper.

'Yes, ma'am,' I replied. 'She has three children – they are lovely. I take them out and meet them from school. Her husband's a minister.'

'Church of England?' asked Mrs Hooper.

'No, Baptist,' I replied.

'Are you Baptist?'

'No, not really. I don't think I am anything,' I replied.

I could see Mr Hooper smiling faintly.

'What did you do before you joined the army, George?,' he asked.

'I worked at Holding's jam factory in Lausanne Road, sir. I was in their laboratory, as they called it. I was learning chemistry at the technical college.'

'Was it nice jam, George?' asked Amelia.

'I thought it was awful. I saw a mouse fall in a vat of jam once,' I said, my face blank.

'Good heavens,' murmured Mr Hooper.

'I told the foreman and all he said was, "It's blackcurrant jam – it won't be noticed once we've stirred it up a bit".'

Amelia and her brother were now smiling, though Mrs Hooper looked horrified.

'How awful. Holding's jam you say. Their blackcurrant jam, I'll remember it, George,' said Mrs Hooper.

'Yes, ma'am, but their plum jam is very good.'

'Is it?' Mrs Hooper's face was a study.

'Yes, ma'am. They are doing very well at the moment, I understand. They've got a big army contract.'

'Good God,' muttered Mr Hooper.

'So, if you have blackcurrant jam in the officers' mess, Edwin, look carefully,' smiled Amelia.

'I will indeed,' replied Edwin, grinning as he looked at me.

'You have brothers in the army, George?'

'Yes, two of my elder brothers are. My sister, Amy, tells me that one has just been posted missing. They were both in Flanders. My other brother is in the navy up at Scapa Flow.'

'Dessert is apple pudding, George. Do you like apple pudding?'

'I'm sure he does, mother,' said Amelia.

When I had swallowed a mouthful of baked potato, I replied, 'Yes, thank you, Mrs Hooper.'

'Do you like your claret, George?' asked Edwin. 'Or would you prefer a whisky?'

'Er, no thank you, the claret's very nice. I've never had it before and it was only the second time that I've tasted whisky,' I replied.

'When was the first time then?' asked Edwin, impishly.

'It was during the summer. A Highland regiment had gone over the top. They were shot to pieces and their piper had got to the German wire. He was badly wounded and when the recall had sounded and the firing died down we could still hear him trying to play his pipes.

'Two of the Highlanders were about to try and get him, but I said I would go, so I took my stretcher poles and waved them and hoped the Germans would not shoot at me. Then as I was making my way over no man's land, I found a wounded German officer half in a shell hole. He had been there from the previous day's German attack. I carried him over my shoulder to their lines and fell in a forward trench with him still over my shoulder. They called him Herr Graff von something or other. A German officer helped me get up and another took out a silver flask and put it to my lips saying, "*Gut schnapps*". It was hot and it warmed me up. The other one spoke English and thanked me, he said to me, "You are a light in the darkness."

'I don't know what he meant, but I told him that I wanted the Highland piper. I think he gave an order to his men not to shoot, so I got out of their trench, pulled the piper off the wire and carried him back. It was so quiet, I thought I heard a bird singing, then I went and fell in our trench – that piper felt like a ton weight. I got to my feet, covered in mud and blood, and a Highland officer pulled out a similar silver flask and insisted that I had a dram, as he put it.

' "It's whisky, laddie," he grinned, so I had a taste.'

'Which did you like best?' smiled Edward.

'I think I preferred the *schnapps*,' I replied, tucking into my apple pudding and custard.

'You are very honest, George,' said Mr Hooper, smiling broadly for the first time. 'A light in the darkness, eh?'

'Yes, sir. A strange thing to say wasn't it, sir?'

'No, George, it was not,' said Amelia, putting her hand on mine and giving it a squeeze.

'More claret, George?' said Edwin, who had got to his feet, and with the bottle in his hand, moved behind me and was topping up my glass before I could reply.

'Thank you,' I mumbled, my mouth full of apple pudding.

The time passed blissfully, and when Mr Hooper was about to return to his office at about two-thirty, I realised that I would have to leave soon.

'Goodbye, my boy,' he said, holding out his hand. 'It's been a pleasure meeting you. Come and see us again before you go back.'

'Thank you, sir, I will,' I replied, shaking his hand.

I heard the front door close and looked at Amelia.

'I suppose I'd better go soon,' I murmured.

'Stay a little longer,' she whispered into my ear.

I could see her mother and Edwin exchange glances, and I'm sure my face reddened, though Mrs Hooper smiled wanly at me. At last I reluctantly said that I had better go and to my joy Amelia said she could do with a breath of air and would accompany me to the tram stop. I thanked Mrs Hooper for my luncheon and she too invited me to visit them again. Edwin shook my hand and even helped me on with my greatcoat.

Fortunately it had stopped raining when we left the house. I carefully shut the drive gate, then quickly walked on the outside of Amelia.

As a precaution, she had brought with her a lady's umbrella, since it seemed that there was more rain on the way. I had hoped she would take my arm, but she did not. After we had gone a few paces, I blurted out: 'Amelia, I can come and see you again, can't I?'

She slowed down before she spoke, touching my arm as she did so.

'George, my dear, I must be completely honest with you.' She stopped walking and looked at me. The private road was quiet and completely deserted.

'Yes, Amelia,' I mumbled, fearing the worst.

'Tell me,' she smiled, 'how old are you?'

'I'm nineteen in five weeks' time,' I replied.

'The end of December?'

'That's right.'

'George, I am a lot older than you,' she said, almost wistfully.

'Are you?' I exclaimed.

'Yes, my dear, six years. In fact I shall be twenty-five in January,' she said. 'So you see...' She began to walk again.

'You don't want to see me then,' I said, miserably.

Amelia put her hand on my arm again and slowed her pace. 'I do, George, very much, but you must realise the difference in our ages.' There was an intense look on her face.

I shrugged my shoulders. 'But what's that got to do with it, Amelia? I just want to see you and,' I paused for a moment, 'be with you.'

Amelia smiled as she replied, 'All right, as long as you know.'

'Ooh yes,' I replied, blissfully.

I hesitantly held up my arm, which Amelia took firmly.

'Haven't you any gloves, George, dear?' said Amelia, noticing my reddened hands. I self-consciously tried to hide them.

'I had two pairs of woollen gloves, but one pair was chewed by rats when I left them out to dry near my billet, and the other pair was so holed by barbed wire I couldn't wear them.'

'I see,' murmured Amelia, thoughtfully.

'Will you be going back to nursing, Amelia?'

'I'm not sure at the moment. It all depends on mother. She is not well, as you could see.'

We were approaching the tram stop, so I quickly changed the subject. 'Amelia, when can I come and see you again?' She looked sidelong at me before she replied.

'That's up to you,' she said, coyly.

'Er, well,' I stuttered, lost for words.

'What about Saturday? You could come to the theatre with us. Daddy has a box at the local repertory company. We have tea about four-thirty then go to the theatre for six-thirty. Come over after luncheon, then we can have a walk on the Heath first, what do you think?'

'That sounds smashing,' I gasped.

'Good,' smiled Amelia, squeezing my arm.

I seemed to be walking on air and was in such a daze that Amelia almost pushed me to the steps of the tramcar when it arrived.

'Goodbye, George. See you on Saturday,' she said, waving to me.

'Bye, Amelia, bye,' I waved frantically as the tram clattered away and continued waving until a bend in the road took her out of my sight, then I found myself a seat. It did not seem ... it was not possible ... that I was going to see Amelia so soon. I thought of every word that she had said to me. What could it mean? I arrived at Amy's house in a daze. I just could not wait to tell her about Amelia. Amy listened patiently as I told her all about Amelia and the invitation for Saturday.

'She sounds very nice, Georgie,' smiled Amy. 'You must bring her here to see us.'

'Can I?' I asked, excitedly.

'Of course you can. Invite her to tea, that would be best.'

'I will,' I said, nodding my head vigorously.

Amelia, however, returned thoughtfully to Cedar Lodge. Had she done the right thing she wondered! How would her parents react, and Edwin? George affected her as no other man ever had. She felt maternal when he was near her, and it was as much as she could do to refrain from embracing him. What was it, she asked herself, after such a short acquaintance? Was it the difference in their ages? Yet in his attitude and beliefs, he was far older than she. He also had the courage of those beliefs, and she could tell that both her father and Edwin respected him. However, inviting him to their home and walking out with him was another matter. How would her parents react?

The house was quiet when she returned. There were sounds from the direction of the kitchen, otherwise all was quiet. Almost silently, she went upstairs to her bedroom and locked the door, then took off her hat and coat. Having done so, she looked in her long mirror and then began to remove her dress and look at herself carefully. It was something that she had not done since Guy Walton had broken off their engagement almost five years ago. Now it seemed unimportant, and after all the tears she had shed over him, it was difficult to remember what he actually looked like – it was a world ago.

Amelia was aware that she was no beauty; her nose was prominent and her teeth uneven, her dark hair was cut short and tended to wave – it was her most attractive feature. Though her hips were broad for her height, her bosom was of more modest proportion but to George, though she did not realise it, her very light blue eyes held his attention, a feature she completely overlooked.

Her mind concentrated on George as she lay on her bed; dear honest George. The more she thought of him, the more she realised that she had fallen in love with him. Almost a head taller than she, with broad shoulders and a narrow waist, judging by the way he tightened his belt. With fair hair, blue eyes and a light skin, which made him appear even younger than he actually was. This concerned Amelia somewhat, in view of her own age. However, she had no intention of letting this put her off, on that she was determined.

As she lay on her bed under a thick eiderdown, a drowsiness came over her and she thought of her brother

James, killed in action at Ypres. Dear self-assured James with his noisy friends, many now dead. Of Edgar, posted missing, the telegram said, and Amelia feared the worst. Of George, who tried to support her for her mother's sake – how different was George? Quiet, modest, didn't like war, would not use a gun, but with a courage few possessed.

Amelia was practical. There were hints that her marriage prospects had not been good before the war; they seemed now almost remote. It worried her and she had no wish to end up being an old maid. Now George had appeared, a private with no prospects or money, yet it did not matter. With his thin face in her thoughts, she fell asleep to be wakened by the maid tapping on her door.

'Miss Amelia, dinner in half-an-hour.'

'Thank you, Alice,' she replied, yawning.

Amelia washed and put on a fresh dress, then joined her parents in the drawing-room.

'Good evening,' said Amelia, brightly, as she entered the room.

'Good evening, my dear,' murmured her father, who was holding a whisky tumbler. Judging by his florid face, he had begun drinking some time earlier.

'Evening, Amelia,' replied Edwin from behind his newspaper.

Her mother, who was sipping what looked like a glass of gin, smiled faintly.

Having decided to take the bull by the horns at the first opportunity, Amelia immediately responded to her father's opening remark.

'You saw your young friend off, I understand, Amelia?'

'Yes, father,' she replied. 'Did you like him?'

Her father nodded. 'Yes I did. In fact I was very impressed.'

'Thank you, father,' said Amelia, sensing her opportunity.

'I hope you don't mind, but I've invited him to the repertory with us on Saturday.'

'Did you indeed?' James Hooper looked steadily at his daughter.

'Hello, hello,' grinned Edwin, lowering his newspaper, 'what's this then?'

Amelia's face began to go red. 'I thought that as we had a box and there would be a spare seat, George might like to go. He only has another week's leave.'

'Isn't he a little young for you dear?' asked her mother, quietly.

'Age does not come into it, mother. George knows how old I am.'

'Does he?' Her mother looked doubtful.

'Yes, mother. I told him,' replied Amelia, her face now flushed.

'It would seem, my dear, that young George has impressed you, too; that being the case,' her father smiled, 'he is most welcome.'

'Thank you, father,' said Amelia, gratefully.

'Mother?' Amelia looked questioningly at her.

'I agree with your father, my dear.'

'Thank you, mother,' she smiled, her face now its normal colour.

'Edwin?' she said curtly, as if expecting his disapproval.

'It's none of my business, Sis,' he replied, folding his newspaper, 'but if you want to know, I like him very much and I hope that if the time comes, I have just half his courage. I shall be pleased to welcome him on Saturday, truly I will.'

'Thank you, Edwin. I hope the time does not come,' said Amelia in a voice a little above a whisper.

'Amen to that,' said Mrs Hooper, tears running down her cheeks.

'Oh, mother!' said Amelia, rising from her chair and

putting a comforting arm around her mother's shoulders.

The dinner gong suddenly sounded, bringing an end to further conversation, though they had, for a number of reasons, little appetite for their meal.

6

In Love

I just could not believe that Amelia had invited me to go to the repertory theatre with her family, and that night, for the first time since I had been home, I found it difficult to sleep.

The following morning I went shopping with Amy as Hector had to visit some sick members of his congregation, so I volunteered to push Jimmy while she looked in the shops and made her purchases in comfort.

'I've been invited for tea first, Amy,' I said, as she looked into the window of a dress shop.

'So you've said, Georgie dear,' smiled Amy, her eyes still on a blue dress that was on a dummy in the window.

'Oh ... er ... yes,' I mumbled.

'What do you think of that dress, Georgie?'

'Um, very nice,' I replied, politely, my eyes on some gloves in the gentlemen's outfitters next door.

'That is a nice dress,' said Amy, her head on one side.

'I've got some money, Amy, if you would like it.'

'That's very sweet of you, Georgie,' she said, patting my arm. 'You keep your money – you've given me enough already.'

'I think I'll look in that second-hand bookshop along on the left,' I said, quickly.

'All right then. I'll meet you there. Shall I take Jimmy?'

'He'll be all right with me. You can go upstairs in the stores with the girls then,' I smiled. Amy nodded gratefully. 'Half-an-hour then.'

I bought some more second-hand books while Amy finished her shopping, then we went home before it became too foggy. Next week we would be in December, then Christmas. Where would I be at Christmas? I shivered involuntarily as I thought of it. Where would I be? Would I be alive? I tried not to think about it.

We arrived home in Lausanne Road as the light was fading. I felt safe and secure as the front door was locked and the curtain pulled across it. I helped Amy with the children as Hector was pretty useless like that, while he looked at the books that I had purchased from the second-hand bookshop.

When the children were in bed, Hector read the girls a story, whilst I told Jimmy one. The smell of our meal wafted up the stairs. I felt hungrier than ever! Amy had again made stewed neck of lamb with dumplings. I loved that. I could crunch the soft bones. I thought of Amelia and the theatre as we ate our meal. I was really happy.

On Saturday I took the children to the park. I think Amy and Hector were glad of that. Both were preparing for Sunday in their way – Hector with his sermon, and Amy, baking.

'Are you going to wear your uniform, or suit, Georgie?' asked Amy. It was one o'clock and I was thinking about getting ready.

'I tried on my suit yesterday, but it's much too big now, it doesn't fit,' I replied.

'I thought so,' she nodded. 'Still, I think Amelia would prefer you in your uniform,' a faint smile appeared on her face.

'Do you think so?' I replied.

'Yes I do. What do you think, Hector?' She turned to

her husband. Hector folded his newspaper before he replied. 'I agree with you, my dear. In fact she might be a little, er ... shall I say disappointed,' he smiled, 'if you did not wear it.'

'But I'm only a private soldier, Hector. Her brother is an officer,' I protested.

'Even so, I should wear it,' said Hector, firmly.

'I'd better clean my boots then and press my trousers. Can I use the flat iron, Amy?'

'I'll press them for you – you clean your boots,' said Amy.

'Thanks, Amy.'

I took my boots and brushes out into the back garden and proceeded to give them a good polish. With the children waving to me from the front room window, I shut the front gate. They had pushed their way under Amy's new lace curtains, and I smiled as I saw Amy appear to scold them.

I went to the greengrocer who had given me the pears, as he sold flowers. He grinned when I asked him for another bunch.

'For a young lady, son?' he asked, his eyes twinkling.

I could feel my face get warm as I nodded.

'Here we are, son, fourpence ter you,' he grinned.

He wrapped the flowers in a piece of white paper as I fished the money out of my purse.

'Thank you,' I said, as I gave him the coins.

As I passed the fishmonger, he waved. 'Want any more kippers, mate?' he chuckled.

'No thanks,' I replied, returning his wave.

It was just half-past-two when I arrived at the Hoopers' residence. This time it was Amelia who opened the front door.

'Hello, George,' she smiled. 'You are nice and early.'

'Er ... not too early,' I said, cautiously.

'No, of course not, come in,' she said.

'I've brought you some flowers,' I said, stepping carefully into the hall.

'That's very sweet of you, George, but you should not keep spending your money like this. I'll just put them in water, then I will get my coat. Mother and father are resting, we can have a walk on the Heath. It's not raining is it? I'll not be a moment,' she said, going in the direction of the kitchen.

I heard voices, then Amelia returned, carrying her coat. She handed it to me as she adjusted her hair in the hall mirror, then picked up her hat from a side table.

'I'll not keep you,' she said, pushing a hat pin into her abundant dark hair. She wore a dark dress drawn in at the waist. It seemed to be of a brocade material, and it looked most becoming and was most practical in this cold weather.

'Thank you, George,' she said, holding up an arm.

I assisted her to put on her coat, the closeness exciting me; she smelt of perfume. I almost shivered. Putting on her gloves, she then picked up her neat umbrella and looked at me.

'Shall we go, dear?' she smiled.

'Er ... yes,' I mumbled. Amelia looked at the front door and I suddenly realised she expected me to open it. I quickly moved forward, my boots scraping on the tiled floor of the entrance hall, and opened the door.

'Thank you, George,' said Amelia, as she elegantly stepped out of the house, whilst I quietly closed the door.

Once in Cedar Gardens and out of sight of the house, Amelia took my arm, much to my satisfaction.

'We go this way, George,' she said, guiding me across the road.

'I was going to wear my suit, Amelia, but it doesn't fit well now. It's gone all baggy.'

Amelia turned her head slightly as she replied, 'I'm

glad that you did not,' she said firmly. 'For an army uniform yours fits very well, and you look very nice in it,' she added.

'Thank you,' I murmured, my face flushing.

'George dear, have you any lady friends? Let me put it this way, have you ever walked out with a young lady? You don't mind me asking, do you?' Amelia half turned and looked wide-eyed at me. I hardly knew what to say, such was my embarrassment.

'Er ... n-no,' I spluttered. 'I haven't. I took out Jeannie Uden once when I worked at Holden's, but that was almost two years ago and we only went to the park.'

'You haven't seen her since you have been home?'

'Oh, no,' I said, quickly.

'Only I would not like to think that you are coming over to Blackheath to see me and also seeing another young lady.'

'Oh, no,' I protested. 'I wouldn't do that, Amelia. Honestly I wouldn't, cross my heart.'

Amelia smiled, 'I believe you, George. Do you like visiting me?'

'Oh, yes, very much, very much indeed,' I said, nodding my head.

'I'm glad, because I like you coming to see me,' she replied.

I said, 'Would you come to my sister's house and have tea with us? Amy told me to invite you.'

'I'd love to, George. I would like to meet your sister,' smiled Amelia.

'What about tomorrow?' I said, eagerly.

'Tomorrow is a little awkward. We have relatives coming for luncheon and it will be difficult to get away, but I'll speak to mother later.'

'Amelia could see the disappointed look on my face. 'I'll really try, I will, I promise.'

We were walking along a path beside the Heath. There was a mist and it reminded me for a moment of the front. It was getting colder and it seemed we were the only ones taking a walk, which was not surprising as the light was already fading. Amelia suddenly stopped and looked around her. There was no one in sight, then she spoke.

'George, take off your hat.'

'My hat,' I repeated, puzzled at receiving such an odd request.

'Yes, dear, remove it,' she commanded. I took off my hat.

'I have not thanked you for my flowers, George. Bend your head a little,' she said, putting a gloved hand to the side of my face. Before I knew it she had kissed me on the lips. My mouth opened slightly in surprise.

'Thank you, George, my dear. Have I shocked you?' she asked, her eyes wide and a smile on her face.

'No, it was nice,' I grinned. 'I'll bring you some more flowers.'

Amelia began to laugh, and I put my arm around her waist and slowly kissed her again. As I released her, I could see the approval in her eyes. For a moment we did not speak.

Quickly Amelia looked around to make sure that we had not been observed, then in a subdued tone said, 'I think we should be getting back.'

'You did ... er ... I mean,' I stuttered. 'It was all right me kissing you again?' I asked anxiously.

'Yes, it was very nice, George, but it's our secret, mind.' She looked at me, her face set.

'Yes, of course,' I replied.

'Not even Amy,' said Amelia firmly.

'No,' I shook my head, 'not even her.'

'Good boy,' she said, taking my arm.

I thought nothing of her last two words at the time,

but I realised years later I was a boy compared to her, not that I minded. I was already very much in love with Amelia and, in spite of the war, had never been happier in my life.

It was dusk by the time we returned to Cedar Lodge. Mr and Mrs Hooper were in the drawing-room, so the maid informed Amelia; of Edwin there was no sign. Mr Hooper was holding a whisky in his hand, and as we entered the room, I noticed that he was almost in the same state that I had last seen my father.

'Good evening, sir, madam,' I said, politely.

'Hello, young man,' replied Mr Hooper, giving me a faint smile.

Mrs Hooper's mouth opened slightly, but no sound came from it.

'Sit down George. I'll find out when tea will be ready,' said Amelia, about to leave the room.

'Four o'clock,' responded Mrs Hooper, looking straight ahead.

'Oh!' said Amelia, resuming her seat.

Mr Hooper took a large gulp of whisky, almost emptying his tumbler.

'Get me another whisky, Amelia,' he said, offering her his glass.

'Tea will be ready shortly, father,' she said, ignoring the glass.

'I am aware of that. I asked you to get me another whisky,' he said, icily.

Without a word, Amelia left her chair and obeyed her father. I could see that her cheeks were pink and she avoided my gaze. I lowered my eyes. It surprised me; I thought it was only in working-class families like mine that people drank.

'George is coming with us to the theatre,' said Amelia at last, her face now its normal shade.

Mr Hooper nodded, 'I shall not be going. I have an appointment with Carstairs at eight-thirty.'

Amelia compressed her lips, but refrained from making any comment.

'Edwin will drive you,' he added.

'Yes, father,' murmured Amelia.

We had almost finished high tea – as it was called – when Edwin entered the dining-room.

'Sorry I'm late, pater,' he beamed.

He bent over his mother's chair and kissed her on the cheek.

'Excuse me, mother, I was at the Sinclairs. Arthur Sinclair is home on leave.' Edwin suddenly flashed a smile at me.

'Hello, George,' he said, affably.

'Good evening, Edwin,' I said slowly, looking at Amelia, who nodded encouragingly at me.

'Father isn't going to the theatre this evening, Edwin, you will have to drive us,' said Amelia, as Edwin took his seat.

'Fair enough,' said Edwin, helping himself to some sandwiches.

'And drive carefully,' said Mr Hooper, looking over the top of his glasses. 'I don't want the car damaged.'

'Of course, father,' replied Edwin, an innocent look on his face.

'How is Celia?' asked Amelia.

'Very well. She is going to the theatre tonight too.'

'Is she?' smiled Amelia. 'And how is Arthur?'

'Does your father have an automobile, George?' interrupted Mr Hooper.

'No, sir, he doesn't need one. My Bessie would bring him home from anywhere in south London, sir, if he was Brahms.'

'Really,' chuckled Mr Hooper.

'Yes, sir. He would shout "Home Bessie" and go to sleep. I've seen him lying on his back in the cart outside the Golden Anchor after Bessie had brought him back from Greenwich.'

'Amazing,' said Mr Hooper, shaking his head.

'Yes, sir. She has got more intelligence than my father.'

This caused Edwin and his father to burst out laughing, even Mrs Hooper was smiling whilst Amelia was trying not to smile.

'Now he wants to sell her to the Army,' I said, sadly.

The laughing stopped and Amelia put a hand on mine.

'She's twelve years old at least,' I muttered.

'Perhaps the Army will not take her, George,' said Mr Hooper.

'They'll take anything with four legs before long sir,' I replied.

There was an embarrassed silence and it was Amelia who spoke.

'You did not say how Arthur was, Edwin.'

Edwin did not reply immediately. He drank some tea, then thoughtfully wiped his lips on his napkin. 'That's just it, Amelia, he said little – not the gay laughing Arthur of old, far from it, he seemed a different chap.'

'He's been on the Somme too, George, East Surreys.'

I nodded as I carefully lowered my bone china tea cup on to its saucer without making a noise. Amelia observed my efforts with approval and from time to time put a hand on mine. I must admit that I would have felt a little uncomfortable eating at their dining-table but for Amelia's attention, and also on this occasion being made aware that Mr Hooper liked his whisky.

'I do not think that I will go to the theatre this evening, Amelia. You young people go on your own,' said Mrs Hooper, as she elegantly removed non-existent crumbs from the corners of her mouth with her table napkin.

'Why not, mother?' said Amelia in a half-hearted protest.

'I have a headache,' she replied, touching her left temple.

'I should have a rest, mother,' said Edwin, 'then perhaps you will feel a little better.'

'Yes, you should,' agreed Amelia.

Mr Hooper, from time to time, looked over his half glasses at the proceedings, but did not seem interested. Once he turned to me and said with a smile, 'Eat up, lad, have another cake, go on.'

'Thank you, sir,' I replied, taking a piece of cake from the three-tiered cake stand.

'Well, you must excuse me. I have some papers to prepare,' said Mr Hooper, getting to his feet and putting his napkin on his plate.

I was about to get to my feet, but Amelia put a hand firmly on my forearm, restraining me.

'Enjoy the theatre, George, my boy,' he said, looking over his glasses.

'Thank you, sir,' I replied.

'The keys to the car are in my study, Edwin, and remember what I have said,' said Mr Hooper, severely.

'Yes, father,' replied Edwin, winking surreptitiously at Amelia.

'You must excuse me too,' said Mrs Hooper, as she left the table. 'Have a nice evening.'

'Thank you, Mrs Hooper,' I managed to reply.

'Can I get you anything, mother?' asked Amelia.

'No thank you, dear,' said Mrs Hooper, leaving the room.

When Mrs Hooper's footsteps could no longer be heard, Edwin spoke.

'What's wrong, Amelia?' he asked, his face serious for once. 'Why is old Carstairs coming this evening?'

'I imagine it's the business. I cannot think of any other

reason. You know as well as I do, things have not been good,' said Amelia as she folded her napkin. 'For the last two and a half years there has hardly been any wine imported – very little French, and of course no German. This was a large part of our business.'

'Yes, I'm sure you are right,' said Edwin, despondently. 'What do you think will happen?'

Amelia bit her lower lip and shook her head sadly, 'I've no idea, but I know father has incurred some debt.'

'How?' frowned Edwin.

Amelia took a deep breath before she replied, 'All three of you went to university and it had to be paid for.'

'Yes, but...' protested Edwin, his voice rising.

'Have you realised just how much it cost father, there are still bills turning up from time to time with an Oxford postmark on them,' said Amelia, her face flushed with annoyance. 'As far as the business is concerned, I do not know what the position is. I don't do any book-keeping now. Father keeps the books in his study, only Uncle Henry sees them, which, since he owns a share of the business, he is entitled to.'

I had been completely ignored, but I had been listening intently. It was clear to me that Amelia had far more business sense, even though she had never been to Oxford University.

'I'm sorry, George,' said Amelia, touching my hand, 'we are ignoring you with our family talk.'

'George doesn't mind – he's busy polishing off the cake,' chuckled Edwin. 'He doesn't have family problems.'

'No. I was just chucked out!' I replied, eating the last of my piece of fruit cake.

'Er ... yes,' said Edwin, somewhat chastened.

'Never mind, George, dear, you are very happy with your sister Amy,' smiled Amelia, patting my hand.

'Yes, I am, Amelia. I only had two pieces of cake, Edwin,' I said, apprehensively.

Edwin began to smile, 'I was only pulling your leg, George. Have another piece.'

'Er ... no thank you,' I said, my face flushing.

Amelia gave Edwin a frosty look, then put the last piece of fruit cake on my plate. As she placed the cake knife on the base of the stand, she said, 'You finish the last piece, George, it will only be wasted if it is left.' She gave me an encouraging smile and I could only mumble, 'Yes, Amelia.'

Edwin winked at me. I think he knew then that I was completely dominated by his sister and even had some idea, given that fate was kind to me, that I might eventually be his brother-in-law.

Mr Hooper owned a Ford motor car, a model 'T' type, so Edwin informed me. It was kept in a wooden shed at the side of Cedar Lodge, though Amelia was quick to inform me that it was a garage. I stood on the gravel drive as Edwin began to reverse the shiny black automobile out of the shed ... er ... garage.

One of the doors began to swing back as the wind caught it. Quickly I moved towards it, stopping it from hitting the automobile.

'You should have held the door, Amelia,' snapped Edwin.

Amelia gave her brother a withering look and pursed her lips. 'Close the garage door, George dear,' she said, sweetly, turning to me.

'Yes, Amelia,' I replied, pushing the doors together.

I could see Edwin grinning as we got into the motor car. Amelia, however, gave him another icy look then took my hand into her own gloved ones. 'Edwin, do you not have a spare pair of leather gloves that George could use. I'll get him some in Lewisham on Monday.'

Her brother half turned in his seat to speak to her, 'I have, but...' he paused.

'Amelia,' I murmured, gently squeezing her hand, 'private soldiers are not supposed to wear leather gloves, only woollen ones,' I whispered into her ear.

'You mean you are not allowed to wear them?' Amelia turned to me, her brow furrowed in annoyance.

'Yes, that's right,' I nodded.

'How ridiculous,' she exclaimed.

'There are a lot of things about the Army that are ridiculous, I can tell you,' I said with feeling.

'I am sure you could, dear,' smiled Amelia.

Edwin had now begun to laugh as the car moved forward.

'Open the gates, George, old chap,' said Edwin, moments later.

'Yes, Edwin,' I said, opening my door and getting out.

'You like young George, don't you, Amelia?' said Edwin quietly.

'Yes, I do very much, as it happens,' she replied, her face flushing.

'So do I. Completely modest and unassuming; but don't get too attached to him, Sis, he does a very dangerous job,' he muttered.

'I'm well aware of that, Edwin.' There was a catch in her voice. 'He's already told me that he has had his nine lives.'

'Yes. I can believe that,' muttered Edwin. 'He didn't get those medals for nothing.'

'But you can't help your feelings, Edwin, no matter how detached you try to be,' sniffed Amelia.

'I understand, Sis, I really do,' he replied, setting the car in motion again.

Having closed the gates, I got back into the motor car beside Amelia, who immediately clasped my hand.

'Thank you, George,' smiled Edwin, looking into his rear-view mirror. With Amelia close to me, I felt wonderful.

The Heath Repertory Company, of which the Hooper family were members, was something of a family affair. Run by a committee of local people, it was non-profit making and had the double virtue of giving worthwhile artistic entertainment and the opportunity to aspiring actors and actresses to learn the basics of their chosen profession.

This, I should add, came straight out of the programme which I ultimately purchased. It consisted of three sheets of paper clipped together and I was charged sixpence for it. In the foyer Amelia was greeted a number of times and I was given friendly nods. Even a Captain, who I noticed wore the Military Cross, said 'good evening' to me.

'Good evening, sir,' I murmured in reply.

Amelia gave the Captain a curt nod, then took my hand.

'This way, George,' she said, leading me to a staircase.

It was the first time that I had ever been in a theatre box. It had six upright padded chairs, of which two had armrests on them.

'We seem to have lost Edwin,' said Amelia as she sat down in one of the chairs with armrests. 'I expect he has gone to see Celia Sinclair. Leave the other chair with the armrests for him, George, it's usually father's chair. I'm sitting in mother's chair,' she smiled.

'Er ... yes,' I muttered, sitting down on the chair next to her. I had left my overcoat and cap down in the cloakroom, yet I still felt warm. I would have unfastened my collar, but there were too many Captains in the theatre to risk it.

'I hope Edwin brings a programme,' said Amelia, taking some opera glasses from her handbag.

'Shall I go and get one?' I asked.

'Would you mind, George, dear?'

'No,' I said, quickly rising to my feet.

'Thank you,' she said, looking through her glasses at people on the opposite side of the theatre.

I obtained a programme and glanced at it as I returned to the Hooper's box. It was a play by William Shakespeare that we were about to see, and it was called *Henry V*.

'Ah, there you are, George!' exclaimed Amelia, turning to greet me as I opened the door of the box. I took my seat and handed her the programme.

'It's *Henry V*,' I said, trying to impress her.

'Thank you, George,' she smiled, opening the programme. 'I thought it was *Henry V* next week. I'm not keen on Shakespeare, are you?'

I did not like to show my ignorance by admitting I'd never seen a Shakespeare or any other play at the theatre before, so I said, 'Not really. Look, I can see Edwin over there.'

'Where?' asked Amelia, putting her opera glasses to her eyes.

'Over there.' I raised my hand to point but Amelia immediately pulled it down below the level of the box.

'You must never point in the theatre, dear, it just isn't done.'

'Er ... um ... I'm sorry, Amelia,' I said, my face going red.

'That's all right, dear,' she said, patting my hand. 'You don't mind my telling you do you?' her eyes opening wide as she spoke.

'N-no, of course not,' I replied.

'Good boy,' she said, smiling and squeezing my hand.

'I can't see Edwin in the Sinclair's box.' Amelia was scanning the theatre with her glasses.

At that moment Edwin entered the box holding the

hand of a pretty dark-haired girl of about his age, which was about three years older than me.

'Hello, Celia,' smiled Amelia, turning to greet her.

'Good evening, Amelia,' replied Celia Sinclair in a somewhat false accent.

'Celia, this is George, a friend of Amelia's,' said Edwin. I stood up a little self-consciously. 'Good evening,' I murmured.

Celia Sinclair looked me up and down as if inspecting me. 'Good evening, George,' she said at last, a faint smile on her face.

I could tell Amelia was watching her closely, and as Celia had not held out her hand, I did not do so.

'Celia is going to watch from our box, Amelia' said Edwin, giving her the chair with the armrests.

Amelia made no comment, but moved her chair closer to mine while Edwin sat at the far end of the box. The lights were suddenly dimmed and the play commenced. I must admit I was not particularly impressed, largely, I think, because I could not understand it, never having learnt anything about Shakespeare at the council school.

To Amelia's annoyance Edwin and Celia spent the whole time talking in loud whispers and even Amelia's shushes from time to time were completely ignored. After the performance, Celia rejoined her parents and as we left the theatre, Edwin remarked, 'I'm seeing Celia tomorrow.'

'I should not have thought that you had anything left to talk about,' said Amelia, tartly. I tried not to smile.

Edwin did not reply until we were driving back to Cedar Lodge. 'We didn't disturb your concentration, did we George?'

'Er ... no, Edwin,' I replied.

'You did mine,' snapped Amelia. 'George is too polite to say.'

'Go on, Amelia, you were as bored as I was,' he laughed.

'I was not,' retorted Amelia.

'Yes you were, I know you! Will you open the gates, George, we're nearly home.

'Yes, Edwin.'

I could see Amelia say something to Edwin as I opened the gates. Having carefully closed them, I assisted Amelia from the motor car. As I did so, Edwin put his head out of his window.

'Open the garage doors, George, old chap.' As I hastened to open the doors, Amelia stood to one side, a fixed expression on her face.

'That's it, George,' grinned Edwin when I had closed the garage doors. I was not sure whether he was trying to annoy Amelia, but from the frosty look she gave him when we entered the house, he had certainly done so.

The maid greeted us in the hall and took our coats with the words, 'Madam has retired and the master is in his study. Shall I serve now, Miss?'

'Yes please, Alice,' replied Amelia.

Having washed my hands, I walked as lightly as I could in my boots, to the dining-room, and carefully opened the door.

'Come on in, George,' said Edwin, cheerfully, as I closed the door.

'Sit here next to me, George,' smiled Amelia, indicating to the chair next to her.

'Do you like steak and kidney pie?' grinned Edwin.

'I'll say,' I replied, my mouth beginning to water.

'Did you tell father?' asked Amelia, who was now busy serving a delicious pie.

'Yes I did. He said we should carry on. Like a drink, George? I'm having a scotch. What about you, Amelia?'

'I'll have a lime and soda water please.'

'George?' Edwin, who was at the drinks cabinet, looked at me.

'Can I try that too, please?'

'No whisky?' grinned Edwin.

'No thank you,' I smiled.

'George isn't a drinker, Edwin,' said Amelia, curtly. 'Let me help you to vegetables,' she smiled, putting a generous portion of carrots and mashed potato on my plate.

Some moments later, Mr Hooper came into the dining-room. He looked unsteady on his feet and almost collapsed on his chair.

'Thank you, Amelia,' I said, quietly.

Neither Edwin nor Amelia spoke to their father. I think they were as surprised as I was at seeing him the worse for drink. Amelia placed a portion of the steak and kidney pie on his plate, then helped him to vegetables.

'That's enough,' he said, abruptly, as Amelia was about to put more on his plate.

'I hope you have not damaged the car,' he grunted.

'No father,' replied a subdued Edwin.

'What did you think of it, George?' he mumbled.

'Very nice, sir,' I replied.

'Better than your horse and cart,' he leered at me.

'Yes, sir. But it won't come home on its own or go round corners on its own, will it sir?' I replied.

He must have thought for a few moments, then he started to laugh: 'No denying that, my boy,' he chuckled.

I think that I relieved the tension, as Edwin grinned and winked at me, whilst Amelia squeezed my hand.

'What did you see?' Mr Hooper asked, peering around the table.

'*Henry V*, father,' said Amelia, coolly.

Mr Hooper looked blearily at me. 'Did you like it, George? Did it inspire you – England and Saint George, eh?'

'No, not really, sir,' I replied. 'But I enjoyed the ice cream that we had at the interval.'

'Ice cream! Ice cream!' said Mr Hooper, his voice rising.

He threw back his head and began to laugh as if I had said something very funny. Both Amelia and Edwin joined in and it seemed to change the atmosphere at the table.

'George, my boy, I like you,' chortled Mr Hooper. 'You are so refreshingly honest.'

I must have looked a little nonplussed, for Edwin gave me a broad wink and Amelia squeezed my hand.

Mr Hooper had gone back to his study, and Edwin left the table before I could speak to Amelia.

'Did you enjoy your evening, George?' she asked.

'Yes, very much,' I replied.

'Really?' she said, her eyes opened wide in surprise.

'Yes, I was with you,' I said, lowering my eyes.

Amelia leaned towards me and kissed my cheek. 'Thank you my dear,' she murmured.

'You will come to tea tomorrow, won't you?' I said at last.

'Well ... I...' Amelia paused, 'I'm not sure.'

'I'll come over and meet you, then bring you home,' I said, quickly.

'All right, George,' she smiled, 'I'll come to tea.'

'Good, that's marvellous,' I beamed.

It was getting late and I had no wish to miss the last tram, even though I could have stayed with Amelia for ever, but my common sense prevailed and I said at last that I should leave.

'Yes, it is getting late,' agreed Amelia. 'I'll get my hat and coat and see you to the gate.'

'Should I say good-night to your father and Edwin?'

'No, I'll do it for you,' she replied.

It was quiet as we left the house, though the noise of our feet on the gravel drive – particularly my army boots – must surely have been enough to have wakened Mrs

Hooper. Cedar Lodge was surrounded by trees and large holly bushes. It was in the cover of a holly tree that we said good-night. I was unsure of myself, but Amelia took the initiative. She moved closer to me and whispered, 'You may kiss me good-night, George.'

I carefully put my arms about her and held her close, kissing her until she said at last, a little breathlessly, 'I had better go in now, George. I'll see you about two o'clock tomorrow.'

'Yes, Amelia,' I gasped as she quickly retraced her steps to the house, giving a wave into the darkness as she closed the front door.

By the time I arrived home, Hector and Amy had gone to bed. Carefully I climbed the stairs, my boots in my hand.

'That you, George?' I heard Hector's voice.

'Yes, it's me Hector. Good-night.'

'Good-night, George,' came the drowsy reply.

The following morning at breakfast, I told Amy that Amelia would be coming to tea.

'To tea?' queried Amy, as she put jam on bread and butter fingers for Jimmy.

'Yes, you said invite her,' I said, a little anxiously.

'I know I did, when is she coming then?' she replied.

'Today,' I said casually.

'Today!' repeated Amy. 'But I'm not expecting her today,' Amy's face flushed. 'I've nothing special to give her.'

'We have winkles and shrimps for Sunday tea don't we?' I said.

'Georgie, people who have servants and live in Blackheath do not have winkles for Sunday tea,' said Amy, patiently.

'Why not?' I said. 'I like them. I've been looking forward to them. I told Amelia.'

Hector was now smiling broadly and Amy started to smile and shake her head.

'You told her, and she is still coming to tea?' frowned Amy.

'Yes, why not? She has never had winkles before. She's got one of those large hat pins. She'll soon get her winkles out,' I replied.

This was too much for Hector. Sabbath or not, he suddenly doubled up laughing until tears ran down his face. This started Amy who put her hands to the side of her face. 'Georgie, what am I going to do with you?' she chortled.

Promptly at ten o'clock Hector left the house wearing his dog collar and long black coat. Amy, the children and I were to follow at ten-thirty.

It was a cold, clear morning when we left the house. I held the girls' hands whilst Amy pushed Jimmy. As was the practice, one of the older ladies amused the children in a side room while the service was being held. I offered to help, but the offer was politely declined, which seemed to bring a smile to Amy's face, so I sat through the service and listened to Hector's sermon, which I thought would never end.

Amy left immediately after the service to attend to the Sunday dinner, while I was detailed to bring the children home. 'Go the long way, Georgie,' said Amy, 'down Gautry Road and then St Mary's.'

'Yes, I know, Amy,' I said, quickly, before she hurried away.

Some of the congregation congratulated me on my medals. I felt self-conscious about it and was glad when I was at last taking the children home. Hector said he would follow later as he had to speak to the caretaker when everyone else had departed. At two-thirty I was walking briskly down Lausanne Road to catch the tram to Blackheath. My uniform neatly pressed and my boots newly polished, I felt spick and span. Amy assured me that she would see the winkle man who pushed his barrow of winkles and shrimps around the streets on a Sunday afternoon.

Amelia had obviously been waiting for me, as she left Cedar Lodge before I could close the wrought-iron gate.

'Hello, Amelia,' I smiled.

'Good afternoon, George,' she replied as she approached me.

Although Amelia smiled, it was strained. I opened and closed the gate again quickly, as she took my arm.

Amelia was wearing a different coat and hat; the colour of the coat matched the long dress she was wearing beneath it. I felt very proud and excited as we walked down Cedar Gardens, yet I could tell that something was amiss.

'Is there anything wrong, Amelia?' I asked, cautiously. For a moment she hesitated.

'Well,' she paused again, then as if having made up her mind, spoke in an almost hesitant voice. 'We have problems at home at the moment and it has not been helped by Edwin going off this morning with Celia Sinclair. Uncle Henry should have come to luncheon, but refused to do so. Father's a changed man, he never used to drink like he does now.' Amelia was close to tears and I put my hand on her, which was tucked in the crook of my arm.

'I'm sorry, Amelia, really I am,' I murmured.

She smiled weakly, then nodded her head.

We walked for a few moments in silence, then I spoke as I had to ask her something that was on my mind. 'Amelia, you won't be cross with me if I ask you something, will you?'

'That depends on what it is,' she said. She stopped walking and turned to face me, her lips taut.

'It's ... er ... um. I mean, have you got a young man,

Amelia? I mean ... er ... besides...' My face, I'm sure, was red.

'You mean besides you?' she asked, a smile appearing on her face.

'Er ... um ... y-yes,' I mumbled.

'No, George, I have not. Does that answer your question?'

'Oh yes,' I beamed. 'When I go back will you write to me?'

'Of course,' she replied.

'That's wonderful,' I breathed.

We continued walking to the tram terminus. Suddenly Amelia spoke, 'Now it's my turn to ask you a question, George.' Amelia glanced sidelong at me, a mischievous look on her face.

'Go on then,' I grinned.

'What made you register as a conscientious objector, George?' she asked.

'Billy Snape did,' came my prompt reply.

'Billy Snape!' exclaimed Amelia. 'What do you mean?'

'Billy Snape was my best friend,' I said quickly, 'and he was a conscientious objector. His family belonged to a religious group that did not believe in killing. I used to go there often for my tea. When my father was full of drink I sometimes stayed at the Snapes' house – they were nice to me.'

'I see,' murmured Amelia, 'and where is your friend now?'

'He's dead,' I said, sadly. 'I don't know what happened. He was called up but would not wear a uniform and there was an accident, so I heard. The Snapes moved, so my sister told me.'

'How sad,' said Amelia, holding my arm tighter.

'Yes, it was,' I replied, my thoughts on Bill, who had been far kinder to me than any of my brothers.

We had reached the tram terminus and I could see a

tram in the distance clattering towards us. Amelia moved closer to me and looked up at the grey sky. 'I think it is going to snow,' she remarked.

'Yes, it's cold enough,' I replied.

I held Amelia's arm as she ascended the two steps to get on the tram.

'Shall we go upstairs?'

'Yes, all right, George, why not?' smiled Amelia.

We clambered up the stairs – it was a little difficult for Amelia with her long dress. We walked to the empty front seats and sat down as the tram lurched forward. I now held Amelia's hand. She squeezed my fingers as she spoke to me. 'George,' she said, looking sidelong at me, 'you look older than your age, you know.'

'Do I?' I said, rather proudly.

'Yes, you do. Very mature at times,' she added. 'Tell me, George, what do you think of the suffragette movement?'

I was a little surprised at the question and instinctively shrugged my shoulders. 'Why do you ask?' I said, in an effort to gain time.

'I want to know your opinion?' said Amelia, firmly.

'I haven't one really. After all, it does not concern me, does it?'

'It does,' countered Amelia. 'When you are twenty-one you will get the vote. I do not get one.'

I could see that Amelia was getting a bit worked up and it was a side of her that I had not seen before.

'Then it's not fair, is it?' I replied.

'I know it's not fair, but do you?' she said, accusingly.

'Yes, I've just said so, and anyway I should get a vote at eighteen, after all I'm in the Army and it's not my choice.'

'That's another issue, George, but it's a valid argument,' said Amelia, soothingly.

'My ex-fiancé did not think so. He said women should stay in the home and not get a vote,' said Amelia, indignantly.

'Is that why you didn't marry him?' I asked, quietly.

'It was mutual. It all happened four years ago. He met someone else – a wealthy heiress.'

'I'm glad,' I said, quickly.

Amelia smiled and squeezed my hand. 'I am now,' she whispered, her face now flushed.

The tram clattered through Lewisham and on towards Deptford. It was going slightly downhill and it swayed from side to side as it gathered speed.

I began to laugh, then Amelia suddenly turned, her eyes sparkling, and kissed my cheek. This emboldened me, and I returned the compliment.

'That's enough, George,' she said, still smiling.

We alighted from the tram in Queen's Road, and I felt very proud as Amelia held my arm and we walked up Lausanne Road.

I could see the girls behind the lace curtains in the front room. The curtains moved as I opened the front gate, and before we got to the front door, Amy had opened it. She was wearing her best dress and her hair was neatly combed. Around her neck was the string of pearls that Hector's mother had given her, which was her proudest possession.

'This is Amelia,' I said, quickly. 'Miss Hooper, my sister Amy; Mrs Ross,' I blustered.

'I'm pleased to make your acquaintance, Mrs Ross,' replied Amelia, gently shaking Amy's hand, 'but do call me Amelia.'

'Thank you, and you must call me Amy. Please come in.'

As we entered the hall, we were greeted by the children. It was obvious that Amelia liked them because she established an immediate rapport, and when she produced a bag of sweets from her handbag and gave it to them, she became a favourite auntie.

I could tell that Hector viewed her favourably by his attention to her. He insisted on taking her coat and gave her the most comfortable chair. His family were of a far better class than mine, perhaps that is why my father resented him. They never spoke unless they came face to face and it was unavoidable, though Hector was always polite to him. I think with Amelia, he considered that they were on the same social level, and there was no doubt that from the first introduction, there was a mutual understanding.

I could see that Amy was watching her intently as we sat by the fire in the front room.

'It's just like Christmas day,' piped up Alice.

'Is it?' smiled Amelia.

'Yes,' she said, digging into the bag of sweets that Amelia had given them, 'having a fire lit in this room,' she said, looking at Amelia.

'Oh!' smiled Amelia, glancing at Amy, who smiled weakly in return, and then stood up rubbing her hands together.

'I'll see if the kettle has boiled,' she said, quietly, and then hurried from the room.

I had been a little concerned as to whether Amelia would get on with Amy and Hector, but I need not have worried. Soon they were chattering away and I was almost a casual observer. Tea had been set out in the parlour with a new tablecloth that Amy had embroidered and I had not seen used before.

'Georgie insisted on winkles and shrimps,' explained Amy, almost apologetically, indicating the two large bowls in the centre of the table, 'but I have alternatives. I'm sure that you would prefer something different, Amelia,' smiled Amy.

'No, no,' protested Amelia, sitting down at the table and eyeing the large bowl of shiny black winkles, warily. 'I've never tried them,' she smiled.

'Never?' remarked Hector, his eyes twinkling.

'No,' said Amelia, looking doubtfully at the bowl of winkles.

As Amy began to put some on her plate with a dessert spoon, Amelia removed her gloves and with my assistance commenced to remove a winkle from its shell.

'You don't eat the cap, Amelia,' I said, quickly, as both cap and winkle appeared on her hat pin.

'The what?' frowned Amelia.

'Its cap.' I pointed to the black oval seal on the end of the winkle. She now looked at the winkle with apprehension. Both Amy and Hector watched with interest as Amelia held the long pin to her mouth and reluctantly ate the winkle.

'Nice, isn't it?' I said, encouragingly.

'Ye-es,' agreed Amelia, cautiously. 'It's certainly different,' she acknowledged.

'Have something else,' suggested Amy, indicating the cold meat.

'No, I'll have another,' said Amelia, elegantly holding a winkle with her left thumb and index finger and probing with her pin. Soon she was eating them freely, as well as the shrimps, which she remarked were more to her taste.

'We go to evening service, Amelia,' said Amy, suddenly. 'One of my cousins comes round to look after the children.'

'Are you taking the evening service, Hector?' smiled Amelia.

'Oh yes,' he replied, blinking rapidly.

'I don't think we will have time to go, will we, Amelia?' I said.

'Why not? I'm in no hurry,' replied Amelia.

I could see Amy trying not to smile at the expression on my face.

'If you say so, Amelia,' I agreed, trying to look cheerful.

Alice, who was sitting next to Amelia, was watching her intently. The perfume and elegant clothes seemed to enthral her; at last she could be quiet not a moment longer.

'Aunt Amelia, are you Uncle George's young lady?'

I could feel my cheeks burning with embarrassment. Amelia, however, took it in her stride and exchanged an amused glance with Amy.

'That's right, Alice,' she smiled.

'Alice, get on with your tea,' said Amy, quickly, 'and don't talk with your mouth full.'

'It's not full,' retorted Alice.

'Just eat your tea,' said Hector, sternly.

Alice looked down at her plate and did not speak again for the rest of the meal, which I think impressed Amelia.

After tea, Amelia washed her hands in the scullery. Amy, who had brought a clean towel for her, said quietly, 'It's very good of you to take such an interest in Georgie, Amelia, it's made his leave; I was worried about him.'

Amelia took the proffered towel, and looked steadily at her. 'Thank you,' she murmured, 'but it is mutual, you know.'

'Is it?' replied a somewhat surprised Amy. 'Then I am very pleased. Georgie is very fortunate,' she smiled.

'I think I am too,' said Amelia, returning her smile.

Almost immediately Amy left the scullery, no further words were exchanged between them, a friendship had been formed, which was to mean a great deal to both of them in the years to come.

Hector's sermon seemed to drag on. As usual, it lasted

longer in the evening when there was no Sunday dinner to consider. I tried to be interested but I found myself stifling a yawn from time to time. Amelia looked at me out of the corner of her eye, but gave no indication that she was not completely absorbed by Hector's sermon.

The service at last came to an end, but then the introductions began. It seemed that I was introduced to the whole congregation and it was almost three-quarters of an hour before we left the church with Amy. Hector wanted to speak to the caretaker, so we left him on the steps of the church to follow on later. It was cold and we walked briskly to Amy's house.

'What did you think of Hector's sermon?' asked Amy.

'He went on a bit, didn't he?' I remarked.

'I hope you will not say that in front of him,' said Amy, sharply.

'Er ... no, of course not,' I replied, rolling my eyes at Amelia, whose only response was a movement of her lips.

'I thought it was very good,' said Amelia at last, 'though there were a number of points that I would like to question him on.'

'You will have your chance shortly,' smiled Amy.

The children were still up when we returned, and the first words that greeted us were from Amy's young cousin Lily.

'Jimmy's pooped his pants!' Cousin Lily was an ungainly girl of about fourteen.

'Didn't he tell you that he wanted to go?' snapped Amy, angrily. She had taken her hat and coat off in almost one movement, before propelling the now crying Jimmy out into the scullery.

'He does pong, doesn't he?' said a laughing Alice, holding a none too clean hand in front of her nose.

'He's a stinker,' added a giggling Ruth.

'That's enough of that,' I said, sternly. I caught Amelia's eye. She was not put out, as I expected, so I winked at her and she smiled at me in response.

Amy put her head round the scullery door and glared at Lily. 'Lily, get those girls ready for bed. Don't just stand there. I'll be with you in a moment, Amelia,' she smiled. 'I'm sorry about this.'

'I understand,' replied Amelia.

'You've got it all to come,' chuckled Amy.

Amelia flushed slightly as Amy disappeared into the scullery. Lily came into the parlour with the girls in their nightdresses. She put her head around the scullery door to speak to Amy.

'They're ready for bed now, Amy,' she said.

'Oh no, they're not,' I heard Amy say, anger in her voice. 'They need a wash first. Bring them out here to me and be quick about it.'

'Will you tell us a story, Auntie Amelia?' asked Alice.

'Yes, when you are in bed dear, I will,' smiled Amelia.

'Ooh, goody,' gurgled Ruth.

When Hector returned some ten minutes later, Amelia was in the girls' bedroom reading to them, and I was telling a story to a rather subdued Jimmy.

'Where are they?' asked Hector as he came into the parlour. 'Have they gone?' He looked at Amy somewhat surprised.

'Reading to the children,' she said quietly.

Hector nodded, approvingly, and put his Bible down on the parlour table in a reflective manner. Amy knew he was thinking of something, and almost apologetically said, 'I'm going to lay for supper dear.' She took a tablecloth from the dresser drawer and Hector picked up his Bible as Amy spread out the tablecloth. At last he spoke. 'I'm very impressed with George's young lady,' he murmured.

Amy nodded, 'She's very nice, but don't you think that she is a bit too old for Georgie?' she said in a whisper.

'No, he is not a boy any more, dear; he's a good-looking young man and a war hero to boot. She must be interested in him.'

'Ye-es,' said Amy, slowly, as she laid out the cutlery.

Having read the children a story, we joined Amy and Hector in the parlour for supper.

'I enjoyed your sermon,' said Amelia, after Hector had said grace.

'Did you?' replied Hector, obviously pleased.

'Yes, though I did not agree with all of it, but it was most interesting none the less.'

'Oh!' Hector was a little taken aback and began to blink. 'Which aspect did you find difficult to understand?' he asked, a little patronisingly.

Amelia smiled, then put down her knife and fork, daintily. 'I understood all of it perfectly well, but I found the points that you made about women in the Bible a little...' she paused, 'shall we say belittling.' Amelia looked steadily at him.

I began to smile as Hector looked a little uncomfortable. Amy too had a look on her face that I knew all too well. She approved of Amelia's remarks, but would not question Hector in any way, least of all make a critical comment.

'Amelia's a suffragette, Hector,' I chuckled.

'So! What has that got to do with it?' bridled Hector. 'It was not my intention to belittle women, I assure you, Amelia,' he said in a conciliatory tone.

'Perhaps not, but in the context of your sermon and the example you gave, it did give the impression women were second class.'

'We are,' chimed Amy. 'We do not get the vote and...'

'Ladies, please,' smiled Hector. 'I'd no idea my sermon

– or shall I say your interpretation of it – was of so much interest to you.'

'It did not fall on stony ground, did it, Hector?' I grinned.

Hector looked at me, curiously, before he replied. 'No George, it certainly did not.' This caused everyone to laugh and took away any ill-feeling that there might have been. We ate a leisurely supper, and I listened with pleasure as Amelia, with at times Amy's support, debated the rights of women.

'Do you go to suffragette meetings, Amelia?' asked Hector.

'Oh yes, very often,' she replied. 'In fact I'm going to one on Tuesday evening, though recently, with our decision to stop demonstrating, there have not been many meetings.'

'Did you go on demonstrations?' asked Amy, her eyes wide.

'Oh yes, in the past, before the war started,' replied Amelia.

'Did your father approve?'

'No, he did not.' From Amelia's sharp reply, I gathered that it had been a contentious issue at Cedar Lodge. I could see Amy and Hector exchange glances; I think that they had formed the same opinion.

'Still, we have been promised the vote,' said Amy.

'I'll believe that when I get it,' said Amelia, her face taut.

'If the war goes on in France a few more years, you will have to get the vote,' I said easily.

Amelia and Amy looked at me curiously but neither spoke.

'There will be no men left to vote will there?' I said.

'Good gracious, George, we do not wish to get the vote on those terms,' said Amelia.

'I should think not,' agreed Amy, quickly.

'You are being very pessimistic, George, if I may say so,' observed Hector in his best clerical manner.

'Perhaps so, but we are almost in 1917 and no nearer winning than we were in 1914. Didn't the Old Contemptibles say that they would be home for Christmas having given the Kaiser a bloody nose. There's been plenty of blood spilt, but it has not been the Kaiser's, and where are the Old Contemptibles, eh? Tell me?'

My words struck home. Amelia had bowed her head for a few moments and I now regretted that I had spoken so bluntly. Amelia turned to look at me, her eyes misty.

'I'm sorry, Amelia,' I muttered, somewhat chastened.

'There's no need to be,' she murmured, 'it's true.'

'You have a point, George,' conceded Hector. 'There seems no end in sight to this terrible war.'

'To think how everyone greeted the war with euphoria,' said Amelia, sadly, as she touched the corner of her eye.

'The Snapes didn't, I can tell you. They said it was wrong and my brother Charlie gave Billy Snape a black eye and a bleeding nose because of it,' I remarked.

'How sad,' said Amelia, quietly.

'Charlie always was hot-headed,' said Amy. 'Still, that is all in the past. He was killed at Ypres about a year ago.'

'So was my brother, James. Such a waste, such a terrible waste,' said Amelia, sadly, her eyes clouding.

'Yes, it seems amazing that it could ever have happened,' commented Hector, slowly shaking his head. 'We must pray for God's guidance and an early victory.'

'Amen to that,' said Amy, dutifully.

'That's what the Germans are doing as well,' I said, drily.

My words seemed to have a stunning effect. All three stared at me in amazement.

'But...' began Hector, then he paused unable, it seemed,

to continue. There was never any doubt in his mind that we were in the right and God was on our side.

'Surely not,' said Amelia, frowning at me.

'I've heard dying Germans praying to God. I've learnt some German, and I once saw a German padre in their trenches,' I said.

'Do you know, I've never thought of that,' said Amy, thoughtfully.

'Neither have I,' remarked Amelia.

'We cannot presume to have the monopoly of God's attention,' smiled Hector, benignly.

'If you had seen what I have seen, Hector, you would get the impression that He was not particularly interested,' I remarked.

There was a heavy silence in the room. At last Hector spoke, 'I find it difficult to answer that remark, George. I'm sure that there must be an answer but at the moment I do not have it other than the fact that the good Lord cannot be held responsible for man's wicked actions.'

'We are getting serious,' said Amy. In an attempt to change the subject, she turned to Amelia. 'Did you see the circus, Amelia, that George made for the girls?'

'Yes, Alice insisted on showing it to me,' smiled Amelia.

It was the first time that I had ever heard Amy call me George, and not Georgie, and it made me feel grown up. Even Amelia seemed to have a more attentive attitude towards me.

'I think we should be leaving soon,' said Amelia, glancing up at the parlour clock and then looking at her watch.

'Yes,' I agreed. 'I'll have to get the tram back, and the last one leaves at about eleven-thirty on a Sunday, I think.'

'It's been very nice meeting you both,' said Amelia, as Hector assisted her with her coat.

'It's been a pleasure to meet you,' said Amy. 'I hope George brings you again while he is on leave.'

'Yes, I've only got another week,' I said, dolefully.

Amelia and Amy exchanged embarrassed glances, then averted their eyes.

'Thank you, Hector,' said Amelia, fastening her coat.

We walked down Lausanne Road, glancing from time to time at the street lamps in the thickening fog. Amelia had pulled a scarf across her face and I had taken the liberty of putting my arm about her shoulder. Far from pulling away from me, she had put an arm about my waist. For the first time in my life, I wished the tram would not arrive. We stood near the tram stop in the shadow of a shop front, my arms about Amelia, and it might seem a little ungentlemanly of me to say so, but Amelia began the kissing!

When the tramcar at last clanged towards us, we were both a little breathless. Amelia powdered her nose as I paid the conductor for our fares. We sat on the lower deck and proceeded at a snail's pace.

'You were different tonight, George,' said Amelia, as she put her powder case into her handbag.

'Oh,' I murmured, curiously.

'Yes, very adult. Your comments were very perceptive. It's made me think.'

'Oh,' I smiled, 'has it?'

'Now you are making fun of me,' said Amelia, looking coyly at me.

'I'm not,' I said, putting my arm about her. She did not tell me to remove my arm, largely I suspected because she was hardly likely to meet any of her friends on a tram, added to which we were in a thick fog.

'Would you like to come to a suffragette meeting?' she asked.

'With you?' I asked, lamely.

'Of course,' she retorted.

'Yes, I'll come. Are you shopping tomorrow?'

'Yes, in Lewisham,' she said above the clattering of the tram.

'On your own?' I asked.

'With my mother, if she feels up to it. Would you like to come?'

'Yes. I'll carry your shopping for you,' I smiled.

'I'll get some gloves if you are with me. You can try them on, then I will have the right size. George dear remove your arm please and hold my hand, we are almost there I think.'

'Yes, Amelia,' I replied.

The fog had become thicker and it crossed my mind that the tram might stop running, as often happened when the fog became too bad. Amelia must have been thinking the same thing when I opened the gate of Cedar Lodge for her, and she said, 'George, I would ask you in, but this fog is bad. You must get back straight away, the trams might stop running. If they do, you must come back, I'm sure father will allow you to use the guest room.'

'No, I'd better walk if they do. Amy will only worry about me,' I replied, though since I could hardly see the house, I wondered if I would find my way home. We walked up the drive to the house, the outline of which suddenly appeared. I began to cough again.

'Will you be all right?' she asked, as she took her key from her handbag and then turned to me.

'I'll ask father now,' she said, a look of concern on her face.

'Oh yes,' I grinned. 'I'll find my way all right and I'm not likely to be shot at in Lewisham or Deptford.'

'Really George,' she murmured. She kissed me briefly, went into the porch and put her key in the lock. 'Goodnight dear, take care,' she smiled.

'Good-night, Amelia,' I replied touching my cap.

'Ten o'clock here, remember,' she said, opening the door.

'Right,' I nodded, 'bye.'

The door closed and I stepped back into the fog and made my way to the gate of Cedar Lodge. I was fortunate, a tram was about to leave as I arrived back at the stop. As I boarded it, the conductor spoke: 'New Cross Gate depot only is as far as we go tonight, soldier.'

'That's all right,' I replied, handing him my fare.

The tram moved at a snail's pace, but at least it was moving and it was not far to walk at the other end. I sat back in my seat, cap over my eyes, overcoat buttoned up. I was a contented and happy young man.

7

Edwin Leaves for France

To Amelia's surprise, both her father and mother were at the breakfast table the following morning when she entered the dining-room.

'Good morning, father, good morning, mother,' she said, brightly, as she took her place at the table.

Her father's reply was indiscernible, and her mother merely murmured, 'Amelia,' as she poked at her breakfast.

'Are you coming shopping this morning mother?' asked Amelia.

'No! I have some business to attend to with your father this morning,' said her mother, sharply.

'Oh!' said Amelia in surprise. Never had she heard her mother speak in such a way before when referring to her father. She turned to her father who was reading his newspaper; his face was haggard. 'He is not well,' she thought.

Now she was beginning to suspect the worst as far as the business was concerned. 'George is going to escort me while I shop this morning. May I invite him back for luncheon?'

'Yes, certainly,' her mother replied.

The maid entered the dining-room and placed Amelia's breakfast in front of her. 'Thank you, Alice, and will you bring some fresh tea please?'

'Yes, Miss Amelia.'

When the maid had left the dining-room, her mother spoke. 'Amelia, you are seeing rather a lot of this young man.'

Unsure of the point of the remark, she replied: 'Do you object, mother?' Amelia's face flushed as she spoke.

'No, not really, but he is much younger than you and his prospects could hardly be said to be good, I mean, an assistant whatever,' her mother made a gesture with her hand, 'in a jam factory,' her upper lip almost curled.

'Mother,' said Amelia, putting down her knife and fork, her face even more flushed. 'George will in all probability be back in the trenches within two weeks. I would say his chances were rather poor.'

Her father folded his newspaper and looked at her over the top of his glasses, his face even more strained. 'You have made your point, Amelia. While he is on leave you may see or invite him here whenever you wish.'

'Thank you, father. Mother?'

'I had no wish to criticise, Amelia,' began Mrs Hooper. 'I like the boy, but...' she paused as if unsure what to say.

'Yes, mother, I understand,' said Amelia, quickly. 'But George is far more intelligent than you think, he's never had any opportunity. I went to the Baptist church yesterday with his sister and George, and heard his brother-in-law preach.'

'Did you, dear?' said her mother.

'Yes, mother. His sister is very nice too, and it was a very pleasant evening,' she smiled.

'Did you hear Edwin come in last night, Amelia?'

'No, father. Was he late?'

'Yes, very. Still, I suppose I should not complain.'

'No, father,' said Amelia. 'After all, he has only one more night at home.'

126

Amelia immediately regretted her choice of words as her mother began to dab at her eyes with her handkerchief.

'Mother, please,' said Amelia, rising from her chair.

'I'm all right, Amelia, excuse me, James.' Mrs Hooper pushed back her chair and rose to her feet. 'Amelia, dear, do carry on with your breakfast,' she said, as she left the dining-room.

Amelia began her breakfast, though with little appetite. She watched her father idly stirring his almost empty cup of coffee. At last, she plucked up courage to ask him outright: 'Is anything wrong, father?' she said softly.

James Hooper continued twisting his coffee spoon as if he had not heard. At last he laid the spoon in the saucer and looked at her, his face lined with worry. 'Yes, Amelia, there is. I might as well tell you now, as later. We have serious financial problems with the business. I have an appointment at the bank this morning. Your mother is coming as well, as she will be required to sign papers. I'm hoping that I will get a little breathing space and that business will begin to improve,' he said tiredly.

'I hope it does too, father,' murmured Amelia.

'Are you going back to your voluntary nursing?' asked her father, suddenly.

'Er ... no, father,' she replied a little taken aback by his question.

'No?' Her father looked hard at her.

'Father, I cannot leave mother and I am not a good nurse anyway. I get too emotionally involved when I see those terrible...' She paused and bit at her napkin, her eyes lowered.

'It's wise to know one's limitations,' nodded her father, 'and your mother needs you as you are well aware.'

'Yes, I know, father. She is far from well.'

'Good, I am glad to hear this. It might seem a little selfish of me, but there it is.'

'I wish to find something to occupy my time, father.'

'That is understandable,' her father nodded.

'I intend to apply for a post as a librarian,' said Amelia.

'A librarian!' her father repeated.

'You have no objection, father?' Amelia's head moved slightly to one side as she spoke.

'After your previous occupation, how could I?' her father forced a weak smile.

'Thank you, father,' said Amelia, gratefully.

At ten minutes to ten, I arrived at Cedar Lodge. The maid answered the door and for the first time called me 'sir' and offered to take my cap and greatcoat. Almost immediately, Amelia came downstairs followed by Edwin in his dressing-gown, looking decidedly the worse for wear.

'Good morning, George, dear,' smiled Amelia.

'Morning, George,' grunted Edwin.

'Good morning, Amelia,' I said, brightly.

My reply to Edwin was a little less familiar. I was still unused to addressing an officer socially.

'Good morning, sir, er ... I mean, Edwin,' I mumbled.

I joined the family who were in the morning room. They acknowledged me as I entered the room; in fact, Mrs Hooper even smiled at me as I bid them good morning.

'Just black coffee for me, Alice,' said Edwin, as he lowered himself into an easy chair.

'We are going shopping, Edwin,' said Amelia, putting on her gloves. 'Do you need anything?' Edwin sniffed, 'Don't think so, ask George,' he looked up at me and grinned weakly. 'What do I need for the trenches, George?'

'Whisky and disinfectant,' was my immediate reply.

'Whisky and disinfectant?' frowned Edwin. 'The whisky I've got, but disinfectant! What do I want that for?' he asked, a puzzled look on his face.

'Rat bites,' I replied.

My reply seemed to leave the company dumbfounded.

'Rat bites! George?' gasped Edwin.

'Yes, I've got lots of them.' I pulled up the sleeve of my tunic and displayed some purple and dark red marks on my forearm. 'Look, they still haven't gone, and it's weeks since I was last bitten. I've got them on my arms and both my legs. If you dab some disinfectant on, they go quicker, Edwin.'

'Oh my God' gasped Amelia, her lower lip quivering.

Mrs Hooper put her hands to her face, whilst Mr Hooper slowly shook his head as if in a daze. Edwin, however, quickly got to his feet and almost ran out of the room, a hand to his mouth.

'George, dear, I'd no idea that there were so many. I knew that there were some.'

'It's crawling with them at times,' I said, quietly.

'But why?' frowned Amelia.

I bent towards her ear and whispered the unpleasant reason. 'The dead bodies and bits of dead bodies lying all over the place. I was lying in no man's land during a barrage the last time I was bitten – must have thought I was a corpse.'

'How awful.' Amelia shuddered as she spoke.

'The general public does not know the half of it, so it would appear,' observed Mr Hooper, sadly.

'No, father, you are right. We will get some disinfectant, George,' said Amelia, turning to me and smiling faintly.

I did not see Edwin again before we left the house. This time Amelia took my arm as soon as we were on the gravel drive and it seemed to pronounce to the whole household that I was her young man.

'I hope I didn't upset Edwin by what I said, Amelia,' I murmured, as I carefully closed the drive gate, as I knew Mr Hooper was rather particular about it.

'I think it was the amount that he drank last night

that upset him; the rats I think just finished him off. Still, it was good advice,' she said, looking sidelong at me. 'Is it really that bad, George?'

'Yes,' I replied, crisply, 'worse in fact.'

'I knew it was,' she said sadly as she held my arm tighter. 'But one just cannot believe it.'

At Lewisham, we went to the big department store – a place I had never visited before.

'First we will buy your gloves,' said Amelia, striding towards the men's department.

'Will they be expensive?' I asked, looking apprehensively at the display of attractively arranged goods on the ground floor.

Amelia must have read my thoughts because she squeezed my arm. 'Father gave me some money; he insisted on buying two pairs of gloves for you.'

'Did he?' I replied, visibly brightening.

'Yes,' smiled Amelia, nodding her head.

'That was very kind of him, wasn't it, Amelia?'

'Yes it was. He is a kind man,' she replied, her eyes suddenly filling with tears.

I put my arm around her shoulders, 'Hey, come on,' I whispered.

She screwed up her eyes for a moment and compressed her lips. 'I am all right, George. Remove your arm, please, I will hold it.'

'Er ... yes, of course,' I quickly replied.

Amelia had quite recovered herself as she sorted through a tray of woollen gloves.

'They must be khaki, Amelia,' I said, hastily.

'These blue ones look very nice, George, or these yellow ones.'

'Amelia, I can only wear khaki,' I said, my voice rising.

'Of course, sir,' said the assistant, who immediately produced another tray of gloves.

'Take your greatcoat off, dear, then I can see how well they fit.'

'Greatcoat!' I frowned.

'Yes, George, take it off, then I can see how far they go up your wrists,' said Amelia, as she sat on a chair facing me. I was aware a young officer was standing near us with two people who were clearly his parents. He looked rather patronisingly at us as he examined some leather gloves. I undid my coat and removed it as Amelia had requested, and immediately noticed him glance at my medal ribbons. As I tried on a pair of gloves, I could see him speak to his parents and nod in my direction.

'Do they fit well, dear?' asked Amelia.

'Yes, fine,' I replied.

'Then we will take two pairs exactly the same,' said Amelia to the elderly assistant who gave me a friendly nod.

While Amelia paid the assistant, I put on my greatcoat, and as we left the counter, the young officer touched his hat to Amelia and gave me a friendly smile. I reciprocated by touching my cap to his mother who also smiled at us as did the officer's father, after raising his hat to Amelia. I now realised why Amelia had told me to take off my greatcoat.

For the next hour or so we went from department to department. Amelia made some small purchases, which I carried for her.

'Would you like some refreshments, George, the orchestra will be playing shortly in the restaurant?'

'Er ... um ... well I'd like to buy some scissors and wire cutters first.'

'What on earth do you need those for?' asked Amelia, a puzzled look on her face.

'To get the men off the wire,' I said, quietly. Amelia's lips quivered and she shook her head quickly. 'Oh, George, dear, we don't understand do we?'

She looked so kind and sympathetic that I instinctively kissed her on the mouth and moved back before she could reprimand me, which she did not.

'How can you?' I smiled.

Without another word, she propelled me to the tool department where we purchased, from a puzzled-looking assistant, some first-class Sheffield-made scissors and wire cutters. Again Amelia insisted on paying, much to my embarrassment, and relief, I should add, as I did not expect them to cost so much.

'The gloves were not as expensive as I expected.' She could tell how I felt and it was some relief when she smiled and said, 'Father gave me the money, dear.'

Amelia then took me to the restaurant and at the door a waiter in a tail coat smiled and inclined his head to Amelia.

'Table for two, madam; this way please.'

The orchestra, which had just begun to play, consisted of an old man at the piano and two equally elderly old ladies on violin and cello; yet I thought it was wonderful as we sat at our own table, with coffee and pastries and pleasant music. It seemed to me to be a thousand worlds away from the Somme.

I had removed my cap and overcoat and in the warm store with the smell of coffee, I felt that I was in a cocoon from which I never wanted to emerge.

'More coffee, George, dear?' smiled Amelia.

'Er ... yes, it's very nice,' I replied. 'I've never been in here before and I could stay here with you for ever.'

Amelia smiled at me. She could understand my feelings.

'When we have had coffee we must get that disinfectant.' I could see her shiver slightly as she said 'disinfectant'.

I kept glancing about the store – it seemed so unreal, but for the occasional khaki uniform it would have been possible to believe that the war did not exist, that the hundreds of men now lying in no man's land crying for help were all part of one's imagination. Yet here I was, sitting opposite a young lady from a good family, dressed in the latest fashion, calmly observing other shoppers as she sipped her coffee.

'You are very quiet, George, dear,' smiled Amelia, as she finished her coffee.

'Yes, it seems so unreal here, you know,' I replied, shrugging my shoulders.

Amelia stretched out her gloved hand and touched mine. 'I understand, my dear,' she murmured.

I was now head over heels in love with Amelia; her kindness and sympathy made me forget so much that was in my mind.

'Shall we go?' she asked, opening her handbag.

'Yes, Amelia, but let me pay.'

The earnest look on my face must have convinced her as she snapped closed her handbag and smiled, 'Of course, George,' nodding to a waitress as she did so.

Having paid the waitress what I considered a lot of money for coffee and a few cakes, we continued with our shopping.

'You are coming home for luncheon?' said Amelia, after we had purchased the disinfectant for which she insisted on paying.

'If ... er...' I mumbled, 'it's all right?'

'Of course it is,' she smiled.

Having completed our shopping, we returned to Cedar Lodge. Edwin was in the drawing-room, a glass of what I presumed to be whisky in his hand. 'Hello, George,' he said, loudly, as I entered the room. 'Come in old boy – the only man I know with any sense.'

Edwin, his now red face accentuating his fair hair, was past the happy stage and beyond caring.

'Edwin, don't drink any more before luncheon,' said Amelia, crossly. 'Where is father?'

'*Pater* is in his study and the *mater* in her room,' replied Edwin, with a cocky grin on his face. His reference in such terms to his father and mother caused me to grin, until Amelia turned on me. 'Don't laugh at him, George, you will only encourage him, drinking at this time of day indeed,' she said with a hint of disgust in her voice.

My face immediately lost its grin until Edwin said, 'I can see she is getting you under her thumb already,' wagging a finger at me as he did so, and looking at me severely.

'Edwin,' said Amelia, her voice rising and her face now red, 'please behave yourself.'

I touched her arm. 'It's his last day of leave,' I said in a whisper.

My words were like a douche of cold water to Amelia, who nodded, biting her lower lip as she did so. 'Yes, George, dear,' she replied lowering her voice.

'We got your antiseptic, Edwin.'

'Thanks, George,' smiled a bleary-eyed Edwin. 'Get him a whisky, Amelia.'

'I'd sooner have a lemonade, Amelia.'

'Yes, of course,' she smiled, going to the sideboard.

'Lemonade!' said Edwin in a loud voice. 'Lemonade! We can't give you lemonade.'

Amelia stood, hands on hips, her back to the sideboard, face flushed in anger. I stepped closer to her and murmured in her ear, 'Don't say anything to him that you might regret,' then in a louder voice I said, as if to settle the argument, 'I'll have a ginger beer then, but I wish to be excused first.'

'You know where it is, dear,' smiled Amelia.

As I left the room, I heard Amelia turn on her brother

and say, 'Do try and behave, what on earth will George think?'

'You like George, don't you, Amelia?' grinned Edwin.

Amelia opened a bottle of ginger beer. 'Yes I do, as a matter of fact,' she replied.

'Very much?' he teased.

'None of your business,' snapped Amelia.

'Ah ha!' he grinned. 'You do.'

'Well, so what?' she replied. 'I suppose you consider him below us,' she added sarcastically.

Edwin, clearly stung by her manner, turned on her, his blue eyes flashing with anger. 'No I do not, I like him and admire him. I only hope when the time comes I have his courage.' Edwin emptied his glass then put a hand across his eyes. Amelia sat down on the sofa next to him and put a hand on his shoulder. 'I'm sorry, Edwin, I do not wish to quarrel with you.'

'No, Sis, but I'm dreading it, really I am. Yet George seems so calm and it makes me feel a coward and a bloody fool,' he sniffed.

'George feels the same as you, believe me,' murmured Amelia.

'This bloody war,' groaned Edwin, his head now supported by his hands. 'When will it all end? It was supposed to be over by Christmas 1914, now we're at Christmas 1916.' There was desperation in his voice.

When I returned to the room I could tell that Edwin was in that nervous excitable state quite common to men losing control of themselves. I felt as embarrassed as Amelia appeared to be about Edwin's condition, and was not sorry when, at Amelia's suggestion, he went to have a lie down.

Luncheon was a sombre affair. Mr Hooper made a brief appearance, but Mrs Hooper stayed in her room. Afterwards, Amelia suggested that I left. She put on her coat and came to the drive gate with me.

'I didn't get a chance to thank your father,' I said, looking a little apprehensively at the house.

'Never mind. Come over tomorrow afternoon, you can thank him then. Edwin will have left by then and we can go for a walk,' she smiled.

'Yes, that would be fine,' I said, brightening. 'I'll see you tomorrow then.'

'Yes,' replied Amelia, who quickly kissed me, and before I could react, began walking back to the house.

I stood almost rooted to the spot until she turned as she entered the house, waved, then closed the door.

Amy was busy with her washing when I returned, and was glad of my offer to meet the girls from school.

'Ma called round this morning to see you,' said Amy, when I had returned from the school with the girls.

'Oh,' I said, disinterestedly, as I took off my greatcoat.

'She said Pa wanted to see you; heard about your medals, I think,' smiled Amy.

'So,' I grunted, unlacing my boots and taking them off. 'That's better,' I sighed.

'Your feet don't 'alf pong,' said Alice, holding her nose.

'They don't,' I protested, glancing at Amy.

'They do a bit, George; change your socks, love,' smiled Amy.

'All right then,' I replied, grudgingly. I picked up my boots and walked out of the parlour.

'Are you?' persisted Amy.

I turned and looked at her, my face set, then I spoke, 'He threw me out, didn't he? Told me not to come back, didn't he?' I said bitterly.

'But it's your Ma and Pa,' said Amy, reproachfully.

'So that's my hard luck, isn't it?' I don't know why he doesn't volunteer for the army, he was so keen on this war, don't you remember? Not so keen now I bet, still I could go round and suggest he joins up, eh?'

Amy looked away for a moment, then she spoke. 'I can understand you being so bitter, George. Perhaps it's best if you didn't go if you feel like that.'

I did not reply as I walked into the hall and up the stairs to my bedroom. I lay on my bed and closed my eyes, my head ached and there was a dull pain in my eyes. I drifted off to sleep and only awoke when Amy came into the room carrying a cup of tea. The landing light was now on as it was almost dark.

'Cup of tea, love,' she said, putting it on the chair by my bed.

'Yes,' I yawned as Amy sat down on the edge of the bed.

'Look, George, I wasn't getting on to you, it's that Ma went on – you know what she's like.' Amy touched my hand, 'All right?'

I nodded now, feeling better, 'Course I know, Amy. It's all right. Always in the way wasn't I? Wanted to give me to old Ma Gibbons years ago, d'you remember?'

I could see Amy nod in the dim light. She had not turned on the bedroom light. 'Oh I remember,' there was more than a hint of bitterness in her voice. 'That was when I lived with Aunt Greta – she gave me a hard time did that one,' said Amy, her voice hardening.

'Aye – unpaid labour,' I replied.

'That's right,' agreed Amy, 'and didn't I work from dawn to dusk. She had me at it; never a moment's peace.'

'Makes me sick, Amy, all these people so keen on the war, d'you remember?' I sniffed.

'I remember all right. Hector and I were two of them, I'm sorry to say; how wrong we were. Pa thought you were mental because you wouldn't join up.'

'Hope they put that on my gravestone if I have one,' I said, picking up my cup and saucer.

137

Amy pretended not to have heard my last remark and hurried from the room. 'We're eating in ten minutes,' she said, as she went downstairs.

Later I played snakes and ladders with the girls until it was their bedtime.

'The paper says we have won a victory on the Somme, George,' said Hector, looking up from his newspaper.

'Probably taken a trench,' I said, sarcastically, as I put the snakes and ladders board back into its box.

'You have become very cynical, George,' said Hector, glancing at Amy, who was darning a sock.

'If you had seen the amount of dead men I have, and the bits of men lying all over the place, and the rats in no man's land eating them and the young men praying to die...'

'I'm sorry, George,' said Hector, quickly, his face now pale. 'I'm sorry George, you have every right to be cynical, I apologise.'

'No need to apologise, Hector, it's just that I have grown up and become old over the past six months; still I'm alive and I've got another six days' leave,' I smiled.

'Yes, you enjoy it, too,' said Hector. 'You saw your young lady today then?'

I felt myself flushing as I replied. 'Yes, I did, we went shopping in Lewisham. The Hoopers bought me some gloves.'

'That was kind of them.'

'Yes it was,' I agreed, 'they are very nice people.'

'Amelia was very nice,' smiled Amy.

'Yes, most charming,' agreed Hector. 'Her brother is going to France tomorrow isn't he?'

'Yes,' I nodded.

'How is he?' asked Hector.

'At the moment I'd say he was a bit Brahms,' I grinned.

138

'Brahms,' frowned Hector, unfamiliar with cockney slang.

'Drunk,' said Amy, giving me a reproving glance.

'I see. Had he been to a party?'

I shook my head. 'No,' I said quietly.

'Oh, I see,' said Hector again.

One thing I liked about Hector, though he did not drink and his church was against it, he did not sermonise about it.

Hector and I spent the rest of the evening reading while Amy darned socks and sewed on buttons. It was restful and pleasant. That night I slept well, with no dreams.

To my surprise, Amelia was waiting for me near the tram terminus when I arrived at Blackheath the following afternoon. She looked very pretty in her light blue coat with a blue dress and hat to match.

'This is a nice surprise,' I said as I approached her.

Her face looked strained and it had been well powdered. I suspected that she had been crying.

'Hello, George,' she said, kissing my cheek.

'Is everything all right?' I asked.

She made an indifferent gesture with her shoulders and took a deep breath.

'As well as one can in the circumstances,' she replied. 'Let's go for a walk,' she said, taking my arm.

We walked in silence for a while; at last I spoke, 'Did Edwin get off all right?'

'Yes, father took him to Waterloo station. Mother and I did not go, Edwin wanted it that way.'

'Yes, I can understand that,' I said, quietly.

'What did you do this morning?' she asked.

'I ... um ... went to my old firm, Holdings, to see my boss – you know, the jam factory.'

'Yes, I remember,' Amelia nodded and smiled faintly.

'He said my old job was there when I came home. I

don't think he wants this war to end, he's never sold so much of his rotten jam. He's got a big contract with the Army you know.'

Amelia shook her head slowly and her lower lip trembled slightly, though she did not speak. We looked casually in some shop windows, then crossed the road and made our way to the Heath. We walked in silence, but for Amelia passing the time of day with acquaintances that we passed. At last Amelia spoke. 'Do you know, George, it seems I've known you a long time, yet it was only a short time in France and now just your leave, surprising isn't it?'

'Yes it is,' I said, reflectively, 'and I feel just the same, as if I've always known you.'

Amelia held my arm tighter and looked affectionately at me. I was beginning to hope that she had as much regard for me as I had for her.

I looked across the Heath. It was so peaceful – no barbed wire. I could see two girls on ponies. I thought of the cavalry charge and the German machine gunners. I shivered.

'Is there anything wrong, dear?' asked Amelia, a look of concern on her face.

'No, it's just those girls on their ponies. It reminded me of that cavalry charge I saw. Could we go, please?' I stuttered.

Amelia suddenly kissed me on the lips; her eyes were moist. 'Shall we go home, dear?'

'Please,' I murmured.

When we returned to Cedar Lodge the house seemed very quiet.

'Father's at the business, I think,' explained Amelia, 'and mother has gone to some friends. It's the cook and maid's day off. Let me take your coat.'

I slowly removed my greatcoat; my ears had begun to ache again.

'Are you all right, dear?' There was a frown on Amelia's brow.

'My ears ache a bit,' I mumbled.

'You poor dear, I'll make some tea, perhaps it will make you feel better. Go into the morning-room, there's a fire in there, we can have our tea by it.'

Amelia hung up our coats in the hall cupboard, then took my hand and led me into the morning room. She suddenly hesitated, then spoke, 'George, if I get a pair of my brother's slippers, will you wear them instead of those horrible army boots?'

'Yes, of course, my socks are clean,' I added, looking at them.

Amelia began to smile, 'I'll go and get some slippers for you.'

I sat down in one of the easy chairs in the morning-room and began to unlace my boots. Having removed them, I glanced about the room. It was much smaller than the drawing-room and it struck me as more comfortable; at least it seemed so to me. Perhaps removing my boots helped, but it was far less formal and I felt more at home. The door opened and Amelia came in holding a pair of slippers.

'Try these on, dear,' she said, handing them to me.

'Thank you,' I replied, taking the slippers and quickly slipping them on. I stood up. 'They fit!' I smiled.

'Good,' said Amelia, her head slightly to one side. 'George, you will not mind if I say something to you? I mean, you will not be offended?'

'N-no,' I mumbled. 'It's not my socks is it?'

'Of course not,' she smiled. 'I've had three brothers you know, it's...' she paused, 'it's well ... it's polite if a young man stands up when a lady comes into the room you know.'

'I ... er ... um ... yees,' I managed to reply, my face

now warm. 'I'm sorry, Amelia, I didn't mean...'

'No, of course not,' she smiled, 'but you will remember won't you?'

'Yes, I promise,' I replied, nodding my head.

'And when my father or mother come into the room, do the same thing. My brothers do ... er ... did,' she said, lowering her eyes. Amelia bit her lower lip and her eyes clouded.

'I'll remember, Amelia, I promise.'

Amelia suddenly kissed me on the lips, 'Good boy,' she whispered, taking my hand. 'Now you can help me with the tea things.'

'Amelia,' I said, putting my arm around her. 'You won't be cross if I say something as well.'

Amelia frowned slightly. 'What is it, George?'

'It's ... er ... I ... er ... I mean, I love you,' I said, lowering my eyes.

She did not reply but put a warm soft hand on either side of my face and looked into my eyes. 'George, my dearest, how can you be sure? You have not known me for very long,' she whispered.

'I am, I feel that I've always known you really. I mean it, honest I do. Amelia, do you like me too – I mean, a little?'

Her soft hands caressed my ears as she whispered again. 'I like you a lot, my dear. If I did not, you would not be here.'

She pulled me towards her and for the first time I put my arms about her when she was not wearing a coat. For me it was a rapturous experience and the long lingering kiss she gave me removed any doubts in my mind, but also convinced me that she was far more experienced in such matters than I.

'Now you can help me get tea,' she said, breaking away, her face flushed. She took my hand and led me from the room down the hall through the pantry and into the kitchen. There I stood watching her as she made some sandwiches.

'Take that tray, George, dear, and get some cups and saucers and plates from the pantry.'

'Yes, Amelia,' I replied, quickly, picking up the tray.

'Do you like seed cake, George?'

'Yes please,' I replied from the pantry.

I put the tea things on the tray and watched Amelia make the tea. For the first time I studied her without being in a daze. Her dress revealed her shape and size, even though it reached to her ankles. She had broad hips, which seemed bigger than Amy's, even though Amy had borne three children, and they were of the same height. Her arms too seemed bigger and some might have considered her plump, though to me, she was perfect.

'Bring the tray here, George, and I'll put the teapot on it,' she said, bringing me out of my reverie.

'Yes, Amelia,' I replied, picking up the tray.

We sat by the fire eating fishpaste sandwiches and drinking tea; it was the most comfortable meal I had enjoyed at Cedar Lodge.

'Do you like rabbit pie, George?'

'Ooh yes, I had it once at Amy's. My Ma never did it, too many of us,' I replied.

'We are having it for dinner – you will stay?' said Amelia.

It was more of a command than an invitation but I did not mind. 'Is Amy expecting you?'

'I don't think so,' I replied. 'She said it didn't matter 'cos it was cold meat.'

'Good. Another sandwich, George?' Amelia offered me the plate of fishpaste sandwiches. I carefully took one and put it on my plate.

'Are you feeling better now, dear?' she asked.

'A bit,' I replied. 'I feel better when I'm with you.'

'That's sweet of you, George,' she smiled, 'but you must tell the medical officer about your ears.'

'He won't bother. He'll just tell me to get out,' I replied, morosely. 'I don't want to go back Amelia, I want to stay with you.'

'You've got to, my dear,' she replied, sympathetically, her voice in a whisper. 'I'd like you to stay.' She put her hand on mine and I screwed up my mouth and looked away, 'But you must go back or you will be in a lot of trouble. Promise me?' She looked into my eyes.

'Yes, I will. I'd do anything for you, Amelia,' I murmured.

'I know you would, my love,' she said in a hushed voice.

After we had finished our tea we sat holding hands looking into the fire. Neither of us spoke, each with one's own thoughts. Mine were of France, the Somme and dying in the mud; Amelia's, I suspected, were of her brothers – her favourite, James, who was dead; Edgar, who was missing, and Edwin, now on his way to France. The family business too must have been in her thoughts. What would happen to it? I could hear someone in the hall.

'That's father,' said Amelia, letting go of my hand and rising to her feet. Almost at once the door opened and Mr Hooper came into the room. I got to my feet as Amelia had instructed me.

'Good evening, sir.'

'Good evening, George. How are you?' he smiled.

'Fine thank you, sir,' I replied.

'Good,' nodded Mr Hooper, who then sat down in one of the easy chairs and began to light his pipe.

'Tea, father?' asked Amelia, who had flashed me a look of approval.

'Um, yes,' replied Mr Hooper in an undecided tone.

'I'll go and make a fresh pot and put the vegetables on,' said Amelia, leaving the room.

I was aware that Mr Hooper was studying me intently and I felt a little uneasy. At last he spoke. 'Are you enjoying your leave, George?' he asked kindly.

'Yes, thank you, sir,' I replied.

'Is your hearing better now?'

'Sometimes, sir. At other times there's a whooshing sound in my ears and if I lie on one at night the pain wakes me up.'

Mr Hooper nodded sympathetically, then spoke. 'You must see the Army doctor when you get back to barracks.'

'I will sir, but I don't expect they'll be interested. They have got too much to do.'

'I understand,' Mr Hooper smiled, weakly.

'Thank you for the gloves, sir.'

'You found some to fit you in khaki?'

'Yes sir, they fit smashing; nice and warm too,' I added.

'Good, I'm glad of that,' smiled Mr Hooper.

'I've only got four more days left of my leave, sir,' I said, miserably.

Mr Hooper seemed at a loss what to say. He twiddled the fob of his gold Albert chain, then took out his watch, looked at it, then tucked it back into his waistcoat pocket. 'Yes,' he said at last, 'you must enjoy them lad, I'm sure Amelia will.'

'Amelia's wonderful, sir, really wonderful,' I said.

The sincerity in my voice must have impressed Mr Hooper who said, 'Yes she is, my boy, a fine young woman. I'm proud of her.'

'So am I, sir. When she holds my arm I'm the proudest man in the Army.'

'That's a very nice thing to say, George,' murmured Mr Hooper, 'and I'm sure Amelia's a little proud of you too.'

'D'you think so, sir?' I asked curiously.

Mr Hooper smiled and nodded his head slightly. At this point the morning-room door opened and Amelia entered. I rose to my feet.

'Sit down, George, dear,' she smiled, approvingly. 'Shall we eat in here, father, it's much warmer than in the dining-room?'

'Yes, of course,' replied Mr Hooper. 'Will you get me a whisky and soda, dear?'

'Yes, father. George, dear, put all the tea things on that tray and bring it out to me.'

'Yes, Amelia,' I replied, picking up the tea tray and putting the cups and saucers on it. I could see Mr Hooper was looking at my feet and Amelia must have noticed too for she turned to her father and said, 'I've given George a pair of Jamie's slippers to wear while he is here, father.'

Mr Hooper nodded. 'Sensible,' he muttered. He wiped his eyes with his handkerchief; I could tell that the thought of his eldest son distressed him and I felt very uncomfortable. I looked down at the slippers self-consciously.

Amelia could read my thoughts; she smiled encouragingly at me though there were tears in her eyes, 'Bring the tray out, dear,' she said, walking towards the door. I followed Amelia into the pantry, where I put down the tray. 'I think your father's a little upset Amelia,' I said, quietly. 'Is it because I'm wearing your brother's slippers, 'cos I can take them off – my socks are clean. I know my boots are...'

'No, George,' smiled Amelia before I could finish, 'it's just that father gets so upset when he thinks of the boys; what makes it worse is that he was in favour of this war in the beginning, like most people.' She looked a little apprehensively at me. 'No. You wear the slippers. I'll

146

pour him a whisky and you can take it to him while I put on the vegetables.'

'Yes,' I muttered, as I watched her pour the whisky.

'There we are,' she said, as she put a dash of soda in the whisky glass. 'Put it on that salver, dear, then take it to father. Can you make up the fire, it's getting low?'

'Yes, Amelia. Where's the coal bucket?'

'By the fire. If it's empty, you will have to fill it from the bunker outside, it's at the back of the house.'

'Yes, Amelia.'

'You don't mind, George?' she said, picking up a saucepan.

'No, of course not,' I said, quickly. 'I'd do anything for you.'

Amelia smiled, 'Bless you, George,' she murmured.

I carefully carried the salver into the morning-room where Mr Hooper was staring into the fire. He turned as I came into the room and gave me a weak smile.

'Your whisky, sir,' I said, offering him the salver.

'Thank you, George, my boy,' he said, taking the glass. 'Are you having one?'

'No thank you, sir. I don't really like whisky,' I replied.

'I've no schnapps,' smiled Mr Hooper.

'I don't like that, sir,' I replied.

'I think there's some ginger beer in the pantry – how about that?' he asked, his eyes twinkling.

'Yes, thank you, sir.' I put down the salver and opened the brass coal box. It was almost empty. I put the last pieces of coal on the fire and took the zinc bin out of the box.

'Amelia's finding you jobs to do,' commented Mr Hooper.

'I don't mind, sir, I'd do anything for her,' I replied.

Mr Hooper looked carefully at me before he replied. 'Yes, I believe you would, George, my boy,' he said quietly.

It was the nicest evening that I had spent at Cedar

Lodge. There was a blazing fire in front of which the cook's cat lay stretched out. The table was close to the fire and we had delicious rabbit pie with Brussels sprouts, carrots, mashed potatoes and thick gravy, followed by fruit pie and custard. It became clear to me that Amelia was a most capable cook.

'Do your slippers fit, George?' asked Mr Hooper.

'Yes, thank you, sir,' I replied.

'Good, it will save my parquet flooring,' he smiled, giving me a wink as he did so.

'Yes, father,' said Amelia, who put down her own knife and fork; then, as if it were part of the proceedings, took my knife out of my hand and folded my fingers about the handle in the correct manner. I flushed slightly, realising that I had been holding my knife incorrectly at my previous meals at Cedar Lodge. It was all done so matter-of-factly that it was impossible for me to be actually embarrassed. All she said was, 'That's better, George, dear. You were saying, father?'

Mr Hooper pretended not to have noticed what had happened but I think he drew his own conclusions from it. I realised Hector held his knife the same way and was resolved to do the same.

Mrs Hooper, it appeared, was staying with her sister at Highbury that night in an effort to get over Edwin's departure. I wondered why Mr Hooper had not accompanied her, but it seemed that he did not get on too well with his sister-in-law. The evening passed quickly and before I knew it the grandfather clock in the hall had struck eleven o'clock.

'I'd better go now, Amelia,' I said, reluctantly moving away from the still bright fire.

'Yes, of course, George,' she replied. Amelia left the room while I bade Mr Hooper an embarrassed, 'thank you', and wished him good-night.

'Good-night, George, my boy,' he said, amiably.

I met Amelia in the hall; she was putting on her coat. 'I'll come to the gate with you.'

I pulled on my overcoat and put on my cap. 'Oh! I'm forgetting my boots,' I grinned, looking down at the slippers that I was wearing.

'That will never do,' smiled Amelia, 'slippers with your uniform. What would the Army say? Put them in the hall cupboard for next time.'

'When will that be?' I asked, apprehensively.

'Tomorrow I am going to my aunt's at Highbury with my father. I expect we will bring my mother home. We will stay most of the day I'm sure.'

'Oh!' I murmured.

'And I have a meeting in the evening.'

'Have you?' My face must have brightened.

'It's a suffragette committee meeting and it's at a friend's house, so I'm afraid I cannot take you.'

'Oh!' My face must have registered my disappointment, as Amelia put her hand to my cheek and smiled, sympathetically. 'Can you come over on Thursday?'

'Oh yes,' I beamed.

'Good. Come over for luncheon then.'

'Yes, I will,' I said, eagerly.

We walked slowly down the gravel drive. For once it was bright and clear, though there was the familiar smell of chimney smoke in the air. This time, under the cover of the holly tree, I did not need any encouragement. I put my arms about her and kissed her with a passion that I think surprised her. She responded eagerly and neither of us noticed the heavy frost that was forming or how cold it was in the garden.

At last, we parted, but I watched Amelia enter the house before I left to catch the tram home. The following morning I had a postcard from my friend Vic. He said he had not been well, which did not surprise me, since he had developed a nervous twitch and his hair had been falling out in handfuls. From his card I assumed he was trying to get a medical discharge, and since his father was a doctor, I expected him to get it.

'Are you going to see Amelia today, George?' asked Amy, as I read the card for the third time. I was sitting by the kitchener pleasantly warm with a book on my lap.

'Not today,' I replied. 'She is going to her aunt's at Highbury. Her mother has been staying there overnight after her brother went back after his leave ended.'

'There's a prayer meeting at the church this afternoon,' said Hector, peering at me through his thick glasses.

I pretended not to have heard, but Amy would not let it pass. 'I'm doing the refreshments,' she said to encourage me.

'We are going to pray for an early end to the war,' persisted Hector, peering at me again.

'Do you think it will make any difference?' I asked, my face blank as I opened my book again.

'George!' said Amy in a shocked voice.

'We hope it will,' said Hector, patiently.

'Well, it hasn't done much good so far, has it?' I replied.

Hector and Amy exchanged glances, then Hector lowered his eyes as he spoke to me: 'No, George, it hasn't, but we must keep trying,' he said, quietly.

'I'll look after Jimmy for you and meet the girls from school,' I said, getting out of my chair. I could see that Amy was annoyed with me so I went up to my room and lay on my bed. I could hear voices downstairs. Perhaps I should not have cast doubts on Hector's beliefs, but I could not help it.

'I'm sorry, Hector, for what Georgie said, but he's been through a lot you know,' said Amy apologetically.

Hector slowly shook his head, then began to clean his

150

glasses. 'You've no reason to apologise dear, we cannot blame him for being cynical. After all, he is one of the most honest youngsters I've ever met. Perhaps if there had been more like him there would not have been any war in the first place. If he does not want to come to the meeting, Amy, it's his choice. Don't say any more to him, it will not do any good.'

'No, I won't,' murmured Amy.

Some time later Amy came upstairs with a cup of tea. She looked apprehensive as she opened the bedroom door. 'Brought you a cup of tea, George. You all right, dear?' she asked.

'Yes,' I replied, putting my book on the floor and sitting up. 'Thanks, Amy,' I smiled, taking the cup of tea.

'Are you coming down? Hector has gone round to the church.'

'Is he still cross with me?' I asked.

'No, of course not,' smiled Amy. 'Come on down and talk to me. Are your ears hurting?' she asked, sympathetically.

'No more than usual, and they've not bled for days,' I said, getting off the bed.

We went downstairs and I helped amuse Jimmy by making paper boats. Amy had given me a bowl of lukewarm water and we sat in the scullery with the bowl on a chair floating the boats. I did not hear Hector return. Suddenly I heard a sob and a, 'Oh no, no, no,' from the parlour. I almost jumped off my chair and in three strides or so was in the parlour.

'What's the matter?' I burst out, opening the parlour door so fast I caught the chair behind it with a thump. Amy was so distraught she ignored the knock I had given the chair.

'What is it?' I demanded.

Hector was sitting, head in his hands, elbows on the parlour table, while Amy sat opposite him, tears running down her face, as she explained in jerking sobs.

'He's going to join up, this afternoon – he's going to the recruiting office,' she sniffed.

'Joining up, why?' I gasped.

'That Mrs Minter in Belfort Street stopped him just now and told him he was a coward if he didn't join up.' Amy dabbed at her eyes.

'None of her bleedin' business,' I growled. 'You're not going to take any notice of her are you, Hector? All the Minters have got is big gobs.'

Amy cheered up a little at my words, but Hector, head in hands, still looked down at the green table cover. I pushed my chair next to him and sat down, but he ignored me, so I put my large right hand around his forearm. 'Now you listen to me, Hector, while I tell you a few things.'

Amy sat opposite us, her mouth half open. 'I've always looked up to you, you are the only one in my family that's got any sense. My sisters all married duck eggs who my father liked because they went to the boozer with him. My family, like the Minters, all cheered when war was declared and I was called a coward because I didn't agree. Charlie Minter was a regular, so was his brother, now they are both dead. They wanted this war just like my brothers did.'

'Dickie Minter's dead too; they heard a week ago,' sniffed Amy, wiping her eyes.

'Not so bloody keen on the war now, eh?' I sneered.

'Mustn't swear, Georgie,' said Amy.

'If you go to the recruiting office, Hector, I will think you are as big a fool as they were. Inside a few weeks you will be just one of a pile of rotting bodies waiting to be buried, then what will Amy and the children do, eh, tell me that?' My voice rose.

Hector sat up and took his elbows off the table; he took out his handkerchief and moved to Amy's side, then gently wiped her eyes. 'I'm so sorry, dear, for making you cry. George is right. I will not go to the Army recruiting office,' he said, putting his arms about her.

'Oh!' gasped Amy in relief, kissing him fiercely. 'Thank goodness,' she breathed.

I was about to leave the parlour when Hector spoke. 'Thank you, George,' he said, huskily. 'I look up to you, too, believe me, I do,' he blinked, rapidly.

'Er ... um...' I mumbled, in embarrassment.

As I left the parlour Amy flashed me a look of gratitude.

I was mopping up water on the scullery floor when Amy opened the door.

'We had a bit of an accident,' I grinned.

'I do it,' gurgled a rather damp Jimmy.

I got up and put the wet cloth in the sink. Without a word, Amy put her arms about me and kissed my cheek. 'Thank you, George,' she whispered, her eyes still moist. 'Come on, Jimmy, let's get you dry.' Amy turned and lifted Jimmy into her arms. 'You need a fresh jersey.' She took Jimmy into the parlour while I gathered the now disintegrating paper boats and emptied the bowl of water. I offered to help Hector carry some books around to the church, so at two o'clock we left the house, each carrying a cardboard box.

'I'll be along in ten minutes,' said Amy, 'and don't spill the milk in that box, Hector.'

'No, dear,' he replied, smiling at me.

I walked out of the gate and was about to turn left, which would have been the quickest way to the church.

'Not that way, George, we'll go up to Evelina Road,' said Hector.

'You mean to avoid going down Belfort Road and running into the Minters,' I replied.

Hector's pallid face became even whiter. 'Um … it … er … um,' he began.

'You'll have to face them some time, come on,' I said, striding in the direction of Belfort Road.

Reluctantly Hector followed and I slowed my pace to allow him to catch up. As fate would have it, the first people we saw in Belfort Road were Dan and Elsie Minter. Dan Minter, with his cap well pulled down, had his hands deep in his overcoat pockets. His wife, wearing a black coat with stockings and hat to match, held his arm, her face a picture of woe.

'Taking 'im ter the recruiting office?' sneered Dan Minter, looking at me.

'Why don't you go, you're not too old, you stupid old fool. You were keen on this war, weren't you?' I retorted.

'Er … er … wot's that?' The Minters were taken aback. 'I … er … I…' he spluttered.

'You called my brother-in-law a coward, didn't you, eh?'

I dropped my box of books and pulled open my overcoat and stuck my forefinger against the medal ribbons on my tunic. 'Them's medal ribbons, mate, how many have you Minters got, tell me that?'

They had no reply to my angry outburst and both of them gasped. I held up my right fist. 'He's not joining up because I won't let him. I'll flatten him if he does, get me?'

'Er … yes, mate,' said Dan Minter, hoarsely.

I quickly buttoned up my coat and picked up the box of books. 'You remember, Dan Minter, ter keep a button on your lip about my brother-in-law, see?' I poked at him with my index finger.

'Yes, mate. I didn't know,' muttered Dan Minter.

'Come on, Hector,' I said, pushing my way past the Minters.

Hector followed, mouth half open as if in a trance.

154

We had almost reached the church; neither of us, I think, knew what to say. At last, Hector spoke: 'I do not know what to say, George,' he said, helplessly.

'Nothing to say, is there, Hector?' I grinned. 'The Minters won't bother you again, you can put money on that.'

We went through the side gate of the church and into the church hall. I dumped my box on one of a row of wooden straight-backed chairs. Hector did likewise then straightened his back; he was not used to physical effort. The hall and church were deserted. I held his arm, then spoke: 'Listen, Hector,' I said in little more than a whisper, 'I would do anything for Amy. She brought me up, better than my Ma – she couldn't be bothered with me. Amy's been my mother, so now you know.'

Hector looked at me and blinked rapidly as he replied. 'Yes, I know, George, I've always known that Amy loves you too, you know. Will you stay for the prayer meeting?' Hector looked almost pathetic and I felt tempted to oblige him.

'No, I'll take Jimmy to the park and meet the girls, it will give Amy a break,' I replied.

'Yes, of course,' smiled Hector.

I met Amy coming through the side gate, her small face looked pinched with the cold. I took hold of Jimmy's pushchair. 'I'll take Jimmy to the park and meet the girls, Amy.'

'Isn't it cold in the hall,' she sniffed.

'Bloody freezing,' I replied.

'George, your language,' she admonished. 'Are you coming to the meeting?' she asked.

I turned the pushchair round; the expression on my face must have given Amy her answer.

'I saw which way you came. Did you see the Minters?'

'Yes, they'll not bother Hector again Amy – money on it,' I smiled.

Amy looked happier, then wiped her nose. I thought she was about to cry, and I put an arm around her. 'He'll not go there, he's promised me.'

'Thank you, Georgie,' she said, kissing my cheek.

'Come on, Jimmy, we'll go and see the ducks in the park.'

'Ducks, Unca Georgie,' he gurgled.

'See you later, Amy,' I smiled. 'Enjoy yourself and see you at home.'

Amy was now trying not to smile, 'Be a good boy, Jimmy,' she called, as we went down the road.

The two ponds that the park boasted were frozen and the ducks huddled together in small groups, ignoring us as we passed them. For a moment they reminded me of the groups of men I had seen waiting to go up to the forward trenches. I pushed Jimmy past the ponds. I could not get the war out of my mind, and my leave seemed to be going quicker than ever. Fortunately, I arrived just in time to meet the girls from school, but I could not get past the sweet shop, and after a purchase of three sherbet dabs and a bar of chocolate, we went home.

'For after tea, or I will be in trouble for getting them,' I said to their protests, but I did not give in as we made our way home.

The following day on the stroke of noon I arrived at Cedar Lodge carrying a bunch of flowers. Before I could ring the bell, Amelia opened the door and gave me a wonderful smile. 'Hello, George, dear,' she said, looking quickly from right to left, then giving me, before I could respond, a quick kiss. 'Come on in out of the cold.'

'I've brought you some flowers, Amelia,' I said, giving the bunch of flowers to her when she had shut the front door.

'That's very sweet of you but you shouldn't have done so,' she lowered her voice. 'Shall I tell mother that they are for her? She is a little down today, we had a letter from Edwin this morning.'

'Yes, of course, where is Edwin?'

'The letter was posted in Folkestone, just before he embarked I should think. Put your coat in the cupboard and take your boots off; the slippers are in the cupboard.'

'Yes, Amelia,' I replied unbuttoning my overcoat.

'I'll just put these flowers in water.' Amelia left me in the hall and I had just taken my boots off and put the slippers on when she returned. 'Come on into the morning-room,' she said, taking my hand.

Mr and Mrs Hooper were sitting in easy chairs on either side of the bright fire, which was roaring up the chimney.

'Good morning, sir, good morning, Mrs Hooper.'

'Ah! Hello, George,' said Mr Hooper affably, turning in his chair.

Mrs Hooper nodded and said, 'George,' in a quiet voice.

'How are you, my boy?' asked Mr Hooper.

'All right, thank you, sir,' I replied.

'Sit down here, George,' said Amelia, indicating to the chair next to her own.

'George brought you some flowers, mother,' smiled Amelia.

'I brought them for y....' I began but I did not get any further as Amelia's shoe suddenly struck my shin. Considering how her long dress must have restricted her, it was a surprising blow and it took me by surprise.

'Er ... ouch,' I gasped.

'Yes, dear,' smiled Amelia, sweetly.

'Yes, I brought you some flowers, Mrs Hooper,' I said, quietly.

'That was very thoughtful of you, George,' smiled Mrs Hooper.

Mr Hooper, who was lighting his pipe, was smiling broadly as he had been facing Amelia and had seen what had happened.

'Your sister is well, George?' asked Mrs Hooper, politely.

'She is now, Mrs Hooper, though yesterday she was upset.'

'Oh dear,' murmured Mrs Hooper.

'What was wrong?' frowned Amelia.

'My brother-in-law, Hector, was going to join the Army,' I explained.

'Hector!' said Amelia, her voice rising in surprise.

'Yes, Hector. Can you imagine it with his eyes? They are awful,' I said with some feeling.

'But the Army could give him glasses,' said Mrs Hooper.

'He already wears them,' I replied, 'and they are as thick as the bottom of a jam jar.'

Mr Hooper smiled again before he spoke very seriously. 'But if he thinks it is his patriotic duty, George, after all, the Germans have to be beaten.'

'Why, sir?' I asked.

'Because, George, the Germans would come here and take our possessions,' said Mr Hooper, patiently.

'And they would do all sorts of wicked things,' added Mrs Hooper, her face the picture of woe.

'They bayonet babies, you know.' Mr Hooper looked over his glasses as he spoke.

'I've never seen them do it, sir, and I've never met a man who has either,' I replied. 'If the Kaiser wants to come here and take my possessions, he's welcome. I've only got a few second-hand books and my bed and the mattress is all lumpy. If that would stop the war they can have them,' I said, easily.

'I hardly think, George, that the Kaiser would want your bed,' said Mrs Hooper, a serious expression on her face.

158

'Or your mattress,' added Amelia, endeavouring not to smile.

Mr Hooper was also trying not to laugh as he puffed at his pipe.

'No, I bet he's got a better mattress than me as well, some of the bigger lumps in it I've banged flat with one of my boots.'

At this point Mr Hooper burst out laughing, to be joined by Mrs Hooper and Amelia. All three were doubled up laughing, though I could not see what was so funny.

'Oh, George, dear, I'm sorry,' said Amelia, wiping her eyes with a handkerchief. 'But tell me, what does Amy say when you...' Amelia began to laugh again, 'I mean when you use one of your boots to...' she paused.

'I do it when she is out,' I said, curtly. 'She said I caused a crack in the plaster of the kitchen ceiling the first time I did it,' I said, aware that Mr and Mrs Hooper were still laughing.

'Is your mattress all right now, dear?' asked Amelia, kindly.

'Oh, yes, it's fine now; I like it hard, you get used to it. In the dug-outs there are only bare boards and that's if you are lucky.'

My words were greeted with silence. Perhaps they were thinking of Edwin. How would he fare after the comfortable life that he had enjoyed hitherto. It would be a rude awakening for him, of that I was certain. I did not mind the Hoopers laughing at me; they did not do it unkindly, they were nice people and had been very good to me. As Amelia explained later, it was the first time she had heard them laugh for many months.

After luncheon, Amelia and I went out for a walk. We looked in the shops – one even had some Christmas decorations in the window.

'It will be December next week,' remarked Amelia.

159

I nodded. I was all too well aware of it. I had to report back to Woolwich Barracks on the Monday and it seemed to be approaching ever faster. We did not discuss the war; the news was bad judging from the carefully worded reports in the daily papers. The Somme offensive seemed to be over, having achieved nothing at the cost of an enormous loss of life. One only had to look at the lists in Hector's daily *Times* to know that. In the *Daily Post* there was a report from the eastern front and it caused some consternation. Though the Government tried to deny it, there was no doubt that the Russian army was having considerable problems and men were just going home. Who could blame them, were my thoughts on the matter, though I knew better than to express such opinions.

Both Mr Hooper and Hector had mentioned the article and they took it very seriously. The future looked far from rosy, which made the prospect of going back even more unpleasant. My pay had gone quicker than I had anticipated and I had just nine shillings and fourpence left. It was my intention to buy Amy and Amelia a present and I had decided to buy them something from the pawnbrokers in New Cross Road, but I had to invite Amelia out at the weekend before I went back and I did not want to run out of money. This, however, was solved for me as I was invited again to the theatre by Mr and Mrs Hooper on the Saturday evening, and Amy invited Amelia to Sunday dinner.

On Friday, Amelia had an appointment at Deptford library and I arranged to meet her there at ten-thirty. Before I did, I called at the pawnbrokers. Having spent nearly fifteen minutes peering through the grille on the windows, I had decided on an opal brooch for Amelia, and a ring for Amy. At last I pushed open the substantial shop door and caused two bells to start jangling. A man with long, dark hair and a skull-cap suddenly appeared.

160

'Can I help you, young man?'

I approached the counter, glancing around the shop as I did so. It was filled with articles of every description, from every sort of garment to pots and pans, musical instruments, swords, toys – the list was endless.

'The opal brooch in the window – how much is it?' I asked.

'Ah, yes,' the man held up his hands, 'a beautiful opal set in small diamonds with a strong clip – it's gold, too,' he enthused.

'How much?' I asked.

'It's expensive, soldier,' the man paused.

'How much?' I was getting impatient.

'Let me show it to you,' said the man, moving around the counter to the window. He took it out of the window and held it near the gas lamp that was on the counter, it looked even better.

'How much?' I asked again.

'Ten shillings to you, my dear,' he said, rubbing his hands together.

I shook my head. 'I haven't got ten shillings.'

'How much have you got?' he peered at me.

'I'll give you five shillings,' I replied.

The pawnbroker slowly shook his head, but did not speak.

I turned to leave and as I did so, he said, 'Seven shillings then.'

'No, six,' I replied.

The man paused for a moment and I moved towards the door. 'All right, I rob myself,' he said.

Having quickly agreed a price of two shillings for an amethyst ring for Amy, I gave him the eight shillings, leaving me one shilling and fourpence. Pleased with my purchases, I left the shop and made my way to the Deptford library. I had arranged to meet Amelia in the entrance hall. Her appointment was at eleven o'clock, and from the clock which I noticed as I entered, it was ten-forty.

'George!' I turned, Amelia stood behind me.

'Amelia,' I beamed, stepping forward to kiss her.

'No, George, dear, not here, you could smudge my make-up,' she said, avoiding my embrace.

'Er ... yes of course,' I mumbled, a little deflated.

'Shall we go upstairs?' said Amelia, stepping towards the double doors. I moved forward to open a door for her, then followed up the wide stone stairs. On the walls were posters exhorting men to enlist with the colours. I gave a wry smile.

'What is it, dear? asked Amelia.

'Don't show the trenches in those recruiting posters, do they?'

Amelia shook her head almost wearily, I thought. 'No,' she said in a whisper.

I watched as Amelia entered an office on the first floor. I stood in the corridor outside; she seemed a little nervous, getting the position meant a great deal to her; at the time I just did not realise how much.

Even I, who took little interest in clothes, could not help noticing what a variety Amelia had. Today she was wearing a completely different ensemble – all in dark blue, which I thought looked very becoming.

As I sat on the bench in the corridor, I looked at my purchases. They looked bargains, if indeed they were diamonds and gold. I put them away and as I sat there, members of the staff passed from time to time and I received nods or smiles, depending on whether it was a man or woman, until an older man came past who glanced at me. Then, as he was about to enter the office next to the one that Amelia had entered, he spoke to me.

162

'Who are you waiting for?'

I stood up. 'My young lady, sir, she is having an interview.'

'I see. Are you on leave?'

'Yes, sir. I go back on Monday.'

'My son is on the Somme,' said the man.

'I was there three weeks ago.'

'Were you! What's it really like there?' The man was hoping I was going to give him some comfort.

'You don't really want to know, sir,' I said, quietly.

The man nodded and compressed his lips, then he spoke, 'No, perhaps you are right,' he said huskily. 'Which regiment are you with, young man,' he asked, quietly.

I pulled at the sleeve of my greatcoat so he could see the Red Cross badge, and I noticed him peer at my ribbons as my coat was unbuttoned.

'Ah, I see you are with the Medical Corps. My son is with the fusiliers, the Eighth Battalion.'

'I was recently with the fusiliers – brought some back from no man's land, not sure which battalion they were. They all get mixed up, you know.'

'Quite,' said the man, a choke in his voice.

As the man was trying to recover, I decided to mention Amelia. 'My young lady is hoping to get a librarian's job. I met her in France, she was a nurse but she had to give it up.'

'I see,' said the man, thoughtfully. 'Tell me, we are sending our son a parcel, what would you suggest we put in it?' he asked.

I answered without any hesitation. 'Whisky and disinfectant, sir, and put both in metal flasks so that they don't get broken.'

'Thank you, young man, for your help. Good luck. By the way, what is your young lady's name?'

'Miss Amelia Hooper, sir,' I replied.

The man nodded, said 'Good luck' then disappeared into his office.

I sat down again to await Amelia and some fifteen minutes later she rejoined me, her face beaming. 'What do you think? I've been offered the position,' she gasped.

'That's marvellous,' I said, kissing her cheek. In her excitement she did not reprimand me and we hurried down the stone stairs through the entrance hall and out on to the pavement.

'I've got a present for you, Amelia,' I said, putting my hand into my greatcoat pocket and taking out the brooch, which was wrapped in a piece of tissue paper.

'For me?' said Amelia, her eyes sparkling. She removed her gloves then unwrapped the tissue. 'Oh, George, dear, it's beautiful, you shouldn't have.' Her lips quivered and there were now tears in her eyes.

'You will wear it?' I said, anxiously.

'Wear it! Of course I will, dear, I'll always wear it.'

'Put it on now, then,' I urged.

'You pin it on for me, just there,' she said, pointing to a spot up on her left breast just below the collar.

Having secured it as instructed, Amelia took my arm. 'We will go and have coffee at the department store in Lewisham,' she said, smiling at me. I paused, unsure what to do. 'What is it, dear?' she asked, a look of concern on her face.

'I won't have enough money, Amelia,' I said, my face going red.

'You've spent it on my present, haven't you?'

'I've bought something for Amy, too,' I mumbled.

'You shouldn't have done that. Amy will say the same thing, I'm quite sure,' said Amelia, quietly.

'I wanted to buy you both a keepsake,' I replied.

There were tears in her eyes as she took a handkerchief from her handbag. 'George, my dearest, you should not

164

have spent all your money on me,' she said, carefully wiping her eyes.

'Well, er ... um...' I muttered somewhat at a loss for adequate words.

'Come on, dear, let us go to Lewisham.' Amelia, now recovered, put her arm through mine and almost pulled me to the tramcar stop.

There was that same smell of coffee and the sound of cutlery on plates that greeted us when we entered the restaurant. The head waiter quickly found us a table.

'Do watch those boots of yours, George,' said Amelia, glancing under the table.

'Shall I take them off then?' I said, putting a hand to one.

'No, don't you dare,' glared Amelia.

I began to grin at her and she realised that I had been joking. Amelia smiled, then spoke to a waitress. Again I was fascinated by the restaurant. It was as if the Somme never existed. I thought of Edwin, how was he faring? That's if he was still alive. How many times did you go over the top before you bought it or came back on a stretcher? I was told, but I did not care to remember such things. The life span of a stretcher bearer was no better than an officer.

'George, dear,' I felt Amelia's hand on mine. 'Are you all right, dear?' She looked anxiously at me.

'Yes, thank you,' I smiled.

'Have a pastry,' said Amelia, picking up a plate and a cake fork. 'Which one, dear?' she said.

'Any one,' I replied, my eyes on a large cream pastry.

Amelia, with the experience of having had three brothers, immediately placed the pastry on my plate, much to my delight.

'Thank you,' I grinned, digging into the pastry. 'It's nice in here, isn't it, Amelia?' I said, my mouth full of cream pastry.

165

Amelia smiled at me, almost motherly. 'Yes dear,' she replied, as she stirred her coffee.

'Have you got enough money, 'cos I've got a shilling left?'

'I have enough, George,' said Amelia, patiently. 'Would you like another cake? Remember we shall have luncheon in an hour.'

'I'd better not then,' I said, with some reluctance, as I glanced at the plate of pastries.

Amelia's lips moved slightly and there was a faint smile on her face as she said, 'I don't suppose another one would make any difference,' putting another pastry on my plate, 'but you see you eat your luncheon,' she said with mock severity.

'I will, I promise,' I said, as I filled my mouth with pastry.

'George, did you speak to a gentleman as you waited for me in the corridor?'

I nodded, as my mouth was full of pastry.

'What did he say?' said Amelia.

'He told me that his son is with the fusiliers on the Somme.'

'I see,' said Amelia thoughtfully. 'He was the borough librarian, you know.'

'Was he?' I grinned.

Amelia looked at me curiously, then she spoke quietly. 'Did you know, dear?' she frowned. I looked over my coffee cup, my eyes laughing at her. 'I guessed that it was,' I said, at last.

'Oh why?' she frowned.

'Quite simple really – the door he went into had "Borough Librarian" on it,' I grinned.

Amelia smiled as she glanced at the bill, then opened her handbag. 'I think we had better go now, dear,' she said, putting some coins on a plate, 'before you finish off all the pastries.'

I started to laugh as I put on my greatcoat. I had to admit she did have a point.

It was clear to me that Mrs Hooper was not overjoyed when Amelia informed her of her news.

'Yes well, I suppose it will be something to amuse yourself with for the time being,' she said with a nonchalant wave of the hand. I could tell that Amelia was hurt; her cheeks were flushed and for a moment she lowered her eyes.

Amelia glanced at me and I gave her an encouraging wink. This seemed to cheer her up as she replied firmly to her mother, 'It is a permanent arrangement, mother, and father appreciates the matter.'

'Is it indeed?' snapped Mrs Hooper in an attitude new to me.

'Yes, mother,' replied Amelia, whose manner was equally brusque.

Mr Hooper did not join us for luncheon, and I was not sorry when it was over. There was some tension between Amelia and her mother, and I was sure that it was not just because of her new position. Later, when we walked across the Heath, Amelia made the position clear to me.

'Mother does not think that I should have a position; we had problems with her when I went into nursing. Mother lives in the past, she cannot accept that things change and will not accept the fact that you cannot bury your head in the sand. As matters stand at the moment, I might be glad that I have a position – she will not deter me.' Amelia clenched her teeth.

'You mean because of the family business?' I remarked.

'That's right, dear,' she said, lowering her eyes.

It seemed that I had known Amelia for years, and it did not seem possible that I should know so much of her family's affairs after such a short time. Perhaps the war was making our situation unreal?

We returned to Cedar Lodge as the light was fading. We could hear voices coming from Mr Hooper's study as we entered the hall. It was clear an argument was taking place. Amelia bit her lip. 'I think you had better go, George, dear,' she said, giving me a quick kiss. 'Come over at about two o'clock tomorrow,' she whispered in my ear.

'Yes, all right,' I replied.

'And thank you for my present,' she smiled, opening the front door. 'I'll always wear it, I promise.'

The voices rose and the smile faded from Amelia's face. Before she could move, I held her upper arms and kissed her again, then stepped out into the gathering gloom. 'Bye!' I called, as I hurried down the gravel drive. I heard her call a reply, then the front door closed.

I sat in the tram thinking of the argument I had heard. One of the voices was Mr Hooper's, but the other voices, though male, were strange to me. It worried Amelia, I could tell.

The tram suddenly clattered across some traversing lines and the noise brought back thoughts of France, and there were beads of sweat on my forehead. I had little time left and I was convinced that if I went back to France I would not return.

Amy was out shopping when I arrived home, and it gave me the opportunity to talk to Hector, who was sitting in the parlour. The girls were using their crayons and sketch pads at the table, which gave me a chance to speak to him on his own.

'Hector,' I said, sitting down next to him.

'Yes, George,' he blinked at me as he peered through his thick glasses. Since the affair with the Minters he seemed to take more notice of me.

'I go back on Monday,' I said, quietly.

'Yes, George, I know.' He looked down at the Bible he was reading, almost in embarrassment.

168

'I want you to take care of my savings book. I've got three pounds in it. I gave Amy as my next of kin and I've written a letter here saying she is to have any outstanding pay that was due to me if I don't come back, and the money in my savings book is for her as well.'

I put my savings book and the letter into Hector's hand, it trembled for a moment as he clutched them. Hector swallowed hard and he was blinking more than ever. 'I don't know what to say, dear boy.' His voice was husky and there were tears in his eyes.

'Promise me one thing, Hector,' I said, my face set.

'Yes, anything I can do,' he said eagerly.

'You won't go to the Army recruiting office when I'm gone.'

Hector smiled faintly, then shook his head. 'I promise, George.'

'You swear it,' I persisted, clasping his right hand and pushing it down on the open Bible.

'I swear it. I've got over that little episode now,' he said, as I released his hand. 'Anyway, I doubt whether they would have taken me with my eyesight,' he added.

'Don't you be so sure, they will take anyone who can walk before long,' I said with some feeling.

'Perhaps you are right, George. Anyway, I'll not volunteer, I promise you that.'

'Good, and make sure that Amy collects everything that was due to me.' Before he could reply, Alice burst into the room.

'Daddy, Ruth has scribbled on my picture.'

'I haven't, Daddy,' said Ruth, who had followed her into the parlour.

I rose to my feet as any further conversation would have been quite impossible. 'Shall I make a cup of tea, Hector?'

'Good idea, George,' he smiled.

I smiled as I brewed the tea. Hector had many good points but in the house he was useless, which was not surprising really, since he had been brought up in a house that had servants and Amy almost waited on him hand and foot. Still, I liked and trusted him and he was good to Amy – that was everything as far as I was concerned.

When the children had been put to bed, I gave Amy the ring. Her mouth opened in surprise when I took her small right hand in mine and slipped it on her middle finger.

'Oh! George,' she mumbled, her lips quivering.

Clearly, she was pleased with it and she, like Hector, knew the significance of it. We all exchanged glances but nothing was said. I winked at Hector, who looked most unhappy.

'It's lovely,' said Amy, her voice faltering.

Our evening meal was a rather subdued affair. At last Amy spoke: 'How is Amelia?'

'Fine,' I replied.

'Did she get her position?' asked Hector.

'She seems to think so,' I nodded.

'That will be nice for her,' said Amy, smiling at last.

'Yes,' I said, absently stirring my tea.

'I saw Ma today with sister Mabel,' said Amy.

'What? Were they coming out of the Golden Anchor?'

Hector smiled faintly at my comment but did not speak.

'No,' said Amy, patiently. 'In Queen's Road. They asked after you. Why don't you go and see Ma?'

'I've already told you, I do not wish to,' I said, slowly, grinding out the words. 'And that's final, Amy.'

My jaw set and Amy knew me well enough. It was pointless pursuing the matter, however she had to have the last word. 'Ma's very upset about the boys, Georgie.'

Her calling me Georgie again suddenly irritated me and I took a deep breath before I replied.

'It's what they wanted, wasn't it?'

'Oh, Georgie, no, not that,' said Amy reproachfully.

'Well, what did they think war was all about? People get killed in war on both sides – always have done. Now after all the cheering and flag waving, they start to whine. Who are the cowards now?'

Amy looked down at her plate, her face flushed.

'I'm sorry, George. I will not mention them again,' she murmured.

'Good,' I said, somewhat ungraciously.

Hector was about to speak; instead he compressed his lips and pushed back his chair and rose to his feet. 'I think I will go and finish my sermon, Amy.'

'Yes, dear,' she replied.

I helped Amy clear the table and do the washing up. We did not speak, there seemed little for us to say.

The following morning, I helped Amy with her shopping. By chance, our father came past us, sitting up on his horse and cart. He saw us but looked the other way, which was just as well because I ignored him anyway.

I got to Blackheath at about two-fifteen. Amelia opened the door to me at Cedar Lodge and though her greeting was cordial enough, I could tell that something was wrong. 'I'll get my coat, George, then we can go for a walk,' she said, opening the hall cupboard door. I assisted her with her coat, then she put on her hat and we left the house. She immediately held my arm but did not say what was wrong until we were well away from Cedar Lodge.

'I'm sorry I rushed you off like I did yesterday,' she began.

'That's all right,' I smiled.

'Things are very difficult at home at the moment. You heard my uncle and his accountant yesterday. Our business is going to be wound up almost immediately.

'Wound up?' I repeated, a little uncertainly.

'Yes. Closed down because it cannot meet its obligations.'

'It's gone nap then?'

A hint of a smile appeared on Amelia's face, but it quickly disappeared before she continued. 'Yes, George.'

'What will you do then?' I asked. The concern on my face seemed to prompt Amelia to tell me.

'At the moment, I really cannot say, but I'm sure it's only a matter of time before Cedar Lodge is sold.' Tears appeared in Amelia's eyes and I put my arm about her shoulder to try to comfort her. I then guided her into the doorway of an empty shop. 'Where will you go?' I asked, anxiously.

She shook her head. I had put my arms about her and she leaned forward against me. My lips were level with her forehead and I kissed her.

'I really do not know what I will do, but I intend taking the librarian position, no matter where my parents move to.'

Her words came as a relief to me, this meant she would not leave the area; not that it would make much difference as far as I was concerned since I had only one more day of my leave left. 'If they moved a long way away, I'm sure you could stay with my sister and Hector until...' I paused.

'That's very sweet of you, George, but I receive a little legacy next month on my twenty-fifth birthday.' At the mention of her age, she lowered her eyes, 'And I might buy a small house with it but nothing's decided as yet.'

I nodded my approval. 'If you've got your own place, Amelia, that's best – makes you independent, doesn't it?'

'Exactly, dear. Shall we carry on walking?'

We continued our walk, and Amelia seemed in much better spirits. We carried on a little further, then returned to Cedar Lodge.

172

'Mother and father have gone down to Worthing to see some of our relations,' said Amelia, as she opened the front door of Cedar Lodge, 'so we will have the box to ourselves this evening. I think you will like the play, it's a comedy.'

Having assisted Amelia to remove her coat, I took my own off and put them both in the hall cupboard, then proceeded to remove my boots and put on the slippers provided for me. I could sense Amelia watching me, but she made no comment. We had tea in the morning-room, after which, we proceeded to the theatre.

'We must leave earlier, George, as I cannot drive the car yet.'

I must admit that I did enjoy myself more than on my previous visits, largely because we were on our own. The play did not particularly appeal to me. It was supposed to be a comedy but I could not see much to laugh about, though I politely told Amelia that I enjoyed it.

When I caught the last tram, I was even more loathe to leave Amelia, though I said that I would return in the morning.

On my last day, it was raining and we were eating in the front room, as Amelia had been invited. Hector and Amy were putting on a special meal and I could smell it cooking as I left for Blackheath to collect Amelia.

Amelia was rather subdued when I arrived, and close to tears. We had little to say, though I did notice that she held my arm tightly when we left Cedar Lodge.

I think the children cheered her up; both the girls were keen to show her their new dresses. When she produced sweets from her bag and a box of chocolates for Amy, it caused even more excitement.

'After your dinner, girls,' said Amy quickly.

'Er ... luncheon,' murmured Hector, quickly.

'Yes, luncheon,' added Amy, her face flushing.

'Thank you for the chocolates, Amelia, they are lovely,' said Amy, clearly delighted with them.

It was a day I would never forget, even Hector's sermon in the evening was not too long, though the day went all too quickly.

When I took Amelia home, I was even more loathe to leave her. Before I did so, Mr and Mrs Hooper came to wish me good luck.

My final parting with Amelia was tearful and I told her how much I loved her and when she said that she loved me too, I could have deserted there and then. I knew, however, she would never have allowed me to do it, and when it actually came to it, I would not have done so either.

Monday morning was wet and cold and I left a tearful Amy in the hall at Lausanne Road.

'Thank you for everything, Amy,' I said, giving her a last kiss and a hug. Her reply was inaudible above her sobs; dear Amy. Hector accompanied me to the tramcar stop in Queen's Road, and as my tram approached, we shook hands.

'You will be constantly in our prayers, my boy,' he said, blinking faster than ever to keep back his tears.

'Thank you, Hector.'

'Goodbye, George.'

'Bye,' I replied, grabbing my kitbag and clambering aboard the tram.

8

Marriage and the Somme

I did not know what to expect when I arrived back at
Woolwich. In my mind, I expected to be immediately
put on a train, sent down to the coast on a boat, and
then up to the front line. But no, I was put on hospital
duties without even going to the medical officer about
my ears. I began to feel that my luck was really changing
for the better. True, I was not off duty for three weeks,
but I did not mind that – anything was better than the
trenches.

On 20th December I was given a forty-eight hour leave
pass and three weeks' pay. In high spirits, I made my way
to Amy's. I had written to both Amy and Amelia so it
was not too much of a shock for Amy when she opened
her front door. Her greeting was both tearful and over-
whelming. 'It's wonderful, Georgie, dear,' she said, her
arms about my neck. 'We thought you would be in France.'

'No, thank God,' I muttered.

After a warm welcome from Hector and the children,
we all went into the parlour. Amy quickly made a cup of
tea and we sat around the parlour table.

'Look at the decorations, Uncle George,' said Alice,
pointing at the little rings of coloured paper that Amy
had stuck together with flour and water. 'And our
Christmas tree,' beamed Ruth.

'They're smashing,' I grinned.

'How long have you got now, George?' asked Hector.

'Until 1800 hours on Sunday,' I replied.

Amy frowned, then glanced at Hector.

'Six pm,' explained Hector.

'Well, why didn't you say so, George,' smiled Amy. 'What about Christmas, will you get any more leave?'

I shook my head. 'No, this is my Christmas leave, Amy. I'm lucky to get that, I can tell you,' I replied, my thoughts on the never-ending flow of wounded that seemed to arrive at all hours.

'I saw Amelia in Queen's Road on Monday,' said Hector.

'Did you?' I said, eagerly.

'Yes, she was with a...' Hector paused.

As Amy frowned at him, I could feel my face going red as I said, quietly, 'Who with, Hector?'

'I've no idea. It was an older man. We did not speak, they were on the other side of the road, she just waved.'

'I think I'll go and see her now,' I said, huskily, getting to my feet.

'We are going to eat shortly,' said Amy, quickly.

'I'll have something when I get back,' I replied, as I left the room.

Amy recounted the following, years later:

'Why did you have to say that to him?'

Hector shrugged his shoulders as he replied, 'I'm sure there is a perfectly good explanation, Amy. I have a high regard for Amelia. After all, in my view, she is a lady.'

I said, 'I just hope you are right.'

A chill wind blew in my face as I strode down to Queen's Road, my hands deep in my greatcoat pockets. I did not notice the wind – my thoughts were on Amelia. Who was the man she was with? I tried to think sensibly about it, I had no right to object; she could go out with anyone she chose, though it both hurt and angered me.

176

I had sent Amelia a postcard the previous day, so I was sure she would be at home. The tramcar clattered through Deptford and I could see by the Town Hall clock it was almost six o'clock. Though it was nearly dark, I knew my way to Cedar Lodge well enough, and as I opened the gate, I could feel my heart thumping. I rang the bell and wondered for a moment if the maid would open the door and say Miss Amelia was not available.

'George!' It was Amelia's voice that dragged me out of my gloomy thoughts.

'Amelia,' I gasped, as she came forward to kiss me.

I could not doubt the pleasure on Amelia's face and I immediately felt ashamed of my doubts. I knew in my heart that I would accept Amelia under any conditions.

'Come on in and let me take your coat,' she said, happily. 'There, you see your slippers are still there.' Amelia handed me the slippers as she shut the hall cupboard door.

I could feel the tears in my eyes and my lip quivered. Amelia put her arms about me. Why had I doubted her, I asked myself? 'I was so unhappy, Amelia,' I croaked. 'Hector saw you with a man in Queen's Road,' I mumbled.

Amelia stepped back and looked at me. I lowered my eyes in embarrassment and could feel my face going red.

'Ah! So that's it,' she said, quietly.

'I'm sorry, Amelia, I've no right, I know that, but I love you,' I said, sadly.

Amelia did not speak but lifted her hands and put them on either side of my face. She moved forward and kissed me. 'George, my dearest, I love you too. That was a builder friend of father's and he was looking at a property for me.'

'Oh, er...' I started to mumble.

A smile appeared on Amelia's face as she took my

hand. 'Put on your slippers, dear, and come and say hello to mother and father.'

I sat at the bottom of the stairs and removed my boots. Amelia watched attentively and smiled encouragingly at me.

'The slippers, Amelia, you expected...' I paused.

The smile left Amelia's face to be replaced by a look of anguish. 'I expected you to return to me,' she whispered.

I put my arms about her and kissed her again. She did not attempt to stop me but held me close.

Mr and Mrs Hooper looked older, though they welcomed me kindly. They looked tired, as if everything was an effort, as I suspected was the case.

'We thought that you were going to France, George,' said Mr Hooper, smiling briefly.

'I thought I was, sir,' I replied, 'but I've been on a course at Woolwich, besides doing my other duties. I expect that I'll be sent back to France before...'

'Still, it's nice being home for Christmas,' said Mrs Hooper, giving me a wan smile.

'I'm not,' I replied. 'I go back on Sunday evening. I shall be on duty all Christmas and the New Year.'

'We had a letter from Edwin yesterday,' said Amelia, quickly. 'He is in Flanders. It was posted somewhere near Ypres.'

'Oh, yes,' I replied, glancing at Mrs Hooper, who looked near to tears.

'We have had no news of Edgar, George,' she murmured.

'It takes time, Mrs Hooper, believe me. Half the relatives of the men in Woolwich Army Hospital don't know that they are there, I'm sure. There are so many men, you have no idea who's coming and going all the time.'

'That's what I told mother, George. We must be patient, it takes time,' said Amelia, looking gratefully at me.

'You will have dinner with us, my boy?' remarked Mr Hooper.

'Thank you, sir,' I said.

I noticed that there were no Christmas decorations at Cedar Lodge, which, in the circumstances, was hardly surprising. They must have read my mind as I glanced about the room.

'Has Amy put up any Christmas decorations, George?' asked Amelia.

'Yes – for the children. It gives the girls something to do, cutting them out and sticking them together. I'm sure she would not bother otherwise,' I replied.

'Quite,' nodded Mrs Hooper.

I did not get the opportunity to ask Amelia about the property that she had been looking at until later in the evening when Mr Hooper had gone out and Mrs Hooper retired to her room.

'You are not going to the theatre this evening, Amelia?' I asked, when we were on our own.

'I have not been since I went with you, and mother and father are not interested these days,' she replied.

'Yes, I understand,' I said.

'We will be giving up our box; membership is renewed in the New Year and...' Amelia shrugged her shoulders and sighed.

'You said you were looking at property, Amelia?' I said, quietly.

'Yes.' Amelia paused; she looked unhappy and began to rub her hands together in agitation.

'The fact is, George, I want a home of my own. Does that seem ungrateful to you?'

'How do you mean?' I frowned.

'My mother thinks I should remain at home. I come into an inheritance on my birthday in the New Year and the question arises, should I leave it invested in consols or buy a house? My mother strongly opposes my moving.'

179

And your father, what does he say?'

'I think he expects the worst, though he has managed to support his business for the time being. As far as I am concerned, I think he considers it sensible; after all, I shall be transferred to the Deptford library soon.'

'I thought that's where you were going to start.'

'No, the vacancy was at Lewisham; it was more convenient for me, but it was only a temporary arrangement.'

'Have you decided yet?' I asked, curiously.

Amelia shook her head and again shrugged her shoulders. 'No, not exactly, it depends on what happens during the next two months. I have been to see my uncle, he is also my godfather – he owns a share of my father's business and he said that the two months would be crucial as far as my father's business was concerned. It was a reprieve, as you might say. Even so, I might still buy a property with my legacy as an investment; it's all a problem,' said Amelia, shrugging her shoulders again.

'Er ... yes,' I remarked, a little at a loss what to say.

We sat talking of the war, the subject on everyone's lips. The news was not good and it was going to be a bleak Christmas.

My forty-eight hours went all too quickly and before I knew it I was back at the Woolwich Military Hospital.

Christmas came and went, in what seemed to me a haze of ether and disinfectant, but time went quickly; there was so much to do. I was on duty almost all the time, though I did manage to get away for Amelia's birthday.

They had just heard from Edwin. His letter was most subdued, as Amelia put it. I gathered that he had been over the top a few times, which I suspected accounted for it. I bought Amelia some earrings again from the pawnshop, though I did not tell her where I purchased them. She was delighted, though I am sure she had received some far better presents.

Amelia had a present for me. It was in a nice box – unlike mine, which was wrapped in tissue and brown paper. I carefully opened the box and as I did so my eyes opened wide. It was a magnificent silver hunter pocket watch on a silver chain.

'Cor!' I gasped. 'It's marvellous, Amelia, it's smashing.'

Amelia was beaming at the expression on my face. I held the watch to my ear but I could hear nothing.

'It needs winding, dear, the key's in the box,' smiled Amelia.

I wound and set the watch and carefully put it in my top pocket. 'I won't take it back with me, it's the best present I've ever had, really it is,' I said, kissing her quickly.

'You are not taking it back, dear?' she asked.

'I could get it nicked, couldn't I?' I replied, frowning.

'Oh,' Amelia smiled.

'I'll leave it with you before I go back, Amelia.'

'Are you sure, George?'

'Definitely,' I said, firmly.

'As you wish, dear,' said Amelia, patiently.

I returned to Woolwich, my mind made up. At the first suitable opportunity I would sound out Amelia on my chances as far as her marrying me were concerned.

The news we read of the war seemed to be going from bad to worse. The Imperial Russian Army was collapsing and large units had mutinied. It did not take a military genius to realise how it would affect us. Before long, German divisions on the eastern front would be moved across to face us on the western front. There was talk of a coming German offensive; it did not bear thinking about. One ray of hope was that the United States of America had just entered the war.

9

Marriage

I had been at the barracks almost three months and I was happy. This might have seemed strange considering the amount of suffering going on about me, but I was now hardened to the misfortunes of my fellow men.

I was attached to four of the intake wards and my job was to take newly-arrived wounded from the ambulances to the wards. It was much to my surprise that at this time I was promoted to corporal. Although I tried to hide my delight, it was the pleasure that it gave Amy and Amelia that pleased me most. Good news was a rare commodity in March 1917. To the general public there seemed no end to the war and morale was low. The casualty lists in the national papers seemed longer than ever, and the never-ending stream of wounded from the front was, at times, like a flood, as I could testify.

At times, we had men lying in the corridors, though such things were never mentioned in the newspapers and I had enough sense to keep my mouth shut. I would talk to Amelia and to some degree, Hector, but only on the understanding that they did not repeat what I said to them.

'If it came out that I had said anything to you, Amelia, I would be in trouble.'

Her face clouded as she replied, 'I would not breathe a word, my dearest.'

'I would be sent back to the front, you know.'

There were tears in her eyes, 'Oh, no, George,' she gasped.

Amelia moved closer to me and I put my arms about her; she held me tight and I could feel her trembling. 'I could not bear it, my dearest, if anything happened to you,' she sobbed, her face close to mine.

'What's wrong, Amelia?' I murmured. She lowered her eyes, turned her head and would not reply.

'Tell me,' I persisted. She sniffed and tried to wipe her eyes. I took the lace handkerchief from her hand and gently dried her tears; she tried to smile, but her lower lip quivered again.

'Don't you trust me?' I asked, softly.

'Of course I do, my dearest.' Her eyelids flickered as she looked into my eyes. I had never seen her like this before.

'It's just that everything seems to be going wrong,' she said, wiping at her eyes, her voice close to breaking. 'First the boys, and now our business is collapsing; things are very serious for us.' She was about to cry again and I held her close to me.

'I'm sorry, Amelia, really I am. If there is anything I can do...' I paused, unable to think what to say.

'I know, my dearest,' she murmured, holding me close.

We were in the morning-room at Cedar Lodge. I found it the most comfortable room in the Hoopers' house and happened to tell Amelia. After that, whenever I called on her, I was always shown into it, and when we were on our own, we always ate there.

'Amelia, I want to ask you something.'

She looked at me, curiously, 'Yes, George,' she replied, now more her normal self.

'I've bought you a ring,' I said, lowering my eyes.

'A ring?' Amelia's voice rose. 'For me?' she gasped. 'Can I see it,' she said, excitedly, her eyes now shining.

'It's well, er ... an engagement ring,' I said at last.

'Are you asking me to marry you?' Amelia's eyes opened wide.

I nodded, 'Yes, if you would consider it. I know you could do a lot better than me.'

'I could not, George, my dearest,' she said.

'You mean you won't marry me,' I said, disappointedly.

'I will marry you and I could not do better, so don't you ever belittle yourself to me again,' she said, more her old self.

'That's marvellous,' I gasped, my face wreathed in smiles. I kissed her tenderly until she pulled away, her breathing coming faster and her face flushed. 'Someone might come in,' she murmured.

'Yes,' I said, fumbling in the breast pocket of my tunic. I took out a piece of tissue paper and unfolded it. 'It's not a new one, Amelia,' I said, apologetically, handing her the diamond and sapphire ring.

'It's beautiful, George,' breathed Amelia, 'and it fits!' Sure enough it fitted her finger.

'You will have to ask father.'

'Oh, dear,' I muttered, 'do you think that he will agree?' I asked anxiously, my crestfallen look made Amelia smile.

'I am of age, you know, dear,' she smiled.

'Yes, but what if he refuses?' I persisted.

'He will not, though mother might be a problem; still, we shall have to see. Don't worry, my dearest, I shall marry you, but it will have to be a quiet wedding in view of father's financial problems.

'The quieter, the better for me,' I said, with some feeling, 'but I must go. I must be in barracks at 1100 hours.'

'I'll come with you to the tram stop,' said Amelia, quickly.

'No,' I said, shaking my head, 'it's a rotten night, you will get wet.'

184

'I'll be all right,' she replied, getting to her feet.

'No,' I said firmly. 'Can I have my greatcoat and cap?'

'Yes, of course,' said Amelia, taking my hand and leading me from the room.

I put on my greatcoat, then at her insistence, helped her on with hers, though I did try to have the last word. 'Only to the gate, mind,' I said, firmly.

'Yes, dear,' she said, meekly.

We stood under the holly tree hidden from the house. It was a cold night, but I was warm; the excitement of my new situation caused my blood to race.

'You are sure?' murmured Amelia as she clung to me.

'Sure? Of course I am,' I frowned. 'Why shouldn't I be?' I added. Amelia bit her lower lip. 'George, you know very well,' she said, lowering her eyes.

'I don't, why?' I frowned, now completely mystified.

'I'm older than you; I am twenty-five and you are nineteen.'

'So!' I said, almost aggressively.

'It is important, dear,' said Amelia, patiently.

'Not to me, Amelia. It makes no difference at all. I love you, it's as simple as that and I don't want to hear you talk about it again.'

'Yes, dear. I'll never mention it again,' she murmured.

'Promise?' I grinned, kissing her lips.

'I promise, my love,' she smiled.

'I must go now or I'll miss my tram,' I said, kissing her again and releasing my hold of her.

'Take care, my love,' whispered Amelia as I opened the drive gate and let myself out.

I was aware that Amelia still stood there as I hurried away in the darkness.

The following morning, while I was bringing the new arrivals to 'C' ward, Amelia was telling her parents of her plans for the future and her marriage.

'Are you not being a little hasty, my dear?' said her mother, whose almost acid look made it clear what her opinion was.

They sat at the breakfast table in the morning-room with her father, as usual, reading the daily papers.

'No, mother,' said Amelia, firmly.

'He is much younger than you, after all,' added her mother, with a look almost of triumph on her face.

'I am aware of that, mother, and so is he,' said Amelia, curtly.

'And his prospects are hardly promising are they?' added her mother, in a patronising manner.

'Rather poor, I would say. He could be going back to France at any time now,' retorted Amelia, sarcastically.

'Your mother did not mean that, Amelia,' said her father, sharply, his newspaper no longer of interest.

'Do you object to him, father?' Amelia looked at her father, her manner almost challenging.

'No, I like George, but marrying you is different,' he replied.

'You mean he is not good enough, father,' said Amelia coldly. James Hooper looked uncomfortable. 'It's not...' he began hesitantly.

'It is father, and you know it,' snapped Amelia.

'Amelia!' her mother said. 'How dare you speak to your father in that tone, how dare you?'

Her mother's voice rose until it was almost a squeak.

'I shall marry George whatever you say,' replied Amelia, her cheeks now a bright pink.

'We cannot afford a wedding at the moment,' said her mother, a note of finality in her voice.

'I am not asking for a wedding, as you put it. I do know of father's situation, I do not want a big wedding. George's brother-in-law can marry us at the Baptist Chapel.'

186

'Marry you where? Have you taken leave of your senses?' Mrs Hooper's face was now as flushed as her daughter's.

'No,' smiled Amelia, who was now enjoying her mother's discomfiture.

'We are C of E as you know,' Amelia's mother said, importantly. 'Things are coming to a pretty pass I must say.' She compressed her lips, her face now pale with anger.

'Really, mother! If that's your attitude I will make my own arrangements.'

'What arrangements?' sneered her mother.

'I start my new position at the Deptford Public Library and I will see how matters progress. Let me make it perfectly clear, I have no intention of being left on the shelf until a man comes along of whom you approve. Do you realise that of all the young men who were at Edgar's twenty-first birthday party, only four of them are still alive, and two of them are crippled? Even if that were not the case, I would still marry George. He has never had a chance in life; he is the youngest of nine, and his father, who did not care for him, was drunk half the week. He was working before he was thirteen, but he has always tried to better himself. He is more intelligent than you think,' said Amelia, her eyes full of tears.

'We cannot stop you marrying George,' her father said, kindly. 'You are of age, but do not be hasty, my dear.'

'Father, I am twenty-six next birthday. I have no wish to end up on the shelf like Aunt Polly or Aunt Cissy – two maiden aunts who have nowhere to go at Christmas and whose only interest is their cats. If this war goes on for a few more years, there will be no young men left at all.'

Her parents lowered their eyes and Amelia regretted her choice of words. 'I'm sorry, I should not have been so frank,' she murmured.

Her father looked at her, his face haggard. It seemed

187

that he had become an old man. He sighed, then rose to leave the table. 'Sadly, you could be right, Amelia. If you wish to marry George, so be it. I like him very much and you could do a lot worse, believe me. However, you could also do a lot better, financially, I mean, but unfortunately we can do little to help you in that regard, I am sorry to say. The business will close very soon now – it's inevitable. I am sorry to say our creditors are closing in.'

Since it was as Amelia expected, her father's dramatic statement had little impact. Even her mother's angry glare at her father meant little to her at this stage of events.

'So I can tell George to come and see you, father?' she asked.

'Yes,' he replied, smiling faintly at her.

Amelia left the table and as she passed her father's chair, bent over and kissed him on the cheek. 'Thank you, father,' she said, quietly. However, a quick glance at her mother told her that matters did not have her approval, so without any more ado she left the room.

The following days were full of excitement for me and I was never so happy in my life. The Hoopers gave an engagement dinner for us and I hoped Mrs Hooper had relented in her attitude to our marriage – as yet I did not know my future mother-in-law. At Amelia's insistence, I wore brown shoes to the dinner and I asked Hector to wear his dog collar. 'Naturally, I will,' he smiled, 'and a purple front – their servants might think that I am a Bishop; that should please Mrs Hooper.'

I began to laugh. Hector was no fool at times, and both he and Amy joined in. Amy had a new dress for the occasion and talked about it for days. All I said to her was, 'Just watch Hector at table, Amy, and do as he does; he knows about such things,' I said importantly.

'Yes, George, I will,' she replied, nodding her head quickly. 'I'm so pleased for you, dear.'

I kissed her forehead; I knew she meant it. Amy was a wonderful person and I loved her so much.

About a week after the engagement party I managed to get a few hours off duty and went straight to Cedar Lodge. Amelia immediately informed me that she was buying a property.

'A property?' I gasped, incredulously. 'But why, where?' I spluttered, completely forgetting all that I had been told previously.

'I told you that father had business problems, didn't I?' said Amelia, patiently.

'Yes, of course you did,' I nodded.

'The fact is, it cannot go on any longer, and they may go down to Worthing to live with my Aunt Polly – she lives on her own in a large house.'

'But what about Cedar Lodge?' I said, quickly.

'Cedar Lodge will be sold to pay business debts,' replied Amelia.

'You will not go with them?' I said in a worried voice.

Amelia smiled and shook her head as she said an emphatic 'No'. 'My grandfather, bless him, left me some money, which I received when I was twenty ... er my last birthday.'

'When you were twenty-five,' I grinned.

Amelia's eyes narrowed, then she smiled and wagged a finger at me. 'That was not very nice, young George,' she replied.

'Nor was that,' I replied. She knew that I did not like being called 'young George'.

'Evens,' she laughed.

I nodded and grinned then I kissed her.

'I saw our solicitor, Mr Petters. He said that the money is at the moment in government consols and the yield is only eighteen pounds and ten shillings per year. In view of that I am selling them and buying a house and shop. I shall let the shop and live on the two floors above it.'

'On your own?' I frowned.

'No, our cook, Mrs Cross, is coming with me, she is old and will not get another position. Aunt Polly already has a cook and maid. Agnes will not be my cook, more my friend. I have known her all my life and we had to find her a home; she has no relatives, you see.'

'Where is this place?' I asked.

'By a strange coincidence it's in Queen's Road,' she smiled.

'Cor! Would you believe it,' I replied.

'Amazing, isn't it?' said Amelia. 'Our solicitor is arranging everything. The property belonged to one of his clients.'

'When can I see it?' I asked.

'Tomorrow, before you go back to barracks,' she replied.

'Where shall I meet you?'

If you meet the tramcar at the stop near the fire station, I will try and be there at about ten o'clock,' said Amelia.

'That's not far from Amy's house,' I said, eagerly.

'Yes,' murmured Amelia. 'It's all happened so suddenly. I am wondering if I have done the right thing.'

'I think you have,' I said, quietly.

'Why?' said Amelia in an almost surprised voice.

'You would not want to live with your aunt would you? And it's your house, remember; you have your job to consider too.'

'George, I think I underestimate you at times; those are exactly my reasons for making the purchase,' smiled Amelia. 'In future, I will discuss all my decisions with you.'

'When we are married and I move in, will I have to pay you rent?' I asked, my face serious.

'Of course not, dear,' her voice rose and her face reddened. 'Whatever made you think that?'

I started to grin and Amelia began to laugh, now aware that I had been pulling her leg.

'How's your mother?' I asked; the smile left Amelia's face.

'Proving difficult, to put it mildly. I shall not be sorry when I am on my own. She has been down at Worthing for the past week and I am not looking forward to her return.'

'Oh!' I said, a little taken aback.

'Father's a different man; he's drinking at least a bottle of whisky a day; he cannot go on like that.' Amelia was close to tears. Instinctively, I put my arms about her and she clung to me with a new intensity.

The following morning I met Amelia at the tram stop near to the fire station. I had noticed an empty shop on the other side of the road when I had walked from Amy's house and this, it transpired, was the property that Amelia had purchased.

'Is the roof all right?' I asked, as Amelia put the key in the lock of the front door.

'Our solicitor says it is,' replied Amelia, opening the door.

'H'm ... has he looked, then?' I asked.

'I'd hardly think that he would do that,' she replied, patiently.

'Well, someone needs to before you move in. I looked from the other side of the road and it looks good – no missing slates. I'll look round the back in a minute, from the road at the rear, to make sure. Let's look upstairs and see if there are any leaks.'

'Er ... yes, of course, dear,' replied Amelia, more than a little impressed by my practical ability.

The property was larger than I anticipated. The ground

floor consisted of a shop with a storeroom behind it, a living-room and a kitchen and scullery. Through the scullery window I could see a yard and a small garden.

The first floor was divided into a large front room with two rooms at the rear; between them was a room with a bath in it and a small room-cum-cupboard in between. The second floor consisted of four small rooms, above which was the loft. It all seemed quite dry, though it had that musty unlived-in smell about it.

'Well, what do you think?' asked Amelia, as we looked out of the first window that overlooked Queen's Road.

'It's very nice,' I said, with some enthusiasm, 'but what about furniture?'

'Father says I can have some from Cedar Lodge,' replied Amelia. 'It's sad, but one has to face up to facts – unfortunately mother will not do so, still perhaps she will with Aunt Polly.'

I realised that Amelia was made of stern stuff and that I would be marrying at a disadvantage, still I did not mind, as I loved her so very much.

Having locked up the premises we went to see Amy and Hector, who made it quite clear to Amelia that when she had moved in, he would expect to see her in his congregation.

'We will, won't we, George?' she replied, looking at me.

I mumbled an agreement, but Hector only smiled as he said, 'I shall rely on you, Amelia, to see that he comes.'

'He will, Hector, never fear,' nodded Amelia, a reply that brought a smile to Amy's face.

'It's got cellars and they are dry,' I said in an effort to change the topic of conversation.

'They will be very useful,' remarked Amy.

'Yes, they can be used for storage,' said Amelia.

'When do you expect to move in?' asked Hector.

'Within two weeks,' came Amelia's immediate reply.

'So soon?' said Amy, a look of surprise on her face.

'Yes.' Amelia smiled faintly, 'It's all a slight shock really. Father has found a buyer for Cedar Lodge who wishes to move in quickly. Since the Queen's Road property is now legally mine, it will be convenient to all if I move.'

There were tears in Amelia's eyes. I exchanged glances with Amy who hastily left the room to make some tea.

'It's best, isn't it really, to make the move quickly,' said Hector in his best pulpit manner. 'After all, the sooner you get in, the better, then you will be settled. I am sure your shop idea will be a success, a confectionery establishment there should do very well.'

'Do you think so?' said Amelia, brightening.

'Certainly I do,' he replied.

'And our wedding? How much notice will you require?'

At Amelia's words, I could feel my face go warm, though she seemed so completely self-assured about it.

'I'd need virtually no notice but you will need a licence you know – only Church of England marriages are legal,' said Hector with a wry smile.

'Yes, I appreciate that,' replied Amelia.

At this point Amy entered with a tray of tea things, she must have heard Amelia as she asked Hector about the wedding. 'What about the reception and honeymoon?'

'I shall have it at Queen's Road,' replied Amelia, her face blank.

'Yes, but...' began Amy, as she handed round cups of tea. 'I mean...' Amy looked a little uncomfortable.

'We have no money for a big reception, Amy, and my father certainly cannot afford one. As for the honeymoon, going away will have to wait. George cannot be certain of any leave and he could be going back to France at any time, you know.'

'Ye-s,' said Amy, slowly glancing at Hector.

'You seem remarkably well organised, Amelia, if I may say so,' observed Hector, as he stirred his tea.

'Yes,' agreed a surprised Amy, 'you certainly are.'

After this, things moved quickly. A licence was obtained and Amy got my father's signature on the consent form. Within two weeks, Amelia had moved into the Queen's Road property, along with a large amount of her parents' furniture and household effects. The Hoopers' cook, old Mrs Cross, was also with her along with her cat. I was able to come home for most of my off-duty hours and one evening I arrived at Queen's Road as Amelia and Mrs Cross were having their meal.

'Would you like something, Master George?' asked Mrs Cross, who was about to rise from her seat.

'Er ... no thank you,' I said, quickly. 'I ate in the mess about an hour ago.'

'George, would, I'm sure, like a piece of your apple pie, Agnes, when we have our dessert,' smiled Amelia.

'Smashing,' I grinned.

I could tell that Mrs Cross felt very self-conscious eating with Amelia. She held her knife and fork in what she considered an elegant manner. I knew how she felt, having eaten in the dining-room at Cedar Lodge. Amelia, I could tell, did her best to put her at ease and treat her as a family equal.

'I had a letter from Edwin this morning, didn't I, Agnes?'

'Yes, you did, Miss Amelia,' said Mrs Cross, nodding her head and causing her large chins to move.

'It's not Miss Amelia now, Agnes,' said Amelia, touching Mrs Cross's hand.

'You will always be Miss Amelia to me,' said Mrs Cross, doggedly. 'Always – no matter what,' she sniffed, her lips trembling.

194

I looked down at my boots as I could see that there were tears in Amelia's eyes. There was an embarrassing silence, which I at last broke. 'How is Edwin?' I said, suddenly.

'He seems fine, but...' Amelia took a deep breath then shook her head suddenly; at last she spoke.

'Father wrote to tell him about Cedar Lodge; I suppose he had to really, after all Edwin could suddenly come home on leave.'

There was another uncomfortable silence. Mrs Cross stood up, 'I'll serve the dessert, Miss Amelia.'

'Thank you, Agnes.' When Mrs Cross had left the room with the dishes of the first course, Amelia spoke. 'I wrote to Edwin today, offering him a room with us when he comes home. I know it would appal him down at Worthing with Aunt Polly. I hope you don't mind, George?'

I was taken aback for a moment, unsure what to say.

'You get on well with Edwin, don't you?' Amelia frowned, slightly.

'Er ... yes, but it's not for me to say, is it? It's your house, not mine, isn't it?'

'George, dear, when we are married, as I have already told you, it will be yours, too. I would not offer Edwin a home here if you did not approve.'

'Wouldn't you?' I asked in surprise.

'No, of course not,' said Amelia, in tones that reminded me of her mother.

'I like Edwin,' I said, lamely.

'Good,' smiled Amelia, 'that settles it.'

'He wouldn't expect me to clean his boots would he?'

'Certainly not, dear; the very thought of it,' snapped Amelia.

'What did he say about France?' I asked.

'Not very much. He was most concerned about father's situation. I do not think he believed it could have actually happened; neither did I, come to that.' Amelia lowered her eyes.

'Still, you have a nice house, Amelia,' I said, in an effort to console her, 'and inside, it looks just like Cedar Lodge,' I grinned.

This brought a smile to Amelia's face. 'It should do...' she began. At this point Mrs Cross came into the room, carrying a tray.

'I'm seeing my company commander tomorrow.'

'Are you, George?' said Amelia, curiously.

'Yes. Word is we will be off soon and I am going to ask him for some leave,' I said, my face reddening.

'Good, in that case I think we should get married as soon as you get leave, dear, even if it's only a week,' said Amelia, firmly.

'Where will you go for your honeymoon, Miss Amelia?' asked Mrs Cross.

'We will not go anywhere, Agnes. There is still too much to do here and I need more stock for the shop.' Amelia looked at me. 'What do you think, dear?' she smiled.

'I think it's best to stay here. There's a lot to do and I might not have a lot of time,' I replied.

Amelia bit her lower lip and there was a look of pain on her face and I immediately regretted what I had said.

'We could go away,' she began.

'No!' I protested. 'I don't want to stay in a hotel, Amelia, I'd sooner be here.'

'Yes, of course, dear, we'll stay here. There's lots for us to do and we can have days out,' she smiled.

'And I'll make you a little garden at the end of the back yard. If I clear all the rubbish away I can put some plants in and make a small lawn.'

'That would be very nice, George. Do you not agree, Agnes?'

196

'Yes, very nice, Miss Amelia,' nodded Agnes, her chins wobbling as she did so.

'This apple pie is smashing, Mrs Cross,' I said, my mouth full.

'George, dear, what have I told you?' said Amelia, gently.

'Sorry,' I mumbled.

'Perhaps Agnes will give you a piece to take back with you,' said Amelia, tactfully.

'There's plenty, Miss Amelia. I'll cut him a nice slice,' nodded Agnes, causing her chins to move again.

'Did you call at Amy's first?' asked Amelia.

I nodded, but did not speak; my mouth was again full of apple pie.

'Amy has been very kind and a great help, especially with the curtains,' smiled Amelia, 'even though she has so much to do. She is so sweet, just like the sister I would have liked to have had. Mrs Cross and I went to evening service last Sunday at the chapel with her and afterwards we were introduced to a number of local people.'

'Oh!' I murmured, unsure as to what I should say in reply.

Amelia folded her serviette and slid it into a silver serviette ring, before placing it on the table and smiling. 'I think that we shall be very happy here, George, dear.'

'Yes, I think so too,' I replied, happily.

10

Our Wedding

'So you wish to get married, Corporal Bowman?'

My company commander sat behind a mahogany desk and peered at me over the top of his glasses.

'Yes, sir,' I replied.

'I cannot give you more than eight days, Corporal. We need you and we could be posted any day now, so I suggest you go on Thursday to the following Friday week, though you might get called back, but that's out of my hands; all right?'

'Thank you very much, sir,' I replied, happily.

'See you leave an address if you go away.'

'We are not going away, sir.'

'Very well, Corporal.'

The Major handed me back my papers and I came to attention then gave a smart salute.

'Good luck, Bowman,' he said, quietly.

'Thank you, sir.'

I seemed to be walking on air as I left the barracks carrying my kitbag. I had drawn my pay and received a chaffing from the lads; at that moment the Army was not so bad. The tram stopped just a few yards from Amelia's house and as it was on the way to Amy's, I called there first. Fortunately, Amelia had just arrived home from the library. 'So you have eight days, dear?'

she said, slowly, her mind suddenly made up.

'Yes, Amelia. I think it will be France again then,' I murmured.

'In that case, we will get married on Monday,' she said, firmly.

'Monday! Miss Amelia,' gasped Mrs Cross, 'but it's Thursday today.

'I am well aware of that, Agnes,' snapped Amelia.

'But the master and mistress?' protested Mrs Cross, her loyalty to her late employers still paramount.

'...will probably not be there. Certainly my mother will not, if I know her and I think that I do,' replied Amelia, shortly.

'Mine won't be either,' I remarked, casually.

'Are you sure, George? After all, they only live down Pomeroy Street.' Amelia looked steadily at me.

'I am,' I said, quickly.

'It's up to you, dear,' she smiled.

I suspected she was glad of my decision, since she did not press the matter – quiet wedding was what she wanted and I entirely agreed with her.

Amelia also made it clear to me that it would not be a white wedding in view of all that had happened, and again, I agreed. After having tea with them, Amelia accompanied me to Lausanne Road and it was a surprised Amy who opened the front door to us.

'Monday!' she exclaimed, when Amelia told her of the wedding date; she turned to Hector, 'But it's wash day!' she said, her voice rising.

'Then you will have to wash later in the week,' snapped Hector, a rare note of impatience in his voice. 'I admire your sense of purpose, Amelia; if we have the wedding at eleven o'clock, you will be able to call at the registrar's office before luncheon, then we can have a small reception for you here about midday,' smiled Hector

'That's very kind of you and Amy, Hector, but Mrs Cross is preparing it for me at Queen's Road. Amy has so much to do as it is, but I do appreciate it, really I do,' smiled Amelia.

'I can come and help,' said Amy, in truth, a little relieved.

'Please do,' replied Amelia.

I felt a little superfluous as the arrangements were being finalised, so I went upstairs and unpacked my kitbag.

They were still talking about the guest list when I returned to the parlour.

'No, there will be none of my family there. My brother Edwin would have been, but he is in France. I shall ask Miss Peskett from the library and also Mr and Mrs Hollins – they are from the library as well, though they may not be able to stay long as it will leave the library short-staffed.'

I could see Hector and Amy exchange glances. I think Amelia's cool manner shook them a little and when Amy asked her when the shop would be opened, her answer floored her.

'Next week,' came the calm reply.

'Yes, but...' began Amy.

'I've a girl starting on Monday, maybe even Saturday; everything is ready,' said Amelia in a matter-of-fact tone.

Amy seemed lost for words, but I could see a look of admiration now on Hector's face. Having finalised all the arrangements, I escorted Amelia home. To my surprise I was dismissed at the front door; I received a perfunctory kiss from Amelia as she said, 'It's almost dark now, dear, I cannot have our new neighbours talking, can I? Good-night, George.'

'Er ... no,' I mumbled. 'Good-night, Amelia.'

'Good-night, dear. Come around early tomorrow, I've some jobs for you to do.'

'Yes, Amelia,' I replied, as she closed the door.

Amy was surprised when I returned home so soon and when I told her the reason, I was sure she was trying not to laugh. Hector made no comment, but later he remarked, as we drank our bedtime cocoa, 'I think, George, your future wife is a most capable lady. You are a very fortunate young man.'

'And so is she, Hector,' bridled Amy, for once daring to question his judgment.

'I am fortunate, I know that,' I replied, quietly, 'but for the war, I doubt if she would have looked at me.'

Hector looked a little embarrassed at my words, and Amy arose from her chair and went out into the kitchen.

The following morning, I was at Queen's Road just before nine o'clock wearing some old clothes and carrying my toolbox. To my surprise the shop was open and a young girl was behind the counter, clearly chewing a sweet.

'Can I help you, sir?' she said, almost cheekily.

'I've called to see Miss Amelia,' I said, a little haughtily.

'Oh!' exclaimed the girl. 'She did not say.'

'Should she? We are getting married on Monday,' I snapped.

'Ooh! I didn't know,' said the girl, looking at me curiously, with a smirk on her face.

'That's all right,' I replied, lifting the counter flap and going through to the back of the shop.

'They are upstairs,' said the girl.

Without bothering to reply, I climbed the steep stairs to the living-rooms on the first floor.

'Ah, there you are, George, dear,' said Amelia, greeting me.

I was still smarting a little from my abrupt dismissal

201

of the previous evening and I made no attempt to kiss her. 'Good morning, Amelia. What do you want me to do, I've brought my tools?'

'Um ... yes,' she said, quietly, a questioning look on her face. 'Are you all right, dear?' she frowned.

'Yes, I'm fine,' I replied.

'Did you sleep all right?' she asked.

'Same as usual. What shall I do?' I said, quietly.

'Something is wrong, isn't it?' Amelia compressed her lips.

'No,' I said, shaking my head.

'Yes it is. Now tell me, George.' She lowered her voice and put a hand on my arm.

I lowered my voice and spoke, still not looking at her. 'If you must know, I thought that you could have asked me in last night; Amy and Hector noticed when I went back so soon.'

'Did they? And I suppose, George...' she paused. 'No, I'll say no more,' Amelia's face was now flushed. At this point, fortunately, Mrs Cross came into the room. 'Would you like some more tea, Miss Amelia?'

'No thank you, Agnes. George, would you like a cup of tea?'

'No thank you,' I replied, despondently.

Agnes Cross left the room and Amelia folded her arms, her head slightly to one side. 'Well, George?'

I stood in front of her like an offending schoolboy might do in front of his master. I shrugged my shoulders, then spoke in a meek voice. 'I'm sorry, Amelia, if I offended you but...' I paused.

'But what?' her voice became friendlier.

'I know it's your house. I'll always remember that and I know if there had not been any war you would not have bothered with the likes of me and...' I paused.

'Is that what you think, George?' she exclaimed, sadly.

'Yes. I've nothing, Amelia, just a few pounds, some old books and my toolbox. You are not getting very much, are you?'

'Oh! My dearest.' There were tears in her eyes as she stood up and threw herself into my arms. With hands on either side of my face, she kissed my lips as I held her close to me.

'Don't ever speak like that to me again, my dearest, never. I did not ask you in last night because I was going to wash my hair and have a bath. We have just had a gas geyser installed.'

I did not know what to say, I felt so overcome as I held her close. Tears were now running down my cheeks. 'I'm sorry, Amelia,' I sobbed.

'I was thoughtless, too. Please forgive me, my dearest,' she said, kissing me again before drying my eyes.

After our little misunderstanding, which I think benefited our relationship, I began doing the list of jobs that Amelia had prepared for me. In the cellar was a bench and some wood, both of which came in very useful. Having put up all the shelves that were required, I began to tidy the yard, as the painting had been done by an old man from the church whom Hector had recommended.

Since all the wedding arrangements had already been made, I was rather curious as to what they were, so after our midday meal I tentatively broached the subject. Amelia's cut and dried attitude to it did take me aback somewhat, though I should have expected it, knowing Amelia as I now did.

'Yes, dear, after our wedding we will have a small reception here, then later go on to the theatre. On our wedding night Agnes will stay with your sister and Hector and the following day we will go out for the day, what do you think?'

'Sounds smashing to me,' I grinned.

'That's good,' smiled Amelia. 'Now, dear, is there anything that you would like?'

'How do you mean, Amelia?' I frowned.

'I mean, dear, in the house, something you would like?'

'There is one thing,' I said, thoughtfully.

'What is that, dear?'

'Some lights in the cellar.'

'That seems a very sensible idea.' Amelia nodded her approval. 'We will have that done. Anything else, dear?' said Amelia, smiling at me.

'I'll tell you later, as you do need good locks and bolts for the doors,' I replied.

'That's what I was going to talk to you about. I've bought some bolts, could you fit them?'

'Of course, where are they?'

'In a box under the counter in the shop, dear.'

'I'll put all the locks on and get some bolts for the windows. Amelia, with your stock, you could get a break-in.'

I immediately regretted my words as I did not wish to alarm her.

Amelia, however, was not perturbed as her reply made quite clear. 'Yes, you are quite right, George. Two women on their own, so I've decided to have a dog,' she said, firmly.

'Oh!' I said, a little taken aback. 'What sort?' I frowned.

'A Staffordshire bull terrier,' she replied, calmly.

I started to smile, and Amelia quickly retorted, 'What is so funny, George?'

'Nothing,' I said, shrugging my shoulders as Amelia looked questioningly at me, her lips pursed. 'It's er, well, you are not the bull terrier sort. If you had said a spaniel, I could understand it.'

Amelia began to smile and took my hand as she replied, 'George, dear, I need a dog to protect me, not one that would lick any burglar's hand.'

I burst out laughing, then kissed her on the lips as I replied, 'I think you are wonderful, Amelia, I really do.'

'Then I take it that you approve, dear?' she beamed.

'Very much so,' I replied.

I thought about Amelia and how she had changed in the time I had known her, and I was learning more about her every day. These thoughts went through my head as I fitted the locks and bolts to the windows. Before I knew it, most of the day had gone. At last I was finished, and Amelia, who had watched my progress from time to time, said suddenly, 'George, dear does your sister have a bathroom?'

I flushed slightly at her words, then I replied uncertainly, 'No, I have a washdown in the scullery; they have a tin bath in front of the kitchener.'

'Would you like to use our new bathroom?' said Amelia.

'Yes, please,' I said, quickly, being aware that I did smell a bit after all my exertions.

'I must show you my new bed, er, our new bed after Monday,' Amelia blushed as she spoke and I could feel my face burning.

She took my hand and led me to her bedroom, which I could smell had been recently decorated. 'What do you think of it?' said Amelia, proudly as we entered the room. I was unsure whether she meant the new double bed with its ornate brass fittings, or the curtains and flowered wallpaper.

'Er . . . ye . . . yes, very nice,' I mumbled in embarrassment.

I was aware that Amelia's eyes were twinkling; she had me at a disadvantage, and she was enjoying it.

'There are drawers for your clothes and there's plenty of room in the wardrobe as well.'

'I haven't many clothes,' I said, gruffly, in an effort to hide my embarrassment.

'Oh! Never mind, dear,' smiled Amelia. 'You will have one day. Now I'll show you how to light the new geyser.'

After my bath, I had a meal with Amelia and Mrs Cross and we discussed the arrangements for Monday. It was a bit one-sided really; I just agreed to what Amelia and Amy had arranged. Not that I had any complaints. Amelia was marrying below herself, I knew that from the day she placed the soup spoon in my hand, the very first time I had eaten with her family. Gently and almost motherly, she had tried to show me what I should do and say; I did not resent it, as I loved her. I had nothing, but she never once hinted at the fact, she always said 'we will do this' or 'we will have that.' It was to be our house, our home, even our dog, and I was to be allowed to name it.

'Me, Amelia?' my face beamed.

'Of course, dear, why not?' she smiled. I was just putty in her hands and I think she knew it.

'We will collect it on Wednesday; it will be a dog not a bitch,' said Amelia, firmly.

'If it's going to guard you, it will have to be,' I replied.

'Exactly, and as a puppy it will ignore your cat, Agnes,' said Amelia, turning to Mrs Cross.

Agnes Cross did not look too sure, but Amelia touched her hand as she said with some authority, 'If it's brought up with cats, there will be no trouble, I assure you, Agnes.' She smiled confidently.

'Yes, Miss Amelia,' she replied, doubtfully. It was late that evening when I returned to Amy's house. They were still up and as I drank my cocoa, Amy began to ask questions. We sat in the parlour; I was at the table while Amy and Hector sat on the settee in front of the dying embers of the fire.

'Are Amelia's parents coming?' began Amy.

'She did not say,' I replied.

206

'Didn't you ask?' persisted Amy.

'No, I didn't. It's none of my business, is it?'

'Of course it is,' said Amy, impatiently. 'The father always gives the bride away.'

'Not necessarily,' remarked Hector, putting down his book.

For once, Amy completely ignored him as she persisted stubbornly. 'You should have asked Amelia,' she snapped.

'Yes, Amy,' I replied, tiredly, trying to stifle a yawn. 'I didn't like to. I think she is hoping her parents will arrive – they have been invited.'

'I see,' said Amy, somewhat mollified. 'Let's hope they do, for Amelia's sake,' she added.

'I hope so too. It's strange how they have just split up; I hope it's not through me,' I said quietly.

'Of course it isn't, Georgie,' smiled Amy, sympathetically.

'Surely the failure of their business accounts for that, George. You have no bearing on the matter. They made it clear at the engagement dinner they gave that they welcomed you to their family, so put those thoughts out of your head,' said Hector.

'Yes, but she is so independent now,' I said, helplessly.

'No doubt her new situation has made her like this, after all, she now has a shop, a position at the public library and after Monday, a husband to look after,' smiled Hector. 'I think that you are very fortunate to be marrying such a capable young lady.'

'I know that, Hector,' I said, quietly.

Amy glanced at Hector but did not speak. I wondered what she was thinking, but she remained silent.

The following day, being a Sunday, I expected to be hauled off to church, but on this occasion Amy sent me down to Amelia's to do last-minute jobs, much to my relief. Amelia was reading a letter when I entered the sitting-room.

'Good morning, Amelia,' I said, approaching her; she looked up.

'Good morning, George, dear,' she smiled.

I bent down to kiss her. After she had returned my kiss, she spoke, 'I've just heard from my parents, they are coming to the wedding.' Her face was now wreathed in smiles.

'That's good,' I replied, happily, as I knew how much it meant. 'When will they arrive?'

'George, dear, do take those awful boots off. We will have no floor coverings before long; use those brown shoes of yours, dear. Father says that they should arrive for about midday which will be just in time, then they will catch a train about five and return to Worthing.'

'Do they still like it there?' I asked.

'Ah! That is the question.' Amelia compressed her lips. 'They have moved into a cottage near Aunt Polly and are going back to Aunt Polly's for meals, apparently.'

'Um,' I murmured, making no comment.

'Mother can scarcely boil an egg,' remarked Amelia, folding the letter and carefully putting it in the envelope. 'I had better get a bottle of whisky for father,' she said, rising to her feet.

'I think I had better get it. You know that it's in short supply, and I am more likely to get it in uniform than you.'

'Yes, dear, I had not thought of that,' said Amelia. 'What did you intend to do today?'

'I thought that I would start on the yard and the bit of garden,' I replied, 'so you can have some flowers.'

'That would be nice, dear, and Agnes has a clothes line that needs to be put up as soon as you can,' smiled Amelia.

'I'll do it, leave it to me,' I replied.

For the next three hours I worked solidly in the yard,

clearing away a pile of rubbish and putting it in a hole that I had dug in the small garden. With the excess earth and some large stones that I had found, I made a rockery, and when Amelia came out to see my efforts, she was delighted. 'It will make a nice little garden, dear. We will get some plants and flag stones, it's too small for a lawn, George.'

'Yes, I suppose it is,' I agreed, reluctantly.

'You have done well, now come in and have a wash before luncheon, and I should sweep up the earth, George, or it will tread into the house,' Amelia remarked.

'Yes, Amelia, but I want to put up the clothes line first.'

'All right, but don't be long, luncheon is nearly ready,' she replied, going towards the back door.

'Five minutes,' I replied.

I was aware that Amelia was watching me from an upstairs window as I fixed the washing line to the hook on the back wall. I tied the line to the hook then began to sweep up as Amelia abruptly left the window, satisfied, I think, that I had obeyed her.

Mrs Cross had made a steak and kidney pudding – it was delicious.

'Amy told me that it was a favourite of yours,' smiled Amelia, as I scraped my plate.

'It is,' I said, putting down my spoon, suddenly aware that my table manners were not all that Amelia might have desired, and using my dessert spoon on my dinner plate was not quite the thing to do.

'George, I've invited some friends to the wedding,' she paused.

'Oh, yes,' I said, somewhat disinterestedly, as Mrs Cross was now bringing in the pudding.

'Yes, dear, they are friends of mine from the suffragette movement.'

'Are they?' I said, my eyes on Mrs Cross's apple pie.

'You do not mind?' asked Amelia, sweetly.

'No. Why should I mind?' I looked across the table at Amelia.

'The fact is that my father does not approve of them and would not let me invite them to Cedar Lodge.'

'Why not?' I asked.

'Because, George, dear,' said Amelia, with affected patience, 'they questioned our system with their actions.'

'So did I, didn't I?' my face blank as I replied.

'Er ... yes, but...' began Amelia, her brow furrowing.

She looked carefully at me, but when I began to smile she playfully kicked me under the table.

'George, you are teasing me,' she smiled.

'Am I?' I said, innocently.

'You know you are. It was different in your case; you may have questioned the system, but you have proved yourself on the front line and that, in father's and Edwin's eyes, is everything.'

'Um,' I grunted, unmoved.

'You do not mind, dear?' asked Amelia, looking steadily at me.

'No, of course not,' I said, shaking my head.

'Thank you, dear,' she smiled.

I felt flattered that she had asked for my approval. I was quite unused to such consideration and I loved her for it.

For the rest of the afternoon I busily engaged myself on laying out the little back garden and tidying up the yard. The day passed quickly and by four-thirty it was almost dark, at which point Amelia suggested I had a bath. This I did without any question; I was now completely under her spell and had never been happier in my life.

After my bath we had a meal, then Amelia suggested that I went to Amy's to collect my belongings.

210

'I haven't got very much, Amelia, a pile of books mainly,' I said with some embarrassment.

'Never mind, dear, you can bring them,' she smiled.

'Yes, I will. I can put up some bookshelves for them, can't I?'

'Of course you can,' said Amelia.

'I have asked some lady friends here this evening, George. Were you going to do anything?'

'Er ... no,' I replied.

'I see,' said Amelia, looking carefully at me. 'Still, I expect you have things to do this evening.'

'No, I haven't,' I replied.

'Well, George, dear, I must be frank; this is my evening and only ladies are invited – you understand?'

'Yes, of course, Amelia,' I grinned.

'Amy has been invited by the way,' smiled Amelia.

'Has she? Then I expect I shall have to read to the girls,' I replied, still grinning at her.

'Have you no friends that you wish to meet?'

'No. There were only the Snapes and they moved months ago.'

Amelia seemed to relent, as she then said quietly, 'If you bring your things down at about ten, you can then escort Amy home; that would be best.'

'Yes, Amelia. I'll see you later, then,' I said, kissing her cheek and hurrying out of the sitting-room.

As I entered the parlour, I noticed that Amy was wearing her best dress and her hair had been neatly set.

'Have you eaten, George?' were her first words to me.

'Oh yes, thanks,' I replied. 'You look very smart, Amy – going anywhere?' I grinned.

'Don't be cheeky,' she laughed.

Amy rarely went out, even with Hector, and it was obvious she was looking forward to this rare treat.

'Hector's upstairs reading to the girls,' said Amy, as she noticed my glance at his empty chair.

'Is he?' I nodded.

'Will there be many there, Georgie?' Amy asked, nervously.

'I'm not sure – some of Amelia's suffragette friends, I think. They might ask you to chain yourself to a railing somewhere – that would please Hector,' I grinned.

Amy burst out laughing, showing her perfect set of teeth. 'Oh really, Georgie, they have stopped doing that. We have been promised the vote after the war.'

'Oh, yes,' I said, thoughtfully.

I had forgotten the war for a while, and it brought me back to reality with a jolt. It seemed that there was no end to it.

'They'll have to, won't they? There will only be you left.'

Amy now looked serious; she began tidying up and pretended she had not heard my reply. I took off my overcoat and hung it up. I collected my few possessions together and put them in the hall near the front door. My books were in some cardboard boxes and my clothes in a battered old suitcase.

'Are you all right, Georgie?' asked Amy, as she watched me putting the boxes against the wall, in case anyone tripped over them. Amy came close to me and spoke quietly. 'Amelia will be good to you, I know that. See that you are good to her; take care of her, she loves you a lot.'

'Look, Amy, I love her too, and I'd do anything for her,' I said, breathing deeply.

Amy knew me well enough not to press the point and proceeded to remove her apron. 'I'll get my coat now,' she said, quietly.

'Right. I'll go down with you; take some of my things and bring the rest when I come to meet you.'

Amy went upstairs to say good-night to the girls and Jimmy, whilst I pushed the trolley outside the front door. I could hear her speaking to Hector, then she came down the stairs. I carried a small box of books and my suitcase, while Amy pushed Jimmy's trolley which was also full of books.

A chill wind blew up Lausanne Road, right off the river, so it seemed. We did not speak, there was little to say; it seemed that our old relationship was now coming to an end. I glanced at Amy and she too could sense my feelings. Her eyelids flickered and her mouth tensed. I bent forward and kissed her cheek. Amy smiled with some difficulty then looked away from me, though we still did not speak. We did not need to speak to express our feelings for each other, we were far too close for that.

11

Wedding Day

I awoke early on Monday morning; in my half sleep, I wondered where I was. At last I collected my thoughts – today was my wedding day. I slipped out of bed and parted the thin window curtain. It was not raining and the day looked clear; it might even be sunny later, I thought. I looked over at Jimmy, he was still asleep, his thumb in his mouth.

Reluctantly, I got back into bed as I was sure Amy would not welcome a cup of tea at this time of the morning. As I lay in bed, I thought of the wedding and it occurred to me that I knew little of the day's arrangements. I was not even sure if Amelia would be wearing a wedding dress. I drifted back to sleep to be awoken by the words: 'Wake up, sleepy head, you are getting married today.'

I opened my eyes to see a smiling Amy holding a cup and saucer.

'Thanks, Amy,' I yawned, sitting up in bed and taking the cup of tea from her. 'Did you enjoy yourself last night?' I asked as I yawned again.

'Yes, it was a lovely evening. You were asleep when we got back.'

'Yes,' I said, drinking my tea. 'Hector seemed to be gone ages, so I came to bed, I was going to meet you, you know.'

'Yes, dear, but Hector wanted to confirm the final arrangements should Mr and Mrs Hooper not arrive. You can wash and shave first. There is some hot water, so come down right away, there's a lot to do,' said Amy as she left the room. 'Try not to wake Jimmy, the longer he sleeps, the better.' Amy said the words with some feeling.

I grinned as I looked at the still sleeping Jimmy, his right thumb in his mouth and not a care in the world. I carefully dressed with a clean shirt and underwear that Amy had laid out for me, then crept downstairs.

'Wear your black shoes today, George,' said Amy, pointing to the neatly polished black shoes in front of the kitchener. For a moment I did not recognise my shoes and turned to Amy.

'Are they mine, Amy?'

'Yes, I've had them repaired and cleaned,' she replied.

'Cor, thanks. I'll pay you, but...' I hesitated.

'Amelia made it quite clear that she was not marrying you in those army boots,' smiled Amy.

'But regulations, Amy!' I protested.

'Sod regulations,' she whispered, 'it's your wedding day. Now get a move on before Hector comes down; he takes an age to wash and shave and if he gets in first we will be all behind.'

I grinned, it was the first time that I had ever heard her criticise Hector in any way.

'All right, I'll not be long,' I said, going into the scullery.

Just before eight, cousin Lily arrived. She was the smartest that I had ever seen her and I knew the reason why, for Amy examined her carefully as she came into the parlour.

'H'm, I suppose you'll do,' she said, grudgingly. 'Now you know what I told you,' said Amy severely.

215

'Yes, Amy,' sniffed Lily, as she was about to wipe her nose on the back of her hand. I could see Hector wince and look away.

'Don't you do that, you dirty girl,' stormed Amy. 'I've told you before. Haven't you got a handkerchief?'

'No, I ain't,' replied Lily, truculently.

Amy did not reply, her face was white with anger and she produced a handkerchief from the dresser drawer. Without a word she thrust it into Lily's hand. Lily took it with a grin and blew her nose loudly.

'If you have to make that noise, Lily, go into the yard,' snapped Amy glaring at her.

'Gawd, strewth, there's no pleasing,' said Lily, cheekily.

'Any lip from you, my girl, and you'll feel the weight of my hand,' said Amy angrily. 'Now make a start on the washing up.'

Lily, still wiping her nose, hesitated, until Amy without any ceremony bundled her out of the room. Amy, her face now flushed, tidied the parlour table. 'I'll get the children down now,' she said, quietly.

'That's all right, dear,' said Hector, 'I'll get them for you while you make their breakfasts.'

'What shall I do, Amy?' I asked, getting out of my chair.

'I've got plenty for you to do,' smiled Amy, now her normal self.

The morning went quickly and before I realised it Amy was giving Lily last-minute instructions.

'See they have their dinner at one, and make sure they are clean before you go to the park. The girls should be at school, so don't go down Waller Road or the school board man might see you.'

'What if it's raining?' sniffed Lily.

'You don't go out,' said Amy, her voice rising, 'and see Jimmy uses his potty before you do go out.'

216

Hector had already gone to the church when we left the house. Amy looked sidelong at me, a smile on her face.

'Nervous?' she asked.

I shrugged, my face I could tell was beginning to flush.

'Amelia will take good care of you, George,' said Amy, now serious. 'You are very fortunate to have met her.'

'I know,' I said, gruffly.

'She'll give you fine children, I'm sure of that; she has the hips for it. Child-bearing will be no problem to her.'

My face, I'm sure, was now even redder and Amy started to grin. 'I'm embarrassing you, Georgie,' she chuckled. 'Never mind, after tonight that will all go. Tell me, you never have ... with a woman ... have you?' Amy lowered her voice.

'No, of course not,' I protested, my face burning.

'I'm sure Amelia hasn't either, she implied that to me,' said Amy in a matter-of-fact way.

I was just too embarrassed to speak and I almost walked into a lamp-post, such was my confusion.

'There's no need to worry about it, Georgie, my sweet. Amelia will guide you I'm sure. Women have a natural knowledge of these things.' Amy touched my arm and smiled reassuringly.

Later I realised Amy was trying to be kind and understanding, but at the time I wished I had walked round to the church on my own; I was sure my face was red, such was my embarrassment.

The ladies of the Baptist Church had decorated it with the first of the spring flowers. I caught a faint odour of their scent from time to time, mingled with the smell of dust that seemed to be ever present in the church hall.

I did not have a best man and Amelia did not intend to have any bridesmaids. It was to be a simple ceremony.

I noticed, as I stood at the top of the church steps,

that some of the residents of Gautry Road were standing at their front gates watching the guests arrive.

'Don't stand there, George,' said Amy, sharply. 'You should be inside.' She pulled at my arm and I went back into the church, almost reluctantly.

Amelia arrived, accompanied by her father. Of her mother there was no sign. This did not bother me as I felt she did not approve of me anyway.

I had been under the impression that Amelia would be wearing a wedding dress, but at the last minute decided against it. I think the loss of her two brothers, and Edwin now at the front line, added to her father's misfortune, took much of the happiness of the day from her. Instead she wore a smart suit with a hat of the same colour to match. I had to admit I was very proud when I looked at her – she did look lovely.

There were about twenty in the congregation – all Amelia's guests and, of course, Mrs Cross, to whom I was becoming rather attached. Perhaps it was because we were lonely people, though I'm sure our mutual love for Amelia had much to do with it. Agnes Cross smiled reassuringly at me as I passed her in church, and I winked at her in reply.

The ceremony was brief and seemed to be over before I could fully comprehend what was happening. Before I knew it, I was being congratulated and kissed, then we were ushered out of the church to a waiting car for the journey to the registry office.

I caught a glimpse of my mother on the pavement on the opposite side of the road, but I pretended I had not seen her. I had been about to wave, but I stopped; after all, they had not even sent us a card – not that I had expected them to send us one.

At the registry office we were accompanied by Amelia's father, Hector and Amy, Amelia's friends, Irene Peskett,

Maud Littleton and Kate Jackson. Having been officially married, we returned to Queen's Road, where Agnes Cross, with two assistants, was welcoming the guests. All the drink had been provided, not surprisingly, by Amelia's father, and each guest was greeted with a glass of sherry as they entered the house.

I was still in a daze as I escorted Amelia back to Queen's Road. I felt so different; perhaps it was wearing my new black shoes. Amelia had declared firmly, 'George, you are not marrying me in those awful Army boots.'

The first floor front room had been laid out as a reception-cum-dining-room and there Amelia and I received the congratulations of the guests. Apart from Amelia's lady friends, Irene Peskett, Maud Littleton and Kate Jackson, the guests, beside Hector and Amy, were all strangers to me.

Mr Hooper took me to one side and shook my hand as he said, 'George, my boy, I'm very proud to have you as a son-in-law.' I could tell he meant it, as there were tears in his eyes.

'Thank you, sir,' I mumbled; his words had brought a lump to my throat. 'I'll always take care of her, sir.'

'I know you will, my boy, and she will always take care of you, of that I am quite certain,' he replied.

I had good reason to remember his words long after he had died. They were absolutely true. Amelia was to be the one sure thing in my life, the one reason why I was to persevere, in spite of all the pain I was to suffer in the years to come.

I had never seen so much food in all my life – where Amelia had obtained it all was beyond my comprehension. Unfortunately, the excitement had taken the edge off my appetite. I managed to eat something as I murmured to Amelia, 'I don't feel very hungry, Amelia.'

219

'Never mind, dear, don't force it down or you will be sick, and we don't want that, do we?' she replied.

'No, Amelia,' I said.

Amy, who was sitting to my left, must have heard her words, as a smile suddenly appeared on her face and I could feel my face flush.

Happily the wedding breakfast was soon over and the guests began to depart. I was not sorry to see them go, though I wondered who was going to wash all the dirty dishes, but I need not have worried as Amy had arranged for cousin Lily and her two sisters to do it, 'and if there are any breakages, my girl, you will get your ears boxed and you will pay for them,' hissed Amy, who did not seem to like cousin Lily.

Mrs Cross was to supervise proceedings and then go to Amy's, where she would stay until Wednesday evening.

It was the intention of Amelia's father to return to Worthing, and much to his surprise, Amelia announced that we would see him off from Waterloo Station.

'But my dear!' he protested, 'it's your honeymoon...'

'We are going to the theatre after we have seen you off, so we will not be going out of our way,' said Amelia, firmly.

Mr Hooper looked at me and smiled as he said, 'See what you have let yourself in for, George?'

'Yes, sir,' I grinned, 'but I don't mind though.'

Both Amelia and her father burst out laughing; it was the happiest that I had ever seen them together. We put on our coats and left the house after Amelia's father had said an affectionate goodbye to Mrs Cross.

Waterloo station was crowded with khaki uniforms. We exchanged anxious glances when we saw them; in another week I could be with them. Amelia's lower lip trembled, but she quickly gained control of herself as she looked up at the train indicator board. 'Your train is on platform five, father, it's in now.'

'Yes, I'll get on board, my dear, and let you two get off. Really, I should be seeing you off on your honeymoon.' He shook his head.

'I shall be fine, father, so you take care,' replied Amelia, 'and give my love to mother,' she added casually.

'Yes, my dear, enjoy the theatre,' said her father, giving her a hug and a kiss.

'Goodbye, my boy.' He shook my hand and gave me a sad smile. 'Take good care of her.'

'I will, sir,' I replied quickly.

'And you take care, too,' he added. I could see Amelia biting her lower lip as he spoke.

'Yes, sir,' I nodded.

We watched him board the train and waved as it moved away in a cloud of steam, and his carriage disappeared from view. Amelia took my arm and squeezed it, then looked up at me, 'Let's go to the theatre, husband,' she said, cheekily, her face wreathed in smiles.

I tried to remember over the years what we saw at the theatre, but was never sure. It all passed in a blur of happiness.

It was dark when we returned to Queen's Road; a small light on the stairs had been left on and there was a fire burning in the sitting-room. A cold supper had been laid out for us and there was a saucepan of soup on the stove.

'You go and unpack your case, dear, while I prepare our supper,' said Amelia, as she put on her apron.

We ate our supper almost in complete silence and I for once was not hungry. Our wedding night was more wonderful than I could have imagined, yet I awoke from a nightmare. I was back in no man's land lying next to a dying man. He kept touching my face. I pushed him away, it was warm and gentle.

'No, no, no.' My eyes opened.

In the dim light I at last realised where I was. The sweet smell of Amelia's hair on the pillow made me shiver. The foul water in the trench loomed before my eyes, the rats running into holes; I could hear the wounded. I dozed off; I was warm but the dream came back.

There were rats near me, one touched my foot and I awoke. Suddenly I was sitting up. Amelia moved, her foot touched mine. My forehead was damp. I looked at Amelia, she was fast asleep. It all came back to me, I was now married. The trenches disappeared; I was a happy man.

Once it was eight o'clock, I made Amelia a cup of tea. Yet, as I made the tea, I thought of Flanders; each passing hour would bring it closer to me. I entered our bedroom holding the cup and saucer.

'You are up, my dearest,' Amelia brought me out of my thoughts. She stifled a yawn as she smiled at me, pulling the bedclothes up to her chin.

'I've made you a cup of tea,' I said, handing her the cup and saucer.

'That is sweet of you, dear.'

'I was wondering,' I began, then I paused. Amelia looked at me over the rim of her cup, a slight frown appeared on her brow.

'What is it?' she said, softly.

'Well, it's about the dog you are getting – when are you...?' I did not finish, as Amelia cut in.

'Tomorrow, dear, we will collect it,' she beamed.

'Tomorrow,' I grinned.

'Yes. Have you drunk your tea, dear?'

'Yes,' I nodded.

'So have I. Take my cup and saucer, dear, remove your night attire and come back into bed,' she smiled.

'Yes,' I said, huskily, as I hastened to obey her.

My impatience to collect the bull terrier puppy was all too obvious. I mentioned it as Amelia prepared breakfast. She smiled as she cut some bread then put it under the grill.

'Would you like to collect it today, dear?' she said.

'Yes, please. Could we?'

'I see no reason why not,' replied Amelia. 'One day will make no difference. Is the yard completely secure – it must not get out.'

'I'll make sure after breakfast,' I said, eagerly.

'I thought we might go out for the day, George. Is there anywhere that you would like to go?' she asked.

I whispered in her ear and she blushed slightly and smacked playfully at my hand.

'Really, we have only just got up,' she said with mock severity, then she began to smile and blushed even more.

'Perhaps later,' she conceded.

As we ate our breakfast, Amelia talked to me for the first time about our finances.

'I had thought we could go out for days this week, but after I have paid for all the stock for the shop and the reception, I shall have little left,' said Amelia, her face set.

I stopped eating and looked at her. Money had been the last thing that I had thought about.

'And my salary from the library is not due until the end of the month. I'm hoping we take enough money in the shop to pay the girl and there are other small bills.'

'I will get a married allowance from the Army, don't forget,' I said.

'I know, dear, but I shall not get that until you go back and show the paymaster our marriage certificate,' she replied.

'How much will the puppy cost?'

'The man is asking seven shillings and sixpence for the dogs and five shillings for the bitch ... er ... lady dogs,' she said, her face colouring slightly.

'I could pay for it,' I said, getting out of my chair and taking my wallet and savings book from my Army tunic pocket. 'I had meant to give it to you before, Amelia.' I took ten one-pound notes from my wallet and handed them to her, together with my savings book.

'What's this, George, dear?' Amelia's mouth opened slightly.

'It's my pay. I saved it up. I gave a pound to Amy before I left; she did not want to take it, but I insisted.'

'Of course,' nodded Amelia.

'And it's my savings book. Hector has been looking after it, but he gave it back to me yesterday. He said I should give it to you. There's six pounds eight and sixpence in it.'

Amelia looked hesitant and almost reluctantly she opened her handbag and put the money and savings book into it.

'Are you sure, dear?' she murmured, her eyes moist.

'Yes,' I grinned. 'I've got fourteen shillings left.'

'Thank you, George, it will be most useful. After breakfast we will go and get the puppy,' she smiled.

'Where are you getting it from?'

'It's a neighbour of Irene Peskett near Brockley Park,' said Amelia, as she rose from the table.

As we washed up, I whispered in her ear, 'Can we? Before we go out?'

Amelia started to giggle and blushed slightly as she dried her hands, then she turned and kissed me. 'I think that is a good idea, my dearest,' she murmured.

'What would you like to do when we have collected the puppy, dear. Where shall we go?' asked Amelia as she looked submissively at me.

We were about to leave our bedroom and Amelia was adjusting her hair as she glanced at her dressing-table mirror.

'I would like to finish off the yard and garden for you and go to Kew Gardens,' I replied.

'Kew Gardens, dear?' Amelia looked surprised.

'Yes,' I said, as I stooped to tie up my shoe laces.

'Kew Gardens would be nice, but we would need to leave early. We could go tomorrow.'

'Fine, and I can get some plants and things for the garden on our way back from Brockley. I'd like to go to the New Cross Empire as well.'

'The New Cross Empire?' smiled Amelia. 'Why not, dear,' she nodded. 'We will if you wish to.'

'It's not expensive and seats up in the Gods are only threepence, and you can buy bags of rotten fruit to throw, from the barrows near the theatre.'

'Bags of rotten fruit?' Amelia mouthed the words.

'Yes, only a penny a bag. It's not like your theatre at Blackheath. You can have a good night there, particularly if you can get bad eggs as well. Mind you, you need to be careful with them if they break when you take them in, you smell a bit.'

Amelia was lost for words and she looked at me, her eyes wide. 'George, you are not going to throw rotten fruit and eggs in my company – whatever next? I can hardly believe my ears,' she said, staring at me in disbelief.

I began to laugh and her face began to soften, then she too began to laugh as well. 'George, you were pulling my leg, you beast,' she said, striking at my chest with both clenched hands.

'Yes, I am,' I replied, lifting her off her feet and kissing her. 'They search you when you go up to the Gods,' I chuckled.

Her arms were around my neck as she clung to me,

and her perfume would remain with me in the months ahead as I would try to ignore the stench and horror of the trenches.

'Is this the one, Mr Smailes?' asked Amelia, as she peered at the two puppies that were lying comfortably in the corner of a butter box.

'That's right, Miss,' came the reply.

'It's Mrs Bowman, if you don't mind,' retorted Amelia.

I pretended not to hear the exchange as I made a fuss of the puppies, but I felt proud all the same, as Amelia corrected Mr Smailes.

'Seven shillings and sixpence, I think you said.'

Amelia opened her purse and took three half-crowns from it.

'That's right, Mrs Bowman. The other one's a bitch and that's five bob. I'll probably keep that one now for breeding.'

'Quite,' said Amelia, giving Mr Smailes the three half-crowns.

I picked up the puppy and put him inside my greatcoat so that he nestled against my chest. He seemed perfectly happy now and I grinned at Amelia. 'I think he's going to sleep, Amelia.'

'That's good dear. And you've written down what we should give him to eat, Mr Smailes?'

'That's right, Ma'am. Here we are.'

He gave Amelia a piece of paper, which she put into her handbag. 'And make sure he doesn't go out for some weeks yet, if possible, or he could catch something.'

'We have a yard, Mr Smailes, which he can play in,' I said quickly.

'That's fine, son, keep him on his own,' nodded Mr Smailes, as he pulled knowledgeably at his grey moustache.

I held the puppy close to me as we made our way home.

'I want to call in at Amy's,' said Amelia, suddenly.

I was a little surprised by her remark, but I welcomed it none the less as I could show the girls the puppy.

'I'm going to suggest to Agnes that she comes home tonight. I am quite sure that she did not sleep too well in your bed, George. I think that she would prefer her own bed. I hope you do not mind, dear; she is getting old.'

'Me, Amelia?' I said in surprise.

'Yes, you dear. Do you object?'

'No,' I murmured, a little taken aback.

'After all, you did say yourself that your bed was not very comfortable, didn't you?' smiled Amelia.

'I did, but I'm used to hard beds; I don't suppose Aggie is.'

'Quite. It's Agnes dear,' replied Amelia, sweetly.

'D'you know, Amelia, he looks just like Buster Miller in my unit,' I said, looking down at the sleeping puppy.

'Does he?' reflected Amelia. 'Buster, that's a very good name for a bull terrier, George, dear, I think we will call him that, what do you think?'

'That's a good idea,' I said, enthusiastically. 'We'll call you Buster,' I said, touching the puppy's nose.

Agnes Cross did not need asking twice when Amelia suggested she came home with us. She was up the stairs packing her small suitcase before Amy could put the kettle on. The girls were still at school and Jimmy was out with Hector, so the house was quiet.

'We thought that Agnes would prefer her own bed, Amy,' smiled Amelia, as she stirred her tea.

'It's a bit hard,' I added. 'Amelia's bed is much nicer and it's got springs, Amy.'

'Our bed, George, dear,' said Amelia, her face flushing.

Amy was doing her best not to laugh, but it was too much for her, and she put down her cup and saucer then put a hand to her face. 'Really, Georgie,' she laughed.

'Well it is, isn't it, Amelia?'

'I've no idea, George. Do be quiet, dear, about our bed.'

Amelia's face was now almost bright red and her patience was wearing thin – this made Amy worse and she was now almost doubled up laughing, much to Amelia's annoyance.

'I fail to see what is so humorous, Amy,' she said, quietly.

'I'm sorry, I should not laugh,' said Amy, wiping her eyes.

'But you are,' I said.

At this point Agnes returned to the parlour carrying her small suitcase and wearing her hat and coat. 'I'm ready, Miss Amelia.'

'Very good, Agnes,' said Amelia, rising to her feet.

'Thank you for the tea, Amy. You must bring the children down to see us. The shop will be open tomorrow and I'm sure they would like some sweets.'

'But you are on your honeymoon,' protested Amy.

Amelia, now her normal self-assured manner asserting itself, calmly put on her gloves. 'The girl I have engaged will be there. George and I will be going to Kew Gardens for the day – that's if the weather is reasonable.'

'Oh!' Amy seemed surprised.

'We're going to the New Cross Empire tonight,' I beamed.

'Yes. George wanted to go,' smiled Amelia.

'Did he?' said Amy, her eyes twinkling.

'Are you ready, George?'

'Yes. I think Buster's waking up.'

'I expect he will want feeding shortly,' said Amy, as she stroked the puppy's head.

'And he might want to do something,' observed Amelia.

'Do you think so?' I said, with some concern.

'Yes, dear,' replied Amelia.

I needed no further urging as I quickly left the house. 'Bye, Amy,' I said over my shoulder as I opened their front gate.

Amelia was still talking to Amy as I strode down Lausanne Road, and I only stopped when I heard Amelia call: 'Do wait for us, George.'

I stopped and walked back to her as I looked anxiously at Buster.

'Take Agnes's case dear,' she said, smiling at me.

'Yes, Amelia,' I said, holding out my hand for the case.

'It's quite all right, Miss Amelia,' said Agnes, still firmly holding on to the case.

'It's not, Agnes. George will carry it for you,' said Amelia.

I winked at Agnes and took the case from her. We both knew that it was pointless disputing the matter with Amelia.

Agnes's cat, Arthur, had now settled in at Queen's Road. The big ginger tom looked at the puppy suspiciously when I put it near his blanket. At first Arthur ignored Buster, but then, to our surprise, accepted him – even allowing him to share his basket.

'Well I never,' said Agnes in relief. 'Would you believe that, Miss Amelia?'

'I am agreeably surprised,' smiled Amelia.

So began the strange friendship between Arthur, the cat, and Buster, the Staffordshire bull terrier.

My leave passed all too quickly and I was now dreading the thought of leaving Amelia. We did not speak of it, but I knew it was constantly in our thoughts. I seemed to love her more each day. I never questioned anything she told me to do; this was not the blind obedience of love, but a simple recognition of her intelligence and capability. I knew she was clever; her father had hinted

229

to me that she had been the brightest in the family, quite unlike her mother who had seemed a little stupid to me and who was now never mentioned by Amelia. I think the fact that she would not attend her wedding hurt Amelia and it seemed to widen the void between them.

The fact that Amelia had received a legacy on her twenty-fifth birthday prompted me to ask her if her brothers would receive a similar amount.

'No, dear,' she replied.

'Why not?' I asked curiously.

'Because my grandfather – that is my mother's father – died before my eldest brother was born. He made his will before his last voyage; he was a ship's master. I was his only grandchild then and I was less than two years old. His ship sank in a storm off the Scilly Isles and he and all his crew were lost. So you see, George, Edwin has no expectations with the exception of Aunt Polly and I think her will is made out in favour of an animal organisation. That is why I have to offer Edwin a home if he needs it, you see.'

'I understand, Amelia. My father has made out his in favour of the brewers,' I grinned.

'So I understand.' Amelia's light blue eyes twinkled.

Our honeymoon was almost over. For the last two nights I could hardly sleep. I awoke early, uncertain what hour it was; I could see a faint light through the bedroom curtains. I slipped out of bed to look out of the window; it was the light of the street lamps. I crept back into bed, careful not to disturb Amelia, and as I snuggled into her back, she spoke.

'Are you all right, my dearest?'

'I didn't wake you, did I?'

'No, dear,' she replied, turning on her back. 'Is it France?' she murmured.

'Yes,' I sniffed. 'It's not the trenches, Amelia, it's leaving you. I love you so much.'

'Oh, my precious,' she sobbed, putting her arms about my neck.

I clung to her – the most important thing in my life. Words could not describe my feelings for her. In her arms, I went back to sleep, only to awaken to the fact that my leave was ebbing away. For my last two days, I did not want to leave the house. I was almost Amelia's shadow but she did not complain; she understood. She would hold my hand and fuss over me, like a hen with one chick.

My last day arrived all too quickly. I had to be at Woolwich by noon. We sat at the kitchen table drinking tea; neither wanted any breakfast. Agnes was packing a parcel for me. Amelia held my hands, there were tears in her eyes; we seemed lost for words, but at last Amelia spoke. 'I could come to Woolwich,' she sniffed.

'No. We'll say goodbye here,' I croaked, my head shaking.

Amelia nodded; she knew in her heart that it was best. Woolwich would be crowded with men.

'Have you packed everything, dear?'

I nodded and sipped my tea, holding both her hands in one of my own. I lowered my cup and looked into her tearful eyes. 'Yes, everything is packed. I've got the stamped addressed envelope to send back our marriage certificate as soon as the paymaster has seen it. I'll only draw a small allotment of my pay, so you can get it with your marriage allowance.

'Oh, George, dear.' Amelia's lower lip quivered. 'I'll not need it, my dearest,' she murmured.

Amelia compressed her lips but the tears began to appear on her cheeks. I left my chair and bent over her, enfolding her in my arms. Agnes, seeing Amelia's distress put her hands to her face and left the kitchen.

231

'I'm sorry, George, dear,' she said, drying her eyes on her apron. 'I should act better, I know I should.'

'Why? It shows you love me,' I said, kissing her damp face.

'If only you knew how much,' she whispered.

'If it's just half as much as I love you, I'm the luckiest man in the world,' I said, softly.

At this, she kissed me with a tenderness that I could never forget and which I was to remember in the dark days ahead.

I had said my goodbyes to Hector and Amy the previous evening. They knew I was leaving at eleven o'clock, so I said goodbye with a big hug and kiss to Aggie with instructions to take good care of Amelia and little Buster.

'I will, Master George,' she sobbed. 'You take care, too.'

I left the house, carrying my kitbag, accompanied by Amelia. 'Do make sure that girl keeps the passage door shut, Amelia, or Buster will get out on to the road and get run over. That yard's plenty big enough for him, you know.'

'Yes, dear. I'll make sure she does,' replied Amelia, dutifully.

As we approached the tramcar stop I could see Amy hurrying towards us – she waved a hand.

'It's Amy,' I said, dropping my kitbag near the tramcar stop.

'Yes,' said Amelia, her lips hardly moving.

'I had to come, Georgie,' said Amy, breathlessly.

'Yes, of course,' replied Amelia, trying to appear normal.

Words were difficult to find and before we knew it a tram clattered towards us. I could catch any of them as I had to change trams at New Cross Gate, and they all went there. We said our farewells; Amy in tears and Amelia struggling to hold back her tears. Usually the tram did not wait, but the driver and the conductor could see what was happening and for once waited patiently. At last, I climbed aboard; the conductor took my kitbag as I leaned out to kiss once more a now weeping Amelia.

The tram ground forward with a screech of metal on metal. Amy took Amelia's arm and I waved until they were out of sight. I brushed my eyes with the back of my hand and stumbled to a seat, completely forlorn and, resting my head against the cold glass window, my mind became a complete blank.

At New Cross Gate, I got off the tram. As I did so, I offered my fare to the conductor but he refused to take it.

'That's all right, old son. Good luck,' he smiled.

I nodded, a lump in my throat, then picked up my kitbag, and with a wave to the conductor, made my way to the Woolwich tramcar.

12

Back to Army Life

The barracks at Woolwich was full to overflowing, and my unit was expected to move out almost immediately.

Having reported to my company commander, I sought out the paymaster with my marriage certificate. Having made the necessary entry in my pay book (whilst making a crude remark), and noting my new next of kin, he gave me back the certificate. This I put in the stamped addressed envelope Amelia had given me and gave it to my company commander.

'Writing already, Corporal?' he asked, raising an eyebrow.

'No, sir. It's our marriage lines; my wife wants them back.'

'I see.' He gave them a cursory glance then sealed the envelope and put it in his post tray.

'Report to Sergeant Lane, Bowman, we should be moving out in the morning.'

'Yes, sir.' I saluted and left his office.

I stowed my gear in my billet, glancing down the barrack room as I did so. I could tell that a lot of the men sorting out their gear were new recruits; most seemed younger than me, though some were old enough to be my father.

I had not met Sergeant Lane before and he was quick to tell me that it was his first posting to France. He was

234

a large man in his late thirties; his belt must have been twice the length of mine or it would never have gone around his waist. His fat face seemed to droop over his collar and his bald head seemed to be permanently covered in a film of sweat. It was clear to me that he was dreading the thought of the trenches, even more than I was. He was continually smoking and his small office was filled with smoke.

'Do you smoke, Corp?' he asked, offering me his packet of Players.

'No thanks, Sarg. I stopped last when I got a niff of gas; it makes me cough now and my chest hurts when I do.'

'You got the DCM and MM, I see,' he said, peering at my tunic.

'Aye, but they could have them back if they sent me home,' I replied, morosely.

'Not much chance of that, mate, we are moving out.'

'I was lucky to get my leave,' I said, my thoughts on Amelia.

'You was. The Major's a good skin, some would have sent for yer days ago, I can tell yer.'

'Yes, he's all right,' I nodded. 'Are you a regular, Sarg?' I asked.

'Nar. Used ter be a butcher in West Ham,' he replied.

'Looks like the Army got you in the right place,' I remarked.

'Right ... wad'yer mean?' he said, frowning.

'You'll see plenty of blood with this unit,' I said, easily.

Jack Lane peered at me, unsure how to take my remark. He stubbed out his cigarette and sniffed. 'Maybe so. From what I hear, a new battle is building up in the Ypres sector.'

'Is it? My brother-in-law is there, I think.'

'You might see 'im,' said Jack Lane, laconically.

'Aye, you never know,' I murmured.

'It's George, isn't it?'

'That's right,' I replied.

'I'm Jack when we are on our own. I'm relying on you, George, to put me wise when we get up to the front. Most of our company consists of new recruits; the crowd you were with moved out with a new unit last Tuesday. They'll be in Flanders by now, I shouldn't wonder.'

'Have this new lot done any training?' I said.

'Just the usual,' replied Jack Lane. 'Basic first aid and how to lift, that's all. Four of them were medical students, so they should know something.'

'That's helpful, I suppose,' I remarked.

'Anyway, dinner time,' said Jack Lane, looking at his watch. 'Come on, let's get down to the sergeants' mess.'

'Righto Jack,' I said, familiarly.

To my shame, Amelia passed out of my thoughts as I enjoyed the benefits of being an NCO. I found Jack Lane easy to get on with and he seemed quite popular with the men, who were a mixed bunch from widely differing backgrounds.

The four medical students were from a medical school in Scotland and obviously very intelligent, and I suspected they were now regretting their patriotic fervour. They looked at me with a mixture of curiosity and faint respect. I could tell that they were waiting for the opportunity to ask me what it was like at the front. They knew that I was not as well educated as they were, and one asked me, almost patronisingly, why I was in a medical unit. I think my answer shook them because after it they always treated me with some deference.

'I was a registered conscientious objector,' I said, curtly.

'And you've got medals,' sneered one of the older men.

'You'll get the chance too, once you've been up to the

236

German wire a few times,' I smiled. 'And I'll see you get the chance. What's your name?'

The man mumbled something and I could see two of the medical students were grinning, but I did not press the point as the man did not make any further remarks – not in my hearing, that is.

I sat on my bed and wrote to Amelia. I had to tell her that I was now with the 56th Field Ambulance Unit, attached to the 14th Field Hospital. It was difficult for me to put into words my thanks for all the happiness that she had given me, but she would understand what I was trying to say to her.

I handed my letter in at the company office, unsealed, and then returned to my billet. My bed, as was custom, was in the corner at the far end of the barrack room.

The men eyed me warily. Giving them orders came easily. It was only in Amelia's company that I remained silent.

'Where do you think we are going, Corp?' asked the ginger-haired lad in the bed next to mine.

'France,' I replied, flopping down on my bed.

'I bloody know that, but where?' he demanded.

'How the hell should I know?' I replied, irritably.

Since there was nothing else to do, I read a book for the next two hours. All our equipment was packed; there was no doubt that we would be off in the morning. I slept poorly and it seemed that I had only just got to sleep when the barrack room lights were switched on. There was no bugle call, as we were close to the hospital.

'Come on, come on,' bawled the duty sergeant, his heavy boots crashing down on the barrack room floor as he strode down the centre aisle between the rows of beds.

I sat on the side of my bed and peered out of the window. It seemed a pleasant morning, even the sun was coming out. Thankfully, as a corporal, I had a separate bowl. I was grateful for that as I leisurely washed and dressed. I had nearly finished when Sergeant Jack Lane appeared and glared around the barrack room.

'I want this place spic and span before any man goes to the mess,' he bawled. 'When I'm satisfied, you line up outside. Corporal Bowman,' he looked over at me.

'Yes, Sergeant?'

'A word with you if you please.' He nodded towards the barrack room door and I grabbed my cap and followed him out.

'George, two of the men tried to desert last night.'

'Did they?' I said, in surprise.

'They did, but the guard stopped them. Did you notice anything?'

I shook my head and breathed heavily. 'The bloody fools,' I snapped.

'That's a fact. Anyway, the Major's decided to give them a month's loss of pay and it will be entered in their records.'

'So if it happens again – the bullet,' I said, quietly.

'Right in one,' nodded Jack Lane. 'We will be moving out at 1100 hours. Lorries will be here at 0900 hours for all our gear. If you notice anything that we should have, let me know straight away, George.'

'Will do, Sarg,' I replied.

'Now go and roust out those lazy bastards, then I'll inspect the barrack room.'

'Righto Sarg,' I said, trotting back into the barrack room.

The men were standing about in groups and it was clear the subject of conversation was the two missing men. They turned to look at me as I entered, as if expecting some news.

'Is it cleaned up in here?' I said, in a loud voice. There was a blank silence, so I spoke again.

238

'Cary and Francis,' said a voice, 'did they get away?' asked the man who had been sarcastic to me the previous day. He leered as if it was a dig at me.

'No, they didn't, and let me make a couple of points clear to you lot, so gather round,' I said, curtly. The men formed a half-circle around me, with little enthusiasm.

'They will get a loss of pay and it will be entered in their records.' My remark caused a number of sarcastic grins to appear and a couple of indifferent shrugs. 'That means that if they try it again on the other side of the water, they will be shot.' I could tell that the men did not believe me and I was getting annoyed. 'Let me make it clear that stories you have heard are true. You will be shot for desertion. Not long ago I was detailed to take two men away who had been shot. It's not an unusual event – it happens every week in France. So those two in the guardhouse ... the next time, will be their last time.

'Now get this place cleared up before Sergeant Lane comes back, or you will miss your breakfast.'

My words seemed to spur them into action and the barrack room became a hive of activity. When Sergeant Lane returned, he found nothing amiss.

The lorries arrived promptly and our equipment, which was stacked in neat piles, was quickly loaded. I had expected that we would be going to the station but the Captain who was in charge said we would travel to Dover by lorry.

'We might break down,' said a voice, hopefully.

I smiled to myself – a little different from last year; some of them could not wait to get there then, now feelings had changed. Half of them would have cleared off if they could have got away with it, and I would have been one of them.

We got away early and it appeared we were part of a

239

long military convoy that seemed to stretch for miles and hardly caused any interest to passing pedestrians. A group of young boys might wave to us and sometimes an occasional woman, who would then put her fingers to her mouth as if remembering a loved one who would not be returning.

The war was no longer popular and the sight of us was an unpleasant reminder of the fact that too many had died already. Thousands more were listed as missing and wounded men could be seen in every town and village.

The sun was shining and the war seemed so far away as the lorry wound its way through the lovely Kent countryside. I felt like jumping over the tailboard and disappearing into one of the little woods we passed from time to time. At least I was spared the singing, which was something I suppose. At midday we stopped near a pub, as it happened. The unfortunate landlord and his wife were almost flattened by the avalanche of men who descended on them. I did not bother. It seemed a little pointless and I sat by the side of the road, chewing on a large issue biscuit that was hard enough to flag our yard.

Our cook had started to boil some water and I was interested in getting my tin mug filled with tea. I noticed Jack Lane emerging from the throng outside the pub. I started to grin. He was holding a pint of beer in each hand. He came towards me, beaming, and held out one of the pints while he drank the other.

'Drop of beer, George?' he said, affably.

'No thanks, Jack. I'm waiting for a brew,' I said, nodding in the direction of our cook.

'Hoped you'd say that, son,' he replied, as he finished the first pint with a flourish.

I grinned; I was beginning to like our Sergeant Lane and I think that the feeling was mutual.

We started to embark at Dover at about 1600 hours. A stiff breeze was blowing up the Channel and the sky was darkening. I could feel spots of rain and it seemed our crossing could be rough. This proved to be the case, and once we left the shelter of the harbour wall, the ship began to roll. One of our first casualties was Sergeant Lane. We had not reached mid-Channel when he had parted company with his two pints of beer and much else besides.

Those men who were not similarly affected thought it a huge joke, particularly the Scottish medical students and our two erstwhile deserters. I tried to help Jack Lane, but there was little I could do, other than put a cold compress on his forehead.

The sky became darker and the weather worsened. I leaned over the rail, almost indifferently. I now wore my oilskin cape and water ran off it in streams.

'Hello Corp,' said a voice in my ear. I turned to see one of the medical students.

'Hello,' I replied. 'It's Duncan, isn't it?'

'No, I'm Graham. Alistair Dunlop is the dark curly-haired one.' He grinned, running a hand through his wet reddish hair, 'Davie Graham,' he said, holding up his wet hand.

I shook it with my equally wet one, though somewhat surprised. 'George Bowman,' I replied.

'Sea doesn't bother you then?' he asked, in an almost accent-free voice, which I associated with the Scottish upper class.

I shook my head and leaned over the rail, then grinned at him. 'The sea doesn't shoot at you Davie,' I replied.

'No,' he said, thoughtfully. 'What's it like, George?' he asked, softly.

I could see that he was worried, yet had the honesty to admit it.

241

'Don't think about it – won't make any difference, believe me, Davie. When the time comes you'll be all right,' I smiled.

'No, I suppose you are right, George,' he said, morosely.

'You'll soon get used to it,' I said, easily.

'Did you?' he frowned.

'Had no choice.' My reply seemed final and seemed to answer him.

We watched the white-crested waves in silence. My thoughts were of Amelia and little Buster, and it reminded me of Buster Millar and Vic who, if he had not got a discharge, would have gone ahead with my old unit, or what was left of it. I thought of Amy and Hector, of Alice, Ruth and little Jimmy. God! When would this war end, I asked myself?

'I'd better have a look at Sergeant Lane,' I said, suddenly.

David Graham, who had been staring at an escort destroyer, turned to me, 'There's nothing you can do, George,' he said.

'I know, but I'd better look at him all the same,' I replied.

'I expect he thinks he's dying,' grinned Davie.

I made my way down to the deck below where I found him. Sergeant Jack Lane was sitting on the deck, his back supported by a wooden crate. Davie Graham's guess was not far short of the mark, for Jack Lane did indeed think he was dying. His plump face had an almost green hue to it and from time to time he clutched at his stomach and tried to vomit. There was no doubt he was ill, and we would be docking within the hour; it was clear to me he was in no condition to give orders.

'How are you, Jack?' I asked, kindly.

'Bloody awful, son,' he groaned.

'We'll be landing soon,' I said, though the deck was still heaving and the air full of spray.

'I don't care if we bloody sink,' came the desperate reply.

'You stay there, Jack. I'll get the men organised for going ashore.'

'Thanks, lad,' he gasped, as he grabbed at his stomach again and began to retch.

I made my way warily across the deck. Davie Graham was talking to one of his chums.

'Davie, have you seen Captain Mason or Lieutenant Ames?' I asked.

'No, George,' he replied.

'Lieutenant Ames was down below a while ago spewing his heart up,' smiled one of the medical students who had just joined us.

'Oh well, I'd better look for the Captain,' I said, grinning.

I found Captain Mason in a bar reserved for officers; he didn't look too good, but he was on his feet. 'Ah! Bowman,' he said, as he spotted me. 'How are the men?'

'Half of them are seasick and Sergeant Lane is quite ill, sir.'

'Lieutenant Ames is *hors de combat* too, so I understand.' The Captain sniffed and downed his glass of whisky. 'Bloody fine start, I must say. Well, you had better get the men organised for going ashore, Corporal.'

'Yes, sir,' I replied, saluting and leaving the Captain to struggle up to the bar again.

With the assistance of Davie and his chums, I managed to get the men together. Since the ship was packed with Army personnel, this was no mean achievement. At least six of the men had to be assisted to walk and this included Sergeant Jack Lane, who seemed the worst of all. Of Lieutenant Ames there was no sign; it transpired he was in the officers' lounge, lying on a sofa.

'Shall we get a stretcher for him, Captain?' asked a voice.

The Captain did not take too kindly to this suggestion. 'No,' he bawled. 'Corporal, go and inform him we are making ready to disembark.'

'Yes, sir,' I replied.

I found Lieutenant Ames after another search, leaning over the rail on the upper deck.

'Sir!' I said, saluting him. 'Captain wants you to fall in.'

'What?' he said, looking at me with a pallid face.

'I mean down below, sir. We are making ready to disembark.'

'Oh!' He gave me a faint smile.

'Feeling better, sir?' I asked.

'A little,' he replied.

'Have any of the men been sick, Corporal?'

'Quite a number, sir. Six have been ill with it, but Sergeant Lane was the worst – he can hardly stand up.'

'Poor bastard,' murmured Lieutenant Ames, as he gingerly left the rail and made his way unsteadily to the stairway.

It was almost nightfall before our lorries and equipment were unloaded. We could hear the sound of gunfire in the distance and it did not exactly spur us to the height of activity. We made camp in a field just outside Calais. After a reasonable meal we slept under our lorries. I lay there looking up at the stars thinking of Amelia. When would I see her again? Would I ever see her again? The thought made me shiver ... would I?

At first light we broke camp and joined a convoy of lorries that appeared to be going north-east. The further we progressed, the louder became the gunfire and the more subdued became the men. Sergeant Jack Lane had now recovered from his seasickness ordeal and was his old self. It was generally agreed that a new offensive was building up and we were in an unending stream of vehicles, horses and carts, lorries, staff cars, artillery teams – there was no end to it and it stretched for miles. If anything broke down it was just pushed off the road by the Provost-Marshal's men who were stationed at regular intervals. We now knew we were going in the direction of Ypres; it caused hasty discussions among the men. I made no comment; what we thought was of no consequence to the powers that be.

It was now 6th June and it had begun to rain. I looked gloomily out of the back of the lorry as it bumped and swayed on the uneven road – each yard taking me further away from Amelia. At last we stopped at a village just outside St Omer. We left our lorries and were given a meal at an Army field kitchen. It was supposed to be a stew and it was burnt – at least mine was, but the bread was fresh, which made up for it. The rain became heavier so we took shelter in a barn.

It was not long before we were ordered to get back into the lorries that had been refuelled and checked. As we moved off our places were immediately taken by others. The gunfire became louder; I had almost forgotten the awful noise. Our progress was slow; the road was a continuous line of traffic. Some miles to the east of Hazebrouck, our lorries stopped and we were told to get out. We had reached our immediate destination, which was the 14th Army Field Hospital, and it was still raining.

It was now late in the afternoon and we were informed that we would be moving up to the front the following morning. We were allocated billets, then given jobs to do as the hospital staff had been on duty two, even three days without sleep. Needless to say, they were pleased to see us.

I got to my bed just after midnight and fell into a deep sleep. It was just after three in the morning when I was awakened by an almighty explosion. The noise was unbelievable; windows were broken by the blast and there was glass everywhere – my bed was covered in it. Yet we were some miles from the front. No gun made such a noise; I could only think that it was an ammunition dump, but whose?

There was no more sleep that night, as we tried to clear up the glass without getting cut to ribbons. We were to find out later that it was the result of our sappers tunnelling under the enemy lines and planting a huge quantity of explosive, and detonating it all at once. It was said that the Prime Minister heard it in his rooms in Downing Street, such was the noise of the explosion. This great mining operation took place at a place called Messines and it involved a small hill about 200 ft high, which ran south of our lines at Ypres. For the past two years it had been held by the Germans and it gave them an unrestricted view of our positions. Though we had tried to take it on a number of occasions and had suffered heavy losses in doing so, it had remained in their hands. Our commander in that sector fortunately realised that sending men uphill without cover was suicide and so decided to use some conscripted miners, who dug over a hundred feet below the ground to plant dynamite and lay charges. The effect was incredible. The previously impregnable enemy defence positions were completely blown away – how many men were sent into oblivion was anyone's guess.

Our infantry – already on alert and ready to move forward – immediately occupied the enemy positions without loss.

My ears were still ringing when we moved up to a front line position early the following morning in preparation for the expected enemy counter-attack. It was still raining and it was supposed to be summer. I had never seen so much mud; men and animals were getting bogged down in it.

246

'It's worse up the front,' said a driver of a horse ambulance whom we had passed a half a mile from our trenches.

Before we could reply, the shells began to fall about us. We immediately ran for cover and the air seemed to be filled with earth and muddy spray. Just as suddenly the shelling stopped. Of the horse ambulance there was no sign, but I knew an enemy attack would soon start as I could hear the rat-a-tat of a Vickers machine gun. Another day of slaughter had begun as other machine guns began to sing. These birds of death haunted the cold dawn air.

We were allocated our positions in the forward trenches, already with six inches of water in them. After a few days it seemed as if I had never been home and Amelia was just a dream. It was during the first week of July that we were relieved and pulled back to a base hospital, and the 29th Field Ambulance took over from us.

We had lost six of our men to shell fire and it was a subdued Davie Graham that tramped by my side as we made our way to a cleansing block, called a bug house by the lads.

All of us had picked up lice, even in that short space of time, and our feet were also in a state from standing in cold water for long periods. The warm shower seemed to come straight down from heaven as I rubbed the carbolic soap into my hair. It was wonderful; I could have stayed there all day.

The most important event for us was the mail distribution. We did not parade like some units – it was quite informal. There were few of us and our unit was an easygoing affair, which was something to be grateful for, I suppose. It was Lieutenant Ames who handed out the mail and we stepped forward when our names were called, as we stood in a circle around him waiting expectantly.

He began by giving some letters to Sergeant Lane standing by his side, who immediately stuffed them into his tunic pocket.

'Send these back, Sergeant,' he said curtly.

We knew whose letters they were; the six men who had been killed.

'Anthony,' he began.

'Thank you, sir,' said Jimmy Anthony taking his mail.

'Corporal Bowman.'

'Thank you, sir,' I said, gratefully taking my letters.

'That was nice work yesterday, George, bringing back that officer from the Hun wire. His unit has thanked the CO.'

'Sir,' I mumbled, stepping back among the other men.

'Carstairs.'

'Oh, thank you, sir,' said Claude Carstairs in his posh accent.

So the distribution went on until all the letters had been distributed, but not before a humorous exchange.

'I say, chaps, what do you think?'

'You've put the vicar's missus up the stick,' said a cockney voice.

'Really, how disgusting you are, Chivers,' said Carstairs to further laughter.

'No, it's...' began Carstairs.

'You've put the vicar up the stick,' cut in Chivers.

'It's from the publisher of my encyclopaedias. I've made the first payment, now they want to know where to deliver them.'

'Ave 'em sent 'ere, mate,' said Chivers.

'You could stand on 'em in the trenches and keep yer feet dry.'

Carstairs' reply was inaudible due to laughter – even Lieutenant Ames was chuckling as he left us.

Once all the mail was given out, the men dispersed to

what little privacy there was to read their letters. I had three letters from Amelia and one from Amy and I crouched down behind some packing cases to open them.

For the next half hour I read them again and again; nothing else seemed to matter. I was with Amelia. From one of her letters, I gathered Edwin was in the same area as myself, but our chances of meeting were small.

There was a constant stream of men and equipment moving up, surely there would be a big offensive soon? After the success at Messines, it was inevitable.

We had returned to our front line positions less than a week, when a massive barrage started. Our gunfire seemed to blot everything out for me. It was on the second day that I lost my hearing completely. The third battle of Ypres began on 31st July; or as it was more commonly called, the Battle of Passchendaele.

From the beginning our casualties were appalling and what made it even worse was the mud – almost waist deep in places. Getting men back from no man's land was, at times, almost impossible. Sometimes wounded men just drowned in the sea of mud.

The rain fell incessantly and the mud became worse. I watched the new tanks being sent forward just slide into a shell hole, then to disappear in the mud at the bottom. One just sank into the mud until only the top of its side turret was showing. Fields were just seas of mud and still it rained. On the sixth day of the battle I was struggling back to our lines with a wounded man over my shoulder when I was hit by a shell splinter. Strangely, I did not feel a great deal of pain, but it sent me forward on my face; fortunately on a hard piece of ground.

Davie Graham and his pal, Angus Muir, saw me fall and immediately came to my assistance. I tried to rise, but my left side was numb. Davie spoke to me, but I could not hear him. They put the wounded man on their stretcher and I staggered after them to our lines.

In our forward trench I tried to ascertain my wound. At least I could walk, I told myself, but it seemed as if a large knife had gone right through my greatcoat and battledress on my left side under my arm. I was bleeding profusely and one of my unit helped me to a dressing station. Quickly I was examined, my uniform removed and the wound dressed.

'Only a flesh wound, mate,' said an orderly. I was learning to lip-read, as my hearing had not yet returned.

I was sent back to the Field Hospital and given a new tunic and greatcoat then given light duties to do. I did not mind this as I was dry and out of the mud.

Every minute of the day and night men were brought in. It was an endless procession of blood-stained khaki, mud and blood. When would it ever end?

Lieutenant Ames came to see me. He looked at my wound, had it re-dressed and sent me to a rear rest camp.

'You cannot lift a stretcher with that, Corporal,' he said.

I was grateful to him; a week later he was killed. What a sad waste of a fine officer and gentleman. The rest camp was a hotchpotch of wooden buildings at the edge of a village. It was crowded with men of every nationality and the village now seemed to be one large café.

I was allocated a bed in a hut for walking wounded. I kept hoping that I would be sent home, but there seemed no chance of that. The only men going back were dead ones, and there was a constant flow of them.

My left arm was in a sling, but I was able to get about and the duties I was given caused me no discomfort. I wrote to Amelia but did not tell her that I was wounded as I did not wish to worry her. I said I was at a rest camp. I also wrote to Hector and reminded him of his promise, and thanked him for his prayers, which I knew would meet with his approval.

Being almost completely deaf now had its compensations (though my ears bled at times and were always aching), in that I could hardly hear the guns at night and there were heavy batteries less than a half a mile away, so I was told. But now my ears had stopped bleeding and when my chest did not give me pain, I slept well, so I was fortunate.

One evening, I left my billet to go to the village for a drink. I had just heard that I had been awarded a bar to my Military Medal and decided to have some cheap red wine to celebrate. The village was crowded and each house seemed to have tables and chairs outside to cater for our men. I could see Australians, Highlanders in their kilts, gunners, infantry men of many regiments, even spurred cavalrymen. Suddenly I saw a bunch of officers around a table that was strewn with bottles and glasses – then I saw Edwin, I was sure of it. I pushed my way towards him – it was!

'Edwin,' I shouted. He did not react to my call – was it him?

'Edwin.' He turned and put down his glass.

'George,' he grinned, leaping out of his chair, his arms about me. 'It's good to see you, old chap.' There were tears in Edwin's eyes and I felt moved by his welcome.

'It's good to see you too, Edwin,' I sniffed.

'What's happened to your arm?' said Edwin.

'A shell splinter,' I replied.

'This is my brother-in-law, chaps,' said Edwin, introducing me to his brother officers, 'Corporal George Bowman, DCM and MM,' added Edwin, with pride.

'And bar,' I added.

'A bar, George?' enthused Edwin.

'Yes, a bar to my MM,' I grinned.

251

'Congrats, old chap,' beamed Edwin, shaking my hand. 'When did you hear?'

'Today.' I tried to appear nonchalant.

'Bravo, old fellow,' said the officer to my left. He stood up and began shaking my hand like mad. He was followed by the others and I was quickly found a chair and given a glass of wine. Edwin looked much older. His boyish manner had gone and his face was drawn; lines had appeared and he seemed ten years older.

I gathered, by the comparatively good state of their uniforms, that Edwin's unit was moving into the line, but I thought it wise not to ask.

'What are you doing here, George?' asked Edwin.

'I'm on light duties at the field hospital up the road – slop bucket detail for the surgeons as a matter-of-fact. I can use my right arm, you know.'

I could see Edwin and his friends exchange glances. I did not need to enlarge on my duties.

'More wine, George?' said a Captain near me.

'Just a little, thank you, sir.'

'Have you heard from Amelia lately, George?' asked Edwin.

'What's that, Edwin? I can hardly hear now, so would you speak slowly and let me see your lips move.'

Edwin looked at me and spoke again. 'Really, old chap?' He looked concerned.

'Hardly a bloody thing now. I can sleep through a barrage, too. I sleep like a top; it's only if I get blown out of bed that I wake up.' I could see that Edwin's companions were trying not to laugh.

A faint smile had appeared on Edwin's face as he said again, 'Have you heard from Amelia, lately?' He spoke slowly and emphasised his words and I understood him. I nodded and took a letter from my tunic pocket and handed it to him. He shook his head and would not take it.

252

'I don't wish to read it,' he said, abruptly.

'You read it,' I said, putting it on the table in front of him.

'Are you sure, George?' he frowned.

'Yes, it's your sister,' I said, easily.

'I know that but...' he paused.

'Go on – tell me what she means?'

Edwin looked curious, then picked up the letter and opened it. As he read it a smile began to appear on his face. He turned to me and grabbed my hand again.

'It means, old chap, that she thinks she might be expecting and she is going to see her doctor about it,' grinned Edwin.

'I thought it might be that, but she only said that she was going to ask her doctor to confirm something she suspected,' I muttered.

'She cannot make it any clearer, can she, old chap?' smiled Edwin.

'More wine, *garçon*,' shouted one of the officers.

At that point I gathered that a shell fell nearby as three of them suddenly dived off their chairs; even Edwin crouched down, his hands on his head.

I was drinking my glass of wine. I had not heard a thing; the others looked at me in amazement. Edwin shook his head, then grinned. 'George, does nothing bother you, old fellow?'

'I told you, Edwin, I can't hear a bloody thing,' I replied.

One of the officers refilled my glass, then raised his own.

'To Amelia,' he said, looking round the table.

'Amelia, Amelia, Amelia,' they chorused.

I was beaming, but I think Edwin was a little embarrassed. I was as happy as a dog with two tails.

'How long were you in the line, George?' asked one of Edwin's companions.

I held up my right hand and spread my fingers. 'Five weeks, sir. I've been here nearly three. Are you going in the line?' I asked.

Edwin nodded, then shrugged his shoulders and smiled weakly. 'We've been in the reserve for six weeks; now it's our turn again.'

'You watch those puddles, then. Go in some of them and you will go straight down. I mean it. I saw a tank go in one and the water covered it; in the shell holes – you won't get out.'

They looked at me in disbelief and one started to laugh.

'All right, sir, if you don't believe me, ask those Highlanders. They have just come out of the line. Edwin, keep close to any tree stumps and out of the shell holes.' The wine had made me talkative, but I could see that Edwin's brother officers were listening to me and I knew Edwin would take my advice.

An RSM came to the table, saluted, then informed the senior officer that the men were ready to move. They all stood up and Edwin clasped my hand.

'Goodbye, George. Take care of yourself, old son,' he said.

'Bye, Edwin. Keep your head down. Remember what I said and watch the blackcurrant jam as well,' I grinned.

For a moment Edwin frowned, then he burst out laughing. 'I'll remember, old son,' he chuckled.

The other officers all nodded to me as I stood to attention and saluted.

'Goodbye, Corporal Bowman,' said the senior officer, briefly returning my salute, 'and good luck to you.'

'Goodbye, sir, and good luck to you,' I replied.

Edwin waved briefly then disappeared in a throng of men. I watched them go, then picked up a half-full bottle of wine, pushed a cork into it and slipped it into my greatcoat pocket. I walked slowly back to my billet, elated with Amelia's news. I sat on my bed and wrote to her again, though I did not mention Edwin was going into the line, only that I had seen him and he was well and I was at a rest camp.

I lay back on my bed. I was in my own silent world. The pain in my side seemed a little less and the wine made me feel better. I thought of Amelia and Amy, and of course, Buster. My thoughts turned again to the mud – I was now dreaming of it. The thought of drowning in that stinking mud was a nightmare to me. When I go, I pray it's quick and I know nothing. I think we all pray for that. I drifted off to sleep until I was awakened by a hand shaking me.

'Come on, George, you are on duty.'

Though I could not hear, I was now able to lip-read quite well.

The battle, if you could call it that, went on all through July. No ground of any consequence was taken, but our men died in their thousands; it was a nightmare that would not end. August began and still the battle continued relentlessly – more casualties – a never-ending cycle.

I had heard nothing of Edwin. His regiment, the Royal Fusiliers, had many battalions; his, I think, was the tenth, and it seemed impossible to get any news of him.

13

Good News from Amelia

During the second week of August I received a letter from Amelia. I sat on my bed reading it. Though I was unable to hear a thing, I could almost see Amelia talking to me as I read it.

'I must leave the Town Hall library soon, dear, and I am looking forward to the baby's arrival. I would like a little boy, but really, I'll be happy if it's a little girl; sounds a bit silly doesn't it, George? I am busy knitting and Amy is helping me, so is Agnes. She sends her love to you, dear.

'Amy is so kind to me, just like the sister that I would have liked to have had. Hector has not been well; he had a fall. His eyes are not good, you know, I think that if he had joined the Army he would have been something of a liability with a rifle!'

I smiled at Amelia's dry sense of humour, but there was no doubt that she was right in her judgment.

Buster, the dog, it seemed, was a good companion and Amelia felt safe with him, which was a relief to me. My own problems seemed to be my only concern at times, but things were not easy for her. It seemed that her relations with her parents were cool and she did not see them at all these days.

'Agnes and I go regularly to hear Hector preach. At times he is very good, but he does tend to ramble.'

I smiled at her choice of words. Amelia was being polite – I found Hector boring, even though I liked him. Amelia said little about what happened at home. She knew all too well that all letters were censored, particularly in my case, being a registered conscientious objector. It was clear to me what people wanted, from my last leave alone. Gone was all the euphoria for the war. Every family in the land now had a relative who had died or who had been badly wounded, yet there was still no prospect of it ending.

I put Amelia's letter carefully away, to read again when I felt down – which would not be too many hours away – and went back on duty, having first had my dressings changed. There was a continual stream of ambulances going to the hospital trains that were some miles to our rear, and another column of men moving in the opposite direction up to the front line. My side was beginning to heal, I could feel it start to itch, which was a good sign, but my chest was still hurting; when I coughed, the gas seemed to have permanently affected my lungs. This I put down to all the wet weather we were having; it seemed to make it worse.

What it was like now up at the front did not bear thinking about. I tried not to think about it but I could not stop my dreams and they would haunt me – the dead faces, the smell of rotting flesh and the screams of agony.

I knew I would not be sent home with my wound. I was still on slop bucket detail and I would stay on it until I could lift a stretcher again. I was getting four hours sleep at night and there was no off-duty period. Even so, I counted myself fortunate to be in the dry and getting a hot meal each day. This could go on until the end of the war, as far as I was concerned.

During the first week in October, we had a visit from

the General Staff. They all had neat uniforms, smart collars and clean knee-length leather boots. I wandered past a group a number of times, carrying my bucket, when one officer beckoned me to him. With one arm in a sling I could not salute him and before I could put the bucket down to do so, he nonchalantly flicked off the lid with his swagger stick and peered into the bucket.

'What are you wandering about with that bucket for, Corporal, eh?'

Inside the bucket were the remains of two arms and two feet cut off just above the ankle. He jumped back in alarm when he saw them and his face now had a look of horror and disgust on it.

'I am the surgeon's slop bucket orderly, sir. It's light duties.'

'Urgh ... be orf with you – how revolting,' he muttered.

I put down the bucket and replaced the lid that he had removed, and having saluted, I left them. They watched me go in the direction of the deep hole that had been dug to receive the contents of the bucket. It was an awful job, but I was now immune to it. Someone had to do it and I did not give it a thought.

Our attack continued. Fresh regiments were thrown in. It still rained. How many died or just disappeared was anyone's guess. There were so many wounded at times we just could not cope. By the first week in November I think it dawned, at last, on Army headquarters that nothing was being achieved. Our gains could be measured in yards and our casualties in thousands.

Our last attacks took place during the second week in November. Again nothing was accomplished but the death of more brave men. The front then lapsed into a period of inactivity. It had turned colder; there were frosts and conditions became worse, if that was possible, in the trenches.

I returned to the 56th Field Ambulance – or what was left of it. Lieutenant Ames was dead; Captain Mason was hobbling about with the aid of a stick; he had been wounded and was awaiting a replacement. Davie Graham had been made a corporal and his chum Angus Muir a lance-corporal. The other medical students had been carrying a wounded man on their stretcher when a shell struck them and no trace of any of them was ever found.

The two men who had tried to leave camp in London had been killed accidentally by our own men, so Sergeant Lane told me – what a twist of fate. Almost half the unit was dead.

Sergeant Jack Lane was now almost slim, though he looked twenty years older, but there was no doubting his friendly welcome.

'Good ter see yer, son,' he said, shaking my hand. 'OK now?'

'Wouldn't say that,' I replied. 'I'm as deaf as a post – can't understand a word unless you speak slowly and look at me; my chest is bloody awful. I'll never lift a stretcher,' I wheezed.

'Ah well, never mind, mate, we'll find yer something ter do.'

'Have you been out of the line, Jack?'

'Aye, twice since you left,' he sighed, his face twitching. 'And we've 'ad two lots of replacements as well.'

I nodded, sympathetically. There was little I could say – what unit wasn't down to half its strength?

It became colder and keeping warm became a number one priority. I think it would have been impossible to have made the men advance through the semi-frozen mud and even the guns were silent, so I was told.

The final attack of the so-called offensive took place on 7th November in thick fog, resulting in the Canadians

259

capturing the village of Passchendaele. What good that was I will never know. There was nothing left but piles of rubble and stumps of trees and how many men had given their lives for that? It must have been thousands upon thousands. While our sector of the front tried to keep warm, 45 miles further south, a new attack had begun on 20th November.

The tanks in our sector had been a disaster; they just sank in the mud, but at Cambrai, where the new attack was mounted, the ground was rock hard with the frosts. Three hundred and eighty tanks swept through the enemy lines to a depth of five miles on a four-mile front. This was hailed as a victory and the church bells rang at home to tell everyone the fact. However, since our infantry could not keep up with the tanks, little was achieved. The enemy was able to recover and the initial advantage was lost. Within ten days all the ground taken from the enemy had been regained by them and the line was much as before.

An army enquiry was later held to find out what went wrong, and the poor blighters in the front line got the blame as usual.

It was December and the front was quiet. Sometimes a patrol was sent out on our sector, but that was all. I had told the medical officer about my ears, but he dismissed it, saying my hearing would return in time. I had been told that before and in all honesty it had done, but this time I was worried; there was no sign of it getting better.

It was about 10th December when I had a letter from Amelia. She made little mention of how she was, but she was most concerned about Edwin. It appeared he had been wounded and was in a hospital just outside St Omer and could I possibly see him? There seemed little prospect of my going home for Christmas, so I immediately wrote back to Amelia, saying I would try to visit him when I was next at a rest camp.

Thanks to Captain Mason pulling some strings for me, two weeks later, on Christmas Eve, I was in the back of a lorry bumping along a road to St Omer.

I was a little apprehensive – after all, Edwin was in a ward for officers and I was unsure how I would be received.

Though the ward sister looked something of a dragon, she seemed reasonable enough to me.

'You are Lieutenant Hooper's brother-in-law, Corporal?'

I could not hear her and she began to speak again.

'Sister, I can't hear you; I cannot hear a word,' I said.

The sister was an experienced nurse. She nodded briefly then ushered me down a ward and pointed to a bed, the occupant of which was lying on his back.

'Lieutenant Hooper,' she said, slowly, and moving her lips to emphasise her words.

'Thank you, Sister,' I said, grateful that my journey was not a waste of time.

The occupant of the bed turned his head towards me and spoke: 'George, George, my old son,' smiled Edwin.

'Hello, Edwin,' I grinned, stepping forward and taking his hand.

'Good to see you, old chap,' said Edwin, clearly pleased to see me.

He looked ill and I could tell that he was in pain. From the shape of the blankets on his bed, it appeared that he had not lost a limb, so I assumed it was his back.

'I'm unable to move, George,' he began.

'I can't hear you, Edwin. I'm as deaf as a post, please speak slowly,' I said in a louder than normal speaking voice.

'Sorry, George,' replied Edwin, sympathetically. 'I said I cannot move,' Edwin spoke slowly.

'Not at all?' I frowned.

'No,' said Edwin, shaking his head.

'Maybe movement will come back – like my hearing?' I suggested.

Edwin shook his head again and I could see tears in his eyes.

'I shall be lucky to be in a wheelchair,' he choked.

'You'll get better,' I said, confidently. 'At least you'll go home now. I wish I could go – Amelia's going to have a baby as you know.'

Edwin smiled and grabbed my hand again with enthusiasm.

'Congratulations, George.'

'Thank you,' I beamed.

'It's great news.' Edwin seemed genuinely pleased and I was glad. 'I knew already, of course – you let me read Amelia's letter to you, but it's wonderful news and I really mean that.'

'Thanks, Edwin,' I said, happily.

'When did you come out of the line, George?'

'Yesterday afternoon.'

'What's it been like, recently?'

'Quiet. Most of my time is spent with the burial squad. God, what an awful job!' I said with some feeling.

'I'm sure,' murmured Edwin.

I slowly shook my head as I thought about it. Edwin looked away almost in embarrassment.

'You've no idea how many men have died,' I muttered.

Edwin held my hand and squeezed it, then suddenly released it.

'I know, George, believe me, I know,' he said, huskily.

We lapsed into silence as if in respect to all those killed in the third battle of Ypres.

'Ask Sister for a chair, George, and take your greatcoat off, it's warm in here.'

'Yes, I will, it is a bit,' I replied.

For the next half hour we talked. Edwin made it clear that as soon as there was a place for him on a hospital train, he would be going home.

'You might go home to get your medal,' suggested Edwin.

'Stuff the medal,' I retorted, my voice rising. 'I want to see Amelia and Amy and Buster.'

Edwin turned to the patient in the next bed who appeared to be laughing, but since I could not hear and his face was covered in bandages, I could not be sure.

'Who is Buster?' grinned Edwin.

'It's our bull terrier – he's smashing but he piddles everywhere. Amelia's not very happy about that, I can tell you.'

Edwin was now laughing for the first time.

'Why do you call him Buster, George?' asked Edwin.

'Well, he looked like Buster Millar, in my old unit, the 23rd Field Ambulance, but he's dead now – got hit by a shell, someone said. They saw one of his stretcher poles disappearing in the direction of the French sector, but we didn't find anything of Buster. Still, I named our puppy after him; well Amelia did really.'

'I'm sure he would have been pleased about that,' said Edwin, turning to wink at the man in the next bed, who seemed to be laughing again.

'Anything else happen of interest up the line, George?' grinned Edwin expectantly.

'We had a visit from a Staff General, but he didn't stay long.'

'Why was that?' queried Edwin.

'He fell in a hole,' I replied.

Edwin was smiling; he turned to the officer in the next bed, said a few words and then spoke to me. 'Tell us what happened, George,' he chuckled.

'A staff car pulled up outside my billet and this General with red tabs got out. He came towards our billets and there was a large hole, which looked like a puddle. I was saluting him as he stepped into it – he went in up to his waist.'

Edwin was now laughing, banging his right hand on his bed as he did so. 'Marvellous,' he chortled. 'Why didn't you warn him?' he said at last.

'I was saluting, wasn't I? I couldn't speak to him.'

Edwin and the officer in the next bed laughed even more.

'I gave him a hand to get out of the hole, then I said there were deeper holes further up the line and that he had been lucky. Then he swore at me and squelched back to his car and drove away.

I could see tears running down Edwin's face. 'Wasn't very grateful, was he, Edwin?'

'No,' gurgled Edwin.

At this point the sister came striding down the ward. I could not hear her speak, but from her looks and the movements of her mouth I gathered that she thought I was causing a disturbance and was about to tell me to go. However, she relented when Edwin told her I was better than any medicine and he was supported in this by the Major next to him.

'Very well, Corporal, you may stay a little longer,' she nodded.

'What's that, Sister, I can't hear you?'

'I said...' she began to mouth the words and I could understand her without any problem.

'Any chance of any dinner, Sister?' I asked.

'What?' She seemed suddenly lost for words.

'I won't get any dinner otherwise. I've got to get the lorry back soon,' I explained. This, however, was lost on the sister.

'Where do you think you are, Corporal, at the Ritz?' she snapped.

'One could be forgiven for thinking that,' grinned Edwin.

'I'll say,' said the Major, sarcastically.

'Another fifteen minutes, Corporal, then you must go,' said the sister, who then turned and swept off down the ward.

'There's a canteen here, I think, George,' said Edwin. 'Have you got any money?'

'Yes. I've got a shilling,' I replied.

'Is that all? Have you been in the café, George?'

'No, I haven't,' I replied. 'I only take sixpence a week of my pay; the rest goes to Amelia. She'll need it when she has to leave the library to have the baby, you know.'

'Er, yes, of course, George.' Edwin seemed a little chastened. 'By the way, Amelia offered me accommodation at your house,' he added, somewhat subdued.

'I did not get all that, Edwin, look at me,' I replied.

With some difficulty Edwin explained what he was trying to say and at last I understood him.

'Yes? I know!' I grinned. 'I hope you come.'

'Do you mean that, George?' Edwin, his head on one side, looked at me, curiously.

'Of course I do,' I said, quickly.

'Do you realise, George, I might never walk again?' There was a choke in Edwin's voice and he quickly turned his head away.

'I'm sure you will, it's early days yet,' I replied.

'That's what I've been trying to tell him,' said the Major.

'What if I don't?' Edwin turned to face me again, his face twisted in anguish.

'Amelia said she would always have a home for you,

Edwin,' I said in a low voice. 'I agreed with her and there were no conditions – honest.'

'I believe you, George, you could not tell a lie if you tried,' said Edwin, a choke in his voice.

'I'll help you, Edwin, you know that,' I said, softly.

He gripped my hand, close to tears, and we sat in silence for a short while. Neither of us mentioned Christmas; it was far from our thoughts, so as I said goodbye to Edwin, I did not mention it.

'Take care, George, old son,' said Edwin, clasping my hand in both of his. There were tears in his eyes and I was a little moved.

'Bye Edwin; give my love to Amelia,' I said, turning quickly and marching off down the ward. I managed to get a bully beef sandwich at a mobile canteen and then I found a lorry going back to the front.

By late afternoon, I was in my rest camp billet at a table, writing to Amelia, or to be strictly correct, trying to think what to write to her. What could I say about Edwin? Should I tell her of his injury. I did not want to worry her, in view of her condition. It was a problem. In the end I decided to be vague. I would just tell her that we had a talk and that he would be home soon. What more could I say?

On Christmas Eve we were asked to help at a nearby military hospital, even though we were supposed to be resting. Some of the nursing staff had been taken ill and they were desperately short-handed. I did not mind as I had nothing else to do, though some of the lads who had found a local hostelry that had plenty of wine and willing girls, were none too happy at having to work.

We quietly celebrated the New Year, each of us wondering what it would bring. Would the war ever end, we asked ourselves?

14

The Somme Again

On 14th January we were sent back to the line – not as we anticipated, but south in the direction of Amiens, almost into the French sector. We were back on the Somme and it was worse than ever.

I remember the mud was everywhere, almost as bad as Ypres, and the smell – it was now awful enough to make some of our men sick.

The sector was quiet but for the occasional patrol clash. I gained the impression from gossip that an enemy attack was expected and in consequence there were extra machine gun posts in our forward trenches.

It was a bitterly cold night in January when I had my first involvement with the French. Our trenches virtually joined the beginning of theirs and I was on duty with Davie Graham, Angus Muir, Jackie Hastings and Charlie Bolt. A French patrol had gone out and run slap into a German one. There had been numerous bursts of firing and what was left of the French patrol almost fell into my trench. Almost immediately two French officers came hurrying towards us and after talking to them in an animated manner, started shouting at them and waving their arms about. Davie Graham, who could understand French, told me that they had left their wounded Captain out in no man's land and now refused to get him.

Discipline and morale were low in this French unit and the officer of the unit to which we were attached spoke to me.

'I can't hear a thing, sir,' I said, before he got going, at which he turned to Davie.

'Will you lads try to get him back. As bearers, you stand a better chance, you know. It's not an order, mind, but we don't want to see a mutiny along the line.'

The French looked uncomfortable and the two officers, who I am sure could understand English, seemed somewhat embarrassed.

Since we did not seem to have much choice in the matter, Davie and I put on our white helmets and gingerly climbed out of the trench clutching the stretcher poles.

'We'll look for a wounded Hun, Davie,' I said, when we were clear of our trenches.

'Aye, George,' he nodded. 'The "Froggies" said they were on the far side of no man's land.'

Davie grabbed my arm and pointed. By the light of the moon I could see a German stretcher party. We moved towards them; they were about to run, but saw our white helmets and white armbands and continued to put a man on their stretcher. Their greeting was friendly enough as we joined them. Two French officers lay near them. I bent over them to find that only one was alive and in spite of his pain, he tried to smile. To me it seemed ghostly quiet. I was sure the Germans were watching me, but nothing happened.

We laid the man on our stretcher and made our way back. It was bad enough during the day, but at night it was far worse. At times clouds obscured the moon and it was pitch black. We stumbled and staggered to our wire, just as flashes lit the horizon. The guns had started; I did not hear them, but Davie gave me a good indication by beginning to trot.

The French officers greeted us like two long lost brothers, after we had lowered the man into the trench. They insisted on giving us cognac and asked for our names and numbers. It appeared we had brought back a Captain – the patrol commander. Davie explained that the other man was dead.

The two French officers thanked us again, then with a wave, disappeared along their own trench with the wounded Captain.

The trenches affected every man in one way or another, but in the case of Sergeant Jack Lane it was all too obvious. I know I was deaf, but he was even worse. His hands were continually shaking and he looked as if he was at least seventy. But for the fact we were so short of men, he would have been sent back, so Davie explained to me. Davie seemed to speak to Captain Mason a great deal and I am sure it was because they were both educated.

'You should be sent home, too, George,' said Davie one day as we sat on a box eating our breakfast.

'What's that, Davie, speak slower.'

'I agree about that,' I said, when I understood what he had said. 'Amelia will be having the baby in April and that's only two months away. I'd like to get home for that, I really would,' I murmured.

'You never know your luck,' smiled Davie.

The days seemed to pass quickly. I measured the time by the changes of underwear and baths I had and they were none too frequent. Everything and everyone seemed to smell. They said that you would get used to it, but I never did, the stench haunted me.

It was now the second week in February and it was cold and wet. We had a bit of news yesterday. Davie and I had been awarded a war medal by the French for bringing back their wounded Captain. The lads pulled

269

our legs about it and Jackie Hastings remarked, 'A French General will kiss yer when he gives it yer.'

'I won't mind if it's in Paris,' replied Davie, grinning at him.

Though the front was quiet there was no leave for anyone for any reason, and rumour had it that a big German attack was about to take place. Our forward trenches had been reinforced in anticipation of it and more patrols were being sent out. Davie explained to me that they were trying to find out what divisions had been brought from the Russian front, which, now that Russia had been knocked out of the war, no longer existed.

Overhead we watched aeroplanes having aerial fights, sometimes they would swoop low over us, at times even firing at both ours and the enemy positions. The German attack and subsequent offensive began on 23rd March, but before that happened certain events were to take place that would change my life.

It was 15th March – I remember it so clearly. The day began badly for us and it seemed to fill me with apprehension. A patrol of the Rifle Brigade had gone out and it seemed that they had run into trouble. What was left of the patrol almost fell into our trench. Jackie Hastings and Charlie Bolt had gone out to bring in the wounded, when they were mown down. It sickened us as we thought the Huns respected stretcher bearers and it made us even more apprehensive about the future.

At midday I received a letter from Amelia and I found a corner in which to read it – much like a dog with a bone. Having read it six times I put it in my breast pocket, just as I saw Davie Graham and Angus Muir going over the top with their stretcher.

A few minutes later a barrage started, though I could not hear it, and what was left of another of our patrols almost fell on top of me. I expected Davie and Angus

270

to follow them, but there was no sign of them. Perhaps they were in a shell hole, I thought.

The time passed. It was past four-thirty and the light was beginning to fade. Someone had to go and look for them. When Captain Mason came hobbling down the trench towards me I knew what he was about to say. By pronouncing his words slowly I understood him; he seemed apologetic and said he would try and get me some leave. I nodded and thanked him and walked towards the parapet. I picked up a stretcher pole. The lad going with me was called Jimmy Langley, newcomer to our unit. He picked up the other end of the stretcher and followed me up the ladder, just as I had climbed out of our trench.

I must admit that I had never felt so apprchensive. It was as if I had a premonition of what was to happen. We made our way forward, crouching as we did so. There were plenty of dead men lying about, but there was no sign of Davie and Angus.

The shelling appeared to have stopped and we were well into no man's land. The smell of rotting corpses was enough to make you retch. Jimmy Langley grabbed my arm and pointed. Sure enough it was Davie. We hurried towards him; he must have seen us as he tried to wave to us. At this point Jimmy Langley was sick; it was understandable, as it was his first time out. I waited until he had finished. We crouched down to keep our heads below the top of the ridge in front of us. Strewn about were the bodies of our infantrymen; some in grotesque positions, others as if asleep. Among them I noticed Angus Muir – or what was left of him. Davie Graham was lying on his side, he had been shot in the thigh. He had managed to tie on a tourniquet, which had probably saved his life, though he was fortunate that we had found him in time. Without a word, we quickly

271

put him on our stretcher and made our way back to our forward trench as fast as we could.

I was at the front of the stretcher and did not notice Jimmy Langley fall. I felt the stretcher go and turned as Davie fell on the ground. My quick examination of Jimmy told me he was dead – what sort of bastard would do that? I asked myself angrily. I grabbed the writhing Davie Graham and swung him over my right shoulder and began to trot. Fortunately he was a lightweight and my anger spurred me on. There were flashes in the sky and dirt fell on me from a shell, which must have landed close by. I then felt a terrible pain in my face and left arm and seemed to be propelled through the air, though I still seemed to be running. How I got past the wire and into our trench, I'll never know. I saw a look of amazement on Captain Mason's face, then everything went black.

I regained consciousness about a week later in an Army hospital outside Amiens. I lay, unable to collect my thoughts, due to the terrible pain in my head, which was heavily bandaged. I could see out of my right eye, but there was a searing pain in my left eye which was covered by the bandage.

A nurse appeared by my bed. She spoke and smiled at me then put her hand on my right wrist. I tried to speak but felt myself slipping into a merciful sleep. When I awoke again it was dark and it was the warm fingers of the nurse, again feeling my pulse, that caused me to open my eye. I still had a terrible pain in my head, though it seemed a little better. The nurse spoke. I could not hear her but from the movement of her lips I think she was asking me if I wanted a drink. I tried to move my head, but it hurt me to do so. The nurse understood – my lips were cracked and there was a vile taste in my mouth. She held the spout of a feeding bowl to my mouth. Never had water tasted so good. Why was this? The thought went through my mind as I sucked at the spout.

I felt tired again and drifted into a sleep. When I awoke it was daylight and I was aware of activity going on around me. I was now able to form some idea of my condition. There was also a bandage around my left arm and shoulder, but where was my left arm? I was seized with panic. No! It couldn't be. I tried to feel with my right hand; my mouth moved but I could hear nothing. It was all a nightmare!

The nurse appeared, then another. They spoke but I could not understand. But at last I learned the awful truth. My left arm had gone from above the elbow. I moved my right foot, then my left. I had them both, thank God, but the pain in my left eye made me feel sick. Strangely, I felt relieved and I think I spoke to the nurse.

'I can't lift a stretcher any more.'

'You will go home, Corporal,' she smiled.

In spite of the pain, I felt good, but so weak. A lady volunteer orderly came with a feeding bowl of warm soup. She held the spout to my mouth and I gratefully sucked at it. The lady was French and very patient with me. She spoke slowly, but I could not understand her. I touched my right ear with my forefinger then moved my fingers. She immediately understood. 'Mon pauvre ami,' she bent forward and moved her lips slowly. I could now understand her. When she left me she informed the sister of my hearing condition and it made communication easier as the sister later came to me and mouthed the words she was saying to me.

That evening I had my first solid food and it made me feel a lot better, and I was even given something for the pain in my eye. It was two days later that I discovered

273

I had lost my left eye. It was all so matter-of-fact – as if I had lost one of my boots. The sister removed my bandages and I almost screamed with pain as she took them off. When they at last came away and I still could not see, I said simply: 'My eye, Sister?'

'It's gone, Corporal,' she mouthed – just like that, nothing more.

A doctor examined me, nodded, then my bandages were replaced.

I lay back in bed in a kind of exhaustion. It had been more of a shock than finding out about my arm.

The following day I was told that I would be sent home on the first available transport. This news pulled me out of my lethargy and my first feeling of elation was mingled with thoughts of how Amelia would react to my condition.

I had forgotten about the front, of Davie Graham and the unit, but what brought them to mind was the fact that the expected German offensive began at dawn on 23rd March, this time without the usual heavy artillery barrage.

Making their advance through thick early morning fog, the enemy infantry had overrun our forward line before our men had got their eyes open. With our forward machine gun posts wiped out, the German infantry advanced through our second defence line. Soon the whole sector line was crumbling or in retreat.

I, of course, learned all this much later, but in that early offensive, the 56th Ambulance ceased to be. Captain Mason and Lieutenant Ames's replacement, a Lieutenant Black, were both killed, as was Sergeant Jack Lane and the rest of the lads. Only Davie Graham survived of the whole unit and he was in another ward of the same hospital as I was in.

Since the British reserve units were too far north,

some French divisions were thrown into the battle to give us support, and this seemed to stabilise the situation.

In order to provide beds for the expected influx of wounded, we were immediately moved out. We were put aboard a hospital train at Amiens on 29th March, the same day that Amelia was brought to bed for the birth of our son, Edward.

I do not remember much of the journey home. I had picked up some kind of fever and I had spells of unconsciousness, which was a relief from the constant pain in my head. After a period of about two weeks, much of which was a blur, I was transferred to the hospital at Woolwich, so I had now completed a full circle.

The first person I saw at Woolwich was Sister Greening, who I had known quite well when I had been on the intake wards before going back to France. In spite of my bandages, she recognised me.

'Hello, George,' she smiled, as I was carried into B Ward.

'Hello, Sister,' I mumbled, as she looked at my card, which was attached by a pin to my blanket. Quickly reading it, she put her hand gently on my forehead, then smiled.

'Your fever's gone, George. Put him down on bed eight on the right,' she said briefly to my stretcher bearers.

Her words cheered me up. The further up the ward you were placed was an indication of your recovery chances and Sister Greening, from my knowledge of her, was never wrong. If she had said one or two on either side of the ward I knew that there was a good chance that I would leave the ward in a wooden box.

Later I had a visit from an Army padre. My first thought was that for once Sister Greening had got it wrong and I hurriedly assured him that I was feeling a lot better. He smiled as he carefully placed a folding chair by my bed. 'I am sure you are, Corporal, but I am the bearer of good news, I am pleased to say. It makes a pleasant change for me these days in this sad time.'

The padre, a red-faced man in his forties and who smelt of a mixture of alcohol and tobacco, leaned forward on his chair. 'First, I must congratulate you for being awarded a bar to your DCM, and also the French award of the *Croix de Guerre*; you also have a bar to your MM, I understand – magnificent!'

He took my hand and shook it vigorously. Since he sat facing me and spoke slowly, I could understand him. He must have been told I was stone deaf. 'Well done, my boy, an incredible achievement,' he beamed, 'and last, but not least, I have to tell you that your wife gave birth to a baby boy three weeks ago and both are well.'

'A boy, sir, a baby boy?' I gasped, my eye filling with tears. 'It's wonderful, padre,' I sniffed, wiping my eye.

I think even the padre was a little moved. He patted my hand as he rose to his feet. 'It is indeed, old chap. Here are some letters for you.'

He placed a packet of letters on my bed, then folded his chair and placed it against the wall of the ward. 'Goodbye, Corporal, and good luck,' he smiled, as he left me and walked down the ward.

I was too overcome to reply. As I clutched my letters my eye was again full of tears. There were six letters from Amelia, one which said she would come and see me as soon as she was allowed. There was also a letter from Hector and Amy and one from Edwin, who, it seemed, was in an Army convalescent home near Guildford in Surrey. Apparently, he was in a wheelchair and would be confined to it. Even with that prospect, Edwin's letter was remarkably cheerful – I think he was just glad to be alive.

15

A Royal Visit and Home

The next few days passed quickly and I seemed much better. My fever had gone and I was now eating normally. I thought we were due for an inspection when, one morning, we had twice the amount of staff fussing about us. Our sheets were changed and I was given a clean pair of pyjamas. Sister Greening even combed my hair, much to my embarrassment. It caused ribald remarks from down the ward, which stopped when she said sharply, 'If that was you, Private Pope, I will put you on a charge.'

'Nar, it weren't me, Sister,' said the same voice.

Just after eleven o'clock, the padre and a Captain appeared at the end of the ward; the Captain pointed his swagger stick at me and nodded. I instinctively tried to slide down in my bed, 'Was my face dirty; what had I done, I wondered?'

Still further officers appeared, then the senior medical officer. By this time Sister Greening was hovering about them, her face now a shade of dull pink. Having been instructed by an officer standing at attention, 'Those sitting up sit up at attention,' the inspection began. When I saw Sister Greening make a curtsy to a young man in army uniform, I knew it was no ordinary army inspection. I realised it was the Prince of Wales.

He quickly traversed the ward, speaking to those who

could reply and nodding to those who could not, followed by three aides, one of whom had a stiff leg, the other carrying a small blue velvet cushion.

They came at last to my bed and stopped. The Prince smiled. 'And this, Sister, is Corporal Bowman?'

'Yes, your Royal Highness,' she replied, rubbing her hands together, nervously.

'How are you, Corporal?' he asked in a quiet voice.

'I can't hear you, sir. I can't hear a bloody thing,' I replied.

I could see smiles appear on their faces, so I spoke again. 'I can't hear a thing, I've not been able to hear for weeks, sir.'

The Prince turned to the senior medical officer and spoke. I could not see the Prince's lips move, but I could see the senior medical officer shake his head. The Prince turned to me and smiled. 'Never mind, I will speak slowly, then perhaps you can read my lips. Is that better?'

'Much better, sir. I wish everyone spoke like that,' I replied.

I could see two of the other officers exchange glances, faint smiles on their faces.

'How are you feeling now?'

'A bit better, sir, thank you.'

'The padre tells me that your wife has just presented you with a baby boy,' smiled the Prince.

'Yes sir, a boy, smashing, isn't it?'

'Wonderful news for you, and what will you call him?'

I paused for a moment, then I replied. 'I think I'll call him Edward, sir, after you, if you don't mind?'

A broad smile appeared on the Prince's face, then he nodded. 'I should be honoured, Corporal,' he replied, with a faint inclination of his head. 'And now it is my pleasure to present you with a second Distinguished Conduct Medal and a second Military Medal.' The Prince

278

turned to his aide holding the velvet cushion. The officer bent forward for the Prince to pick up the first of the medals that were lying on the cushion. As he did so I recognised the other officer who walked with a stiff leg. It was the Guards officer who had given me the handkerchief and who I had brought back from the German wire. The officer had, I think, recognised me, as he gave me a friendly smile and a nod.

'I haven't got your handkerchief, sir,' I said.

'Never mind, Corporal,' he grinned.

The Prince looked mystified; he paused in the task of pinning the medal on my pyjama jacket and turned to his aide.

'Enlighten me,' he said.

'Your Royal Highness, it was Corporal Bowman who brought me back from the enemy wire, and on the previous day he brought back Colonel Sir Charles Bailly Stewart.'

'Did he indeed?' nodded the Prince.

'On that occasion I gave him a handkerchief to wipe his face – he was in something of a state.'

'I understand,' smiled the Prince, who stepped forward to pin the second medal on my jacket.

'Congratulations, Corporal Bowman, you thoroughly deserve it,' he said, shaking my hand.

'Thank you, your Royal Highness,' I replied, a little overcome.

As the royal party began to move down the ward, the officer who had spoken to me put a hand into his breast pocket and took out his pocket book. He held it with difficulty in his left hand and took out some notes with his right. He folded the notes then put his pocket book away and stepped towards me. Quickly, he took my hand and pressed the notes into it, then he folded my fingers over them.

'Buy your baby son a present for me, Bowman, there's a good chap.' He patted my shoulder and smiled. 'Good luck for the future. Here's my card; if ever I can help you, let me know.' He pushed the card into my hand then turned and limped down the ward to rejoin the royal party.

When they had left the ward I opened my hand. First I looked at the card; it read: *MAJOR THE EARL OF WARENNE, MC, GRENADIER GUARDS.*

I then opened the notes; my jaw dropped. I had never seen fifty pound notes before. There were two of them. A hundred pounds! I could not believe it. I was still staring at them when the Sister returned to my bed. She must have seen what had taken place and I think her curiosity got the better of her. 'What did the Major give you, George?' I could see her eyebrows rise as she saw the value of the money.

'It's to buy the baby a present, Sister, so the Major said.'

'He must have considered himself in your debt,' she smiled.

'We were lucky to get back, Sister,' I replied.

'I can believe that,' she said, quietly.

'Will you look after it for me, please?'

'I will put them in my safe, George,' she replied.

'Sister, could I have something for my head, please, it hurts rotten.'

Without a word she felt my pulse, then nodded. 'I'll bring you something shortly,' she said.

Nobby Clarke in the next bed had been watching me closely; at last he had to speak. 'He never give me anything, George. You must 'ave got 'im out of the mire mate; should 'ave left 'im in it, if yer ask me.'

'No one did ask you, Clarke. Keep your opinions to yourself,' snapped Sister Greening.

'I only said...' began Nobby.

'Be quiet, Clarke, or you will be on a charge.' Sister glared at the unfortunate Nobby, then hurried to the far end of the ward where something else had caught her ever-watchful eyes. Nobby began to talk to me, but gave up when he realised it was something of a waste of time. Thanks to the tablets that Sister had given me, I slipped into a pleasant doze, and later that day I took my first steps out of bed, which seemed to complete one of the most exciting days of my life.

The flow of wounded from France continued unabated and I was told by the medical officer that I could go to a convalescent home, which did not appeal to me one bit.

'Now your fever has gone, your wife may visit you, Corporal.'

'I don't want to go to a convalescent home, sir. I want to go home, please,' I replied.

The doctor turned to the sister and said something I could not pick up. He looked at me and spoke slowly. 'You may go home next week if your wife can manage you.'

'She was nursing in France, sir,' I said, eagerly.

'In that case you may go sooner. You will come back here for dressings every week. We need your bed,' he added.

'Yes, sir. Thank you, sir,' I beamed.

After the doctor had left my bedside it occurred to me that Amelia might not want me home so soon. My elation suddenly evaporated. Surely she would not say no. The thought began to haunt me; she would not say no, I was sure of it.

I could now get up to wash, but for the terrible headaches I still had, I would have thought that I was improving.

It was two days later that Amelia came for me. I did

not see her approach my bed as I was sitting on the edge of it trying to get my socks on. Nobby Clarke spoke to her first.

'Are you George's missus?'

'I am,' replied Amelia, tartly.

'He's as deaf as a post yer know, but there's nobody 'ere with more decorations than 'im.'

Amelia touched my shoulder and spoke, 'George, dear.'

I turned. I could not speak. My lips moved but I was not sure if I made any sound. Amelia kissed my trembling lips and put her arms about me; there were tears on both our faces.

'I can come home, Amelia?' I sniffed.

'Of course, dear. That's why I'm here, silly,' she said, kissing me.

I was suddenly aware that Amy was with her.

'Amy!' I gasped.

'Oh, Georgie, dear,' she said, kissing my cheek. There were tears in her eyes but she was doing her best not to cry.

Amelia dried her eyes and began to assist me to dress, while Amy put my personal effects in a bag that she had with her. We were joined by Sister Greening, who, it appeared, knew Amelia.

'I was not aware, Hooper, that Corporal Bowman was your husband.'

'We met in France,' said Amelia.

'I see,' replied Sister Greening. 'I have some property of your husband's in my office safe; follow me and I will give it to you.'

'Thank you.' Amelia nodded briefly and followed the sister down the long ward.

'I haven't got to go to a convalescent home, have I, Amy?'

'Not if you don't want to, Georgie.'

282

Amy sniffed as she buttoned up my coat. I think my physical condition affected her more than it did Amelia. Perhaps Amelia was able to control her emotions better.

'Dry your eyes, Amy,' I said, as Amelia and Sister Greening came towards us.

I was now ready to leave. I quickly said goodbye to Nobby Clarke.

'Goodbye, mate,' Nobby winked as he shook my hand.

'I wanted to say goodbye to my friend Davie Graham, Sister.'

'He left for Scotland days ago, George, when you were not so well. He gave me his address for you, it's with the papers that your wife now has,' she replied.

'Thank you, Sister, and goodbye,' I said, holding out my hand, which she quickly shook.

'Goodbye, Corporal, and good luck. You must excuse me, I have another patient for your bed.'

We were now ignored as the sister gave instructions to a nurse who I had not seen before and my bed was stripped before we were half-way down the ward.

We went home on the bus to Deptford then got a tram for the rest of the way. I was wearing the clothes that Amelia and Amy had brought to the hospital. Obviously, the Army did not think it worth giving me another uniform. I was glad of my old overcoat and the thick scarf that Amy had given me, as there was a cold wind. I was, in fact, given another army uniform later when I went for dressings, since I was not officially discharged; why, I did not know, and never did find out.

I could feel the tears welling up in my eye as we walked towards the shop. My lips must have trembled as Amelia turned and smiled, 'Nearly home, dear, it's all over now.'

I nodded and wiped my eye with the back of my hand. My legs felt weak and I was in a daze. I was still very shaky and unused to walking and a tiredness had now gripped me.

'Have there been any callers, Rita?' asked Amelia, as we entered the shop. Rita hastily swallowed before she replied, 'No, Mrs Bowman.' She looked at me curiously as she spoke.

'I hope you have not been eating those marzipan pancakes again.' Amelia looked suspiciously at one of the cardboard sweet boxes on view beneath the display case.

'No, Ma'am.' Rita shook her head.

'I hope not,' said Amelia, severely, 'or I will be stopping it out of your wages.'

'Er, the mineral water man called, Mrs Bowman. He said he would come back tomorrer,' said Rita, in an effort to sidetrack Amelia. This cut no ice with Amelia, who still looked at the sweet boxes, then nodded curtly and swept past her.

We went through the back of the shop and up the stairs. Agnes came out of the kitchen to greet me. She put her arms around me and kissed my cheek, her face screwed up. She did not speak, then lifted her apron to wipe her eyes, and returned to the kitchen just as Buster emerged from it, tail wagging – this brought a smile to my face.

'Buster! Isn't he big now?' I cried, getting down on one knee to pat him. I almost toppled over as I did so. Amelia bent down to assist me and I got shakily to my feet.

'George, dear, there are hot water bottles in bed; you go and lie down for a while and I will bring you a hot drink.'

'Can I see the baby first?'

'Of course you can, dear. He's in the kitchen with Agnes; I'm going to feed him shortly.'

The baby was in a little cot not far from the fire. Buster came and sat next to it; he looked up at me with an expression that seemed to say, 'that is my baby – touch it if you dare.'

I looked down at the happy little face I never expected to see. 'He's...' I could not continue. I felt my shoulders shaking and tears ran down my cheek. Amelia understood and she took my arm and led me from the kitchen and up the stairs to our bedroom.

'I never thought I would see him,' I mumbled.

'I know, dear,' replied Amelia, her eyes full of tears.

I sat on the edge of our bed completely exhausted, while Amelia undressed me and took some warm pyjamas that had been wrapped around one of the stone hot water bottles that were in the bed. In warm pyjamas I climbed into bed and rested my head on one of the feather pillows. I felt warm and safe; nothing mattered any more. Amelia tucked the eiderdown up around my neck and kissed my cheek. 'You have a sleep,' she seemed to say. I tried to smile my gratitude and my eye began to close.

I was home and for me the war was over.

16

Home

I did not awake until late the following morning. Deafness had its compensations; I could no longer hear the trams clattering by in Queen's Road. I know this disturbed Amelia at times, but I was now in my world of silence.

Of Amelia there was no sign. I was now unsure which day it actually was, until Amelia suddenly came into the bedroom. 'You're awake at last,' she smiled. 'How are you, George, my dear? Do you feel better?'

'Speak slower, Amelia, I must see your lips move,' I replied, trying to sit up in bed.

'Of course, dear, I'll remember. Would you like a cup of tea?'

'Please,' I nodded.

'I'll not be a moment,' said Amelia, leaving the room.

I sank back into the warmth of the bed in a torpor of security to await my cup of tea. I must have gone to sleep again as the tea had been put on the bedside table and when I touched the cup it was stone cold. Through the half-drawn curtains I could see spots of rain on the window panes. I thought of the trenches and involuntarily shivered. 'Thank God I am out of it,' I muttered to myself.

Amelia must have heard me talking to myself and came into the bedroom, a look of concern on her face. 'Are you all right, dear?'

'Yes, Amelia. Can I get up now?'

'Would you like your luncheon in bed?'

'No thank you. I'll get up and have a wash first.'

'What about a bath? But you must not get your dressings wet, remember. I'll help you then you can sit by the kitchen fire.'

'With the baby?' I beamed.

'Yes, with him,' smiled Amelia.

When Amelia helped me off with my vest I could see her lips purse as she took a deep intake of breath. Though the wounds to my chest and shoulder had closed, they were still very red and inflamed. Amelia smiled, wanly, as I stepped into the bath.

After a bath and a cup of tea I felt much better. I sat by the kitchen fire and from time to time looked proudly into the baby's cot.

Agnes had prepared stewed lamb and dumplings – one of my favourites, and the smell of it reminded me just how hungry I was. I had not eaten since breakfast the previous day.

'George, dear, the baby must be christened. I would like to call him Edwin after my brother, who I wish to be his godfather, what do you think, dear?'

I looked at Amelia, a little open-mouthed. She thought I had not understood her and started to repeat herself. 'I heard you, Amelia, er, I mean I understood you. I would like him called Edward, like the Prince of Wales. I told the Prince I would like to name him after him and he said that he would be honoured, so that's why I want him named Edward.'

Amelia and Agnes looked at me in disbelief, then exchanged glances, then Amelia spoke. 'George, dear, are you feeling all right, have you been dreaming?'

'I have not dreamed this up, Amelia. The Prince came to the hospital last week and presented me with my medals.'

'Did he?' gasped Amelia.

'Yes, and he knew about the baby,' I added.

'Well I never!' Amelia had her hands to her mouth as she spoke. 'If that's the case, dear, we will call him Edward Edwin George,' said Amelia, firmly.

I shook my head and a slight frown appeared on Amelia's brow.

'No, I don't like the name George. I think it should be James after your father – he has been very kind to me.'

'Very well, dear, it shall be as you say – Edward Edwin James. They will be his names, George, dear,' smiled Amelia, approvingly.

'Yes, Edward Edwin James – it sounds nice, doesn't it?'

'It does, indeed, George, dear,' agreed Amelia, glancing at Agnes.

'Yes, very nice, Miss Amelia. Lovely names,' agreed Agnes.

'I found the hundred pounds with your personal effects – in fact Sister Greening pointed it out to me. It was very generous of Major Lord Warenne, wasn't it? What shall I do with it, dear?'

'Whatever you think is best, I don't mind.'

'I'll think about it,' smiled Amelia.

I lost all interest in the money as I tucked into one of my favourite meals. Amelia had cut up everything for me as I was now only able to use a spoon, but after a few mouthfuls I was unable to eat any more. I put down my spoon and looked unhappily at my plate.

'What is it, dear?' asked Amelia, a look of concern on her face.

'I can't eat any more,' I said, miserably. 'I want to, it's lovely.' My hand began to shake.

'Never mind, dear, have it later,' said Amelia, now

holding my hand. 'Go and sit in the grandfather chair by the fire.'

I did not need telling twice. I could look at the baby as I sat in the chair and the chair was very comfortable as well. The warm fire sent me off to sleep again, and for the first two weeks at home I spent much of my time the same way.

Amelia understood. She would just put one of her father's tartan travelling rugs about my legs and leave me to sleep. I did not feel any inclination to go out, but I had to, after a week, for my dressings, and I was not looking forward to it.

Amelia accompanied me to the Woolwich hospital and I was immediately stopped by a sergeant-major whom I could not hear, which annoyed him. However, he met his match in Amelia and before I knew it, he was escorting us both to the quartermaster's stores and I was issued with a new uniform, which almost fitted me. Besides which, I received a cap badge and ribbons to sew on my tunic. It was all some kind of miracle that Amelia had achieved. Finally, the sergeant-major escorted us to the hospital outpatients department, saluting Amelia before leaving us. Since I could not hear what was said as I walked beside them, it was quite a mystery to me.

After an initial inspection of the dressings by the sister in charge, and her conversation with Amelia, they were not touched, so we were able to leave immediately.

'Your pay, dear,' said Amelia, as I walked towards the gate.

'But I haven't ...' I began.

'I have your pay book, dear,' she smiled, handing it to me.

The paymaster's office was as helpful as the quartermaster's and soon my back pay was safely in Amelia's handbag.

It was raining before we arrived home and I felt so tired. My uniform and boots were soon discarded and I was back in the grandfather chair with a cup of tea, where I felt snug and happy.

Amelia had given up her full-time job at the public library and was now a relief assistant. She had little choice in the matter as she had to feed the baby, though there was a possibility she would have her position back in the future.

The fact was we needed the money, though Amelia never worried me with such matters – she handled all our finances. I had been given my full pay for the next month, then I was to get a disability award, so I was told. Amelia made it clear that she would go with me when it was awarded, and I must admit that I was glad.

Edwin was in a convalescent home at Dorking in Surrey and I gathered from Amelia that he was not happy there. He had progressed to a wheelchair and he would spend the rest of his days in it, so the doctors had told him.

I felt very sorry for Edwin – so keen to join up and win a medal. Now he was a cripple with no future.

As the days passed I felt much better. I found little jobs to do and even helped in the shop. I still had an ache in my head, which would not go away and was very painful at times. One morning Amelia had a letter from Edwin; she read it a number of times at breakfast before she told me of its contents.

'Edwin's very unhappy, George,' she said suddenly.

'Is he?' I frowned.

'Yes, dear. He wants to leave the convalescent home and mother and father cannot have him; neither of them are well – they could never lift him, even with some help.'

'I see,' I murmured.

'So he wants to come here,' said Amelia, with a sigh.

'I see. Still, you did offer him a home, didn't you?'

'I know, George, but that was before he was crippled. How could we manage him, dear?' she frowned. I did not reply. I think Amelia took my silence as some sort of reproach, but that was not the case.

'How could we manage him, dear?' Amelia looked unhappy as she asked the question again.

'Downstairs there is just the shop and stockroom. His bedroom would be on the second floor, he cannot sleep downstairs.'

'He would have to have two wheelchairs,' I said, suddenly.

Amelia frowned slightly, then she spoke slowly and emphasised her words with some patience.

'George, dear, did you understand what I said? I was saying Edwin...'

'I understood you, Amelia. I said two wheelchairs because I could not get him up the stairs in a wheelchair with one arm, and you could not do it either.'

'No, dear,' murmured Amelia.

'I could carry him up and down stairs over my shoulder and if you held his wheelchair steady I could put him in it.'

'Could you, dear?' Amelia looked doubtful.

'Yes, with a wheelchair for upstairs and another for going out, it would make him easy. I could get him in and out of bed for you.'

'You make it sound very simple, George,' said Amelia, biting her lower lip, still unconvinced.

'You can't leave him in there, Amelia. You promised him a home. He mentioned it to me when I saw him in the hospital in France. He was thinking about it then, and I said you meant it.'

'Was he dear? What did you say?'

'I said I did not think it would make any difference. You cannot make conditions now, Amelia, he expects you to have him.'

There were tears in Amelia's eyes as she bent forward to kiss me. 'George, my dearest, you are the one who will have to manage him. Could you do it? Would you mind doing it?'

'I'd do it because he is your brother,' I murmured.

Amelia kissed me again. 'I do not deserve you, my dearest.'

That evening Amelia wrote to Edwin to tell him what she proposed, and within twenty-four hours she had received his grateful acceptance of her offer.

There was a small room on the first floor that overlooked Queen's Road. At the present time it was filled with a collection of items that had not been given a permanent home, and also stock for the shop.

'The stock can go downstairs and some of these items can be put in the cellar for now,' said Amelia, as we began to get Edwin's room ready.

Moving boxes brought on an awful headache. I sat down on a chair; Amelia looked at me. 'Are you all right, dear?' she asked, anxiously.

'Got a rotten headache,' I replied.

'Go and lie down, George, and I'll get you something for it.'

'Think I will,' I said, getting unsteadily to my feet. I took my slippers off and got underneath the eiderdown on our bed. I felt a little better and did not notice Amelia enter the bedroom. My eye was closed, then I felt her gentle cool fingers touching my forehead. 'That's nice,' I muttered, as I felt myself drifting off to sleep.

When I awoke and went back to the small room that was to be Edwin's, Amelia was busy making up a single bed. She turned as I entered the room. 'Are you feeling better, dear?' she smiled.

'A bit,' I replied.

I watched Amelia finish making the bed. I could not

get over the change in her since she left Cedar Lodge. No task, however menial, was too much for her. She did not mind what she did in the house and amazingly she seemed much happier.

'Do you like it, dear?' she asked, hands on hips, surveying the room.

'Yes, it's very nice,' I replied.

It really did look so different. Gone were all the boxes and half-opened packages. Two tea chests and a roll of lino I had put in the cellar, and instead there was a dressing-table and a chest of drawers, a carpet on the floor and a tallboy in the corner of the room.

'Yes, I think he should be very comfortable,' said Amelia with satisfaction, as she looked at me.

'Did Rita help you?'

'Yes. Agnes went into the shop, and this is the most Rita has ever done since I first employed her,' said Amelia, her lip curling. 'But it all depends on you, dear,' she smiled. 'I told Edwin in my letter that if you could not manage him he would have to return to Dorking.'

'I'll manage him,' I said, confidently.

'On Sunday we will go and see Edwin and make the arrangements for him to leave. Amy is coming too, she will help me with the baby.'

'Amy will like the ride out,' I grinned.

'Yes, of course, dear,' smiled Amelia. 'Amy will enjoy a day out – she does so much and asks for very little in return.'

I nodded. Amelia was right. It pleased me that they were such good friends.

17

Edwin – a Reunion

I had only visited Amy and Hector once since leaving hospital. Hector was both embarrassed and moved by my appearance and I could see that Amy was close to tears.

'They don't want me any more,' I joked. 'You can't lift a stretcher with one hand.'

My attempt at a joke was not a success and Amy put a handkerchief to her eyes. I immediately put an arm about her to try and comfort her whilst Hector began to polish his glasses vigorously, sniffing continuously as he did so. I knew I had to choose my words carefully. 'Still, I'm home – that's one good thing,' I smiled.

'We thank the Lord for that, we really do,' said Hector, his face still showing his anguish.

'Amen to that,' agreed Amy.

'What was that, Amy?' I frowned. 'I can't hear you, you know. I must see your lips move.'

'I know that, George, love,' she said, grasping my hand.

'Bring the children down to the shop after school, Amy, and I'll give them some sweets.'

'But Amelia might...' Amy hesitated. 'I'll pay for them, Georgie.'

'You won't. It's my shop too, you know,' I said, firmly.

Amy smiled and nodded her approval at my words. 'All right, we'll see you later.'

I had some misgivings on how the children would react to me, but I need not have worried. They were more interested in the jars and boxes of sweets than my injuries, and I was almost certain that they would come and see me at every opportunity.

I had now started to read the newspaper again and the news from the front seemed better – that's if you could believe it. The German offensive had run out of steam, so it said, as if they would know. Even allowing for our appalling losses we were managing to hold them, albeit at positions some miles further back from our original front.

Great hopes were being placed on the American Army that was building up in France. Whether we liked it or not, only a blind man would fail to see that the French and ourselves were coming to the end of our tether. Still, it was no concern of mine. It was Edwin and Hector who took it all so seriously.

Amelia had not mentioned the hundred pounds that I had been given by the Major. I know she had put it in a savings bank but I had thoughts of spending a bit of it. I was now feeling a lot better so I was able to give the matter some thought. On the Friday evening prior to our proposed visit on the following Sunday to Edwin, I decided to raise the matter with Amelia. We were just finishing our meal and Amelia was carefully folding her serviette when I broached the subject. 'Amelia, I would like to spend some of that hundred pounds that I was given,' I said calmly.

Amelia looked at me curiously, before she replied slowly.

'George, dear, it was a present for Edward you know,' she said, patiently placing the serviette in its silver ring.

'The Major said that, I know, but he could hardly say "Corporal, here's a ton for bringing me back from the Hun wire and saving my life", could he?'

'A ton?' frowned Amelia.

'A hundred pounds,' I smiled.

I could see a faint smile appear on Agnes's face but she made no comment as she cleared away the dishes.

'Well, if you put it like that, dear,' replied Amelia. 'What do you want the money for?'

'I thought we could build a conservatory at the back of the house. We have already got the two side walls and a back wall – it would not cost much. Edwin could have his wheelchair out there and we could grow plants and the baby's pram could go out there, too. It would not cost more than twenty pounds, maybe twenty-three at the most. We could put a table out there and chairs and even a heater, and we could come in through the back gate and not go through the shop.'

At last, I stopped for breath as Amelia replied – her mind obviously made up 'That's an excellent idea, George, dear. We will do just that. It will make another room – how sensible.'

'What did you think I wanted it for, eh? A penny farthing bike?' I said, grinning at her.

'Really, dear,' she said, clasping my hand, which was having one of its bouts of shaking.

We left early on Sunday morning as we had to change trains twice, then catch a bus to reach the Army officers' convalescent home at Dorking in Surrey.

It was a nice, late, spring morning and Edwin was sitting out on one of the lawns reading a newspaper when we arrived. He greeted Amelia and Amy happily enough, but when he saw me his face changed and he looked almost tearful. 'Oh Christ, George, what have they done to you, old son?' he groaned, as he gripped my hand and put his other arm about me. I was a little taken aback by Edwin's emotional outburst and I could see that Amelia and Amy were affected by it.

'We brought the baby,' I said, breaking free of his embrace.

'Yes, here he is.' Amelia pushed the pram closer to Edwin's wheelchair as she spoke.

'He's fine,' sniffed Edwin, giving the pram a brief glance.

'He's a lovely boy,' said Amy as she cooed at the baby.

'He's smashing,' I beamed.

'We have a small dining-room for visitors,' said Edwin. 'I have booked a table for luncheon.'

'That will be nice, Edwin,' smiled Amelia.

'Father and Mother came yesterday – no, it was the day before. You would not recognise them, they have aged. Father's got the shakes too, and Mother's little better.'

'Oh dear' murmured Amelia.

'Mother's fallen out with Aunt Polly and father's sold the car. I think that went to pay his wine merchant.'

Amelia made a movement of her lips and shook her head sharply. I could see she was annoyed, but she made no comment.

'My father sent poor old Bessie to the Army, Edwin, the old bastard,' I said, my face set. 'She wouldn't have lasted five minutes in all that mud; you know what it was like,' I said, miserably.

'Never mind, George,' said Edwin, patting my arm and smiling, sympathetically, at me. 'Let's go and have luncheon, old chap. They will be serving it soon.' He looked at Amelia.

'You go with Edwin, George, while Amy and I go to the ladies to attend to the baby,' said Amelia, rising to her feet.

I began pushing Edward's invalid chair for the first time, and moved towards the fine mansion that had become a convalescent home for Army officers.

In the large entrance hall I pushed Edwin one way, while Amelia and Amy pushed the pram down a corridor in the opposite direction. At the entrance to the dining-room we were greeted by an elderly maid who smiled at Edwin.

'Good-day Captain Hooper, you have reserved a table?'

'That's right, Mary. For four and one baby in a pram.'

'I'll give you a table near the window, then the perambulator can be put in the bay out of the way, sir.'

'Capital, Mary,' smiled Edwin.

The dining-room had about eight tables, half of which were occupied. Those dining pretended not to notice us as we entered, until we passed a table next to the one allocated to us. It was occupied by a friend of Edwin's and his family.

'Hello, Edwin,' said a young man of about our own age who had reddish hair and a bright pink face. 'Let me introduce you to my family.'

'Thank you, Teddy,' replied Edwin.

The young man, like Edwin, was in a wheelchair and also a Captain. 'My father, General Maxwell, my mother and my sisters, Lucy and Charlotte, this is Captain Edwin Hooper.'

Teddy Maxwell's sisters were in their late twenties and their faces had an almost bored expression when they were introduced. At last, almost as an afterthought I was introduced.

'This is my brother-in-law, Corporal George Bowman,' began Edwin.

I was given patronising nods by the General and Mrs Maxwell and faint smiles by Lucy and Charlotte Maxwell, until Teddy Maxwell said, 'Is he the one with all the medals, Edwin?'

I moved one of the chairs so that Edwin could bring his wheelchair up to our table, then sat on the chair

298

next to him. 'That's right, Teddy, DCM and Bar, MM and Bar and *Croix de Guerre* – not bad eh?'

'Very good,' replied the pink-faced Teddy.

I was aware that they were talking about me but I was not interested, so I looked out of the bay window. I was suddenly aware of Edwin touching my arm and turned to face him.

'General Maxwell is talking to you, George,' said Edwin.

'Er ... what's that, Edwin?'

'George is as deaf as a post, General,' explained Edwin, turning to face Teddy Maxwell's table.

'I said that was a fine achievement, you must be very proud,' said General Maxwell, looking at me.

'I am, sir. I'm very proud of him, he's a lovely baby. You'll see him shortly, Amelia is just giving him his dinner.'

'I said your service record is a fine achievement, Corporal. Were you with the Guards?' The General's moustache seemed to twitch.

'No, sir, the 56th Field Ambulance unit at the end, until it was all knocked out like the 23rd I was with before. I was a stretcher bearer most of the time.'

'I see,' said the General, losing interest.

'You see, sir, I was a registered conscientious objector.'

I could see the General's face going a shade of red and one of his daughters was now smiling at me. Edwin was hiding his face with his left hand as I continued.

'See – the Army won't want me any more, General. You can't lift a stretcher with one arm. With that I moved the stump of my left arm up and down, much like a penguin at the zoo might do. I noticed Edwin and his friend Teddy Maxwell exchange glances. The General had picked up the menu card and was now discussing it with Mrs Maxwell; however, both the Miss Maxwells were now smiling in my direction.

At this point Amelia and Amy entered the dining-

299

room, pushing the pram. I got to my feet as they arrived at our table.

'Sit down, George, dear,' smiled Amelia, as she pushed the pram into the window bay.

The General now pointedly ignored us, so no further introductions were made and as the waitress came to take our order, it took away the snub to some extent.

'What would you like to drink, George?' said Edwin, abruptly.

I looked about the table as I had not seen him speak and did not know what he had said.

'George will have a ginger beer, Edwin,' said Amelia. 'Amy would like a lemonade and I will have the same.'

Edwin ordered the drinks and added a whisky for himself, while Amelia looked at the menu card.

'There is a choice of roast lamb or fish pie, what would you like, George, dear?'

'What's that, Amelia?'

'Roast lamb or fish pie, dear?'

'Yes, Amelia,' I replied, unable to see her mouth move properly.

'What would you like, dear?' asked Amelia, patiently. 'Roast lamb or fish pie?'

By this time Edwin was beginning to get a little annoyed. 'Good God, Amelia,' he began, his face flushing.

'Edwin, you must be a little patient with him, he's completely deaf, you know.'

'Yes, but honestly...'

'Look, Edwin, if you are coming to live with us you must be patient with him, because it will be George who will be looking after you. I cannot lift you, and Agnes cannot help, she is an old lady,' said Amelia, her face now as flushed as Edwin's.

Their voices must have been rising and it was clear that the General's table were listening to the exchanges.

300

'Give George the menu, Amelia,' said Amy, quietly.

'Of course, Amy,' said Amelia, passing the card to me.

'I can still read, Edwin – the Army's left me with one eye,' I said, sarcastically. 'I'll have the roast lamb, please,' I said, looking at the card.

Having ordered our meal we now lapsed into an embarrassed silence, which Amelia tried to overcome.

'Tell Edwin about your meeting with the Prince of Wales, dear,' said Amelia, looking at me.

'The Prince of Wales!' repeated Edwin, in disbelief.

I could tell that the General was now listening to us.

'They wanted me to go to a convalescent home, Edwin, not a posh place like this one – for other ranks; the nearest one was a converted doss-house in Shoreditch.'

'Oh, yes!' grinned Edwin, now looking happier. 'What about the dossers then, George?'

'Put them in the Army; probably made them staff officers, I shouldn't wonder,' I replied, looking up at the ornate ceiling.

Edwin burst out laughing, as did Teddy Maxwell – even the General was trying not to smile.

'Ha, ha, ha,' chortled Edwin, 'that's a good one, George. That reminds me, George, of that staff officer who stepped into that hole at Ypres – the one you told me about.'

Edwin began to laugh again, as Amelia looked at me. 'What happened, George?'

'It was at Ypres, about five months ago. I had just had a spell out of the line and this Staff General came up in his car. He got out and came towards me. I came to attention and saluted, then he stepped into what he thought was a puddle and went in up to his waist.'

Edwin was doubled up laughing as I continued, 'I was still saluting as he had not returned my salute, then he shouted to me to give him a hand, without even returning my salute, so I said, "I'm saluting you, sir" – won't tell you what he said, Amelia.'

'There's no need, dear,' smiled Amelia.

'I gave him a hand to get out and said, "You were lucky, sir. Further up the line you could have gone in and the water would have been over your head," then he swore at me again and went back to his car – the car reversed down the road and disappeared.'

Edwin was now convulsed with laughter, as were Teddy Maxwell and his sisters, though Amelia looked a little puzzled.

'Why did you not tell the General, George, dear?' she asked.

'I was saluting him, wasn't I?' I replied, sharply.

'Even so...' persisted Amelia.

'A corporal does not speak to a General unless spoken to,' I explained.

'That seems a little strange given the circumstances,' said Amelia, as the waitress brought us our drinks.

'Come on, George,' said Edwin, wiping his eyes with his handkerchief, 'let's hear what His Royal Highness said to you.'

'He knew about the baby,' I said, pointing to the pram.

'Did he?' asked Edwin, disbelief evident from his voice.

'Do you think he reads the births and deaths column in the *South London Echo*, Amelia?'

'I very much doubt it,' she smiled.

Edwin was now laughing as I continued with the story.

'Well, he knew all the same,' I said, firmly. 'He was nice and understanding. I said to him, "I'm as deaf as a bloody post, sir. You'll have to speak slower and let me see your lips move."'

'And what did he say to that, George?' grinned Edwin.

'He spoke as I asked him to and I understood him. I told you, he's very understanding; and I said to him that

302

the baby then didn't have a name and could I name him after him, and he said he would be honoured. So that's why he's Edward Edwin and not Edwin George James.'

Edwin nodded and was still grinning at me.

'Then he gave you your medals, George?' said Edwin.

'That's right,' I replied.

'Then the Earl of Warenne gave you a present for the baby, didn't he dear?' smiled Amelia.

'Why did he do that, George?' asked Edwin, now visibly impressed.

'I think our dinners are coming now,' I said, as the waitress came towards us with a tray of dishes.

'I should take your overcoat off, if I were you, George,' suggested Edwin.

'What's that, Edwin?'

'Your overcoat, Georgie – let me help you take it off,' said Amy.

With Amy's assistance I removed my overcoat, which the waitress took from me. 'I'll hang it up for you, sir,' she smiled.

I could see the General glance at me before I sat down. I was sure that I had more medal ribbons than he had on his uniform.

'Amy, put George's serviette under his chin, we don't want any marks on his uniform, he has to go to Woolwich in it tomorrow,' said Amelia, as she looked into the pram.

'Why's that?' asked Edwin.

'He has to have his dressings changed. Don't you dear?' smiled Amelia, now satisfied that the baby was fast asleep.

'What's that?' I asked, putting down my soup spoon.

'Never mind, dear,' smiled Amelia. 'You carry on with your soup. It's just your dressings.'

'Not looking forward to that – it's been three weeks since last time and I had a rotten cold.'

303

'This soup's all right, Edwin,' I said, suddenly.

'Do you like it, George?' grinned Edwin.

'It's fair dinkum,' I replied.

'It's what?' laughed Edwin.

'Fair dinkum – that's what the Australians say. I brought an Aussie back from the wire, and he said, "you're fair dinkum, mate." I asked another Aussie what he meant, and he said it means all right.'

'Well, I hope the roast lamb's fair dinkum as well,' chuckled Edwin. 'You did not tell me why the Earl of Warenne gave you a present for the baby?'

I could see the General move slightly in his chair and glance at me as he heard the name, 'Earl of Warenne' mentioned.

'I brought him back from the German wire when I was on the Somme. He'd been there all day; he would not have lasted much longer. He remembered me – he was with a Guards regiment; he gave me his card and said I was to contact him if I ever needed any help.'

'I see,' nodded Edwin, somewhat subdued. 'He had a very good reason to buy the baby a present, I would say,' said Edwin, now no longer smiling.

'Will you cut up George's luncheon for him, Amy,' said Amelia as she passed a dinner plate to Amy who was sitting next to me.

'I brought back their RSM and Colonel, too. God that RSM was a weight. I hope you are not as heavy, Edwin, if I've got to get you up and down stairs,' I grinned.

'No, no, I'm a lightweight, George,' smiled Edwin.

'I hope so,' I said, as I tucked into my roast lamb.

The meal passed pleasantly enough and when Captain Maxwell and his family left their table they all (to my surprise) came and shook hands with me – even the General, who said, 'I'm pleased to have met you, my boy – very pleased, and good luck for the future.'

'Er ... thank you, sir,' I replied, a little taken aback.

'See you later, Edwin,' said Teddy Maxwell, as he propelled his wheelchair away.

'Yes, of course, Teddy,' replied Edwin.

After our meal, we returned to the gardens, and though it was overcast, it was not raining and we sat on the rustic chairs provided.

'Teddy Maxwell is leaving on Wednesday,' said Edwin, casually.

'Is he?' replied Amelia, taking the hint. 'Well, your room is ready for you, but you will need an additional wheelchair, Edwin.'

'It's already arranged, Amelia,' he replied, promptly.

'Then it's just a question of George being able to get you up and down the stairs, isn't it?' she replied.

'George can manage me easily enough. If he can carry a Guards RSM across no man's land in the mud, he can lift me about,' said Edwin, confidently.

'Perhaps so, but George has been badly wounded recently and he will not have got his strength back yet,' said Amelia.

'He can manage me, can't you, George?'

'Er ... wassat?' I muttered, almost asleep.

'I said, George, you can lift me up,' said Edwin, smiling at me.

'Yes,' I yawned.

'Go on then, do it – just to show Amelia,' he urged.

'All right,' I said, getting to my feet and taking hold of Edwin.

Unfortunately the wheelchair slipped back on the grass and I missed my footing with the result we both fell on the grass. We lay there laughing while Amy stood there also laughing. Amelia, however, looked annoyed as she said sharply, 'Get up, George, at once.'

At this point the assistant matron came hurrying towards

us, but before she reached us, I was on my feet with Edwin over my right shoulder.

Whatever's the meaning of this, Captain Hooper? Have you taken leave of your senses?' she stormed. 'I shall report this to the senior medical officer at once.'

Both Amelia and Edwin, who was still suspended over my shoulder, were shocked into silence, but I understood what the woman had said and I retaliated.

'I'm not doing this for fun, Sister. He can't stay here for ever and I've got to see if I can carry him up and down stairs. I haven't got my medical discharge yet. Still, I can lift him; hold his wheelchair steady, Amelia.'

'Yes, George,' said Amelia, quickly, as I lowered the still silent Edwin into his chair.

'If he's coming home, Sister, we have got to look after him unless the Army is providing assistance.'

'I understand the situation now. The matter is closed, Captain,' she said, turning on her heel and walking towards the mansion.

When the sister was out of earshot, it was Edwin who spoke first. 'Well done, George,' he grinned.

'Yes, George, dear,' said a red-faced Amelia, who looked a little doubtfully at a still smiling Amy.

'When will you be leaving, Edwin?' asked Amy.

'Ah! That, dear lady, is the question,' replied Edwin.

'You can come whenever you wish, Edwin, now that George feels able to manage you,' said Amelia.

'I hope he understands, Amelia, that he will have to get me out of bed. It's a lot to take on, you know,' said Edwin, thoughtfully.

'George understands. I've discussed it with him,' replied Amelia.

Edwin did not look too convinced until Amy remarked, 'George knows, Edwin. I know him and if he says he'll do it, he will – he means it, you know. There are not many like George, believe me.'

'I do believe you, Amy, and I'm grateful to him,' replied Edwin. 'I'll try and get a lift home. We have transport going to Woolwich regularly and I'll come at the first opportunity.'

'That's settled, then,' smiled Amelia.

'I'm going to serve in the shop soon, Edwin.'

'Are you, George?' smiled Edwin.

'Do you fancy that then?'

'Not bothered really, but that bloody girl we've got keeps eating the marzipan comfits.'

'Don't swear, dear,' said Amelia, trying not to smile.

'Why's that?' grinned Edwin.

'Cos she's eaten most of the liquorice whirls, that's why. Before long there won't be any stock left. I bet she's been stuffing herself today, Amelia,' I said, my voice rising.

Edwin was now convulsed with laughter and Amy was endeavouring not to laugh. Amelia, however, was not smiling. 'I will dismiss her, dear, if the stocks are down and I'll stop it out of her wages,' said Amelia, her face set.

'Yes, you get rid of her. She smells, as well you know,' I said.

'I don't think we want to know about that, dear,' said Amelia.

'She does, you know, Edwin,' who was still convulsed with laughter.

'He won't think it funny when he smells her, Amelia.'

'George, will you be quiet about that girl, please. I will dismiss her as soon as you can serve in the shop,' said Amelia, her face now going red.

'I think we had better leave now, Edwin. We mustn't miss that bus.'

'Yes, of course,' said Edwin, wiping the tears from his eyes. 'It's been good to see you, Sis, it really has, and you too, George, and you, of course, Amy – very good of you to come.'

'I hope you will soon be home, Edwin,' smiled Amy.

'It was a seven-pound box of liquorice whirls – they are nearly all gone, Edwin. She's had the bloody lot.'

'George, will you keep quiet about those wretched sweets?' said Amelia, for the first time showing annoyance.

Edwin, however, was now convulsed with laughter again.

'I don't know what's so funny, Amelia, we'll never make the shop pay,' I said in a huff.

'We will, dear, once you are in the shop,' said Amelia patiently.

We left Edwin at the large wrought-iron gates of the convalescent home. He waved to us as we made our way down the road to the bus. He looked so pathetic in his wheelchair; I was glad that I had made him laugh.

I was glad to get home. I felt tired and my head was beginning to ache. Agnes had prepared a nice tea for us in the front room.

'I had better get home,' said Amy, who was about to leave. 'Hector will be expecting me – the children, you know.'

'Stay and have some tea, first,' smiled Amelia.

'I shouldn't really,' replied Amy, glancing at the table.

I could tell what was being said. Amy deserved a break.

'You are staying, Amy,' I said, firmly. 'Hector can manage for once on his own. Come and sit by me.'

'All right then,' smiled Amy, taking off her coat.

'I'll hang it up for you,' I said, taking the coat from her.

I knew Amy had little pleasure and today had been a treat for her and a nice tea would finish it off.

After Amelia had fed the baby and given him his bath,

he was put in his cot. I tried to help as he fascinated me; he was soon asleep, then we had our tea.

'Edwin is looking forward to coming home,' said Amy, as we sat down at the table.

'Yes. I hope George can manage him, and it's not too much for him,' said Amelia, as she cut up some meat for me.

'I'm sure he will,' said Amy, confidently.

'He's getting better each day, aren't you, Georgie?' smiled Amy.

I nodded as I understood the gist of what she was saying.

'I can manage him, that's no problem,' I said. 'What's he going to do all day? That's the problem.'

Amelia put down her knife and fork, then looked at me. 'George, dear, that's a very important point, one I fear I overlooked. Just what will he do?'

'He can't take Buster out, like I can, and if I work in the shop.'

'That's right, dear. Oh well, we shall have to cross that bridge when we come to it,' said Amelia with a shrug.

Afterwards, I took Amy home, which gave me the opportunity to give Buster his evening walk. Amy had enjoyed her day – it had been quite a treat, so she told me.

The following morning, I was due to go to Woolwich Army Hospital for dressings, so Amelia insisted I had a bath and a change of underclothes. I was not looking forward to the dressings being removed from my face and eye again, and as I sat in the bath I tried to remove them, but they seemed to have stuck and it was very painful. I told Amelia of my doubts but she quickly tried to console me. 'They will be very careful, dear, I'm sure,' she smiled.

'I hope so – and what about my fares, will they pay them?'

'Ask the paymaster, dear, when you draw your pay.'

'I will,' I said, firmly.

The following morning, Amelia gave me a shilling for my fares.

'I only need sixpence,' I said.

'You take it, dear. You may need it,' she smiled.

Having passed Amelia's inspection and with a good breakfast inside me, I left the shop and went along Queen's Road to the tram stop. I had to change trams at New Cross Gate and I eventually arrived at Woolwich at nine-thirty.

Having reported to the outpatients' department I found that there were already about eight men in front of me, so I made my way to the pay office. To my surprise, I was given my fares besides my pay, which cheered me up a little and I returned to the outpatients in a better frame of mind.

There were now about twenty men awaiting attention and I found a seat in the passageway outside the treatment room.

I was sitting next to a gunner with one foot missing. He spoke to me, but as I sat next to him I could not see his mouth moving without turning, and I could not tell what he was saying.

'I can't hear you, mate, I'm as deaf as a post,' I said.

My words seemed to strike some of the men as humorous, as there were grins from a number of them – small wonder that they ran into machine gun fire when an officer blew a whistle.

I associated the smell of ether with pain, and I tried to doze off to sleep, my head resting against a wall. I must have succeeded as I felt a hand shake my arm some two hours later.

'Corporal Bowman, it's your turn.' I could make out the words and the uniformed sister who was peering at me. I got unsteadily to my feet and followed the sister into the treatment room.

'Remove your clothes to the waist,' she said, closing the door. I could not understand her and just stood there, unsure of myself. 'Hurry, Corporal, we have not got all day,' she said, sharply.

'I can't hear you, Sister, not a thing.'

The sister nodded, then unbuttoned my tunic and indicated to me to remove my tunic, shirt and vest. A doctor came into the room and sat down at a desk. He opened a folder that I presumed was mine.

'Medical Corps Bowman?' he said, then looked at me.

I did not understand him, but the sister nodded and said something to him, then he spoke again slowly, looking at me. 'An excellent record, Corporal Bowman. A credit to our corps,' he said, closing my folder. 'Sit down and let's have a look at you.' He smiled.

The doctor first examined the scars on my chest and side, then he examined the stump of my left arm, the bandages having been removed by a nurse. It gave me some pain when they were removed, but nothing compared with the pain I experienced when the bandages around my head and eye were cut away. It was as much as I could do not to scream with pain and I'm sure I almost fainted. I could feel myself swaying on the chair, and when at last my wound was dressed, I felt nauseous.

'I get rotten headaches, doctor,' I mumbled.

The nurse helped me to get dressed as the doctor wrote something on a pad. He ripped off the page, much as the sister had removed the dressings on my eye. 'Take this to the dispensary, Corporal Bowman, it will help with the headaches.' He handed me the prescription.

'Thank you, sir.'

'Come again in two weeks,' said the sister, who was drying her hands on a cloth.

'Yes, Sister,' I replied, as I shakily left the room.

As I was leaving, I turned to see the doctor speak to the sister. I thought I could make out him saying to her, 'that man should never have been discharged so soon from hospital.' This spurred me on. I had no wish to go back into hospital, so I hurried in the direction of the dispensary.

Having obtained a packet of tablets, I made my way out of the hospital barracks complex to the tram stop. The fresh air made me feel a little better, but I still felt sick as I sat on a low wall waiting for my tram.

I was unaware that anyone had approached me until someone touched me on the shoulder. I looked up – it was a police constable. 'Are you all right, son?' he asked, kindly.

'Feel a bit sick,' I said, realising what he was asking me. 'Had my dressings done – I feel rotten.'

The policeman's nose wrinkled. I must have reeked of ether. 'Going far, son?'

'What's that? I can't hear you.'

'Going far?' he said, slowly.

'Queen's Road, Peckham; near Lausanne Road,' I replied.

I sat hunched up on the wall, my eye closed in my own silent world, until I felt a hand touch my shoulder again. It was the same constable and with him was a sergeant. 'We'll take you home son,' said the burly sergeant, helping me to my feet.

A police van had drawn up and I was assisted into the front seat. Soon we were driving in the direction of Deptford and in what seemed no time at all, we were in Queen's Road. I pointed out our shop and we stopped outside. My head ached and I felt dizzy. The two policemen had tried to speak to me but I pointed to my ears and shook my head – they understood.

The burly sergeant helped me from the cab and we went into the shop to be met by Amelia.

312

'What is it, George?' she asked, a look of alarm on her face.

Before I could reply, the sergeant spoke. 'We brought him home, ma'am. He was not too well outside the Military Hospital. He should still be in it, if you ask me.'

'Thank you, sergeant. It was most kind of you,' said Amelia.

'It was my dressings, Amelia – my eye,' I mumbled.

'Yes, I know, dear,' she said, unbuttoning my greatcoat. 'He will be all right now, sergeant – thank you once again,' smiled Amelia, taking my arm, and removing the greatcoat.

'Yes, ma'am,' replied the sergeant, touching his helmet.

I could see him looking at my medal ribbons. Then he said, 'You take care, son. We don't see as many medals as that on a corporal very often.'

I guessed roughly what he said before I replied.

'I'd swap them all sergeant, just to hear our baby cry.'

Amelia compressed her lips and there were tears in her eyes. I wished that I had not spoken.

'Aye, lad. We just don't know how lucky we are,' he said, touching his helmet again as he left the shop.

Out of the corner of my eye, I was sure that I could see Rita surreptitiously slip a sweet into her mouth, but before I could speak, Amelia had ushered me upstairs to our living quarters. 'You get into bed, dear, and I will bring you a hot cup of tea.'

Since my head ached terribly, I did not hesitate to do what she said, and having removed my uniform, I climbed thankfully into bed.

'You will feel better later, dear,' said Amelia, as she came into the room holding a cup and saucer.

'They gave me some tablets for my head, Amelia. I'll take some now, they are in my tunic with my pay.' I pointed to my khaki tunic that I had put on the back of

313

a chair. Amelia put the cup and saucer on the chair by my side of the bed, then took the packet of tablets from my tunic.

'Take my pay, too. They gave me my fares.'

'Did they, dear?' First Amelia gave me three of the tablets then took my pay from my tunic pocket. 'Thank you, dear,' she smiled.

'That Rita – I'm sure she's stuffin' herself with those sweets again, Amelia. You'd best go down and see to her.'

'Yes, dear. Take your tablets. Let me hold the cup and saucer – I don't want tea spilt on the sheets.'

I took the tablets and lay down. I felt a little better.

'Are you hungry, dear?'

'No,' I mumbled.

'Have something later,' said Amelia, as she closed the bedroom curtains, and then came to the bed. 'You have a sleep now,' she said, bending over me and lightly kissing my cheek. Then she left the room and closed the door.

I drifted off to sleep, my mind on the trenches with the filthy water up to my knees. Oh to be out of it, I thought. I awoke some hours later and felt much better, though there was a dull ache in my left eye socket. Having decided to get up, I was endeavouring to get dressed when Amelia came into the room.

'Ah! You are up,' she exclaimed. 'Are you feeling better, dear?' she asked, as she began to assist me to dress.

'Yes, much better,' I yawned. 'What time is it?'

'Almost six o'clock. I'm just going to bathe Edward. I've just fed him, then we are going to have our meal.'

'I can watch you bathe him,' I smiled.

'Of course you can. Put these old trousers on, dear, then I'll put your uniform in the wardrobe,' said Amelia.

Putting on my trousers and buttoning me up needed

314

both of us – at least Edwin had two hands and I would be spared that embarrassment every day.

'Are you feeling better now, Master George?' asked Agnes, as I entered the kitchen.

'Yes, much better, thank you, Agnes,' I replied.

I sat, fascinated, as I watched Amelia bathe the baby. 'He likes it, doesn't he?'

'Of course he does,' smiled Amelia, as she kissed the baby's head.

Having been dried and powdered, Edward was put in his cot and he lay there contentedly as Agnes served up the evening meal.

'I had a letter from Edwin at lunch time, George. There is an ambulance going to Woolwich on Friday and it will bring him here. Do you think you will be able to manage him?'

'What was that, Amelia?'

'Edwin is coming on Friday,' she replied.

'Is he?'

'Yes. Will you be able to manage him?'

'Yes,' I nodded.

'Are you sure? I can put him off until you feel better.'

'You cannot put him off, he will think that you do not want him.'

Amelia nodded. 'Yes. You are right, dear, but only if you are sure that you will be well enough to manage him.'

'I will be,' I said, firmly.

'Good. I will write and tell him that we will be expecting him on Friday. I should catch the last post.'

'Do you think he will like it here, Amelia?' I asked.

'How do you mean, dear?'

'Well, it's not like Cedar Lodge, and Queen's Road is not like Blackheath, is it?'

I could see Agnes giving me a sidelong glance. I'm sure she must have thought the same thing.

Amelia compressed her lips for a few moments, then she replied. 'I take your point, George, but he will have to come to terms with it.' She spoke slowly and deliberately in order that I could understand her. 'Our family situation has changed – what there is left of the family.' There were tears in her eyes as she continued. 'We have to face the realities of the position and so must he. I know it is worse for him being in a wheelchair, but at least he has someone to look after him. He will not go to Worthing and will not stay in an army home, so he must learn to adjust. It might sound hard, but if I start to fuss over him it will make him worse.'

Amelia turned to Agnes as she continued. 'Do bear that in mind Agnes, dear, he must learn to do things for himself. He will not have a batman here, you know.'

'Yes, Miss Amelia,' said Agnes, sternly.

'None of the family has offered any help whatsoever, so we must make the best of the situation. I'm sure he will be happy here,' said Amelia, unfolding her serviette.

'I like it – much better than the trenches,' I smiled.

'I would hardly call that a flattering comparison, dear,' replied Amelia, coldly, as she began to cut up my meat for me.

Amelia looked up at my grinning face, then she started to smile, until we both started to laugh as she put my dinner plate in front of me.

'There we are, dear – better than your trench rations, I hope.'

'Thank you,' I said, still grinning at her.

'I've made a jam roly poly for pudding,' smiled Agnes. 'Your favourite, isn't it, Master George? And it hasn't got Holden's blackcurrant jam in it,' she chuckled.

We all began to laugh. Amelia and Agnes exchanged looks – they did all they could to make me happy and I loved both of them.

I felt a lot better the following morning and as we sat having our breakfast I suggested that I did the shopping.

'Do you feel up to it, dear?' asked Amelia.

'Yes. I'm not going far and I expect I will do better than you in the shops,' I smiled.

'George, dear, at times I underestimate you, don't I, Agnes?'

'I think we both do, Miss Amelia. If he can go to the butcher's and grocer's that would be most helpful.'

Since these goods were now on ration, I took our three ration cards and the baby's card when I eventually went out. Most people seemed to know me and when I returned, Amelia was most satisfied with my efforts. 'Very good, dear,' she said, emptying my bag.

'Far more than I would have got,' nodded Agnes.

'I'll take Buster out now, Amelia. We'll only go as far as Amy's and I'll talk to you about the conservatory when I come back.'

'Very well, dear. Take care and watch the road.'

'I will,' I replied, kissing her.

Amy was out shopping when I called and Hector was writing his sermon, so I did not stay long. Though Hector made me most welcome when I called, to the extent of offering to make me tea, I knew that I was an embarrassment to him. This had nothing to do with his not being in the Army, it was my physical state. I could tell that he was almost in tears at times when he looked at me. He knew that he had been wrong in 1914 and should have spoken about it, instead of being all for it. Probably, I would have been the same but for the influence the Snape family had on me through their kindness when I was often locked out of the house.

I knew now that my brothers resented me because I was far more intelligent than they were. I could read and write – only Amy could of all my brother and sisters, and this caused her problems before she married Hector. Now the family – like so many more – was decimated. Two brothers had been killed and two were missing – gone was all the flag waving.

Now I pricked Hector's conscience but at least he was honest enough to have one and I was sorry about that because I admired him in a different sort of way.

'I'm sorry you have missed her, George. You might see her when she comes past you on her way back from school.'

'I'll look out for her,' I replied, having understood most of what he had said.

'Are you coming to church on Sunday?' he asked.

'No point – I can't hear you, Hector,' I replied.

This set him furiously rubbing his glasses with his handkerchief.

'Every cloud has a silver lining,' I grinned.

Hector's mouth screwed up. Then, to my surprise, he hugged me, which took me aback for a moment.

'I'll see you on Sunday, Hector,' I said, quickly, then walked down the hall and left the house.

On my return, I decided to have a talk with Amelia about the conservatory. She was in the shop when I returned, checking the stock while Rita was serving a customer.

'Yes, dear?' smiled Amelia as she wrote on her note pad.

I took her hand and led her back through the shop.

'What is it, dear?' She looked mystified.

I let go of her hand and opened the back door and led her into the yard. Buster came towards us, wagging his tail.

'Buster, don't you dare jump up and mark my dress,' admonished Amelia to the playful Buster.

'See, I came in the back way all right, when it's dry

like today, but if we build a wall across here, then put a roof on here fixed to the walls...'

'Will our neighbours mind, dear?' frowned Amelia.

'I'll ask them. They won't mind. As long as it doesn't cost them anything, it will be all right. The door would be here and another one for the toilet that would be covered in, so Edwin can go without getting wet.'

Amelia frowned as she glanced around the yard deep in thought.

'He won't be able to go upstairs every time, you know, and the WC needs a new pan and cistern and the door is going rotten.'

'Yes, yes, dear, I appreciate what you say,' Amelia held up her hands to try and stop my flow of words. 'But you must realise that it will all cost money, dear. We just do not have a lot to spend. I am no longer at the library; there is only your pay at the moment.'

I knew what Amelia was saying. Money was tight, the shop was showing little profit after paying Rita.

'It will cost about forty pounds at the most, and we can use some of that hundred pounds, and when I'm a bit better I can work in the shop.'

Amelia hesitated and glanced about the yard almost helplessly.

'It will make an extra big room, Amelia, and the WC's got to be mended, plus Edwin will need handles to pull himself up off it.'

'You are right, dear, it must be done,' said Amelia, her mind now firmly made up. 'I will get someone in straight away,' she said.

I shook my head and tapped my chest with my forefinger. 'I'll get someone, Amelia. I know just the man. I'll get it done cheaper, leave it to me.'

'All right, dear, I'll let you arrange matters, but you must not overdo things,' she smiled.

After luncheon, I put Buster's lead on and we made our way to Billy Jackson's yard in Dennetts Road. With something to occupy my mind, I felt better, though I still had a headache. I was wearing my uniform and I was given a friendly greeting by every passer-by that I encountered. This made me feel better as well, though I think it was the fresh air and cold wind really.

I had gone to school with Billy Jackson and two of his sisters. He had six sisters and no brothers, and at school he was always having his leg pulled about it.

Billy, sadly, was killed at the first battle of Ypres and it had devastated his parents. Amy told me that his mother had never got over it. It was a family joinery business; they were also undertakers – another thing that Billy got his leg pulled about.

Billy had been expected to take over the business one day. His father must have seen me as I entered the yard and he came to greet me, holding out his hand. 'Hello! It's young Georgie Bowman,' he said, gripping both my hand and Buster's lead at the same time. 'How are you, son?' He looked at me, sadly.

'I'm all right, Mr Jackson, but I get bad headaches and I'm as deaf as a post. I can't hear a bloody thing.'

'I'm sorry, son. You know about Billy?' He seemed close to tears.

I compressed my lips and nodded, looking down at my boots. 'I heard, Mr Jackson. I'm very sorry,' I muttered.

'It's good to see you, Georgie, very good. What can I do for you?'

I quickly explained what I wanted and the reason for it.

'Didn't know it was your shop, lad.'

'Well, it's my wife's really, Mr Jackson. We have been there about a year now – well almost.'

'Doing well?' he asked.

'It could do better,' I replied.

'Have to get the family to use it. You sell tobacco?'

'Oh yes,' I replied, nodding my head.

At that moment old Mr Jackson came out into the yard puffing at a battered old pipe.

'You remember young Georgie Bowman, Dad. One of young Billy's pals.'

'Aye, I do. How are yer, lad?'

He looked at me with watery eyes and then spoke again. I could not understand him – he had his pipe in his mouth and hardly moved his lips. I turned to his son.

'I can't understand what he says, Mr Jackson.' I touched my ear.

'Georgie's deaf, Dad. It's the guns, most likely.'

Old Mr Jackson nodded, then spat on the cobbles of the yard.

'He wants me to do a bit of work for him, I won't be long.'

'Goodbye, son,' said the old man, holding out his hand. I let go of Buster to shake it and the dog raced up the yard and went behind a shed, just as a cat jumped on it to safety. 'Come here, Buster,' I shouted, but it made no difference; once he was loose, he was a devil to catch.

Mr Jackson, however, managed to catch him and we made our way back to the shop. When I introduced him to Amelia, I could tell that he was surprised.

'I'm pleased to meet you, Mrs Bowman. I heard that Georgie was married from one of his sisters.'

'Quite, Mr Jackson. You will let us know the cost before you commence,' said Amelia.

'Oh, yes. I'll tell you straight away. It will be a good job, you can be sure of that.'

'This way, Mr Jackson,' I said, leading Buster through the shop.

Having shown Mr Jackson what I had in mind, he took out his notebook and tape measure. I held the tape measure, as directed, and he wrote down the measurements in his notebook. At last he spoke. 'It's going to cost thirty-eight pounds for the conservatory and another six pounds approx to cover the rest, and five pounds approx for the toilet, that makes forty-nine pounds altogether.'

Amelia, who had joined us, looked doubtful, but did not speak.

'How much, Mr Jackson?' I asked.

'Forty-nine pounds approx, George,' said Mr Jackson.

'Hm, a bit dear, isn't it?' I replied.

'I don't think so,' frowned Mr Jackson.

'I wasn't expecting forty-nine; nearer forty, more like.'

'Things have gone up with the war, son,' sniffed Mr Jackson.

'Are you tiling the floor?' I asked.

'No, I'm not. I'll put down a screed of cement to make it level,' he conceded.

'Tell you what, Mr Jackson, we'll give you forty-eight pounds cash as soon as you are finished, if you tile it, and I'll help you, how's that?'

A faint smile appeared on Mr Jackson's face, then he spoke. 'The Huns might have knocked you about a bit son, but you've still got all your marbles. All right, lad, as I know you, it's a deal.' He turned to Amelia. 'All right, Mrs Bowman?'

'Yes,' she smiled.

I held up my palm and spat on it as Mr Jackson did likewise, then we shook hands in front of a frowning Amelia. 'Er ... you can start immediately, Mr Jackson?' said Amelia.

'I can, as it happens, we have a big job starting in a week's time, so I can be here tomorrow with two men.'

'Excellent, and how long will you take?' smiled Amelia.

'About a week, I'd say. The glazing is the biggest job, but I've some cut pieces left over from another job so I can use them, it will save time.'

'That sounds fine, Mr Jackson,' said Amelia. 'We will see you tomorrow, then,' she smiled.

'You will, ma'am,' he said, touching his cap and walking down to the back gate.

'Bye, George,' he called, as he closed the gate.

'Cheerio, Mr Jackson,' I replied.

That evening I got my diary up to date. Amelia watched me writing on the kitchen table, a faint smile on her face.

'Are you still keeping a diary, dear?'

'What's that, Amelia?' I asked.

'I said, are you still keeping a diary?'

'Yes. I'll always keep one, I think.'

'Why, dear?'

I shrugged my shoulders and shook my head, then I smiled. 'I don't know, Amelia, but you can always read it.'

Amelia started to laugh as she replied, 'I'm pleased to hear that, dear.'

The army ambulance caused some stares when it pulled up outside the shop on the following Saturday afternoon. I had been watching for it, sitting in a chair placed by the window of what was our lounge-cum-dining-room overlooking Queen's Road. It was directly above the shop and the people on the top deck of the tramcars seemed almost opposite us.

'He's here, Amelia,' I called out, getting out of the chair.

'Yes, I heard you, dear,' she said, as she removed her apron upon entering the room.

Amelia glanced out of the window as the passenger door of the ambulance opened and a khaki-clad figure got out.

'Yes, that's him, dear,' she said, leaving the window.

'I'll make sure Buster doesn't get out; he should be in the yard, but Mr Jackson's men might let him out.'

'Yes, do that, dear, and ask Mr Jackson when he expects to be finished.'

'About next Tuesday, he said when I asked him this morning,' I replied, as I followed her from the room.

The two army orderlies soon had Edwin out of the ambulance and into the shop.

'Have you got all my gear and the spare wheelchair?' said Edwin to one of the orderlies.

'Yes. It's all here, sir,' the man replied.

'Good. Leave the spare wheelchair here and perhaps you would kindly take Captain Hooper upstairs,' said Amelia.

'Yes, ma'am,' said the orderly.

Edwin and his gear were soon upstairs and the orderlies in their army boots clattered down the stairs and out of the shop.

When Agnes greeted Edwin she burst into tears.

'Oh Master Edwin!' she sobbed. 'That it should all come to this,' she said, putting her arms about him.

I think that I understood her correctly and got the impression that her choice of words were a little unfortunate, judging by the way Amelia compressed her lips in annoyance. However, Amelia, who had already greeted him, made no comment.

'How are you, George?' said Edwin at last, shaking my hand.

'A bit better,' I replied.

'Would you make some tea, Agnes, while we take Edwin to his room?' said Amelia, as she picked up one of Edwin's cases.

'Yes, Miss Amelia,' sniffed Agnes.

We took Edwin to his room. As Amelia opened the

door she said, 'We brought your bed from Cedar Lodge, also your dressing-table and tallboy. There's also a built-in cupboard in the room. In it are most of your old clothes, too.'

'Fine, thanks, Sis. Looks almost like my old room,' said Edwin, as he pushed himself into the room.

'I'll help you unpack, Edwin,' said Amelia, as she put one of his cases on a chair. There was little space in the room for me as well, so I made an excuse to leave.

'I'm just going downstairs, Amelia.'

'Yes, all right, George,' she replied.

'Let me know if you want anything.'

'I will, thank you, George,' smiled Edwin.

I thought Edwin looked a lot older. His face was lined and his hair had started to recede.

In the yard I met Mr Jackson. The work had progressed well. The WC was finished and most of the woodwork.

'Should get most of the glazing done tomorrow and what's left done on Monday, with the painting,' explained Mr Jackson.

I nodded. I understood what he had said.

'We'll be finished Tuesday dinner time at the latest. Can I have my money, then?' He spoke slowly and I understood what he had said.

'Yes, I'll tell Amelia, but we won't know if it leaks,' I remarked.

'It won't leak. If it does, I'll come back and fix it,' said Mr Jackson, who looked none too pleased at my remark.

'All right, Mr Jackson, I'll get it for you.'

'Who is the officer in the wheelchair, George?'

'It's my brother-in-law,' I replied.

'I see. We are cementing the floor before we go tonight, then we can tile it Tuesday morning, so don't walk on it.' He pointed to the cement being mixed and I nodded my head.

'Keep that dog of yours off it and that wheelchair – all right?'

'I understand, Mr Jackson.'

I went back into the shop. Rita was serving a customer who could not make up her mind what to have.

'I should have some wine gums before she eats them all,' I said, a little unkindly. Rita's face went red and I could sense she called me something by the expression on the customer's face.

I looked around the shop. It was quite big. Part of it we did not use at all and it seemed a pity that the space was not put to good use, and I began to think about it. I went back upstairs, ignoring Rita. I did not like or trust her, but then that was Amelia's affair – she took her on.

'While Mr Jackson is here, George, we must get him to put another handrail on the stairs, it might assist getting Edwin up and downstairs,' said Amelia, as I entered the kitchen.

When I had fully understood what she had said, I agreed. 'Yes. If he holds it, I might be able to get him up and down in his wheelchair instead of carrying him.'

That evening I began what was to be, for some years to come, my ritual for assisting Edwin to go to bed and get up in the morning. Since time was of no consequence to us, the fact that we took over an hour did not matter. I had intermittent headaches so I would sit in a chair while Edwin had a bath or washed and shaved himself.

As I expected, Mr Jackson made an excellent job of the conservatory and yard. Amelia was very pleased with it and told me on a number of occasions what a good idea it was to have had it done. Edwin sat out there for hours reading his paper and smoking his pipe. I was glad of that, as his pipe made me cough, but he was considerate most of the time with it.

'Made a good job, did Jackson,' said Edwin, pointing to the roof with his pipe. To which I replied with a grin, 'He's an undertaker as well, Edwin.'

'I feel all right, young George. Did you hear that, Amelia?' he said in mock horror.

'Yes, Edwin, worth remembering,' she laughed.

With carpets, curtains and a wrought-iron table brought from Cedar Lodge, Amelia made it most comfortable. When Amelia put an oil lamp in it as well, Buster also took up residence. I do not know what financial arrangement Edwin had come to with Amelia, but she said to me that she was very satisfied. This was just as well because the shop was not doing too well according to Amelia. This surprised me because there was always someone in it. The reason for this did not come to light until the day after Hector baptised Edward Edwin James at the chapel.

Amelia's parents came to the christening and they both looked very ill. When Mr Hooper saw Edwin and me together he burst into tears, much to our embarrassment.

After joining us for tea, which would have been a miserable event but for Amy's children, they returned to Worthing.

On the Monday morning after the christening, Rita did not turn up for work, so I worked in the shop. It was a busy morning and Mr Jackson called in for his own and his father's week's tobacco. He gave me a five-pound note, which took most of my change, though I soon made it up as I was busy.

Rita turned up at dinner time. She said she had been to the doctor's. Amelia was rather curt with her, though I did not see what was said. That evening when we were having our meal, the subject of Rita came up, which caused Amelia to frown.

'She's getting fatter than ever,' remarked Agnes.

327

'I expect she is stuffing herself with toffees now all the marzipan comfits are gone,' I remarked.

'I don't think they are the cause of the problem,' said Amelia.

Edwin was now laughing and it increased as I remarked, 'It's probably the liquorice whirls – they are all gone, too.'

'It's not that either, dear,' said Amelia, patiently.

'Edwin – it's not a laughing matter, snapped Amelia.

'It's not, Edwin – she'll soon finish the toffees. It's a good job she doesn't smoke,' I said in an aggrieved tone. 'I sold a lot of tobacco this morning, Amelia. Mr Jackson gave me a five-pound note – he bought a lot.'

Amelia almost dropped her knife and fork; she looked intently at me as she said, 'You took a five-pound note, dear, what did you do with it?'

'It's in the till with the pound notes I took. There were three of them and the five-pound note when Rita took over from me – it was busy today.'

'When I checked the till after she went, there was no five-pound note and only two one-pound notes,' said Amelia, her face white.

Edwin had stopped laughing, then he spoke, his face set. 'Now you know why you don't make much money in the shop, Sis. In future, George and I will run it, won't we, George?'

I nodded. 'Never did like her and she still smells, Amelia, even after you telling her,' I growled.

'I shall see her when she arrives in the morning. If she does not return the money I shall call the police,' said Amelia, her face still white with anger.

Rita was now temporarily forgotten as Edwin began to read from the evening paper. The news was bad; the German offensive had taken them to within fifty-three miles of Paris. 'They'll push us into the Channel, you mark my words,' said Edwin, sombrely.

I did not comment. It was no longer of any interest to me, not that it had ever been. My deafness had its small compensations, I could just ignore any subject that did not interest me by just looking away from the speaker.

Edwin touched my arm. I put down my spoon and looked at him. 'George,' he said slowly, 'the Huns are only fifty miles from Paris. They could take it by the weekend.'

'They're welcome to it,' I sniffed. 'You tell me when they're at Deptford and I'll be interested.' I picked up my spoon and continued with my pudding.

Edwin was a little taken aback and turned to Amelia. 'So much for the *entente cordiale* as far as our George is concerned,' remarked Edwin, folding his newspaper.

'George did not go to Paris, like you did,' smiled Amelia. 'He did not enjoy the doubtful delights of Parisian life as you did, I am pleased to say.'

Edwin started to laugh, then he became solemn as he said, 'Just as well, in the circumstances, I suppose.'

Amelia pretended she had not heard his remark as she picked up my pudding bowl. 'Have you finished, George, dear?'

'Yes, thank you. I'm just going round to Amy's. Hector's got a book for me. I'll take Buster for his evening walk at the same time. Do you want to go downstairs, Edwin?'

'I'll come with you, if you don't mind.'

'I don't mind as long as you hold on to Buster. You could go to the prayer meeting with Hector if you like. I'll push you round to the chapel and collect you at about ten o'clock when it's over.'

'I don't think that's funny,' said Edwin, a grin appearing on his face.

'It's not meant to be, Edwin. Hector's prayer meetings and sermons are never funny,' I replied.

Amelia was now laughing as she collected the dishes from the table. Edwin turned to her. 'Did you hear him, Sis? A prayer meeting until ten o'clock – whatever next?' said Edwin, now taking me a little seriously.

'Sometimes he finishes at half nine,' laughed Amelia.

'Does he? Well, he'll do it without me,' said Edwin, sharply.

'Never mind, you can go on Sunday and hear his sermon,' I said.

'Can I? And what about you, George?'

'No good me going, I can't hear him.' I shook my head.

'You can lip-read – you do it very well,' smiled Edwin.

'Not there. It's always too dark in the chapel and he's too far away, but you will be all right. I'll push you there,' I grinned. 'He'll be pleased to see you, Edwin. I expect he'll ask you to join the men's committee; they organise games.'

'Games? What games?' Edwin frowned.

'Well, that one where they sit around in a circle and they have numbers in a hat of all the hymns in the hymn book. Then you take a number, call it out and each has to guess which hymn it is, and the one who guesses the most is the winner. You could play – in fact, it's ideal for you,' I said.

For once Edwin was completely lost for words. He looked at me, his mouth half open, while Amelia had turned away to put the tablecloth in the sideboard drawer.

'How do you fancy it? Mind you, I think you will have to polish up on your hymns to stand any chance of winning.'

'I've never heard such rubbish in all my life,' exploded Edwin.

'You don't fancy it, then?' I persisted.

'No, I bloody well don't,' said Edwin, his face now red.

I could see Amelia's shoulders shaking as she was trying not to laugh at Edwin.

'Well, when you are on the men's committee you can suggest other games, if you don't fancy that one,' I said, easily.

'He won't get the chance to get me on any committee, I can assure you of that,' said Edwin emphatically.

Amelia now turned to face us and burst out laughing and Edwin now realised that I had been having him on.

'Right, young George, I owe you one,' chuckled Edwin, shaking his head and pointing at me.

'Still, you can go to the service. Amelia likes Hector's sermons – she sometimes tells him where he goes wrong, don't you, dear?'

'That, I can believe,' chortled Edwin.

'I do not, George,' said a now red-faced Amelia. 'That's not correct, you know it isn't.'

'Do you remember before I went back to France the last time I could hear him, you told him afterwards that you thought his sermon was all wrong.'

'I did not exactly say that, dear. I said I did not agree with certain aspects of his arguments,' said Amelia, patiently.

'Was this during his sermon, Sis?' grinned Edwin. Amelia did not bother to answer him as she turned to me. 'George, dear, you had better get a move on or Edwin will be late.'

'Yes, dear,' I said, getting out of my chair.

'I'm not going to any prayer meeting, and that's final,' said a concerned Edwin, whose face was now a shade of pink. 'Just get me downstairs, George,' he snapped.

'Yes, all right. Still, once we get to Amy's you might want to go,' I suggested.

'That's quite possible, but it will be to the toilet and

not a prayer meeting, so come on,' said Edwin, pushing his wheelchair away from the table.

We were now quite adept at getting downstairs. Edwin held the two handrails to take his weight and I would lower the chair slowly down the stairs.

'Come on, Buster,' said Edwin, waving the bull terrier's lead. The dog needed no urging and he came to Edwin, who leaned forward and grabbed his collar. 'That's it, George, off we go,' said Edwin, turning to face me.

With Buster pulling on his lead, we made our way down Queen's Road. The local residents now knew us and we always received cheery waves and smiles.

Edwin and I got on well. We both tried to be patient with the other as we were fast becoming interdependent; I was his legs and he was my ears and eye. We now did all the shopping. Meat and groceries were now rationed, though bread, fish and vegetables were not. This helped to eliminate queues for food, but I feel bound to say we always got fish and plenty of vegetables, even though there might be none displayed on the marble slabs. Mr Siddenham, who had given me the crab when I had first come home from France, always made a fuss of me and was always very patient, even though other customers might be waiting.

Amy was pleased to see us, though I could tell from the sorrowful expression on her face that the sight of us caused some pain. Hector would always talk to Edwin, largely because talking to me was hard work, and also, I'm sure that the fact that they came from the same social class had something to do with it. Amy was always most concerned about me, asking how I got on at the hospital and when did I have to go again?

'That Rita has been pinching money out of the till, Amy.'

'Has she? How do you know?' asked Amy, frowning. I

told her about the five-pound note, at which Amy nodded her head and then remarked,

'I'm not surprised. She was sacked from Holden's for pinching their jam, didn't Amelia know that?'

'I've no idea, Amy,' replied Edwin.

'She's had plenty of our sweets, according to George. Hasn't she, George?' Edwin looked at me, mischievously.

'What's that?'

'Rita has been taking our sweets,' said Edwin, grinning at me.

'Eaten nearly all the marzipan comfits and liquorice whirls – look at the size of her,' I replied.

'It wasn't the marzipan comfits or liquorice whirls that got her to that shape,' said Amy, a faint smile on her face.

'No, it wasn't,' chuckled Edwin.

Hector immediately changed the subject and I could tell he said 'prayer meeting', which prompted Edwin to say that we must be off, and after Hector and Edwin had their obligatory five-minute discussion about the war situation, we left.

'Tell Amelia I will pop round to see her tomorrow, Edwin,' said Amy, as she kissed me goodbye.

'Yes, all right, Amy. Don't I get a kiss too?' he grinned, cheekily.

Amy blushed, then bent down and kissed his cheek. 'Goodbye, Edwin,' she smiled.

The following morning, Amelia was up earlier than usual and the baby had been bathed and fed before Rita arrived at a quarter to eight.

I did not see and could not hear what took place, but within two minutes of her arrival, Rita left the shop, only to return a few minutes later with the five-pound note and three other one-pound notes, which she gave to Amelia, who then sent her packing.

'I made it quite clear to her that I would call the police if the money was not returned,' said Amelia at breakfast, her face still a little flushed.

'George and I will take over the shop now, Sis, won't we, George?' said Edwin, with some enthusiasm.

'What's that?' I frowned.

'We will run the shop now,' repeated Edwin.

I nodded my agreement, well aware that Edwin might get brassed off with it after a few days behind the counter. However, it proved a blessing in disguise as it gave Edwin something to do during the day, and was to be a big addition to our income in due course.

I was now discharged from the Army and the allowance I was given was only half my army pay, and that was little enough. Edwin was much more fortunate, being a Captain. Amelia did not say what he gave her, but she did say he was most generous to her.

18

An Idea

It surprised me that Edwin and Amelia did not mention their parents. In my case it was understandable – my father had thrown me out, but their circumstances had been quite different. I did not raise the matter, after all, it was none of my business and I had enough problems of my own.

Although Amelia saw her friends from the public library regularly, she did not get her old position back. This, I think, touched her pride more than the loss of income, as Amelia assured me that we were managing quite comfortably and did not need the money.

'All the same if we did,' I growled.

'Exactly, dear,' nodded Amelia, patting my hand.

It was a sunny July morning and I was serving in the shop. Edwin was in the bath reading his *Times* and *Morning Post* while Amelia and Agnes had just pushed the pram through the shop to go to the butchers.

'We will not be long, dear,' said Amelia, moving her lips so that I could understand her perfectly.

'Yes, all right,' I had replied.

Later a Mrs Butler called in. She was a woman in her sixties and lived further down Queen's Road.

'Morning, Mrs Butler,' I smiled.

'Good morning, dear,' she replied. 'A quarter of mints and a half ounce of St Julian, please.'

I tucked the jar of mints under what remained of my left arm and unscrewed the lid with my right hand. Having weighed out the mints on the little scale, I held a paper bag in my right hand and with the same hand tipped up the brass ladle of the scale and emptied the mints safely in the bag. I had been practising this for days and with Edwin's encouragement had almost perfected the manoeuvre. Mrs Butler watched with interest and at last she spoke.

'Is Mrs Bowman still at the public library, George?'

'Where?' I frowned.

'At the public library – is she?' Mrs Butler peered at me.

'No.' I shook my head. 'Why, Mrs Butler?'

'I was going to ask her if she would take my library books back. Got to go all the way to Deptford on the tram and it's a penny each way, you know.'

After she had explained again I understood her. She produced the book – it was only a cheap romance and the book was well worn. 'I like a nice romance and my Ted likes a western, but it's a nuisance having to go all that way,' she explained.

'Yes it is, Mrs Butler,' I said, giving her the mints and tobacco with her change.

Mrs Butler left the shop with her purchases and I sat on my stool behind the counter deep in thought. I served two more customers, then Amelia returned, and I was still deep in thought.

'I'm putting the pram in the conservatory, dear,' said Amelia, as she pushed the pram through the shop.

'I'd better get Edwin out of the bath, Amelia, he's been in it for nearly an hour,' I replied.

'Yes, dear, do that. I'll go behind the counter when the baby is settled,' she smiled.

Getting Edwin out of the bath was no easy matter and

336

if he touched my head it gave me a bad headache. However, he always tried to help me and after a bit of puffing and blowing and a little spilt water, I would get him into a chair. Edwin would sit there a little self-consciously, not because he was naked – that did not bother him – but what did worry him was the fact that his legs were getting thinner through lack of use. He had been an athletic type, having won a Blue at Oxford; now he was to be confined to a wheelchair for the rest of his life. I could read his thoughts and tried to cheer him up.

'At least you have not lost them,' I said, moving the stump of my left arm up and down and trying to grin.

'Might just as well,' he replied, mouthing the words so that I could understand.

I did not reply but carried on trying to help dry and dress him. But for the fact that I was as disabled as he was, I am sure he would have made sarcastic remarks. Edwin could be very caustic at times, though I was always spared his tongue. Perhaps being deaf had its compensations, anyway we got on very well.

At last I got him downstairs and comfortable in his wheelchair. Amelia was behind the counter in the shop and was just giving a customer change.

'Thank you, sir,' she said to an elderly man who was leaving the shop. 'Ah, there you are,' she smiled.

'We'll take over now, Sis,' said Edwin.

'I'll make you both a drink,' she said, coming from behind the counter.

'Amelia, Edwin, I've an idea that I want to tell you about.'

They both looked at me, curiously, then I explained. 'Mrs Butler came in earlier with her library books. She wanted you to take them back to the library, but I told her that you were no longer there.'

'But what is the idea?' asked Amelia.

'I'll show you – come over here.'

Amelia followed me across the shop while Edwin pushed his wheelchair forward.

'See all these display cases along the wall with all those dummy sweet boxes in them?'

'Yes, dear,' said Amelia, patiently.

'I want to take them all out and put bookshelves in their place, right the way along the shop and right up to the ceiling.'

Amelia looked at me and frowned, as she said somewhat tersely, 'What on earth for, George?'

There was a note of impatience in her voice – I could tell that by her pursed lips.

'So we can start our own lending library, that's why! If we get a lot of second-hand books, the type that people like Mr and Mrs Butler like, we can loan them out for a penny a week. Most of the books in the library never go out anyway. We can get the popular books, which people read.'

Amelia put her forefinger to her lips as she thought of my idea, but Edwin was more forthright.

'Well, I think it is a damned good idea; we haven't got a paper business and it would fit in well, he enthused.

'But would the Town Hall like it?' Amelia looked pensive.

'Bugger the Town Hall,' retorted Edwin.

'Edwin, please, your language,' frowned Amelia.

'What do you think, Amelia?' I asked, excitedly.

'I'll think about it, dear, but we must consider the cost.'

'Oh!' I murmured, a little disappointed at her lack of interest.

'I'll pay for it. You and I will do it together, George. We'll get the books and you can get your friend Mr

Jackson to put up the shelves for us,' said Edwin, winking at me.

'Yes.' I beamed at Edwin.

Amelia was too intelligent not to acknowledge that she had been out-voted and since Edwin had insisted on paying the cost, there was little point in her objecting.

It was a fact, and we both knew it, that Edwin would only spend about a half an hour behind the counter. As I pointed out to Amelia, he was far too intelligent to serve sweets for long. He soon became bored and this could be the answer for him.

'If that is what you wish to do,' she smiled, 'I'll leave it in your hands. Now I'll make you both a drink.'

'Will you make up a list of the most popular authors – those whose books were always going out at the library, and we'll need a card system and stamper like they have,' I enthused.

'George, my dear, the more I think of your idea, the more I realise how good it is. I certainly will organise matters.' She stepped forward and kissed me, which caused Edwin to smile and make a remark, which I did not hear, though I did gather Amelia told him to behave himself.

Having told Mr Jackson what we intended to do, it was his suggestion that we made a doorway in the dividing wall so that the shelves could be extended through to the back room and go the full length of the building. 'If I put up a false wall across here, you will be able to put up more shelves here, though you will lose a piece of the back room – it will be about four feet narrower,' said Mr Jackson.

'Sounds good to me,' said Edwin, who had thrown himself wholeheartedly into the project.

'How much will it cost, Mr Jackson? I shall be paying for the alterations and the shelving.'

Mr Jackson made a few notes on a piece of paper, then added up some figures. At last he spoke, 'I'd say about nineteen to twenty pounds altogether, sir.'

'H'm,' grunted Edwin.

'There's a lot of wood, sir.'

'All right, twenty pounds maximum it is, Mr Jackson. When can you start?' queried Edwin.

'I can get a lad in to measure this afternoon, then get all the timber cut so we can start next Monday.'

'Excellent, Mr Jackson,' smiled Edwin. 'How long will it take?'

'About three days, I would say, sir.'

'Very good. Then we can get started, George,' grinned Edwin.

With the assistance of the list that Amelia had made for me, I began to scour the second-hand bookshops, sometimes with Edwin, but mostly on my own. Edwin would look after the shop and cut out cardboard pockets to stick in our fast growing collection of books, which would be neatly piled up ready for me to place on the shelves allotted to them.

Amelia began a card index system and had even obtained a date stamp and ink pad for when we commenced our lending library. At Amy's suggestion, I even went to jumble sales, which became a useful source of books.

Though I obtained most of the books for virtually nothing, they still cost money, which Amelia gave me, and I know Edwin contributed towards their cost at his insistence, I should add. By the time that the alterations were complete and the shelves fitted, we had obtained some hundreds of books.

Three further electric lights were installed and after everything had been painted and allowed to dry hard, we were ready to put out the books that were now in the conservatory and the back room of the shop.

'People will buy more from the shop when they come in for books,' I said, as I assisted Amelia to put books on the top shelves.

Amelia now had a small table and chair in the part that had been the back room. On the table there was her indexing system, date stamp and pad, and even a small till.

In the week before we opened the library, I think I went into every second-hand bookshop in south London. I even had a small trolley that I pulled behind me – it was very useful and enabled me to bring home larger amounts of books.

Edwin became occupied in looking for first editions and it gave him that interest, which he did not have before. Now over half of the shelves were filled and we opened the library, having had a poster in the shop window for the previous three weeks. The question arose about what we should call our new lending library. I suggested the Amelia Bowman lending library, but Edwin was adamant. 'Bowman's lending library, that's what it should be. It was your idea, George, old son,' he said, patting my arm.

'Quite right, Edwin,' agreed Amelia.

'We'll have it on a sign outside. I'll get Jackson to do it,' said Edwin, eagerly.

Much to our surprise, on the first day of the library being opened, we had eleven people join, including Mr and Mrs Butler. Between them all they took out sixteen books at a penny each and with the joining fee of threepence each, we took over four shillings profit on the first day.

Amelia was delighted with this initial success as she only received ten shillings for a full week's work at the library.

'And they buy more sweets and tobacco while they are browsing here,' I pointed out.

'That's quite right, dear,' smiled Amelia.

Edwin was now completely involved with the library. He would give me a list of the books we required and I would go round the second-hand bookshops with Buster, and sometimes Alice, who was now growing bigger and was able to carry a bag for the books. I would give her some sweets to take home and sometimes a bar of chocolate for Amy. On one occasion, Amelia saw me.

'I ... er ... was giving Alice a small bar of chocolate for Amy,' I said, a little sheepishly.

Amelia smiled, then went to a stock cupboard and opened a box and took out a large bar of chocolate, which she put in a paper bag. 'Give that to mummy, Alice,' she said.

'Thank you, Aunt Amelia,' said Alice, offering her the small bar that I had given to her.

'No, you keep that, dear; share it between Ruth and James.'

'Thank you, Aunt Amelia,' beamed Alice.

'Bye.' She kissed Amelia, then myself and turned to leave.

'I'll see you across the road, dear,' said Amelia, taking her hand.

'I got a copy of *Little Women* today, Edwin, and two Dickens and four westerns,' I said, as I approached him, sitting in his wheelchair behind the little table, studying the *Morning Post*.

'Very good, George. Just reading the news again – it's not good,' he shook his head and grimaced.

'Not calling up one-armed stretcher bearers, are they?'

Edwin's eyes twinkled as he replied, 'Not yet, old son,' he chuckled.

'That's all right then,' I grinned.

Edwin smiled and shook his head; at times I think he could not understand me.

Time passed pleasantly enough. The library membership increased each day and Mrs Derby, our daily, brought in her young daughter to assist Amelia. Daisy was the girl's name and she was to prove very useful to Amelia, helping her with the library and shop and also giving assistance with Edward.

On 15th July, the Germans launched what was to be their last offensive of the war. They had now reached their nearest point to Paris and the papers were full of it. Our lines gave way and the enemy moved forward until, on 18th July, the French struck at the exposed German flank. Then the situation changed and the news got better, and by the middle of August, the French, Americans and ourselves had gone on the offensive.

This again involved us in heavy losses, but though we did not know it at the time, it signalled the end of the war. The German Army had had enough. Their losses had been enormous and now they were facing shortages of equipment and food. Indeed, we read that there were chronic shortages in Germany and food riots had taken place. It was now said that the German Government was concerned about their whole system breaking down. This was affecting the German Army, so we were told, but could you believe the newspapers, I asked myself?

All this was avidly discussed by Amelia, Edwin and Hector. I preferred to read Dickens in my world of silence. I was still getting pains in my ears from time to time and my eye socket was even worse. Amelia understood when I suddenly went to bed during the day. This, thankfully, was becoming less often and I seemed to be improving, though I did need the pills for my head most days. Every Sunday, Amy, Hector and the children came to tea. I looked forward to it and told Amelia so.

'I know you do, dear,' she smiled.

We would have winkles and shrimps besides cold meats.

Alice would sit next to me at table while Ruth would sit next to Edwin, who always made a fuss of her.

Each week, Amelia would invite her friends Irene Peskett and Maud Littleton to tea. Both their young men had been killed in the war, which seemed to draw them to us. They were kind and considerate young ladies. It seemed that the man with the scythe would affect their lives too. Mr and Mrs Hollins no longer came to visit us. I think our library did not meet with his approval and he made rather disparaging remarks about it, to which Edwin had retorted 'Bloody old fool.' With the success of the shop and the lending library, Amelia was now able to extend her social life. Now a leading figure at the Baptist Church and on a number of committees, she was becoming well known locally, a fact, I think, she was now enjoying.

I was not particularly religious myself, and one church was the same as another, but it did surprise me that Amelia made this complete change from the Church of England. Once, when I questioned her, she said, briefly, that the Baptist Church had shown her kindness whilst her own church at Blackheath had completely ignored the family's change in circumstances. Not a word of sympathy had been given to them. I never raised the matter again. It was clear to me that it brought back painful memories. Amelia was happy now and that was all that concerned me.

It was much the same as far as women's suffrage was concerned. This was rarely mentioned after I had remarked, 'If this war goes on much longer you will have to have the vote, there won't be any men left.'

'Mr Lloyd George has promised us the vote, George, dear, and I believe that he is an honourable man.'

'A politician?' sneered Edwin.

'Yes – we will get the vote,' retorted Amelia.

It was fortunate that the lending library absorbed much of their interest and energies, otherwise I am sure Edwin and Amelia would have fallen out quite frequently.

One cause of friction was Edwin's drinking. This had become progressively heavier and at times Edwin was drinking almost a bottle of whisky a day. This did not bother me unduly, even though it was me that emptied his urine bottle thoughtfully provided by the Army – this saved me a few trips to the toilet.

It was just as well that I was able to give him a lot of attention, because Amelia and Agnes could never have managed him.

19

Edwin Falls in Love

We had developed a routine – Edwin would make a list of books he thought we should have; Amelia would comment on it, and if they agreed, I'd be given a copy to keep in my pocket, to refer to when I did my rounds of the jumble sales.

Though Edwin would accompany me to the second-hand bookshops, he would never go to a jumble sale. I did not mind. I was glad to be on my own and not pushing a wheelchair.

With our shopping and walks out – which inevitably meant a trip to the pub or off-licence – our weekends were fully occupied. On Saturday morning, Edwin would take me to the eel and pie shop in Peckham next to the undertakers – or to be precise, I would push him there after we had done Amelia's weekend shopping. It was a particular favourite place of mine, since I was rather partial to stewed eels and creamed mashed potatoes with a hot meat pie on top of it.

Edwin would grin as I attacked the bowl of food in front of me with my spoon. He would have a hot meat pie and look at his watch from time to time. I knew he was impatient to get to the Bunch of Grapes pub, just past the undertakers. I would ignore these hints as Amelia made it clear to me that the less time Edwin spent in the pub the happier she would be. It became quite a ritual as we entered the shop. The seating was in cubicles with a table in between, and since Edwin could not get on to the bench seat, I would push his wheelchair to the far end of the shop and he would have his plate at the end of the table. Sometimes it would cause some inconvenience to other customers, but they took it all in very good humour, though Edwin's, 'I do apologise old chap, and please excuse me madam,' caused a few grins from the regulars.

On the first occasion I took Edwin there, I went to the end of the shop to get Edwin settled and then to the counter. I could tell that the owner and his wife were talking about us, but in the bustle of the shop, assumed that I could not hear. However, I could see their mouths move and knew roughly what they were saying about us.

'Who are they?' said the man.

'I recognise the one with the eye patch and one arm, that's young Georgie Bowman,' replied the woman.

'Who?'

'Georgie Bowman – old Bowman the carter's youngest son; the one with all the medals, you know.'

'Ah! I've gotcha,' nodded the man. 'Poor sod, not done 'im much good, has it?'

'Nar, and there's plenty more like him,' said the woman.

'That's a fact.' The man smiled as I approached the counter. 'What's it ter be, son?' he asked.

'Stewed eels and mash for me, with a meat pie on top. My brother-in-law wants a meat pie and two mugs of tea, please – both no sugar.'

'Righto, son. I'll bring them all over to you,' smiled the woman. 'You go and sit down, dearie.'

I returned to my seat next to Edwin, who looked about him with some disdain. 'There's a bloody awful smell in here, George.'

347

'What's that?' I said, leaning forward.

'Doesn't matter, George,' he said, shaking his head.

'Can you smell the hot vinegar, Edwin?' I asked, my face now red from the warmth of the shop.

'Unfortunately,' replied Edwin, drily, a faint smile on his face.

I understood what Edwin had said and grinned broadly. 'I'll let you have a taste of my stewed eel.'

Edwin made a grimace at my offer, which caused my grin to become even wider. He was not happy in the eel and pie shop and was only there under sufferance.

The woman behind the counter came to our table with our order. Other customers looked questioningly at us as everyone collected their own order from the counter.

'That's tenpence please, gents,' she said, as she put two plates of food on the table.

Edwin immediately took a coin out of his waistcoat pocket.

'I've got some money, Edwin,' I said, my hand diving into my jacket pocket.

'My treat, George,' he smiled, as he handed the woman a coin.

Edwin peered at the green-rimmed bowl that was on my plate. It was filled with stewed eels and mashed potatoes and covered with parsley sauce, on top of which rested a hot meat pie. My mouth watered as I smelt it; I picked up my spoon and carefully put a large piece of eel on it, then I held it in front of Edwin and grinned at him, 'You try that, Edwin,' I said, encouragingly.

'It looks bloody revolting,' he replied, screwing up his face.

At that moment the woman brought us our teas and she must have heard him as her face clouded. Edwin, never short of a reply, turned to her and smiled. 'Delightful pies, madam, I've never tasted better.' He took another bite of his meat pie. 'Truly delicious, ma'am.'

The woman was now beaming as she carefully placed our mugs of tea on the table. 'There we are, gents,' she said, handing Edwin his change. Edwin shook his head and refused the money as he smiled again. 'That's quite all right, ma'am.'

'Ooh! Ah!' she exclaimed, all flustered. Quite unused to such manners and never having been given a tip before had almost taken her breath away.

'Thank you, sir. Most kind of you, I'm sure,' she replied, her face now quite red.

I watched all this with some amusement. Even if he had not been in his wheelchair, Edwin would have stuck out like a sore thumb in the eel and pie shop. I knew very well that he did not like the place and was only there as a favour to me. I appreciated that, but I would not ask him again; it would only be if he insisted on coming with me.

Fate, however, suddenly took a hand in the guise of the daughter of the owners of the establishment, who suddenly appeared at our table with two more hot pies on a plate.

'Here we are, gents, me ma thought you might like another pie.'

We both looked up at the voice, even with a white overall and head scarf, she looked very attractive. Edwin obviously thought so, judging by the look on his face and the fact that for a moment he was lost for words. 'Thank you, my dear,' he said at last. 'Most kind of your dear mother,' he smiled.

'You're welcome, I'm sure,' she replied, a faint smile on her face.

'What's your name, my dear?' asked Edwin.

'Iris, sir,' replied the girl, who I guessed to be about the same age as ourselves.

'I'm Edwin, that's George,' he smiled, nodding at me.

I grinned at the girl as I spooned up my mashed potato. 'Hello,' I said, happily.

'Hello,' she replied.

Edwin now began to engage Iris in conversation while I peered into my bowl to fish out the last of my stewed eels. I did not know what he was saying, not that it was of any interest to me. It did not last for long as her mother told her to clear the recently vacated tables.

When we left the shop, the owners made a fuss of Edwin, who was still engaged in conversation with Iris, and it seemed clear to me that Edwin was attracted to the proprietor's daughter. I could well imagine his mother's reaction to any liaison. It made me smile just to think of it.

When we at last arrived home, after Edwin's obligatory trip to the Green Man public house, Amelia was at her little desk checking library tickets while Agnes was serving behind the counter of the sweet shop.

'I'm glad you are back at last, I have been so busy,' she said, as I inched the wheelchair over the step and into the shop. I could see that Amelia looked none too pleased with us.

'I'll serve behind the counter as soon as I have had a pee,' said Edwin, much to Amelia's obvious annoyance.

'There is no need to be so crude, Edwin,' she hissed, her eyes flashing at him.

'George, push me through to the conservatory,' he said, turning in his chair to face me. 'Hello, Aggie,' he said, cheerfully, as we went through the shop. He knew Amelia disliked him calling Agnes 'Aggie', and he always did so when he wished to annoy her – usually when he had had a few drinks.

'Hello, Master Edwin. Did you enjoy your luncheon?' she asked, her eyes twinkling.

350

'It was only a meat pie – it was George here who had the luncheon, if you can call it that,' grinned Edwin.

'Edwin made up for it in the Green Man,' I retorted.

'That, I can believe,' said Amelia, tartly.

In the conservatory, I gave Edwin his urine bottle. He looked uncomfortable as he used it – not out of any embarrassment, we were past that sort of thing long since. I was the one who got him in and out of the bath. Suddenly it dawned on me.

'Have you peed your pants, Eddie?' I asked, in what I thought was a whisper.

He nodded, all the bounce now gone out of him. Instead, he looked the pathetic cripple that the war had made him.

'I'll go and get you some clean pants and trousers, then.'

He grabbed my arm as I walked past him. 'George, you won't tell Amelia, will you? I'm not going back to that home, you know.'

There was a look of anguish on Edwin's face and I felt desperately sorry for him. 'No, I won't tell her. I'll wash your pants out and put them on the line, they'll soon dry,' I replied.

'Stout chap, George,' said Edwin, winking at me.

Having obtained some clean underpants and trousers from Edwin's bedroom, I assisted him to change in the conservatory, then I took his wet garments into the outside scullery to wash them. This was becoming a regular occurrence and I suspected that Amelia knew what was happening, though she did not mention the matter.

A few days later, it happened again, and while I was in the scullery she came in as I was rinsing Edwin's underpants.

'What are you doing, dear?' she asked, saying the words

351

so clearly I could understand each word so well, yet she was as silent as I was in my silent world.

'It's Edwin,' I said, in what I hoped was a quiet voice. 'He has little accidents and doesn't want you to know – it's very embarrassing for him.'

My right hand began to shake, as it was prone to do at times, since I came out of hospital.

Amelia gently held my hand as she said, 'We'll not tell him I know, dear,' she smiled.

'That's best,' I nodded. As I bent to put the underpants and trousers through the mangle, Amelia kissed my lips.

'What's that for?' I smiled, a little taken aback.

'Because I love you, dear,' she replied, coyly.

There was no doubt that Edwin was taken with Iris from the eel and pie shop. She was an attractive girl, even her overall and head scarf could not hide that fact, and she certainly took notice of Edwin.

At Edwin's insistence we now went there on a Wednesday morning as well. He made the excuse to Amelia that it was a treat for me and Amelia had smiled and said, 'Yes, of course Edwin.'

However, I felt obliged to tell her the real reason at the first opportunity, if only to see her reaction. 'She works in the eel and pie shop?' said Amelia, aghast.

'She doesn't cut the eels up,' I said quickly. 'Her father does that – he's very quick at it and I expect the eels know nothing about it,' I added.

'That is a relief!' Amelia looked at me almost in disbelief as she spoke, unsure, I think, whether to be horrified or angry.

'I don't think your mother would approve – I was bad enough.'

'You were totally different, dear, totally,' said Amelia, quickly. 'And mother did approve of you.'

'H'm...' I grunted, unconvinced.

'Anyway, George, nothing can come of it, can it?' said Amelia.

I answered her enquiring glance by just shaking my head, and the subject was dropped. That seemed to close the matter, but two days later we had a surprise visitor. It was a Friday morning and Edwin was in the shop cutting up some card to make ticket holders for books that I had obtained the previous day. I had just come home with some shopping and was about to take it upstairs to Amelia when Iris came into the shop. For once, Edwin was lost for words. Whether it was a surprise at seeing her or sheer amazement at Iris's elegant attire, or a combination of both, I do not know.

'Hello,' smiled Iris.

'Er ... hello,' replied Edwin, at last. 'Do come in, please,' he added, now recovered from his surprise.

'Hello, Iris,' I grinned, then turned to go upstairs, unaware if she had made any reply.

Amelia was sitting in an armchair that had been her grandmother's until it was put in Amelia's bedroom at Cedar Lodge. It was her favourite chair and she had it placed so that she was able to see all that was happening in Queen's Road and do her sewing at the same time. Agnes had also brought her armchair with her and she sat opposite Amelia with a similar view of Queen's Road. Edward would be close to them in his Moses basket and from time to time they would coo and smile at him.

'Amelia!' I gasped as I entered the room.

She looked up at me, a slight frown on her brow.

'What is, dear?' she asked, in her usual patient way.

'It's Iris, downstairs,' I grinned.

'Iris? Iris who, dear?' she frowned.

'Iris from the eel and pie shop – she's come to see Edwin.'

'Good heavens, whatever next!' said Amelia, rising from her chair, a slight flush beginning to appear on her face.

I could see by the determined look on Amelia's face that Iris Conker (that was her name) was about to get her marching orders. I put my hand on Amelia's arm as I spoke to her. 'Amelia, leave them, please. Edwin's very keen on her and nothing can come of it, can it?'

'I've no idea, George,' she said, looking at me, curiously.

'Believe me, it cannot. It's just a bit of make believe for Edwin, so don't spoil it for him, please.'

Amelia resumed her seat, then looked up at me. I knew she did not know the full extent of Edwin's injuries – matters like that were never divulged to a man's sister.

Amelia stared at me as she held her hands to her face. I could tell she wanted to ask me something, but did not have the courage to speak.

'Iris looks very nice, Amelia. I think you will be surprised.'

She looked at me with the same enquiring expression on her face. 'Now I am curious dear,' she smiled, getting to her feet.

'Remember what I said.'

'Of course, George. He is my brother,' she replied.

I followed Amelia down the stairs as I did not wish to miss anything that might take place. I could tell Amelia was a little taken aback when she saw Iris Conker talking earnestly with Edwin. She was dressed in the latest fashion in clothes that would not have disgraced a West End salon. Iris was unrecognisable from the young woman in a white overall and head scarf that served in the eel and pie shop. There was no doubt that Iris was beautiful. She had long reddish hair set in the latest fashion and bright green eyes that seemed to be permanently laughing.

Her teeth looked perfect when she smiled, which seemed quite often, and it was obvious that Edwin was captivated by her.

'Ah, Amelia, I want you to meet Iris,' said Edwin, moving his wheelchair in order to make the introduction.

If Amelia was surprised, she did not give any indication. 'How do you do, Miss Conker,' she said, holding out her hand. 'I am pleased to meet you,' she smiled.

'I'm pleased to meet you, Mrs Bowman,' replied Iris Conker.

Her confident manner was something of a surprise and I noticed Amelia glance at Edwin almost in approval.

'I was just calling on my aunt and uncle; they live in Drakefield Road, you know, so I thought I would accept Edwin's invitation to see your new library.'

'Oh, yes,' replied Amelia, a little coolly.

'It's very impressive, isn't it?' said Iris, as she looked along the rows of shelves.

'Thank you,' murmured Amelia.

'Iris and I are going out for a while,' said Edwin, airily. 'Look after the shop, George, old son.'

Before either Amelia or I could reply, he had moved his wheelchair towards the shop door. 'Give me a push over the step, Iris.'

'Yes, of course, Edwin,' she replied. 'You will have to hold my handbag and parasol.'

Edwin took her handbag and parasol enabling her to put both her hands to the wheelchair's handles.

'Bye, we won't be long,' said a grinning Edwin, turning in his chair to face us.

Amelia nodded and made no reply, while I raised my arm as I said, 'Bye, Edwin, see you later, Iris.'

Iris was too involved in getting the wheelchair over the step to reply, but at last they were out on the pavement and away.

I went behind the counter and picked up Edwin's morning paper.

'Well, there's a thing!' said Amelia, her hands on her hips.

I could see now that she had been agreeably surprised by Iris, which was understandable.

'She's very nice, isn't she, Amelia? I just hope that Edwin does not expect too much, that's all.'

Amelia looked at me and nodded, her expression then changed to one of sadness. 'Yes, I agree, dear,' she smiled, wistfully.

This was the first of a number of visits that Iris made to us. Amelia invited her to dine with us on more than one occasion and we soon knew all about her and her family.

It was clear that Iris's parents had hopes for her after sending her to a private school. She was, I gathered, about twenty-two years old and had been engaged to a young gunnery officer who had been killed in the first year of the war. Her parents had a house overlooking Peckham Rye and seemed quite well off. She always seemed to be in conversation with Edwin, though I did not know what they were saying unless they happened to look at me and speak slowly.

It was clear to me, however, that Edwin was very much in love with her. He did not drink nearly as much these days because, I suspected, Iris had told him that she disapproved of it. He seemed a changed man – far less irritable and impatient and, with the rapid improvement of the war situation, was almost like the Edwin I had first met at Cedar Lodge.

One Sunday at the end of August, Amelia and Edwin's parents decided to pay us a visit. Perhaps they thought it would be their last opportunity. Edwin insisted that Iris was invited to tea as well, and he did not take kindly to my suggestion that, 'perhaps she could bring some jellied eels with her.' Edwin's face went red and he refrained from replying with some difficulty, and Amelia, trying not to laugh, said quickly, 'Of course, Edwin. She is most welcome.'

I grinned at Edwin who now realised that I had been pulling his leg. He raised a hand and pointed an index finger at me, 'And don't you dare tell my parents,' he said, slowly.

I did not speak and Edwin, unsure as to whether I had understood, began to repeat himself. 'They would not believe me even if I did, Edwin,' I said, glibly. 'I was bad enough.' I could see Amelia's face flush and her tongue ran along her lips in agitation and I regretted my words.

'George, dear, that...' she began.

'I'm sorry, Amelia, I shouldn't have,' I leaned forward and kissed her cheek. Amelia nodded briefly and gave a weak smile, and the subject of her parents was not mentioned again.

When the Hoopers did eventually make their visit, to Agnes it was as if royalty had arrived. This, I think, irked Amelia at the time, though she made no comment. Though they looked much older, and Mr Hooper had the shakes far worse than ever I had, they were still much the same. Mrs Hooper, I could tell, was moaning from the moment she arrived. Small wonder their relatives were fed up with them.

I must say that they were very nice to me and told me that they liked the library, and they certainly approved of Iris, so their visit turned out better than expected.

I could tell Amelia was glad when they had to leave. Edwin, Agnes and I accompanied them to their tram, whilst Amelia stayed with the baby. There was no doubt that the feelings Amelia might have had for her parents

357

in the past were no longer there, particularly where her mother was concerned. This I put down to Amelia's grandfather's legacy, which her mother thought they should have had to try and save the business. I did speak to Edwin about it and he explained it simply to me.

'It would not have paid off a half of the firm's debts, old son, that's a fact. I saw the last accounts. Amelia did the right thing, believe me. Where would we all have been if she hadn't bought this place?'

'Thanks, Eddy, I had nothing and look at me.'

Edwin did not speak but smiled almost sympathetically and clasped my hand before he spoke, 'Come on, old son, let's take Buster out.'

The subject of Amelia's legacy and the Hoopers' domestic situation was never again mentioned in conversation; it was all water under Tower Bridge, as far as we were concerned. Though I did not know it, the Sunday visit of the Hoopers was the last time I was to see them together. I was never sure what they actually thought of Queen's Road, as I could not hear them talk, and Amelia only told me what she wanted me to know.

The war had been as crippling to them as it had been for Edwin and me; its vicious tentacles had spread through society and there did not seem to be any end to it. Though we did not know it then, the end of the war was drawing near. At the time it was hard to imagine it ever happening. Our offensive in France began on 8th August and heralded the end of the war. Not that it immediately achieved anything, but it signalled to the now demoralised German Army, that they could not win the war. The German offensive had now fizzled out; they had made small gains but the cost in human life had been enormous. They had been told that this last attack would break the Allied armies and the war would be over. Instead, with the assistance of a large American Army, the Allied counter-offensive took place.

However, to our intense disappointment, it achieved little; true, we retook the ground we had lost, but our losses were appalling. By the end of September, unexpected events in Germany completely altered matters; the situation was out of the civil authorities' control.

We knew little of these matters, and I really did not care as I did my rounds of the second-hand bookshops. I knew every shop from Lewisham to Dulwich. I would take Buster with me and have a canvas bag over my back like a postman.

It was during September that Iris Conker told us that she was leaving Peckham to take a post as a nanny in Hampshire. Edwin took the news badly at first; he said he would never speak to her again, then he was at her shop every day. I was getting fed up with stewed eels and told him so.

'Will you stop moaning,' he said, irritably.

Amelia spoke to him, but he rounded on her and she was in tears. I did not know what he had said and Amelia would not tell me, so I refused to help him until we found him on the bathroom floor in a soiled state. This, I think, brought him to his senses as I made it clear to him, 'You upset Amelia again, Edwin, and I'll never do another thing for you – I mean that.'

Edwin nodded. He knew that I was his legs and without me he was helpless. I did not enjoy the situation, but we had to make the best of things, whether we liked it or not.

Unfortunately, the matter did not end there. I met Iris's cousin, Frank, in Queen's Road. He was on leave from the navy. I was at school with Frank and he told me that Iris did not have a job but was staying with relatives in Hampshire as Edwin had mentioned marriage to her.

'He can't marry her, Frankie,' I said, aghast.

'We know that, Georgie, but he seems set on it,' replied Frankie.

'I didn't know, honest,' I said, shaking my head.

'Anyway, my uncle and aunt are selling the shop and are buying a village store down in Hampshire.'

'Best thing, too,' I replied. 'Bye, Frank, best of luck.'

'And you, George.'

Iris's cousin strode off in the jaunty manner that sailors seemed to have, while I returned thoughtfully to the shop. I told Amelia what I had learned, but Edwin must have overheard me. He propelled his wheelchair into the room, his face twisted with anger, as he began to call Iris unpleasant names.

Amelia looked at me in horror at this outburst, which was so unlike Edwin, and I felt bound to say something. 'I thought you were an officer and a gentleman,' I began.

This made Edwin even worse and he turned on me, his face red. 'Why my sister ever married a fool like you, I'll never know. Half of you missing and as deaf as a post, it's hard work making you understand, you ignorant guttersnipe,' he raged.

Amelia burst into tears, but she was angry as well. 'How dare you speak like that to George. You have no right to, after all he does for you,' she said, drying her eyes.

'I didn't want this war, Edwin,' I snapped. 'You did, and now you're whining about the results of it, you deserve all you bloody got.'

My words seemed to calm him. Suddenly he turned his wheelchair and pushed himself out of the room. Amelia was dabbing her eyes with her handkerchief and I put my arm about her as I said, 'I'm sorry, I should not have said that to him.'

She sniffed and wiped her eyes and tried to smile. 'It's not your fault, dear,' she said, clasping my hand.

Edwin stayed in his room for the rest of the day while I was downstairs in the shop. I made no attempt to go up to see if he wanted to come down, and it was Amelia who acted as a go-between. 'He's very sorry, George, dear,' she said, as she brought me a cup of tea and placed it on the counter.

I pretended not to have understood as she continued, 'He did not mean it, really.' Amelia's lovely eyes were misty and I knew she was close to tears.

'He did, Amelia. I know him now, but I'll do whatever you want me to do,' I replied.

Amelia bit her lip and lowered her eyes. At last she spoke, 'Go up and bring him down. He cannot stay in his room all the time, can he?'

I shook my head, then picked up my teacup and drank my tea. 'No,' I said, carefully placing the cup in the saucer.

Edwin looked warily at me as I entered his bedroom.

'I'll take you downstairs,' I said, gruffly.

'Thank you, George,' he replied. 'Sorry about what happened,' he said, easily.

'You called me a guttersnipe – I understood that and I won't forget it,' I said, lifting him into his chair. 'I'm doing this for Amelia, not you; I'd fling you down the stairs, so help me.'

Edwin did not reply, but gave a curt nod as he pushed himself forward. I held the door open as we left his bedroom. For days the atmosphere between us was strained, not so much because of what we had said, but rather what we now knew we thought of each other.

Amelia tried to heal the rift, to no avail. As Shakespeare says, 'What is done cannot be undone.' Now there was an uneasy silence between us. It was unfortunate and I must take a good portion of the blame for the situation.

Edwin began drink more, when he could get to the pub or off-licence to get it. He had a letter from Iris

361

that seemed to make him better for a few days, but then he drank more than ever. There had been an epidemic of what was called 'influenza'. Many people had died of it. Then we heard that Mrs Hooper had caught it and was very ill.

It was on a Saturday morning that Edwin said he did not feel well and did not want to get up, which was not like him. I had taken him a cup of tea and he did not look too good. He was coughing and wheezing and my immediate thoughts were influenza and baby.

'I think he's got that influenza,' I said to Amelia, who was sitting in the kitchen with Agnes.

Amelia pushed back her chair and was about to rise to her feet. 'I'd better go and see him,' she began. My hand descended on her forearm, pinning it to the table.

'George, dear,' she protested, 'my arm, you are hurting me.'

'I'm sorry,' I said, releasing my hold. 'You don't go near him. If you catch it, little Eddy will catch it, so you stay away from his room.'

Amelia's hand went to her mouth as she gasped in horror. 'Yes, you are right, dear. I must be careful.'

The doctor was called and he confirmed it was influenza. He made it quite clear that Edwin was to be isolated with myself in charge of him. Perhaps it was a blessing in disguise, because during the following days when Edwin was very ill, the antagonism that had built up between us completely disappeared. I struggled to change his wet nightshirt so many times; there was disinfectant everywhere and I smelt of it, even when I changed into fresh clothes.

'Where's Amelia, George?' asked Edwin, weakly, one morning.

'She mustn't come in, Eddy, or the baby might catch it,' I replied.

'Quite right, George. They must not catch it,' he nodded.

'You look a lot better this morning, Eddy. Would you like some breakfast?'

'Think I will – just a little,' smiled Edwin, more his normal self. 'Bring me my papers, George.'

'What?' I frowned, staring at him.

Edwin held up his hands and moved his head from side to side.

'Oh, the paper!' I said, vaguely.

'That's it, George, and the ones I've not read.'

'What's that, Edwin?'

'All of them, George, old son.'

At last I understood. I had a headache and could not concentrate. Having taken him his breakfast and papers I went back to our bedroom. The bed was unmade, so I took off my slippers and trousers and got back into bed. I must have dozed off because I awoke to see Amelia bending over me, an anxious look on her face. 'George, dear, are you all right?' she gently shook my arm.

I struggled to open my eye, my headache was no better. 'Got a rotten headache, Amelia,' I mumbled.

'You have a little sleep, dear. I'll bring you something for it and a hot water bottle.'

'Is the little chap all right?'

'Yes, dear, he's fine. He is going to have a sleep too,' she smiled.

'Good,' I replied, sleepily.

It was well past midday by the time I awoke. When I had collected my senses I realised that I felt much better. The stone hot-water bottle felt cold and putting it to one side I got out of bed and struggled into my trousers.

Amelia was in the front sitting-room reading the paper when I entered. She made to get out of her armchair. 'Are you feeling better, dear?'

'Yes, don't get up. Where's Agnes?' I asked.

'Down in the shop. It makes a change for her. The girl is doing some ironing for me. Edwin wants to get up – he is much better.'

'Slowly, Amelia. What was that?'

'Edwin is much better, dear. He would like to get up, could you manage it?'

I nodded, then sat down. My legs seemed weak today.

'Are you hungry, dear?'

I nodded again and Amelia touched my hand, which was moving. 'You stay here, dear. I'll get you something.'

I picked up the paper that Amelia had been reading as she left the room, and peered at it. The headlines made much of the French advance in Salonica; an attack had been launched on 15th September and the Bulgarians were in full retreat. It seemed clear from the descriptive map that if the enemy did not plug the gap, an awkward situation would arise for them.

Edwin was also full of it when I went into his bedroom. 'If the French push forward, Georgie, they could get behind them; that would give the Huns something to think about, I tell you,' said Edwin, enthusiastically.

Later, when we were in the kitchen having a meal, Edwin repeated his views. I agreed out of politeness; it was of little interest to me.

Edwin was definitely better and itching to get back among the books. He now had a card index system of every book we had and a list of books I was to try and get.

'Edwin, you must wear your greatcoat when you are down there, it's draughty and you have been very ill, remember.'

'Yes, all right, Sis. Don't fuss, old thing,' replied Edwin breezily.

'I mean it,' said Amelia, firmly, none too happy with the 'old thing', I suspected.

'I'll see he does,' I said, before Amelia could continue.

'Thank you, dear,' she said, smiling at me, having first given Edwin a cool glance, which he completely ignored.

The library membership was growing all the time and it was now a full-time occupation for one person, which Edwin capably handled. He was now interested in first editions and advertised for book collections in the local papers.

This, I think, took his mind off Iris and enabled him to make use of the education he had received at Oxford University. He was in touch with an antiquarian bookseller in the City of London and from time to time sold him a book. When he made such a sale, he always gave Amelia and me a share, and it was on an equal basis.

Edwin was often moody and at times I could have lost my temper with him, but there was a generous side to his nature. I am quite sure he would have given me his last penny if I had needed it, which is why I tolerated his moods.

The war – though we did not know it – was nearing its end. Six days before Bulgaria sued for peace, Mrs Hooper died of influenza. Perhaps it was as well; the world she had known had already collapsed about her and their situation was now parlous.

Edwin, assisted by two of his army friends, went to the funeral accompanied by Agnes, which took place in Worthing. Why Amelia did not go, I was never sure. She said at the time it was the baby, but that was not the real reason – I was convinced there was another reason. I did not question her; my lack of hearing left me at a disadvantage, and besides, Amelia could be very stubborn if she did not wish to tell me, and that was an end of it. I was sure it concerned either myself or the inheritance from her grandfather – perhaps both.

Mr Hooper sold what was left of their home and moved

into a small guest house. I am sure Amelia would have had him with us, but he made it clear to Edwin that he preferred Worthing, before any offer was actually made.

I felt very sorry for Mr Hooper. The war had broken him in every way possible and he had little to look forward to.

20

The War Ends

On 4th October Germany formally asked for an armistice. We knew it was the end, but it did not seem possible. It was happening and it was hard to believe. Public euphoria began to build up, but I was left with an empty feeling – my arm, eye and hearing would never come back. I said as much to Edwin. He grasped my hand in his, nodding briefly, his eyes full of tears.

We understood each other, but coming to terms with our disabilities was not going to be easy. In wartime it would keep us out of the trenches, but peacetime? What could we expect? Edwin, who could have expected a fine career, was now a prisoner of his wheelchair. How would he cope? I know Amelia thought of it, but we rarely discussed the matter. On one occasion she did say, however, 'We have all had to adjust to our changed circumstances, George, dear. Edwin will have to as well, we cannot turn the clock back, as much as we might like to.'

It had taken some time for her to tell me that, and I thought long over it afterwards. She might have sounded hard, even callous, but I knew her, she was neither.

Amelia, since the demise of her father's business, had changed and was now a practical businesswoman with her own family. The business and our financial affairs were entirely in her hands. I never questioned anything. If I needed money she gave it to me and always more than I required. To me she was just the same and fussed over me even more and I loved her for it.

The days now passed quickly. The war was almost over, but still it brought tragedy. It was during the last week in October, a Tuesday morning, I recall. I had taken the midday post upstairs to Amelia, who was sitting in her armchair by the front room window nursing the baby and looking down into Queen's Road.

'Post, Amelia,' I said, handing it to her.

'Thank you, dear,' she smiled as she took the letters.

As I crouched down to touch the baby with my forefinger, I noticed out of the corner of my eye the telegraph boy stop on the other side of the road. 'Oh Lord,' I murmured, slowly standing up and peering out of the window.

'What is it, dear?' asked Amelia, clasping my hand.

'The telegraph boy is going to the Winters,' I said, slowly.

At first Amelia did not realise the significance of it. 'Well?' she frowned, her arms now about the baby.

'Sammy Winters is in Flanders with the Rifle Brigade.'

My words had an immediate effect. Amelia's mouth opened slightly, 'Oh, no. He is their only son, she is always talking about him when she comes to the library to change her books.'

I watched the telegraph boy get on his bicycle and pedal away, then moments later the curtains were drawn in the Winters' front room. This told the world of their grief, an all too frequent happening in the neighbourhood.

I looked at Amelia, who put a hand to her mouth. I could see tears in her eyes as she, too, shared the Winters' grief. 'Poor Mrs Winter, she is such a dear, too,' she murmured.

I bent down and kissed Amelia's cheek, then the baby's

forehead. 'I am going back down to the shop to help Edwin, he has some books to sort out.'

'Yes, dear. Will you go to the butchers for me? Agnes has rheumatism this morning and it is painful for her.'

'Butchers? Write it down, Amelia.'

'Yes, dear. I'll bring it down in a minute.'

I nodded as I understood her. She always pronounced her words so precisely for my benefit. People sometimes smiled when they saw her do it, but she ignored them, though my face would redden. I could smash my fist into their stupid faces for laughing at her.

'Did you know him, George?' asked Edwin, when I told him about the Winters' telegram.

'Oh, I knew him. He was a mate of my eldest brother – didn't particularly like him, though,' I replied.

Edwin smiled as he drank the cup of tea that I had just brought to him, for Agnes was busy in the kitchen.

'No one can say you are not honest,' he chuckled.

'Maybe, but he thumped me more than once at school, did Ginger Winter. Still, that's all in the past,' I muttered, a little ashamed that I had mentioned it.

'That's a fact,' replied Edwin.

On 11th November an armistice was signed and the war was over. The day was declared a public holiday and the streets were filled with cheering people. Many, however, like the Winters, felt that they had no reason to celebrate and nothing to cheer about, just some photographs and all too recent memories.

When I went round to Jackson's yard in Dennitts Road, Mr Jackson sat in his workshop, slowly puffing on his pipe. He had a coffin that he had just built resting on two trestles awaiting french polishing, the pot of which was slowly warming on a stove.

'Good morning, Mr Jackson. Any firewood, please?'

'Aye, lad.' He pointed in the far corner of the workshop

with his pipe, then stirred the french polish pot. 'Not celebrating, son?' he asked.

I peered at him for a few moments, then he spoke again. 'Aye, you've as much to celebrate as we have, son,' he said, sadly.

I filled my bag then sat on a stool next to him, staring at the beautifully made coffin, my thoughts on the many burial details that I had been on. 'The worst part of it, as far as I am concerned, Mr Jackson, is that it should never have happened. What had it got to do with us?'

Mr Jackson took out a handkerchief and wiped his eyes. 'Aye, son, you are right. No doubt about it,' he nodded. 'How many will think that, I wonder. You certainly didn't lose your marbles.'

I left Mr Jackson still thinking and mourning for his only son, and went back to the shop deep in thought.

When Mrs Winter came to the shop the following day, I felt even more ashamed as she showed me the telegram informing her that Sergeant Samuel Winter, MM, had been killed in action. I did not know what to say to her, as I handed her back the notification from the War Office. She seemed to understand my embarrassment as she gave me a brief hug, then quickly left the shop.

I felt miserable. Perhaps it was the realisation that I would never again see so many familiar faces of my youth. The war was almost over, but for me the world had changed for ever. I sat on my stool behind the counter, brooding on the fact until a hand touched mine. I had not seen and could not hear Amelia approach me carrying a cup of tea; she looked concerned. 'Are you all right, dear?' she asked.

'I am, as long as I've got you, Amelia,' I mumbled.

'You always will have, my dearest,' she said, kissing me.

I immediately felt better and my mood left me. The

war, after all, had its compensations as far as I was concerned.

The shop was still not open and I thought something was wrong, until Amelia informed me that we would not be opening today. 'Irene Peskett and Maud Littleton, and Amy and Hector are coming round for drinks and snacks, dear.'

'Oh,' I said.

'We did open but I decided to close. People will be drinking and celebrating.'

I would have thought that would have been the time to stay open, but I did not say so to Amelia.

'Edwin has started already,' I grinned.

Amelia compressed her lips – a sure sign that she was annoyed, but she made no comment. We sat in chairs around the two front room windows watching the people down in Queen's Road. There were no trams or buses, and people were milling about, no doubt waiting for the pubs to open. Amelia had opened a bottle of sparkling wine. 'Will you have some, Edwin?' she asked.

'No thanks, Sis, I'll have a whisky,' he replied, helping himself to the whisky decanter again.

'As you wish,' said Amelia, coolly.

I knew that Amelia was unhappy with Edwin's drinking. Since the Iris affair, at times it was a whole bottle of whisky a day. Some days it was even more than that. It just could not go on.

Irene Peskett and Maud Littleton had joined us, so had Hector. 'Amy's following with the children. I had to call on the Winters first,' he explained.

'Yes, very sad. I called on Mrs Winter yesterday. She is heartbroken, but what can you say to her?' remarked Amelia.

'Very little, I would imagine,' commented Edwin.

'I tried to give her some words of comfort,' murmured Hector.

'More wine, ladies – Irene, Maud?' smiled Edwin.

'No thank you,' they replied, almost in unison.

I could tell that they were talking of what would happen now. All the men would soon be coming home; the parties and celebrations had been planned.

For Edwin and me it all seemed something of an anticlimax; I could tell it was as far as he was concerned. There was something in his manner that seemed to tell me that he was facing his future for the first time.

21

A *Land Fit for Heroes*

The Government was not slow in discharging its army of conscripts – a fact appreciated by the men who quickly made their way home to their families.

After the initial celebrations took place, people suddenly became aware of the realities of peace. What the men did not realise was that the statement of 'a land fit for heroes' was nothing more than journalistic verbiage. After a few weeks, when their pay had been spent, they began to look for jobs and to their surprise there were none to be had. For a short while their thoughts were taken off their problems by the proposed victory parades. To this end we had a visit from the local secretary of the newly formed Army Association. I was out with Buster at the time and when I returned, the man had gone; not that it was of any interest to me. When Edwin explained what had been the reason for the visit, I merely nodded.

'You don't seem very enthusiastic, George, if I may say so,' remarked Edwin, glancing at Amelia as he spoke.

I could see a faint smile appearing on Amelia's face, as I replied laconically, 'What do you want me to do, Edwin, burst into song?'

'No, but you might appear keener. It is a victory parade, even if it is a locally held one.'

'What have I got to parade about? I couldn't even hear the band if I was marching with it.'

I could tell that there was an uncomfortable silence, then Amelia turned to me and smiled.

'Your ability to lip-read is amazing, George, dear,' she put a hand on either side of my face, then kissed my lips.

'It's because you are patient, Amelia, that's why,' I said, my eye watering.

Amelia kissed me again, then helped me to remove my overcoat. 'Of course George will, Edwin. I want him to, as Mr Hall said he has more medals than anyone else in the district.'

'You would never think so,' grinned Edwin.

'Perhaps not,' replied Amelia, 'but that's George, isn't it?' she said, smiling at me.

22

The Victory Parade

We now frequented a pub called The Pilgrim's Rest. Edwin liked the pub and Queenie, the barmaid, and I approved because it was close to an eel and pie shop.

Every Saturday we were there at lunch time and, two weeks before the victory parade, we had called in there for a drink. As we entered the saloon bar, customers greeted us; two held open the door and assisted me to bring in the wheelchair, while another immediately ordered drinks for us.

'Here, steady on,' protested Edwin, as the wheelchair propelled over the step by willing helpers almost spilled its owner on to the saloon bar floor.

'Hang on, Eddy,' I said, steadying the wheelchair.

At last we got to an empty table as Queenie the landlady came to us with a tray of drinks.

'Here we are, Captain,' smiled Queenie, a big, buxom lady, who I think had a soft spot for Edwin and myself. Queenie placed a pint of bitter beer and a glass of whisky on the table, as Edwin eased his wheelchair against it.

'Thank you, Queenie, my darling,' grinned Edwin.

'Ginger beer for you, George?' she smiled.

Before I could reply, Edwin spoke, 'Young George will have a pint of beer today and a whisky,' he said firmly.

'Me, I'll have...' I began.

'Sit down. I've ordered,' said Edwin, pointing to an adjacent chair.

'Do you want to go to the eel and pie shop, Edwin?' I asked.

'No, I bloody well don't,' he retorted, downing his whisky in one gulp and then banging his glass on the table.

I was a little taken aback by his change in attitude, and I think the expression on my face caused him to relent.

'You can have a meat pie here, and some pickles.'

'The pies are dearer in here and they are not as fresh,' I replied. 'Besides, I like stewed eels,' I retorted.

'Will you shut up about eels. The smell of hot vinegar makes me feel ill,' snapped Edwin irritably.

'You never said that when we were going to...'

Edwin glared at me and I took the hint and did not continue.

'Queenie, Queenie.'

'Yes, Captain Edwin?' smiled Queenie, ignoring another customer who was trying to catch her attention.

'A meat pie and pickles for George, please.'

'Certainly, in half a minute,' she replied.

'And another whisky for me as well.'

'Righto, Edwin,' she called out as she pulled a pint of beer.

The saloon bar was beginning to fill up and our table was soon covered with glasses and plates. I was drinking far more than usual; ginger beer would only be my first drink, then I would drink bitter, though Amelia never commented on the fact.

I was feeling in a happy state while Edwin was putting away his drinks with a speed that left me bewildered. 'Hey, Edwin!' I laughed, tipsily. 'We haven't got your bottle. I hope you won't pee in your pants.'

He turned. His face, already red in the warm bar became even brighter. Then, for an instant, it was white with anger. 'You ignorant oaf,' he roared, snatching a glass of whisky off our table and throwing it in my face, the neat spirit causing me to cry out in pain.

After that, there was a commotion that I could neither see nor hear, until I felt a soft hand which smelt of beer touch my face. A warm cloth was dabbing gently at my face and eye. At last I could partly open my eye, then Queenie brought an eggcup and I used it to wash out my eye with a bowl of warm water. At last I opened my eye and blinked at the other customers who had been standing around our table.

'All right now, old son?' asked an elderly man, kindly.

I nodded, but my head had begun to ache abominably and I was feeling sick.

Edwin, I think, was apologising, but I would not look at him. I got a little unsteadily to my feet and moved towards the saloon bar door, clutching my cap.

'I'm going home,' I muttered. Customers spoke to me but I do not know what they said. I clasped the brass handle of the door and pulled it open to feel the cold winter air on my face. Outside in Queen's Road it felt even colder and I pulled my overcoat lapels across my chest. I felt better, though I could hardly see. I almost bumped into someone as my sight seemed to become even worse and I felt sick. 'Sorry,' I mumbled.

'It's OK, son,' I seemed to discern.

The shop was closed for lunch when I returned. I let myself in and went upstairs where Amelia greeted me.

'Where's Edwin, dear?' she asked, well knowing the reply.

'Still in the Pilgrim's Rest,' I replied.

Amelia compressed her lips, her arms crossed. 'Luncheon's nearly ready, dear.'

'I don't feel well. I'm going to bed, Amelia.'

Amelia came closer and touched my wet collar, then frowned, 'What happened, dear?'

'Nothing,' I replied, my eye blinking.

'What's the matter with your eye? It's all red,' she asked, gently touching the side of my face.

'Nothing. Nothing. My head aches. I'm going to bed.'

'Yes, you do that. I'll bring you a hot-water bottle, dear.'

I went to the bathroom and removed my still wet whisky-smelling shirt and washed myself, then I went to our bedroom and put on a clean vest and shirt.

Amelia brought me a hot-water bottle and something for my headache. As I got into bed she looked at my eye again, but made no comment. She knew something had happened but did not press me. Perhaps she knew her brother better than I realised. I dozed off to sleep and was not aware of Edwin's return.

Amelia told me later what had happened. The first I knew that something was amiss was when she shook my shoulder to wake me up. Edwin had been brought home at closing time by one of the pub's customers, a little the worse for wear. Amelia had watched, tight-lipped, as the man, also well oiled, had got Edwin upstairs.

'Be careful, for Christ's sake, Charlie,' chortled Edwin, as the man struggled to get the wheelchair upstairs.

'And do watch the wallpaper, please,' snapped Amelia.

'Damn your wallpaper. I want to get upstairs,' retorted Edwin.

'How your brother-in-law gets you upstairs with one arm, Gawd only knows,' gasped the struggling Charlie.

'Well, he does,' glared a now ungrateful Edwin. 'Where is George, anyway?' demanded Edwin.

'He is in bed. He does not feel well,' replied Amelia, coolly.

'You were right out of order there, Captain,' said the

puffing Charlie as he continued to struggle. 'Throwing that glass of whisky in his face, and he was right too, your trousers are wet through.'

Amelia's mouth moved in her effort to control herself in front of a stranger. Edwin was now at the top of the stairs and even less grateful than ever. 'It's none of your goddam business,' he growled.

'Oh, if that's how you feel, Captain,' the man emphasised the word 'Captain' sarcastically.

Amelia quickly intervened and said to the man, 'Thank you for bringing him home, I'm most grateful to you. Let me show you out.'

'That's all right, ma'am. I did it for George, really. I hope he's soon all right.'

Charlie touched his hat as Amelia opened the shop door for him. 'George will be fine when he's had a sleep,' she smiled. 'Thank you once again.'

Amelia closed the door and slid the bolts. As she climbed the stairs her face changed and her lips narrowed with anger. Edwin was in the bathroom sitting on the toilet trying to remove his wet trousers and underpants. 'Amelia, get me some clean trousers and underpants,' he called. 'The door is open.'

To his surprise the door opened immediately and Amelia appeared. 'Did you throw whisky in George's face?' she hissed.

'Yes I did,' replied Edwin.

'Why? Why? After all he does for you. You should be thoroughly ashamed of yourself.'

Amelia's face was white with anger.

'He said something silly and I resented it,' replied Edwin.

'So you did that to him; it could affect his eye. What sort of life would he have then?' Amelia's eyes filled with tears.

'I know, damn it, I know. Don't you think I'm ashamed of myself to do it to George of all people?' blurted out Edwin.

'He thinks the world of you. He looks up to you and you treat him like that, after all he does for you,' said Amelia, angrily.

'I know. I know, damn it. He should look up to me? One of the most decorated men in the Army. He was almost a legend, Sis.'

Edwin wiped his eyes on the back of his hands. 'How many men owe their lives to him, we'll never know and I do that to him. I'm so bloody ashamed of myself.'

The tears were running down Edwin's face and it seemed to cool Amelia's anger. 'I'll get your clean clothes,' she said, quietly.

After Amelia had assisted him to put on his underpants and trousers he got into his chair and pushed himself towards his bedroom.

'Will you get my case down off my wardrobe, Sis?' he asked, his voice just a broken whisper.

Amelia lifted down the case and put it on his bed without a word. Edwin pushed his chair against the bed then opened the case. Amelia hesitated as she left his bedroom and half turned to watch her brother out of curiosity.

From the case he took out the leather holster containing his service revolver, then removed it from its polished case.

'What do you want with that?' asked Amelia, her voice rising.

Edwin turned his tear-stained face, twisted in anguish. 'I'm going to end it, Sis. I cannot go on like this for the rest of my life. Go and get George, I want to apologise to him first.'

'Edwin, please put it away,' sobbed Amelia, her hands to her face.

'Go and get George, quickly,' he shouted.

Amelia scuttled from the room and when she woke me her anguished state immediately cleared my head. I was able to deduce what was wrong and I rushed into Edwin's bedroom without even putting on my trousers. 'Stay outside,' I said curtly to Amelia as she attempted to follow me into the bedroom.

I closed the bedroom door, then turned to face Edwin, who held the revolver to the side of his head. 'I want to apologise, George, for what I did to you,' he began. I did not react but just stared at him.

'Do you understand, George?'

I nodded, then held out my hand. 'You want to leave me on my own, Edwin? What will I do without you? Have you thought of that – me in my world of silence. You do explain things and most of the time you are patient. I will be lost without you, do you realise that?'

Edwin had lowered the gun and his mouth opened slightly. 'I had not thought of that, George, and there are no hard feelings – honestly?'

I shook my head and pointed to the gun. Edwin put the gun on the bed, then grasped my hand and shook it. I knew then that I was closer to Edwin than I had ever been with any of my own brothers. I smiled and picked up the revolver.

'Let's have some dinner, shall we?' I said.

'Right. Be with you in a minute,' he replied.

Amelia and Agnes were standing outside the bedroom, both had their hands to their mouths in anguish. I pushed the safety catch on with my thumb then I smiled, 'I'm going to hide this and then Edwin and I are going to have something to eat.'

Amelia put her arm about me and kissed my lips. The corners of her mouth moved and I could tell she was almost in tears. She released her hold on me, then, controlling herself, said, 'George, dear, go and put on your trousers.'

Before I could reply, Agnes stepped forward and kissed me for the first time on my lips, smiling and winking at me as she did so. I got on very well with Agnes and I think she had a soft spot for me.

I put my trousers on and we had dinner, during which the upset was not mentioned, though Edwin was subdued, and for some days afterwards.

After the incident with the revolver, which, incidentally, I hid in the loft out of Edwin's reach, my relationship with him changed. Until now it seemed to me that he was a little patronising and at times he almost treated me as his batman; in fact, Amelia had reproved him for it more than once. I tended to take no notice of him; being deaf had its advantages at times, and he was good in other ways. He helped in the shop every day, looking after the lending library, and I know he refused to take any payment from Amelia. Further to this, a large portion of the books in the library were purchased with his money and I know he refused to take any of the library profits from Amelia.

Now he was more patient and considerate towards me and treated me as an equal. This, I am sure, was noticed by Amelia, as she seemed to signal her approval by being more sympathetic to him.

We were now looking forward to Christmas, and Amelia had invited Amy and Hector with the children to spend Christmas Day with us. Other than writing to her father, Amelia had no contact with her family – much like myself, though for different reasons.

Amelia had decided to open the shop for two hours each evening, in order that people who worked and were members of the library could change their books. The weather was cold and it occurred to me that we could sell hot baked potatoes during the evenings.

'Hot baked potatoes, dear?' asked Amelia as she cut my dinner for me. 'Do you think we could sell them?'

I nodded as I picked up my spoon. 'Yes, I do. The kids will buy them and people coming for books. I could buy a sack and Aggie could...'

'Agnes, dear,' smiled Amelia.

'...could put them in the oven,' I continued.

'Seems a good idea to me,' remarked Edwin, stirring his tea.

'All right, dear, we will try it,' nodded Amelia.

'We need a sign in the window.'

'I'll make that, George,' smiled Edwin. 'I'll have it done for this evening,' he added.

'The hot potato man at New Cross Gate charges a halfpenny and a penny for a big one and I counted how many potatoes you get in a pound and it works out at four hundred per cent profit,' I said.

Amelia and Edwin looked at me in amazement as Agnes remarked, 'So that is what you wanted my scales for, Master George.'

I nodded and grinned at her.

'Well I never,' said Amelia at last, her eyes twinkling.

'Four hundred per cent,' breathed Edwin.

'If it turns out as well as the library dear...' Amelia paused as she looked proudly at me.

'I'm sure it will, Miss Amelia,' said Agnes. 'I'll help scrub the potatoes.'

'Scrub them?' frowned Amelia.

'Yes, they will have to be scrubbed first,' a faint smile appeared on Agnes's face as she spoke.

'Er ... yes, quite so,' murmured Amelia.

I now realised that Amelia knew nothing of potatoes baked in their jackets; in fact, I doubted if she had ever had one in her life.

The hot potato idea was an instant success; in fact, on the first evening we had sold out within an hour of opening.

'I am amazed,' said Amelia, as she counted the money that had been kept in a separate tin. 'If I take the money for the sack of potatoes – and there are still two thirds left – we are left with two shillings and sixpence halfpenny.'

'We must do more tomorrow, Aggie,' I said, enthusiastically.

'Agnes, dear,' chided Amelia with a smile.

'Yes, we must dear,' smiled Agnes, who was far more familiar with me than she was with Amelia or Edwin, which was understandable.

Edwin, who was reading the paper, suddenly put it down and grinned. 'You will make our fortunes yet, young George.'

'You could be right, Master Edwin,' said Agnes, soberly.

Amelia looked at me and smiled. She made a movement with her lips as if to kiss me. I now had a broad smile on my face. I was a happy man.

23

Mabel

I was well aware that it was a trying period for Edwin. Twenty-two years of age and confined to a wheelchair for the rest of his life took some getting used to and I could understand his frequent moods.

If he was rude or even sharp to Amelia or Agnes, and I understood what he said, I would hold my fist under his nose and say, 'I'll drop you in a bath of cold water, Captain.'

'You would too,' growled Edwin.

I could see Amelia trying not to smile as she ignored us and spoke to Agnes, then it would all be forgotten.

I have already mentioned that he was becoming very interested in antique and first edition books. This now became a consuming interest and he began to teach me what to look for when I was rummaging through the piles of books on the stalls in the market or in the second-hand bookshops.

Edwin was now able to put his arts degree to some use. Our lending library, which was growing all the time, occupied most of his time and he knew virtually every book that we possessed, which had now reached a substantial figure.

Our days seemed to pass quickly, and with the disability pensions we were now given, Amelia was able to organise her budget on a permanent basis, as she put it. I let her handle all our financial affairs and she confided to me that she was very satisfied with matters. This was a relief to me as I wanted nothing to do with money, and I would get even more headaches if I started to worry.

The next event to be remembered was the local victory parade, and one of the organisers called to make sure we would be there. This we assured him of, though with some misgivings, I should add. All the local shops closed and for five hours the trams stopped running, which was just as well because the parade assembly point was near the tram depot.

'I hope we are not going very far,' I said to Edwin, as I polished one of my boots, as we were all to wear our uniforms. Before Edwin could reply, Amelia attracted my attention.

'Wear your shoes, dear, they are far better than those awful boots,' she said, smiling at me.

I dropped my boot, which was under my left arm, aware that Edwin had a broad grin on his face.

'I fail to see what is so humorous, Edwin,' snapped Amelia.

'You wouldn't, Sis,' he chuckled.

'I shall be standing with Agnes outside the shop, Edwin. Since you will be passing by it's pointless standing anywhere else.'

'Makes sense,' agreed Edwin, as he adjusted his tie.

'You could go to Deptford Town Hall,' I remarked.

'I'll do no such thing after what happened,' retorted Amelia, her cheeks flushing.

'Oh!' I muttered.

'I doubt if I would be welcome anyway,' she added.

'In the circumstances, it might prove embarrassing, Sis. I think you would be better outside the shop.'

'I agree, Edwin.'

386

I think Amelia regretted speaking sharply to me and she began to straighten my tie and comb my hair. 'There, that's better, dear,' she smiled, kissing my cheek, 'and wear your scarf, George, it's very cold out. Where is it?'

'It's in Buster's basket, I think,' grinned Edwin.

'Good heavens, whatever next?' snapped Amelia.

Amelia hurried from the room and went downstairs to the small back room behind the shop where Buster had his basket, as he had the run of the downstairs at night. During the daytime, if it was cold, he would lie in front of the kitchen fire or, if it was sunny, in the conservatory on an old rug.

'Look at the state of it, covered in dog hairs,' snapped Amelia, as she returned to the room shaking the scarf.

'I thought Buster was cold the other night, Amelia. He was shivering a bit,' I explained.

'So you covered him with your scarf?'

I nodded, aware that Edwin was grinning broadly at me.

'I will give you something to cover him up,' said Amelia, patiently, as she put the scarf around my neck. 'There, that's better, isn't it?'

I nodded again as she carefully tied the scarf for me. At that moment Buster came in wagging his tail. 'He thinks he's coming too,' I said, bending down to stroke him. 'I'll take you out later, old son.'

'Yes, go and get in your box, Buster, there's a good boy; we'll be tripping over you if you are under our feet,' added Amelia. 'There's not much room in here.'

Buster didn't move, he looked up at me with his 'what about me?' expression on his face.

'Go on, move, Buster,' said Amelia.

'Perhaps he wants George's scarf,' chuckled Edwin.

'Are you ready, Edwin?' asked Amelia, sharply.

'Yes, Sis. Medals as well. Have you got yours, George?'

'Dunno, Edwin. I think they are in...' I began.

'They are here, dear,' smiled Amelia. 'Put your coat on and I'll pin them on.'

Amelia helped me on with my greatcoat, then pinned on my medals. I could see her eyes fill with tears as she did so. She did not speak and when she had finished I bent my head to kiss her forehead. As she straightened my tie she kissed my lips, completely oblivious to Edwin and Agnes who were watching us. 'There!' she said, at last satisfied that I looked presentable.

'Amy and Hector will be with Agnes and me. If it's too crowded on the pavement and the children cannot see, we will watch from the sitting-room windows.'

'That would be the best place to be, Sis,' said Edwin. 'Get a better view as well.'

'Yes, I agree, Edwin. George, dear, we will be at the windows,' said Amelia, slowly emphasising her words so that I could understand.

'That's better. You won't get pushed and shoved then,' I nodded.

'Ready, George?' asked Edwin.

'Yes, I'm ready,' I replied.

So began our daily ritual of getting Edwin downstairs, which we accomplished without any mishap, which was not always the case.

The parade was to begin at Peckham Rye, then go down Rye Lane to us veterans at Queen's Road police station. There were four bands and some Army units and a Naval detachment, and we were to fall in behind one of the bands.

I was not looking forward to pushing Edwin all the way from Queen's Road police station to Deptford Town Hall where the Mayor and civic dignitaries were to take the salute. There did not seem to be much choice for me so I had to make the best of it; at least it was on the flat.

By the time we arrived at Queen's Road police station, the pavements, though they were wide at that point, were crowded with people. This did not prove a problem, as people quickly made way for the wheelchair, some nodding appreciatively as they did so. We were met by Mr Frost, who had invited us to take part in the parade. He was in his old army uniform wearing his medals. 'You are in the front rank of the veterans, George,' he said, as soon as he saw us.

'Captain Hooper will be with the wheelchairs some way back.'

Edwin now had a frown on his face as he looked up at Mr Frost.

'I'm pushing Edwin's wheelchair, Mr Frost. If I am on the front row, so is he,' I said, firmly.

'But, George, those in the front rank are the ones with the most medals, only our two VCs have got as much as you and neither of them have got four medals for bravery and a French one as well.'

'I don't care. If I am in the front rank, so is Eddy,' I said, stubbornly.

'You go on, old son, it's all right,' smiled Edwin, giving me a wink.

'No I bloody won't,' I said, my voice rising.

Mr Frost held up his hands as if in surrender as he said, 'All right, George. The Captain is with you on the front rank, so fall in behind the band when they form up.'

'What's that, Mr Frost?' I asked.

'I said, er, never mind, George – you heard me, Captain?'

Edwin smiled and nodded, then Mr Frost moved off to speak to another group of veterans.

'It's going to be a good march to Deptford, George,' said Edwin, looking round at me.

'Er, what's that Edwin?' I frowned.

'To Deptford, George, a good way,' said Edwin.

'Yes, I think it's going to rain too,' I replied.

'I didn't say rain, I said it's a good march to Deptford,' said Edwin, who was now getting a little exasperated.

'Oh, Deptford! Yes, it is a good walk and if the wheels of your chair get in those tram lines you could end up in the tram depot at New Cross Gate,' I grinned.

Edwin did not find it particularly funny as his face did not change. I think my alluding to the chair still embarrassed him.

The band began to form up and we received friendly nods from the bandsmen as we manoeuvred the chair into position behind them.

'We'll keep to the inside rank, it might be less bumpy on these cobbles,' said Edwin, pointing to the camber of cobbles in the centre of the road.

At this point Mr Frost came hurrying towards us. 'Ah, lads!' he said, a little breathlessly. 'Glad I caught you before we started. The Mayor has invited you three to the reception in the Town Hall afterwards. You two gentlemen,' he said to the VC holders, 'and George here,' he added.

The men nodded and I had managed to get the gist of what he had been saying. 'What about Edwin?' I asked.

'Sorry, Captain Hooper, we are limited for numbers, you understand,' smiled Mr Frost.

'Yes, I understand,' replied Edwin, a slight flush on his cheeks.

'What did he say, Eddy?' I asked.

Mr Frost had now rejoined the column some way behind us and I glanced curiously in his direction. Edwin explained with some difficulty what he had said.

'I'm not going on my own and that's flat,' I retorted.

Before Edwin could reply we moved off and I needed all my concentration to keep the wheelchair straight on the cobbles. Fortunately, from time to time, we missed the cobbles, which was just as well, as I could tell that Edwin was having a most uncomfortable time.

Since the shop was on the left-hand side of the road, Amelia and Amy would have a good view of us as we passed just below them. I would look up as the parade approached them, as I was beginning to enjoy the enthusiastic reception we were being given along Queen's Road. This changed when I saw Amelia and Amy, who were both leaning out of the window, but they were in tears. They had handkerchiefs to their eyes and Amy had an arm around Amelia's shoulders as if trying to comfort her.

I tried to wave and push the wheelchair at the same time, but we had passed before I realised it. The sight of them in tears took away all the interest I had in the parade. I felt quite miserable, and Edwin, who had half-turned in his chair, must have understood how I felt. He put a hand on mine for a moment and winked.

When he resumed his position in his chair, I bent forward and said into his ear, in a voice he must have heard despite the band, 'I don't want to go to Deptford, I've had enough.'

Edwin, I thought, nodded his agreement. I could not be sure, as we were on cobbles again and he was being cruelly shaken.

At the junction of New Cross Road and Queen's Road the procession came to a halt in order to join up with another parade coming down the Old Kent Road. Before I could do anything to stop him, Edwin slew his wheelchair round and was pushing towards the kerb. I helped him to get up the steep kerb with the willing assistance of people on the pavement who were watching the parade.

'Had enough, mate?' asked a man.

'I'll say,' replied Edwin with feeling.

391

Mr Frost had now seen what had happened and came rushing towards us in an agitated state. 'Where are you going, lads?' he asked, excitedly.

'To the First Aid post just around the corner, we'll catch you up. I feel a bit dicky. You understand,' explained Edwin.

'All right then,' he replied, reluctantly, 'but don't forget about George's appointment, Captain.'

'I'll tell him, Mr Frost,' said Edwin, breezily.

Mr Frost seemed about to argue, then the parade began to move again so he turned and hurried back to his position in the column.

After seeing Amelia and Amy in tears, I was not sorry that Edwin decided to adjourn to the saloon bar of the Pilgrim's Rest. It upset me, and having got Edwin's wheelchair to a table, I slumped down on the next chair to him. I sat staring dejectedly into the bright fire of the saloon bar.

'What's the matter, George?' asked Queenie, touching my arm.

She had brought a tray of drinks that Edwin had obviously ordered, and a look of concern appeared on her good-natured face. 'Ah, never mind, dearie. It's because they were both proud of you – look at all your medals.' She put a gentle hand to my face.

'Sod the medals,' I said, bitterly. 'I've never killed anyone; I didn't want to go in the Army.'

'We know that, George. That's why it makes you so special,' said Queenie, tears in her eyes. 'My young brother was killed at Arras. We don't even know where he is buried. He was called up when conscription came in. Have your pie, George, they are fresh today.' Queenie patted my hand then returned to the bar while I continued to stare morosely into the fire.

At last I turned to face Edwin, who looked almost

affectionately at me. 'Eat your pie up, old son,' he smiled.

I picked up my pie and was about to bite when Edwin spoke again. 'Amelia is very proud of you, George, believe me.'

'What's that, Edwin?'

'I said, George, that Amelia was very proud of you.' Edwin spoke slowly and I was able to understand him.

'Honest, Edwin?' I stopped chewing my pie.

Edwin nodded, then took a sip of his whisky before replying. 'And why not, George? She has every right to be proud of you. I'm proud of you, believe me, I am.'

'You are?' I frowned in disbelief.

'Of course I am, and why shouldn't I be?'

'Well, I er,' I was not sure if I had understood Edwin.

'Come on, drink up,' grinned Edwin, nudging my arm. 'You have got to get to Deptford Town Hall to see the Mayor.'

'I'm not going there,' I said, stuffing the last of my meat pie into my mouth.

'You are not?' queried Edwin.

'No, I'm bloody not,' I grunted.

'Are you sure, George?'

'Of course I'm bloody sure. After the way they treated my Amelia,' I snapped angrily.

'All right, old son, I only asked,' said Edwin, holding up his hands.

'Another drink, Eddy, and then we are going home,' I said, firmly.

I had expected Edwin to protest, but he just nodded his agreement as I picked up our two empty glasses and went to the bar to be greeted by a smiling Queenie.

'What is it, George, same again?' she asked, slowly.

'Yes, Queenie, and three bags of crisps please.'

I had not noticed a young woman standing at the bar

on my left. It was my blind side and she suddenly moved away and went and sat next to Edwin.

'I'll give you a tray, dear,' smiled Queenie, as she put the packets of crisps and drinks on one of the brewer's trays.

I was surprised to see this young woman in deep conversation with Edwin when I returned to our table.

'This is Mabel, George,' said Edwin, as I put down the tray.

'How do you do, George,' she said, an almost apologetic smile on her face.

'Er ... how do you do?' I replied, sitting down.

Mabel, I guessed, was about twenty-two with dark hair and blue eyes. She wore a wedding ring and was well dressed and it seemed strange that a presentable young woman such as she appeared to be, was in a public house on her own. On the sleeve of the brown coat she was wearing was a black armband. Now I had an idea why she was in the pub; she was not the first young woman that we had seen trying to drown her sorrows.

'Mabel's husband was in my old regiment,' said Edwin, breezily.

I nodded casually, a habit I had picked up when I was not certain what anybody said to me.

'Oh, yes. Here's your whisky, Edwin, then we are going home.'

'You're not going to eat those potato crisps as well as that pie are you?' grinned Edwin.

'No, they are for Amy's children,' I replied, shortly.

'Our luncheon is at two, remember.'

'I know,' I snapped.

I could see Mabel smiling and I felt, quite wrongly as it happened, that she was laughing at me.

'Why are you laughing at me?' I said, looking at her.

The smile vanished from her face and her previous

394

worried expression returned. I immediately regretted my words.

'I do assure you, George, I am not laughing at you, it's just that I am pleased to be in your company, that's all. I have three younger sisters at home, you see. I still live with my parents. Jackie and I never had our own home, we were only married a week before he went back.' Her eyes were full of tears.

'Here, use this, Mabel,' said Edwin, handing her his clean handkerchief. He looked at me, an expression of annoyance on his face as he did so.

'I'm sorry,' I mumbled.

'Go and get some more drinks, George, here's two bob.' Edwin put the florin on the glass-topped table.

'No,' I said firmly. 'We are going home.'

Edwin took a deep breath as he picked up the florin and put it in his pocket. 'At times, George, you are most annoying,' he snapped.

'It's all right for you. If I take you home all Brahms, Amelia will get on to me. She did the last time you fell out of the chair. Told me I should know better. She expected it of you, that's why all you got was one of her looks.'

'That's very nice, I must say, in front of Mabel here,' retorted Edwin.

'It's true, Mabel. My Amelia knows what he's like when he gets the bit between his teeth,' I said, smiling at her.

Our exchange seemed to cheer her up as the smile had returned to her face. Edwin too was now grinning. 'Tell you what, Mabel, come home and have a spot of lunch with us.'

'Me?' gasped Mabel. 'I couldn't. What would your sister say?' she added, as if trying to convince herself that she should accept Edwin's invitation.

'Nothing,' said Edwin, shrugging his shoulders and shaking his head as he turned to me for support.

I felt suddenly sorry for him as he tried to be the Edwin of old. 'Amelia won't mind, will she, George?'

'No,' I said, a look of innocence on my face.

'I should tell my mother first,' said Mabel, eagerly.

'Where do you live, Mabel?' I asked.

'Waller Road,' she replied.

'We could go that way home, it's not near the top is it?'

'No, this end,' she replied.

'Thank God for that,' I breathed. The prospect of pushing Edwin up that steep hill did not exactly appeal to me.

Mabel was now smiling again and she looked rather attractive. 'You can smile, Mabel, pushing him up a hill like that is no joke. He's getting as fat as butter,' I grinned.

'Do you mind, George! My *avoirdupois* is not a matter for general discussion you know,' said Edwin, winking at Mabel.

'Your what?' I frowned.

'My ... er, never mind, let's be off. Bye, Queenie.' Edwin waved to Queenie, who smiled knowingly as she said, 'Goodbye, Edwin, George. You two take care now.'

Mabel held the saloon bar door open while I, with Edwin's assistance, got his chair over the step and out on to the pavement. Mabel touched my arm and mouthed the words, just like Amelia, so I could read her lips easily. 'Can I push him for you?'

I smiled at her as I took my hand off the wheelchair handle. 'Yes. Why not?' I said. I was beginning to like Mabel.

We left New Cross Road when Mabel suddenly waved to a young girl coming towards us, it turned out to be one of Mabel's younger sisters. 'Tell Mum I'll be home later,' she said.

'Dinner's ready and Mum's cross too,' said the girl, who looked a smaller edition of Mabel.

'This is my sister, Joan,' said Mabel, introducing us.

Joan, who was about fifteen, eyed us sympathetically as she replied, 'Are you helping these wounded soldiers, then?'

'Yes, if you want to know. They were in Jackie's regiment,' replied Mabel quickly.

'Oh, can I help?' said Joan brightly.

'No. Just tell Mum I'll see her later,' replied Mabel.

'Righto, cheerio then,' smiled Joan as she turned to leave.

Edwin wisely let me lead the way into the shop, he knew I would smooth the way with Amelia, who I found in the kitchen.

'Hello, dear,' she smiled as I entered.

I quickly kissed her cheek before I told her that Edwin had invited a young lady home for lunch.

'Do we know her, George?'

'No. We met her in the pub,' I replied.

'And he invited her home to luncheon; whatever next? He must have taken leave of his senses.' Amelia's face was now flushed in anger as she moved suddenly, but before she reached the door I grabbed her arm and shook my head. She looked at me as I released my arm and put a finger to my lips. 'Mabel is very nice; don't say a thing, Amelia,' I said.

Amelia paused and looked thoughtful, then she spoke, 'Very well, as you wish, dear. I'll go and welcome her then. Amy and the children are in the sitting-room.'

Now her normal self, she left the kitchen. I followed her, having exchanged smiles with Agnes who was taking a pie out of the oven. Edwin was showing Mabel the library when Amelia and I came through the shop.

Edwin looked embarrassed and before he could speak

397

I effected the introductions, much to Edwin's obvious relief.

'This is Mabel Eltham, Amelia. Mabel, my wife, Amelia.'

'How do you do, Mrs Bowman,' said Mabel, holding out a gloved hand.

Amelia shook her hand as she said, coolly, 'I am pleased to meet you, Mrs Eltham.'

'Mabel's husband was killed in France; they only had a week together, that's all,' I explained.

'Ah, I see,' said Amelia, who suddenly became much friendlier. 'We are having roast pork. I hope you like pork, Mrs Eltham?'

'Call me Mabel, please, Mrs Bowman. I like roast pork very much,' replied Mabel, her face slightly flushed.

'Excellent, and you must call me Amelia. Come, let me introduce you to George's sister and her husband, while George gets Edwin upstairs,' said Amelia, leading Mabel towards the stairs.

Edwin looked at me gratefully. As they left us, he grinned then squeezed my arm and winked. 'Thanks, old son,' he said, as I pushed the chair out to the downstairs toilet before I got him up the stairs.

Mabel seemed to be immediately accepted by all the family, and Amelia, in particular, became a close friend. I think the fact that Mabel lived so near us was one reason why she was so much in Edwin's company.

Mabel worked in the office of the tram depot and I think she found Edwin so different from the type of men she met each day. Being a young widow she was looked on as fair game by many of the men and the fact that she had Edwin's company compensated her to some extent for the loss of her husband.

When Edwin chose to be agreeable he had an engaging personality, and it was soon clear that he was becoming fond of Mabel. Whenever she came to see him he was a different man and I think Mabel, too, was fond of Edwin, though I could not be sure that it was not out of pity.

At the weekends she would push him out in his chair and in the evenings would be downstairs sitting in an easy chair next to his desk while he examined books I had obtained.

I still went out after books at sales and scanned the local newspaper for job lots. I was learning what to look for and I found it fascinating and often most profitable as well. This was largely due to Edwin's teaching. At times he would be most patient with me and I am sure that he would have made an excellent teacher.

24

Christmas 1919

Christmas 1919, for us, was both a happy and a sad time. I must say that for myself, even with my disabilities, I was very happy and I told Amelia so. Her lips moved and she smiled, then she put her gentle hands on either side of my face and tenderly kissed me, then she said, 'George, my dearest, you deserve to be.'

'Are you happy, Amelia?' I asked, with some concern.

'Of course, my dearest. I have Edward and you,' she smiled.

'Aah...' I murmured, contentedly.

Our happy state, however, was not shared by Amelia's father who had been invited to spend Christmas with us. Sadly, just before Christmas he had suddenly been taken ill and a week before Christmas, he died.

I went with Amelia down to Worthing for the funeral. Edwin had wished to but the problems of getting him there made him decide not to attend, and I went in his place. At the time it did surprise me that we left for the train immediately after the funeral, without even a word to Amelia's relatives. However, I thought about it on the train and as the carriage was empty Amelia slowly explained the reason to me. It seemed that her mother's relatives at Worthing had obtained everything through a legal mistake in her grandfather's will, leaving Mr Hooper next to nothing. Further to this, Mr Hooper had also borrowed a sum of money from them and they had asked Amelia to repay it, since her father had not done so. Amelia's legacy from her grandfather had also been the cause of the estrangement with her mother, who had thought she should have given it to her father. Edwin had made it clear to her that such were the debts that her legacy would still not have saved the business.

'Without my legacy, matters would have been very difficult for us. In fact, I do not know what we would have done.' Amelia compressed her lips as she always did when she was annoyed or upset.

'I had nothing, I know that,' I muttered.

'I knew that, dear, when I married you,' she said, her face softening into a smile.

I held her hands in mine. I loved her so dearly.

In the New Year, Edwin decided we should all go to the New Cross Empire. He booked a box and both Mabel and Amy were invited. Hector had declined the invitation because he had to write his Sunday sermon. I, too, was not particularly keen on going as I would not hear anything, but since I was needed to get the wheelchair up the stairs, I had to go.

Mabel was now at the shop almost every day. When she pushed the wheelchair out I would sometimes go along with Buster. They did not mind me as they did not look at me when they spoke. I could not tell what they were saying to each other and I was not interested anyway. What was clear to me, however, was the fact that they were getting serious, and I said as much to Amelia.

'I had noticed that too, dear. She must realise what she would be taking on.' Amelia looked resigned as she said it.

'Yes,' I said, thoughtfully.

'However, it is their concern, isn't it?' said Amelia, as if asking my opinion on the matter.

I nodded. I had learnt enough not to be drawn. It was none of our affair and I made that clear to Amelia. 'You know Edwin better than me, Amelia. Whatever we say will be wrong. It's up to them.'

'I agree, dear,' she smiled.

I was able to go out more with Amelia. I preferred to push the pram as far as Rye Lane so that Amelia could look in all the shops.

I had received a Christmas card from Davie Graham, who had returned to his medical studies at Edinburgh University. Davie, the only one of the four medical students who joined my unit to survive. I heard from him regularly, and though he had now got over his injuries, what had happened deeply affected him, as it did us all. I wrote and told Davie that he must look at it as a bad nightmare or it would always be with him. 'Concentrate on your studies, Davie, then meet a nice girl and get married.' That is what I told him.

He wrote back and said, 'That is exactly what my father advised, George. I think you would have made a fine doctor, too.' This comment really pleased me. If only I had been given the opportunity – if only.

It was during the second week of March that a letter arrived from Germany and it was covered with stamps. Edwin had taken the letters from the postman and he sat at his desk in the library looking at it. 'Look, Sis,' he said, as Amelia and I came through the shop. 'It's addressed to Soldier Bowman of the Medical Corps Stretcher Bearers and it's from Germany – the post-mark is Berlin. 'What do you make of that?' Edwin frowned. 'Who do you know in Berlin, George?' Edwin grinned.

'Brighton? Don't know anyone there, never been there,' I replied.

'I did not say Brighton, George. I said Berlin.'

'Where, Edwin?' I frowned.

'Berlin,' said Edwin, his face reddening.

'Berley? Where's that?'

'Christ almighty,' gasped Edwin. 'Give me strength.'

'Give you patience, would be better,' snapped Amelia, snatching the letter from him.

'It's a letter for you, George, dear,' she smiled.

'Me?' I replied.

'Yes, dear, you. Shall I open it for you?'

'Yes, please. I say, Edwin, there are foreign stamps on it. Looks like a Berlin postmark on it too.'

Edwin had half closed his eyes, a grin on his face, and seemed to ignore me.

'I said...' I began.

'I heard you, George.' Edwin turned to Amelia who had opened the letter with Edwin's silver letter-opener and was looking at what seemed to be a Christmas card. 'Would you believe it, Edwin, it's from the Countess Elizabeth von Konigsberg and her husband, the Count. There is a letter, as well, written by the village schoolmaster of the village of Konigswald.'

As Amelia read the letter she bit her lip and her eyes filled with tears. When she had finished, without a word, she handed it to Edwin, then put her arms about my neck and kissed my cheek. I was completely mystified as I watched Edwin read the letter over Amelia's shoulder. At last Edwin looked up at me and there was no disguising the admiration on his face. 'It's an incredible letter, old son. A letter of thanks for saving the Count's life, and a testimony to your courage.'

'Me?' I gasped.

'Yes, you, old chap. As the Countess says, her husband,

who commanded a regiment of Prussian Guards stated, "He was the bravest man I have ever met and I am for ever in his debt." '

Amelia released her hold on me and picked up the Countess's card. 'I must write to the Countess and thank her.'

'The *Times* ought to see this letter,' said Edwin, firmly.

I understood what Edwin had said and shook my head, 'No, Edwin, the war is over now. I want to forget about it.'

Edwin nodded and put down the letter, then he smiled at me, 'Perhaps you are right, old son. Your medals are testament enough.'

Amelia wrote to the Countess and right up to 1933 we regularly received a Christmas card from her.

25

The Early 1920s

For us the weeks passed quickly. Summer was approaching and we were able to get out more. Amy was now helping part-time in the shop. It was a mutually satisfactory arrangement for Amelia and Amy. Amelia could trust Amy and Amy was glad of the extra money. She made no secret of the fact that she could hardly manage on Hector's stipend.

We were fortunate, we had a shop and lending library to supplement Edwin's and my army pensions, but others were not so well off. It was not the 'land fit for heroes' that the Government had promised the men in the trenches. Far from it. There was unemployment and soup kitchens – some reward after the trenches and the mud of Flanders.

I did not say anything, but Amelia and Edwin would get quite het up about it. Perhaps they thought I expected as much or even did not notice. In my silent world, with one eye, I missed little. Once I said as much to Amelia, she just smiled as she said, 'Dear gentle George, I know, my love, I know.'

I now kept chickens at the end of our back yard. Edwin had helped me build a chicken house. With his two arms and my two legs, we made a good team. I was closer to Edwin than I had ever been with any of my brothers. I would help him physically and he would help me with anything I wished to know. I also kept rabbits. Amelia raised an eyebrow when I had first mentioned it and smiled faintly but when I said, 'I had a rabbit once, but my eldest brother's dog killed it,' she smiled and said, 'If you wish to keep rabbits, dear, do so, but you must feed them. Agnes and I cannot do it.'

'I'll feed them. Mr Sydenham saves me all his old cabbage leaves for the chickens and he has lettuce leaves, too.'

'Very well, dear. There is a customer in the shop.'

'I'll go. We must order more crisps, too. I'm on the last two tins, Amelia,' I said.

'Very well, dear. I will order twelve more tins tomorrow. They are going well, it was a good suggestion of yours to sell them.'

If it were not for my headaches, which at times made me feel ill, I could say that I was more contented than I had ever been in my whole life, thanks to Amelia's love and understanding. I had been discharged from the Army about three years when I received a letter telling me to report to the Army pensions board at Woolwich. Wearing clean underwear and my best clothes, I duly reported to Woolwich as instructed.

The clerk at the pensions board office looked at my letter and spoke, but I could not understand what he said.

'Are you deaf?' he asked, as I stood still in front of his desk. This time I understood and nodded. He took my arm and pointed down a corridor.

'Last door on the right, mate,' he said, pushing me forward.

This time I reported to a corporal, who took my letter and pinned it to a folder.

'Go and sit over there,' he said, pointing to a row of

wooden chairs, the backs of which were lined up against the far wall. Some were already occupied by men in a similar state to myself. I sat down and closed my eye. I caught the smell of army polish which, for some unknown reason, gave me goose-pimples. For an awful moment I was back in the Army again. Someone touched my hand. I opened my eye and yawned. It was the corporal and he was talking to me. 'Come on, mate, follow me.' He pulled at my sleeve. It must have dawned on him at last that I was deaf. I followed him out to another office. He knocked on the door and entered, then came to attention and saluted.

In the office were three officers sitting at a long table. A chair had been placed a few feet from the table and the oldest of the three officers, who sat in the middle, indicated to me to sit down facing them. The officer to his right began to read my file and speak. I had no idea what he said because he was looking down at the file. 'Well?' he said, looking at me. Unbeknown to me, the corporal was now behind me holding two iron frying pans. Suddenly he brought them together less than two feet from the back of my head. The crash made the three officers jump, even though they were expecting it, but from me there was no reaction. I had not heard a thing. This seemed to convince the pension board that I was deaf as the senior officer mouthed his words as he spoke to me. 'Any pain, Corporal?'

'Yes, sir. My ears bleed at times still, and my head, sir. I get rotten headaches behind my eye socket. The doctor gives me tablets and I go to bed, then I feel better.'

'Good,' said the officer, then he looked at my file and smiled as he said, 'An excellent war record – one to be proud of, Corporal.'

'Yes, sir,' I mumbled.

He wrote something in my folder, then handed me a

piece of paper, somewhat apologetically. I took the paper and stuffed it in my pocket.

'You may go, Corporal.'

'Yes, sir, thank you, sir.'

The senior officer flushed faintly and put a hand to his mouth almost in embarrassment.

On the tram home I took the paper out of my pocket and read it. At first I thought I had read it incorrectly due to the tram swaying, but no, sure enough, there it was. My pension had been reduced by ten per cent.

When I arrived home I gave the paper to Amelia before I had taken my coat off. As she read it her face went white with anger. I was about to take my coat off when she snapped angrily,

'Leave your coat on, dear, we are going back. Reducing your pension indeed – we are going back immediately.'

I had never seen Amelia so angry. On the tram she sat bolt upright, her handbag on her knees, looking straight ahead.

The clerk at the admin building was just brushed aside when we arrived. I pointed the way to the medical board office and before the clerk could stop her she strode towards it.

The corporal, though taken aback, tried to reason with her, but it seemed to make Amelia worse and the noise must have been heard by the medical board as the corporal opened their door and then in followed Amelia and I.

I did not hear the initial exchange, but the corporal grabbed at Amelia's arms as if to push her out. 'Out you go, woman,' he began.

'You impertinent oaf,' snapped Amelia, who wrenched herself free. Before the corporal could touch her again, I grabbed him by the front of his tunic and lifted him up in the air. 'Don't you touch my Amelia,' I roared. I pushed forward and held the man up against the wall, his boots some two feet off the floor. The three members of the medical board were now on their feet as Amelia said to me, 'Put that man down at once, George, and go and sit down.'

I suddenly released him and he fell to the floor. Amelia now sat down on the chair in front of the medical board and I went to one of the adjacent chairs.

'Now, what is the meaning of this, my good woman?'

'Don't you "good woman" me, sir,' snapped Amelia. 'My three brothers were all officers and I nursed in France.'

'Er, yes, of course, madam,' said the senior officer, adjusting his tie and looking most uncomfortable. 'Er, um, what is your problem?'

'My husband's pension has just been reduced by ten per cent by yourselves within the last hour. What is the meaning of it?'

'We have to economise, madam,' said the second officer. 'The Government does not have an endless pocket, you know.'

'It can find a hundred thousand pounds for Field Marshall Haig without any difficulty, can it not?' retorted Amelia.

'That is not very patriotic, madam.'

Two of the officers half rose in their chairs, which spurred Amelia, who was now really upset.

'Patriotic! Patriotic! You say that to me. I lose two brothers and another at home crippled and my husband here lost three. Besides which he is completely deaf and has lost an arm and an eye. What did you lose, or Field Marshall Haig? I am sure, if the truth is known, he never went near the trenches in the whole war.'

'Madam!' The senior officer half rose again in protest.

'If my husband's pension is reduced I shall throw my

husband's and my brother's medals from the visitors' gallery in the Houses of Parliament, and I shall make sure that the *Times* newspaper has a reporter and a photographer there,' said a now red-faced Amelia.

'I am sure, madam, that there is no need to go to such lengths.'

'That is entirely up to you, sir.' Amelia rose to her feet and placed the piece of paper I had been given on the table. 'Good-day gentlemen. Come, George.'

I followed her out of the room, aware that the senior officer was wiping his forehead with his handkerchief.

Two days later I received another letter from the pensions board stating that my case had been reconsidered and that my pension was still the same.

26

Edwin and Mabel

It was now October, 1920, and time seemed to me to be passing quickly. The war had been over almost two years. Yet to some, it would never be over. I did not include myself in that unhappy group. In some ways I was fortunate and I knew it. For Edwin the effects of the war would always be with him and this was particularly sad in view of his feelings for Mabel. I had liked her from the first day we had met her in the Pilgrim's Rest, and surprisingly both Amelia and Amy liked her too.

I am quite sure that Edwin would have asked her to marry him, even though he was crippled, but for the fact he was unable to have normal physical relations with a woman. I knew the extent of his injuries since I helped him in and out of the bath each day, but I was quite sure that Mabel Eltham was ignorant of the facts.

Edwin had hinted to me, quite recently, that he had serious intentions as far as Mabel was concerned. I shrugged and pretended I had not understood. What could I say to him? Only recently, after an army medical, he had been told that there was no possibility of him walking again.

I suspected that Edwin wanted his own home and wished to move out with Mabel to look after him. His father had made him the sole beneficiary of his will, leaving him a sum, much to Amelia's surprise, big enough to purchase a modest house and furnish it. I know that Amelia was a little hurt that she and our little son had been completely excluded, but she made no comment. When I told her what I thought, her reply was short and final. 'If that is what he wishes to do, and Mabel will take him on, that is his affair.'

My suspicion proved to be quite correct as some weeks later Edwin informed us that he had asked Mabel to marry him and she had agreed to be his wife. Further to that they had found a house nearby that he had intended to purchase, if the price could be agreed.

Naturally, we congratulated him, but our enthusiasm seemed a little weak in view of the circumstances.

'We can manage,' said Edwin, sharply, as if reading our thoughts.

'We shall live downstairs,' he added.

'Good,' nodded Amelia. 'Does Mabel realise the extent of your injuries, Edwin?' asked Amelia.

Edwin seemed to pause, as if deciding what to reply. 'She knows. She has eyes,' he snapped.

Amelia looked doubtful, but made no comment and the subject was dropped for the moment.

Later, when I discussed it with Amelia, it seemed her thoughts were the same as mine. 'It's their affair, George, what can we say?' Amelia shrugged.

'Nothing, if he has been straight with her,' I replied.

'Exactly, and how are we to find out? We cannot ask her.' Amelia seemed both sad and helpless.

'No, but he should tell her,' I persisted.

'I agree,' she replied.

'But, whatever we do or say, it will only blow back in our faces, it seems to me,' I reflected.

'Exactly so, dear. I think for the moment we will keep quiet. Don't you agree, dear?'

Mabel's parents, however, took an entirely different view of the matter and made their opinions clear.

'You must be mad taking on a cripple!' said her father.

'Could you lift him about?' asked her mother.

Mabel had not replied and it seemed to spur her on to take up the challenge, as it were, so a date was fixed for the wedding, even though her parents made it clear that they would not attend. I felt very sorry for them and told Mabel that I would always be on hand if she needed any assistance with him. Mabel thanked me with the words, 'Edwin said we could always rely on you, George.'

'Yes,' I replied.

The wedding took place in the Baptist Chapel and Hector conducted the ceremony, much as he did for Amelia and me. We had a reception for them at Queen's Road, then they went to their own home in Dennetts Road.

Only one of her sisters attended the wedding and she would not come back to the reception. This hurt Mabel, but she put a brave face on it.

The house now seemed quieter and I had less to do, and what was more important, Amelia had less income, as Edwin had made a generous payment for his keep. Amelia did not seem perturbed, for, as she told me later, 'I have always saved the money Edwin gave me. We can manage quite comfortably, dear,' she smiled.

It was almost Christmas, 1920, and the weather was cold. I spent more of my time in the shop now. Our bookshelves were full, so I collected fewer books and I spent more of my searching time looking for more valuable books, and not without success. I found two first editions and received sixty pounds for them.

'What do you want to do with the money, dear?' asked Amelia.

'Save it for when Edward goes to school. I want a good school for him, Amelia, just like your brothers.'

Amelia did not reply, but put her arms around my neck and kissed me tenderly. So we opened a savings account for the sole purpose of paying for our son's education.

It seemed unreal when I thought about it later, but Christmas, 1920, was the last time we would all be together. It was a wonderful Christmas, even though I had to admit I could not kill the two chickens and a rabbit; we had to ask the butcher to do it. Amelia did not mind, she just smiled and said quietly, 'I would have been most surprised, George, dear, if you could have done. I will take them and Agnes will collect them.'

At the end of February, Amy told us one morning that they were going to Canada. I could not believe it, the news was shattering. It seemed that the Baptist Church could no longer fund a full-time minister and Hector had been offered an alternative post in British Colombia, which he had accepted.

My face must have mirrored my thoughts, and I could see tears in Amy's eyes as she said, with an arm about me, 'You must understand, Georgie, it's a marvellous opportunity for us and the children. We have nothing here, and Hector's stipend is a pittance. We will be much better off with a nice house – we cannot refuse it. Hector has relatives there. We will not be on our own.'

I nodded, my eye full of tears. I could not speak. Amy put her arm around my shoulder to comfort me, but it was no use, the tears ran down my face. Amy dried my face, much as she did when I was a little boy, but she did not speak – what was there to say?

After that things moved swiftly. Within six weeks we were saying farewell to them at Waterloo Station. It was one of the saddest moments of my life, for I was never to see any of them ever again.

We returned to Queen's Road in silence, for Amelia would miss Amy and the children as much as I. Four months later Amy wrote to say she was going to have another baby; she hoped for another boy, but it was not to be, for it died at birth and dear Amy had a fatal blood infection. When we received Hector's letter I was filled with hate for him. Why have another when they had three already, I asked myself? Hector was married again within six months. I never forgave him for it or corresponded with him.

Amelia knew my feelings but tactfully never mentioned the subject, so a chapter in my life was over. My dear Amy, how could I ever forget her?

27

Edwin

Edwin had been married almost two years, and on the face of it, the marriage seemed successful. However, I knew better. Mabel had much to contend with. Edwin had moods and at times was very unkind to her. Once, when Amelia and I were there, he was most rude to her, and Amelia told him he should be ashamed of himself. One day in the shop, Mabel met one of the young sweets representatives and it seemed that it was love at first sight. Within three months, after a bout of Edwin's rudeness, she had left him and gone off with the traveller. It happened when Edwin was in the bath, and by the time he was able to get out and call for assistance, he caught pneumonia. He was taken to hospital and eventually transferred to an army convalescent home.

I did not relish the prospect of Edwin coming back to Queen's Road, though I did not say as much to Amelia, who put into words my thoughts. 'I'm sure that he has become quite unbearable; small wonder Mabel has left him.'

'I agree, but what will you say if he asks to come back?'

'At the moment, dear, I really do not know. How do you feel about it?' Amelia looked questioningly at me.

I shrugged my shoulders and grimaced, then smiled at

416

her. 'It's whatever you decide, Amelia. I'll leave it to you. I'm going to feed the chickens and rabbits,' I replied.

Happily the problem was solved for us, as Edwin decided to stay in an army officers' home in Greenwich.

I suspected that Edwin thought that people would laugh at him if he did come back, and I know that he could not stand that. It was much the most sensible thing to do. He was with his own kind and plenty of assistance was available. I said I would see him every Wednesday, which pleased him, though Amelia's visits were rare as I think each brought back sad memories to the other.

The house in Dennetts Road was put up for sale and before it was sold Mabel came to see us.

She came into the shop somewhat hesitantly, unsure, I think, of our attitude to her. I greeted her affably enough. I was sorry for both of them, having been sure that it would not work out.

'Amelia is upstairs in the sitting-room. I'll take you up.'

The greeting from Amelia was cool but attentive, as Mabel said, 'I am getting a divorce, Amelia.'

'I see.' Amelia's lips compressed as she replied.

'Our marriage was never consummated, you know.'

Amelia's cheeks flushed slightly. I was watching Mabel's mouth carefully, as I was curious to know what she had to say.

'I see,' said Amelia again. 'You did know what you were taking on, didn't you?'

'True, I did, but his moods and bad temper were too much on top of everything else. I am hoping for a quick divorce as I am expecting Alfred's child and want to get married again. On the grounds of non-consummation of the marriage, it would be quick – that's if Edwin will admit it.'

Amelia turned in her chair and looked down on to

Queen's Road. She was about to speak when a tram clattered by – I could see its overhead poles that touched the power cables move past us.

At last Amelia turned to Mabel and spoke, her face tense, 'Am I to assume you would like me to help you to persuade him to put that in writing?'

'Yes,' murmured Mabel, lowering her eyes.

'I'm sorry, Mabel, I cannot help you. I do not think I could even discuss it with him, let alone persuade him.' Amelia turned and looked out of the window again.

I could see Mabel's lip tremble and I felt very sorry for her. I could understand Amelia's reluctance.

'Mabel, didn't Edwin tell you he couldn't before he married you?'

She shook her head and Amelia turned to stare at me as I said, 'If your solicitor writes to the army medical department, they will confirm it – I thought you knew.'

There was a curious look on Amelia's face, but she did not speak.

'I knew, Amelia. I used to help bath him. That burst of machine gun fire took away his wedding tackle, you see.'

Amelia swallowed and her lips twitched, as she looked out of the window again.

'There is no need for us to get involved, Mabel. We shall be seeing him regularly, but you, I expect, will never see him again.'

'Yes, thank you, George.' Mabel arose from her chair, then bent down and kissed my face. 'Dear honest George, thank you,' she smiled. 'Goodbye, Amelia, don't get up.' Mabel turned and walked quickly from the room.

Amelia was now looking absently out of the window again and I thought she was going to be cross with me. At last she faced me. 'Why did you not tell me, dear, about Edwin?'

418

I looked down at my hand, which had begun to shake. I was then aware that Amelia had left her chair and was crouching down in front of me, holding my hand in both of hers. I looked into her eyes, then hesitated, unsure of myself.

'Why not dear? I had my doubts, but was not sure.'

'I just couldn't, Amelia. I like Edwin too much. He is condemned to that wheelchair for life, without you knowing that. I thought he was going to tell Mabel before they were wed, but he could not have done.'

Amelia kissed my lips then returned to her chair, tears in her eyes, to look out of the window again.

'I'll make a cup of tea and take one down to Daisy in the shop,' I said, getting out of my chair.

Amelia nodded, still looking out of the window. She took a handkerchief from the sleeve of her blouse and wiped her eyes. The war was still claiming casualties, I thought.

Mabel was able to get married to her Alfred Carson. I received a birthday card from her a few months later. It was postmarked Tonbridge in Kent, to where, I assumed, she had moved. I met her sisters from time to time when I was taking Buster out for his walk, though they never came into the shop.

I hope Mabel found happiness. She certainly deserved to, though we never saw or heard anything of her ever again.

Every Wednesday I went to see Edwin. I took his clean washing, since he claimed the home used to wash it in the river. Amelia would send sweets and tobacco, and I took in books. I felt less conspicuous there and could now appreciate why Edwin was happy to stay there permanently.

Time passed quickly and I must admit I missed Edwin in the library and our trips to the various pubs that he frequented. He was good company, and I missed much

419

of his wit; still, looking at Amelia's face was a good indication at times of its telling effect. I suggested to her that he came home at times for holidays, but she did not agree.

'He is best where he is, dear. The staff there are paid to listen to his orders, we are not,' she said with a nod of her head. I gathered then that he had upset her, so I made no further comment on the matter.

It was at this time that Davie Graham wrote to tell me that he was getting married to a nurse that he had met in Edinburgh. We did not know what to buy him for a present until I found an early edition of a book of poems by Robert Burns. It was in a pile of books I bought in a junk shop and I felt a bit mean sending it to him. Imagine my surprise when we had a rapturous letter, almost by return, saying how pleased he was and did I realise how valuable a book it was? I then told him that we were pleased he liked it and wished him well for the future.

We had been invited to the wedding, but it was too far for Eddy, though Amelia said I should accept the invitation. I would not go on my own and I wrote and explained our situation to Davie, which I knew he would understand.

Time began to pass quickly. Eddy was growing and in junior school, which he liked, as he seemed very bright – just like Amelia.

The early twenties were hard for most people, though we were more fortunate than most. A general election was upon us and I thought that a change of government would help matters.

When I said to Amelia that a change of government would be no bad thing, she looked horrified as she said, 'The country has rejected dear Mr Lloyd George, after all he has done for it.'

I sniffed and grimaced, but did not speak.

'Did you vote for him, dear?' she asked, curiously.

'No,' I replied, promptly. 'I didn't.'

'Oh?' Amelia looked even more curious.

'Then who did you vote for?' she said at last. 'Was it Tory?'

'I'm not likely to vote for them, am I?' I replied. 'I voted Labour, of course.'

'You voted Labour?' Amelia looked horrified. 'You voted Labour,' she repeated, her eyes wide. 'Well, I never did. I'm surprised at you, dear.' Amelia shook her head, still unable to believe that I had voted Labour.

I think Agnes had heard the exchange as she winked at me and there was a faint smile on her face when I went into the kitchen.

I do not think Amelia was able to believe me as I am sure she told her friends Irene Peskett and Maud Littleton when they called to see her.

Edwin had now settled in at the home and I used to like visiting him as I was made welcome, and one of the sisters always brought me tea and cakes.

Edwin had been at the Greenwich Green Home for disabled officers for almost five years and I thought that he was happy, or as happy as he could be, given his circumstances. Every Wednesday I would go to see him and tell him all our news and anything that might interest him. If I had found an old book, so much the better, as we often sold these on to a dealer in the West End of London. On special occasions I would be invited to stay for parties, and I seemed to be the only visitor there. Amelia always told me to accept these invitations and I began to wonder why only I was invited to them. It made me curious and one Wednesday afternoon I asked Edwin. 'It's the matron – she's keen on you,' he grinned, giving me a broad wink, to the amusement of men who were near us.

'Eh? You what?' I frowned, positive that I had not understood him.

'That's right, George,' he laughed. 'She likes you,' he repeated.

I looked around at the other officers who were, by this time, all smiling at me, and at the grinning Edwin.

'Likes me? She's sure to like me – look at the state I'm in – one eye, one half arm, me ear gorn and as deaf as a post,' I retorted.

It seemed to embarrass the officers near us, who all began to read again, and Edwin's face had lost its grin.

'It's because you are like us, you are invited,' said Edwin, taking my hand and squeezing it gently. 'Look, old chap, you have more medal ribbons than anyone here – you are like us, admired by all of us.'

At this point the matron came into the room. Miss Tanner was a lady in advanced middle age, taller than the average woman, with iron grey hair parted in the middle of her forehead, cut short and neatly pinned under her head-dress. Her face was thin and lined, but she had nice features and deep blue eyes. When she walked about the home she had her hands clasped in front of her and nothing missed her eyes.

I stood up when she came near and I always received a smile and kind word from her, and for this reason felt that I could always approach her.

For about four weeks Edwin did not seem his usual self. It seemed that he was getting worse, and I was concerned.

He asked me to bring him a book, and as soon as I had got it, to take it to him straight away. This I did and it was on a Monday morning that I took the tram to Greenwich.

'Take him this chocolate dear,' said Amelia.

'I'll be back before it's dark to feed the animals, Amelia.

I'll not stay long as he'll want me to go on Wednesday as well.'

'Be careful, dear,' said Amelia, as she tied my scarf for me.

'Yes, I will,' I replied, kissing her.

Edwin was sitting on his own when I entered the large reading room, and having exchanged friendly greetings with the other officers, approached him. He did not reply when I spoke to him, and looked quite miserable. When I gave him the package containing the book and chocolate, he did not say anything.

'Amelia sent the chocolate, Eddy.'

'Who told you that you could call me, Eddy. Edwin is my name,' he almost shouted.

All the other officers heard him, though none spoke, but when he opened the package and threw the book across the room I could see one say 'shame', whilst another pushed his chair towards us. This officer immediately told Edwin to behave himself, and an argument started whilst I, now embarrassed, retrieved the book. As I returned to Edwin, I could see him apologising and wiping his eyes with a handkerchief. I pulled up a chair and he clasped my hand. I knew then that something was wrong, and when I left him a half hour later, having promised to come on the Wednesday, I went to see matron.

Fortunately, she was in her office and I was immediately taken in to see her. I think she knew the reason for my visit before I spoke.

'Matron, it's about Edwin. He's not himself, you know.'

'Yes, I am aware of it, George, but there is little I can do. All the men get depressed at times, you know. I expect you do too.'

She spoke slowly and pronounced her words and I had no difficulty in understanding her.

'Not like him, Matron. I get bad headaches, but I'm not unhappy,' I smiled.

'Could you have him back?' she asked. The matron sat, her hands still clasped, resting on the edge of her desk, staring at me. I thought of Amelia and the problems we had last time.

'Did you understand what I said, George?'

'I understood, Matron. I would have to speak to my Amelia. He is not easy, you know.'

'I can well imagine,' she smiled faintly.

'It was his choice coming here. I know he had a row with Amelia before he did, but it's me that has to hump him about. I don't mind that as long as he's not rude to her.'

'Quite. He is very fortunate to have you, George,' she smiled.

'Edwin's been a good friend to me. I like him a lot. I'll speak to my wife, Matron.'

'Thank you, George. It could be the answer for him – at least I sincerely hope it is.'

'I will tell you on Wednesday, Matron.'

'Thank you, George,' she said, rising to her feet.

For the first time she shook my hand, then I left her office.

Amelia did not look too pleased when I told her the news.

'We have no choice, dear, I suppose,' she said, looking at me, 'though it's you, dear, who will have to manage him. Do you mind?'

'I will as long as he is not rude to you,' I said, quickly.

'Do you know he wanted me to go to Cedar Lodge?'

'Whatever for?' frowned Amelia.

'To tell him what it looks like now,' I replied.

'That's ridiculous,' snapped Amelia.

'I thought so too, but I'd better go, just to satisfy him.

424

I said I would and he wants us all to go and see him on Wednesday.'

'Are you sure, dear?' Amelia looked at me curiously.

'Yes, all of us. I have promised him,' I blinked.

'Very well, dear, we will have to go.'

There was some resignation in her manner. I knew that it would be embarrassing for her. I had not mentioned that Edwin had been emotional before I had left. When I told him about coming home he had cried and put an arm about me, but then he surprised me. 'I know that you would look after me, Georgie, you are my best friend. No, I am not coming back with you, Georgie, you understand, in this chair every day the bloody same – you understand, don't you?'

I thought that I had understood him and his present problems and nodded. As the matron had said, they all get depressed at times.

The following morning I caught the tram to Blackheath, much to Amelia's surprise, though she made no comment. It seemed that the years rolled back and I felt a little miserable as I got off the tram. I soon snapped back to reality when I reached the avenue in which Cedar Lodge was situated. There was some activity in the road, and it seemed to be lighter. I thought I was in the wrong avenue because Cedar Lodge was no longer there and a large building site was in its place. I peered up at a board on it. Flats, as they were called, were being advertised for sale. I could not believe it. Having ascertained that I was in the right place, I looked at it again, then retraced my steps to the tram stop. I was secretly glad, as it did not seem right that anyone else should be in Amelia's house.

'Well, dear, is it the same?' were Amelia's first words when I arrived home. I thought she looked close to tears.

'No, it's gone,' I replied, 'and I'm glad it's been knocked down. It was your family's home, now they are building flats on it.'

Amelia put her arms about me and gently kissed me, then said, 'I agree, my dearest, that was the best thing that could have happened to it.' It cheered her up and Cedar Lodge was never mentioned again.

After luncheon, as I called it now, we all went to see Edwin, leaving the girl to look after the shop. Edwin was very pleased to see us, particularly Edward, his little godson, but I could tell he was just the same. We did not stay long and he was not surprised about Cedar Lodge. It seemed that an orderly had told him, and I was sent there to confirm it. Though Amelia said he could come home he declined, shaking his head and thanking her as he did so.

Edwin and Amelia found it difficult to talk, and Edwin, having given Edward two five-pound notes, kissed us all and said that we should leave.

It was very emotional and I began to suspect something, though I did not make my thoughts known to Amelia. Perhaps Amelia thought the same, though she did not say as much to me. In fact she did not mention her brother at all.

It was four days later that we received a message from the home telling us that Edwin had had an accident in his bath. Amelia just cried, no fuss. I held her for a few moments, then she comforted Agnes whilst I sat and gazed at the fire. Neither of us was surprised in our hearts. Edwin really died, like so many more, in the trenches of France and Flanders.

I went to make the identification. I had to spare Amelia that, and again I found myself in the matron's office to collect his personal effects.

The matron looked at me curiously for a moment then

426

spoke. 'Mr Bowman, you have not asked me about the ... er ... accident?'

'The message said it was an accident in his bath, Matron. That is enough for us. He must have fallen asleep and drowned.'

'You will not ask for an enquiry then?' said matron, her hands, clasped as usual, seemed to tighten.

'It will not bring him back, will it?' I replied.

Slowly the matron shook her head, then lowered her eyes.

'Then we will leave it. He would have liked a military funeral – he is entitled to that, Matron.'

'I will arrange it with the senior medical officer at the military hospital, Mr Bowman. I must say that you have made a wise decision. You were in the Medical Corps and highly decorated, so I need not tell you that to some men there comes a time when they decide that they have had enough – it's understandable. Your brother-in-law is not the first, and most certainly will not be the last, I'm sure of that, so we must understand them.'

I knew then that Edwin had committed suicide. It was simple enough – bathrobe stuffed behind the door to stop the water seeping into the corridor. Bottle of whisky, some pills and fill the bath, simple enough. No enquiry, an accident, all over.

Yet it was only now that I felt upset. I sat wiping my eye, then I was aware that the matron was beside me wiping my face with a scented handkerchief. I held her hand for a few moments, then I composed myself, feeling somewhat guilty as the matron poured out some tea.

'Sugar?' she smiled.

I shook my head, 'No thank you, Matron.'

We sat talking for a short while. I told her about my family and the lending library and she told me of her cottage in Sussex where she would retire to with her sister.

I left her office feeling a lot better. I knew that she would arrange the funeral as Edwin would have desired.

On my return home I told Amelia of the arrangements.

'That's as he would have wished, dear, and to which he is entitled as a disabled officer,' she said, firmly. 'I shall not inform any of our relatives, dear. They are not interested in us these days and Edwin was not in touch with them as far as I know. They could well have moved by this time, even if I wished to do so. We will get you a new dark suit. After all, you must look your best. There will be all Edwin's officer friends there, and a bowler hat.'

'What was that, Amelia?' I frowned.

'A bowler hat, dear,' she smiled.

'A what?' I asked again.

'You understood, dear, and you are wearing one,' she said, firmly.

I could see Agnes, who was peeling potatoes, begin to smile and I knew that I would have to wear a bowler hat.

'Did the matron mention any will, George?' asked Amelia.

'Yes. He had made one, which she will open in her office after the funeral. She was a witness to it.'

'Really?' Amelia looked curious. 'I do not suppose he has left very much after that divorce. What a fiasco, it's as well mother knew nothing of that.'

'It's in the past,' I said, shortly.

'Yes, dear, as you say,' she smiled.

Thanks to matron's kind efforts, the funeral was to take place in Woolwich Regimental Chapel and internment in the military cemetery. Pallbearers would be provided by his old regiment, even a firing party would be at the graveside.

Amelia, Agnes and I were the only family mourners,

but what we lacked in family was more than made up by all the officers from the home. All wore their uniforms, medals and black armbands, and each was pushed either by an army nurse or an army batman in his best parade uniform.

I was glad I had a new suit and was wearing, at Amelia's insistence, my medals, which along with my service medals issued after the war, made, even if I say it myself, quite a display. I noticed more than one officer peering at them and felt quite proud with Amelia clasping my arm. Edwin too would have been proud of the funeral. It stopped traffic for almost ten minutes as all the wheelchairs got across the road. I had never seen so many of them in one place. Passers-by stopped as well to watch out of curiosity.

The service was moving, but I could not hear it as the padre was not looking at me, but I thought of Edwin, who was a brother to me. I had loved him as much as Amelia, now he was gone and I was on my own.

I now had only one connection with the war. Davie Graham, who had qualified in medicine at Edinburgh, and was now a GP in the Scottish Highlands. Davie came to see me once when he was at a medical conference in London. He stayed for dinner and I know that he was a little taken aback when he saw me. When he saw Amelia cut up my dinner, he became upset and quickly left the table until he recovered. I told him that I was a very happy man and he should think of that and not remember me as I was.

Davie had written to me all the time he had been at medical school telling me what happened there. I had said that I would have liked to have had the opportunity. Amelia and Davie exchanged glances. 'You would have made a fine doctor, George,' smiled Davie, at which Amelia heartily agreed. It made me feel so proud – better than any medal had done. Davie invited us all for a holiday at his home in the highlands, but I doubt that we will ever go.

I felt a jab in the ribs from Amelia. The service had ended and the pallbearers had picked up the coffin. We stood up and filed out after it into the damp mist. Though Amelia and Agnes jumped when the shots went off over the grave, I did not hear a thing. We threw a handful of soil into the grave and as I did so I thought of the thousands of men who did not have any graves. Faces of men that I had known appeared in my mind and who were now nothing. I had indeed been very fortunate.

Miss Tanner, the matron, had arranged for refreshments at the home, where Amelia and I shook hands with everyone. Afterwards, Amelia and I went to matron's office where she produced Edwin's will. I stood by Amelia's chair as Miss Tanner read it, looking at me and speaking slowly as she did so:

I leave my entire estate to my godson Edward Edwin James Bowman for the purposes of paying for his education at my and my late brothers' school the Haberdashers Askes. My gold Albert, which once belonged to my late father and grandfather, to my brother-in-law George Bowman for whom I had such a great admiration. I would also like to thank him for all his kindness and patience, which at times, I did not deserve. I would also like to thank my sister for all her love and kindness to me, which I did not always appreciate. Finally, my love to Agnes to whom I leave eight pounds ten shillings in cash, and my love and thanks to matron who is a wonderful lady.

This, my last will and testament, signed Captain Edwin Charles Hooper.

The matron put down the will. Amelia and Agnes were

wiping their eyes. It was now clear to Amelia that Edwin had planned to take his life, if she had any previous doubts. Amelia took the will from the matron and, after thanking her, put it into her handbag, after which we thanked matron for arranging everything for us.

Before I left, I said goodbye to all the officer residents who all wished me well. 'You can still come in and bring me tobacco and sweets, George,' grinned one. 'Me, too,' laughed another. I said goodbye to them and then returned to matron's office.

'Come in, George,' she smiled.

'Goodbye, Matron.' I held out my hand, as I held hers I bent forward and kissed her cheek, then she kissed my mouth.

'Goodbye, George,' she smiled, stepping away from me, 'and good luck for the future.'

'Good luck to you, Matron,' I grinned.

Amelia, who had collected Edwin's belongings was waiting for me. 'Where have you been?' she frowned.

'Saying goodbye to Matron,' I replied.

'Hm, carry that case, dear, and let's get home.'

For the rest of the day I could tell that Amelia was itching to question me and I knew the reason – it was Edwin's death.

That night, when we were in bed, I opened the subject because it was easier for me to talk. 'It's Edwin's death, isn't it?' I began.

Amelia nodded, her lips quivering. 'Yes it is. You should have told me, George. I had a right to know.'

'I thought you did know,' I replied.

'I suspected, but was not sure,' she sniffed.

'The matron hushed it up. There could have been an enquiry. Nothing would have been gained, no military funeral and I doubt whether he would have been buried in the military cemetery. Look, he died, he'd had enough and he decided what to do. He knew he could come back here, but he made his decision and that's the end of the matter, Amelia. Do you understand?'

Amelia looked at me then nodded and left the room.

Later she came to me with the Albert that had been her father's. 'It will look well on you, my dearest. My grandfather would have been very proud of you. I will not mention Edwin's death ever again,' she said, kissing me.

'No, it's best. I loved Edwin too, you know. He meant far more to me than any of my brothers, far more,' I sniffed.

Amelia clasped me, tears running down her cheeks. Dear Eddy, how I would miss him, oh that awful bloody war.

Yet we were not to lose our connection with the officers' home completely, and it happened in the following manner. It was almost my birthday, and just before it at breakfast one morning, Amelia said to me, 'George, dear, what would you like to do on your birthday?'

Suddenly I said, 'I'd like to go to those stores in Lewisham where we had coffee and pastries before we were married and where we bought the gloves that your parents paid for, and have coffee and pastries.'

For a few moments Amelia did not reply, then tears suddenly coursed down her cheeks. She used her napkin to dab at her eyes as she said in a choking voice, 'Yes, dear, we will do that, it would be nice.'

'And we will go on the tram,' I added.

'Yes, dear,' she smiled.

Since our marriage, Amelia had never gone to Lewisham to shop. It brought back too many painful memories, I suspect. Instead we had gone to the department store in Peckham. I would sometimes persuade her to come into Edwin's eel and pie shop with me, but she would always complain that the smell was such she would need to have her coat cleaned. I would prefer to go on my own as it reminded me of Eddy, and tears would run down my cheek. I would tell Amelia it was the hot vinegar, but she knew, and put her hand on mine.

On my birthday morning, after we had taken little Teddy, as I called him (Amelia always called him Edward) to his school, we caught the tram to Lewisham. We sat with Amelia holding my hand, our thoughts going back, saying little. Both of us had lost a great deal – Amelia, her whole family and a comfortable way of life. In my case life had its compensations and I was happier now than I had ever been, strange as it may seem.

We walked about the store and I could tell that Amelia was not really interested and I was beginning to think that it had not been a good idea, when I suddenly felt a tap on my shoulder. I turned to see the face of the matron at Edwin's old home. For a moment I was not sure it was her without her starched cap.

'Good morning, George,' she smiled.

'Ah, yes, it's Edwin's matron. Good morning, Matron,' I replied. 'You met my wife, Amelia, didn't you?'

'Yes. Good morning, Mrs er ... I'm sorry, I'm not sure of your name.'

'Bowman, Matron. Good morning to you,' smiled Amelia.

After the initial introduction, it seemed that the matron and Amelia got on very well indeed, and since I was walking behind them, could not see what was said. By the time we reached the restaurant my suggestion that the matron joined us was quickly agreed upon and we were conducted to a table near the orchestra.

'This is nice, isn't it, dear?' smiled Amelia.

I was about to say that I would have preferred one near the balcony so that I could see the people down below, but I refrained from doing so, instead I nodded and smiled.

Amelia and the matron were now on Christian name terms and I felt a little out of it. I could only tell if the orchestra was playing if I saw the violin bow was going up and down. I was beginning to think my idea was not such a good one after all, and that Kew Gardens would have been better, when the matron asked about our library.

'Amelia has been telling me all about your library, George. That was a good idea,' she smiled.

'You must come and see it, Matron,' I replied.

'Emily will see it when she comes home for luncheon dear, and don't eat too many of those or you will not eat any,' said Amelia, looking at the fast emptying cake stand.

So Emily Tanner became a regular visitor to Queen's Road, usually on a Wednesday, which was her day off.

Other than meeting Emily Tanner, our visit to Lewisham was not a particular success. You cannot turn the clock back and it is silly to try to do so.

The matron became a close friend of Amelia's. They had much in common. Besides coming from the same background, they were lonely for similar company. I did not feel out of things. I knew that I was hard work at times, being completely deaf put me in my own world, which only my books and animals could penetrate.

My one concern was that Amelia was happy. This, she always assured me, was the case, so I was content and satisfied with my lot. I had nothing whatever to do with my own family, even though most of them lived but a stone's throw away from me. Amy had told them not to enter the shop years ago, and thankfully none of them ever did.

And this war to end wars, what did it achieve? Nothing.

434

It left widows by the thousand, families ruined and a generation of young men dead or crippled. I should be bitter, but I am not. It gave me Amelia; but for it, I would never have met her, so in spite of my disabilities I am content. Yet sometimes, when I sit by the fire, I look into it and see the faces of the men that I served with in the Medical Corps. Captain Mason, Lieutenant Ames, Angus Muir, who would all now be enjoying successful careers. Sergeant Jack Lane in his butcher's shop, and many more – all gone. Just names on war memorials somewhere; not even a grave. Only Amelia can read my thoughts at such times. I know that she thinks of her three brothers – what a terrible waste. I hope mankind has learnt something from it, but I doubt it.

Amelia and I pray that our son is never involved in such a war – never could mankind be so stupid ever again.

I am finishing my diaries now. I think that I only began them to record what I had seen. It kept me sane to some extent, otherwise I would have thought that what I had seen was just some hideous nightmare. Yet, if you asked people how did it start and what were the reasons, nine out of ten people could not tell you. This, sadly, is the worst part of the nightmare. What was it all for? No one can give me the answer.

28

The Present Day

I put down the last of my grandfather's diaries. I could feel dried tears on my face. What an incredible man he must have been, and my grandmother, in her own way, no less a person. I felt very proud to have been their only grandson.

My mother had told me the end of the story a number of times, so it was still fresh in my mind. Mother had met my father in 1939 when she had been living with her parents in Gautry Road, and they became engaged in 1940, just after he left university, having obtained a degree in law. He joined the army and was commissioned in the Royal Fusiliers, as his godfather and uncles had been, much to my grandparents' apprehension.

During the blitz of London, a firebomb went through the roof of the shop in Queen's Road, causing extensive damage and destroying the library. My grandfather, in trying to save some of the books, had a bad fall and banged his head on the pavement outside the shop. Perhaps there was a splinter of metal still in his head from the war wound that moved when he fell. Sadly he died in my grandmother's arms on the pavement outside the shop. Before he died he must have seen the flashes in the sky, because he thought he was in Flanders again.

436

'What are you doing here in no man's land, Amelia? Go back to Cedar Lodge,' he had whispered.

My parents were married soon after and my mother moved into the part of the shop which was repaired. The library was never replaced, as my grandmother had lost all interest in it when my grandfather died.

My grandmother never got over my grandfather's death and when my father was killed in action, it was the end for her. As my mother put it, she just lost the will to live.

I looked at the now tarnished medals and faded diaries and felt suddenly very ashamed. I did not know where my grandparents were buried, or even if they had been buried. I would ask my mother when she was well enough to talk. I looked at my watch. It was just four-thirty and getting light. I yawned and stretched my legs. The hospital had not rung. I went out into the hall and dialled the hospital.

'I would like to speak to the sister on intensive care please, concerning my mother, Mrs Bowman.'

'I'll put you through.'

Moments later I heard the sister's voice. 'I'm sorry to have to tell you, Mr Bowman, that your mother passed away at three-twenty this morning. She did not regain consciousness, or we would have rung you.'

'Thank you, Sister.' I replaced the telephone. None of my questions would ever be answered, I told myself. I went into the kitchen and made myself a cup of coffee without milk. I could not get the diaries out of my mind, and sat thinking about them.

The following morning I made the funeral arrangements and discussed the future of my mother's cats with her neighbour. I locked up the house. I returned home, taking with me mother's personal effects and the contents of her tin trunk. Liz was naturally sympathetic. I had

437

said little on the phone to her and nothing about the diaries.

'Have you eaten, Teddy?'

'No, I'm not hungry. Cup of tea, shower and bed. Ring up Graham at work and tell him the situation for me.'

'Yes, of course,' replied Liz.

'Read my grandfather's diaries. They are in that tin trunk I brought back with me.'

'Family skeletons?' queried Liz, a smile playing about her mouth.

'Not exactly, but worth reading all the same,' I replied.

'Will do. It's starting to rain. I'll bring up that tea.'

After my shower and tea I went straight out and did not awake until early evening. I went downstairs to find Liz in the sitting-room engrossed in the diaries.

'Hello, feeling better?' she smiled as I entered the room.

'Much. What do you think?' I said, kissing her.

'Incredible. I've been reading all afternoon.'

'Where are the kids?' I remarked, aware the house was so quiet.

'Out. Edward is at extra tuition and the girls are out; they should be home shortly,' she added.

'What do you think of them?' I asked.

Liz closed the last of the diaries and stretched out her arms.

'Do you know, Teddy, other than your mother, I know nothing of your family. I started to read them out of curiosity, then I could not put them down.'

'Gripped you like that, too?' I smiled.

'What incredible people, Teddy. I would have liked to have met them,' said Liz, yawning again.

'They made them tough then,' I remarked.

'No question about that,' she agreed.

'Edward was fascinated with the medals,' said Liz.

438

'I'm glad now that we called our son Edward,' I said, suddenly.

'So am I. It was a close thing, I recall. Glen or Martin, wasn't it?' she smiled.

'What a man,' I murmured.

'True, and your grandmother was something else,' smiled Liz.

'I'm going to offer grandfather's medals to his regiment. I was thinking about it on my way home.'

'That would be nice,' said Liz, as she rose to her feet.

'Sort of a permanent memorial,' I reflected. 'They must be worth something, too, but I just could not sell them. I'd feel cheap doing it.'

'You cannot sell them after reading his diaries. I feel as if I know them both.' The intensity in her voice surprised me.

'No, his regiment is the best place, that's if they want them. I'll get the diaries typed out as well.'

'What a futile waste of life that was!' said Liz.

'Unbelievable, wasn't it?' I replied, following her out into the kitchen.

The following day, during my lunch hour, I made a number of calls and was at last put in touch with a Sergeant Millett of the Royal Army Medical Corps at Aldershot. I quickly explained the reason for my call to him. 'You see, Sergeant, I would like his regiment to have them.'

'We would like to have them too, sir. Corporal Bowman is a proud part of our history – a very proud part, I might add. I've read about him, Mr Bowman. Who hasn't in our Corps? But to be quite honest, we do not have the money in the kitty that the medals, diaries and letters would fetch on the open market.'

'I've no intention of asking for any money for them, it would be an outright gift to his regiment.'

'In that case, sir, we would be honoured to have them,' came the reply.

'Even though he was a conscientious objector?' I remarked.

'Even more so, in my opinion, Mr Bowman. To believe as he did and yet risk his life every day to save other men's lives, makes him something special.'

'Yes, ye-es.' There was a catch in my voice.

'I'd be very proud if he had been my grandfather,' said the voice.

'I am, I assure you, Sergeant. I will be in touch. Nice talking to you.'

'And you too, Mr Bowman.'

I put down the phone and leaned back in my chair, my thoughts still on my grandparents, as I reflected on the diaries. It occurred to me that my grandfather had never once said anything derogatory about the Germans – not once had he cursed them and yet he had every reason to do so.

That evening I mentioned it to Liz as we were having our evening meal. She put down her knife and fork. 'I noticed that, too, yet he seemed so bitter as far as his parents were concerned.'

'Bitter?' I remarked.

'Yes. There appears to have been no reconciliation. He had nothing to do with them and yet they only lived around the corner, as it were.'

'That's true. Still you can hardly blame him given the circumstances, can you?' I smiled.

'Perhaps not,' agreed Liz.

'Still, I will not mind paying VAT so much in future.'

Liz frowned, then smiled at me. 'What on earth do you mean by that?'

'One of the reasons the Common Market was formed was to make us interdependent and eliminate the

440

possibility of war between us and the Germans ever happening again. General de Gaulle's words, not mine, I might add, and our VAT mainly goes to finance it, I understand.'

'Does it?' smiled Liz. 'I don't think many people appreciate that.'

'People's memories are very short,' I remarked.

'That's true,' agreed Liz.

'Where are the kids?' I asked.

'Doing their homework upstairs, I hope,' said Liz, glancing at the ceiling.

'Sounds like it,' I smiled, as the sound of the latest pop music came from above our heads.

'Will you sort them out when you have had your pudding? Do check their homework,' said Liz, taking my dinner plate.

That night I did not sleep well. I kept thinking of my grandparents and my father, who I had also never met but who was now lying in an Italian military cemetery. War – the futility of it all. Pray God it never happens again.

The following day, after the contents of my grandfather's diaries had been put on tape, I had them all packed carefully in a box with his medals and letters. I took one last look at the medals as they lay in the velvet-lined presentation cases and felt immensely proud of the grandfather who I had never seen. What a brave man he had been, in every sense of the word.

I had spoken to an officer of his regiment on the telephone and he assured me that they would be on display at the regimental museum, along with the diaries and the photo taken at the shop in Queen's Road.

I also sent a picture of my grandmother in her VAD nursing uniform, with the stricture that her picture should be alongside my grandfather's as he would have wished.

441

It seemed to compensate for the fact that we have no record of what happened to their mortal remains.

Unlike so many of their generation now completely forgotten, their stories lost in the mist of time, they would be remembered and I hope respected for what they had been.

I had a very nice letter from the Army inviting me to visit the museum at any time, but I will never go – like my grandfather, the medals do not interest me. I have copies of the sepia coloured photographs now in silver frames, and if ever I feel a bit down I read the diaries and it makes me realise how fortunate I am. My problems seem to fade away as I think of my grandfather, Corporal George Bowman, RAMC.